Praise for *The Italian Divide* by Allan Topol

"A fast-paced page turner perfect for beach and cabin reading."

—Yale Alumni Magazine, July/August 2016

"If you're looking for a thriller immersed in politics, revenge and intrigue, unfolding in an international stage, start reading."

—*Ambassador Magazine* of the National Italian American Foundation, Fall 2016

"Allan Topol is a master at pulling together several pieces of current events and creating a fast paced, tight action spy-thriller novel…a perfect start to an early summer vacation."

—Night Owl Reviews, April 29, 2016

"The Italian Divide is a "highly charged and electrifying novel by the internationally famous and award winning author Allan Topol . . . the ending will leave you speechless."

—Fran Lewis, Just Reviews/MJ Magazine

"The Italian Divide is an international thriller of the highest order, one which this reviewer eagerly recommends for those who love this dynamic genre of writing."

—Crystal Book Reviews, April 10, 2016

"The characters are eerily believable…Topol spins such a captivating tale that it is hard to put The Italian Divide down before the nail-biter of an ending."

—Mystery Maven Blog, March 31, 2016

"Topol's latest Craig Page thriller is an electrifying foray into the world of international intrigue."

—Book Reviews & more by Kathy, March 16, 2016

"The Italian Divide is a thriller I recommend to everyone who enjoys adventure and intrigue in the high stakes world of international banking, reeking with power and revenge, and a hero who is real, daring and dedicated to finding justice . . . 5 stars and counting! Bravo!"

—Fresh Fiction Review, March 15, 2016

"The Italian Divide is a real page turner!"

—Outnumbered 3 to 1 Review, March 17, 2016

"Allan Topol's latest Craig Page thriller is an electrifying foray into the world of international intrigue."

—Teddy Rose Book Reviews, March 15, 2016

Praise for *The Washington Lawyer* by Allan Topol

"Pity the poor political novelist. After all the real-world skullduggery of recent decades—Nixon's Watergate, Clinton's intern—how can fiction possibly compete with reality? Washington lawyer Allan Topol can't beat those odds, but in *The Washington Lawyer* he's given us a lively insider's portrait of political mischief featuring a senator who is a traitor and perhaps a murderer, a nominee for chief justice of the United States who is desperately trying to cover up his own misdeeds and a gang of Chinese spies eager to bribe or, if necessary, kill our politicians to obtain the Pentagon's innermost secrets . . . Topol's version is entertaining and at times has the ring of truth."

—Patrick Anderson
"Book World," *The Washington Post*

"*The Washington Lawyer* is a thrilling tale of intrigue and revenge at the highest levels in the American government—told from an insider's point of view. The action is nonstop, from the gripping prologue to the satisfying end. Not to be missed!"

—Joan Johnston
New York Times best-selling author of *Sinful*

"Archeologist professor Allison Boyd doesn't believe her beautiful twin sister, congressional aid Vanessa Boyd, drowned in the Caribbean while away for the weekend alone. Vanessa was many things but 'alone' was never one of them. Convinced Vanessa was murdered, Allison heads to Washington to uncover the truth. As she finds herself caught up in a tangled web of power players, she begins to realize how far some people will go to keep a secret. No matter the cost.

Fast-paced and action-packed, Topol's novel expertly weaves together power, murder, and intrigue to paint a chilling picture of the sinister underbelly of Washington politics. A thrill ride that doesn't let up."

—Beth McMullen
Author of *Original Sin* and *Spy Mom*

"Rich with international intrigue, *The Washington Lawyer* bristles with insider details, heart-stopping action, and memorable characters. This is Washington politics at its most revealing, told by a top attorney who knows where the truth—and the bodies—are buried."

—Gayle Lynds
New York Times best-selling author of *The Assassins*

"Morals, ethics, values, and integrity often go out the window when temptations come your way. What happens when two men let their greed and desire for wealth and power overtake their moral compasses, and find that one simple indiscretion leading to one wrong choice can bring down your entire world? . . .

Once again author Allan Topol delivers a plot and storyline that will keep readers in suspense from start to finish . . . When the truth is revealed whose damage control wins out? Find out when you read this five-star novel."

—Fran Lewis
Author, creator and editor of *MJ* magazine, and host on Red River Radio Show and World of Ink Network

"*The Washington Lawyer* is a thrilling tale of intrigue and revenge at the highest levels in the American government—told from an insider's point of view. The action is nonstop, from the gripping prologue to the satisfying end. Not to be missed!"

—Joan Johnston
New York Times best-selling author of *Sinful*

WASHINGTON POWER PLAY

Also by Allan Topol

FICTION

The Fourth of July War
A Woman of Valor
Spy Dance
Dark Ambition
Conspiracy
Enemy of My Enemy
The China Gambit
The Spanish Revenge
The Russian Endgame
The Argentine Triangle
The Italian Divide
The Washington Lawyer

NONFICTION
Superfund Law and Procedure (coauthor)

WASHINGTON POWER PLAY

A Political Thriller

ALLAN TOPOL

SelectBooks, Inc.
New York

This edition published by SelectBooks, Inc.
For information address SelectBooks, Inc., New York, New York.

First Edition

ISBN 978-1-59079-425-8

Library of Congress Cataloging-in-Publication Data

Names: Topol, Allan, author.
Title: Washington power play : a political thiller / Allan Topol.
Description: First editon. | New York : SelectBooks, [2017]
Identifiers: LCCN 2016047177 | ISBN 9781590794258 (softcover)
Subjects: LCSH: United States–Relations–China–Fiction. |
  China–Relations–United States–Fiction. | Government
  investigators–Fiction. | Women detectives–Fiction. |
  Conspiracies–Fiction. | Political fiction. | GSAFD: Suspense fiction. |
  Mystery fiction.
Classification: LCC PS3570.O64 W375 2017 | DDC 813/.54–dc23 LC record
available at https://lccn.loc.gov/2016047177

Manufactured in the United States of America
10 9 8 7 6 5 4 3 2 1

Dedicated to my wife, Barbara, my partner in this literary venture

Acknowledgments

I am very fortunate to be working with Kenzi Sugihara, the founder of SelectBooks. *Washington Power Play* is our fifth novel together, and once again Kenzi offered sound advice and enthusiasm from the time that I raised the idea of doing another Washington novel. I was thrilled when Kenzi judged *Washington Power Play* to be a gripping story on his first reading, and I could not ask for more from a publisher.

Nancy Sugihara and Molly Stern did a superb job of editing. They were relentless in raising queries that forced me to focus on numerous details for this intricate plot, while at the same time they smoothed the sentences and caught those pesky grammatical errors.

Kenichi Sugihara, the marketing director, has again developed an amazing cover. He has led the marketing effort with energy and creativity.

My agent, Pam Ahearn, played a critical role in helping me shape the story and providing valuable editorial suggestions. She is an outstanding editor, and I am grateful to have her assistance.

Again with this book, I have enormous gratitude to my wife, Barbara, for her help with the story and her encouragement.

"As China asserts itself as a naval and air power,
and as America responds, the risks of confrontation are growing."

—*The Economist*, May 30, 2015

PROLOGUE

December, in Bejing

Liu Guan was anxious about his meeting with Yao Xiao, the president and supreme leader of China. That was an unfamiliar feeling for the powerful head of the Ministry of State Security, or MSS, China's top intelligence agency. Mired in heavy traffic, Liu was riding alone in the back of a limousine.

"Use the siren and flashing lights," Liu called to his driver. "I want to get there today."

"Yes, sir."

An hour previously, Yao's aide had called to summon Liu to the presidential office in Tiananmen Square as though he were a misbehaving schoolboy. Ever since the call, Liu thought about the approach he should take with Yao. Though the Chinese president hadn't told him the purpose of the meeting, he had no doubt Yao would rip into him for his failure to obtain the Pentagon's Five Year Plan for Asia from US Senator Wesley Jasper.

In response, Liu had no intention of telling Yao what had happened to Jasper. That would only magnify Liu's failure. Instead, he planned to shunt that aside and move on to a new operation, which was sure to appeal to Yao. This new operation would address the difficulties the Chinese president was currently facing.

The Chinese economic miracle, launched by Deng, Mao's successor, was running out of steam. The intervening presidents, Jiang Zemin, Hu Jintao, and Xi Jinping, had kept it sputtering along while at the same time building the country's armed forces. The prevailing view among those three presidents and the Politburo was that as long as China's economy continued to expand and the people enjoyed prosperity with an accompanying increased standard of living and a rising stock market, the pressure for freedom and human rights would simmer at a low level. If, on the other hand, the economic juggernaut came to a halt, the pressure would build.

Yao's solution to this dilemma was conquest throughout Asia. By dominating its neighbors, China could ensure additional markets for its exports while at the same time obtaining cheaper raw materials. And there was something else. Conquest and domination of the rest of Asia played into the Chinese people's nationalism, which in turn was a powerful salve for a weakening economy. Yao saw Asia as a single monolithic ship with China at the helm. China's military was strong enough to achieve this result. He faced only one obstacle: the United States and its Asian treaty commitments.

When Liu entered Yao's ornate office, Yao didn't rise from his seat behind the large, red leather-topped desk. He motioned to the empty chair in front of the desk, and Liu sat down.

The sixty-four-year-old Yao looked weary, Liu thought. He had marked creases on his face and bags under his eyes. Liu had learned from a servant in Yao's house that the president rarely slept—at most an hour or two a night. Yao would either be at his desk reading documents or pacing the house. Sleeplessness took a toll on anyone—even the mighty president of China wasn't exempt.

"What happened in Hong Kong?" Yao asked.

"I was forced to turn the army loose on the protesters, they left me no choice. Several dozen protesters were killed. Many more wounded. We rounded up and imprisoned the organizers of the so-called student protest movement who were not really students but agitators. Some of them were from Japan. We also arrested journalists who were instigating these people. I made sure we blocked any media coverage. I think Hong Kong will be quiet for a while now. How long is difficult to say."

"You made the right decision," said Yao. "We had to nip this early. Otherwise, the protest movement would spread to the mainland."

"That's what I told the leaders in Hong Kong," affirmed Liu. "They agreed we had no choice. If we hadn't moved decisively, it would have been worse than 1989."

Yao got up from his desk and walked over to the window facing Tiananmen Square. Liu guessed Yao was replaying in his mind what happened there in June 1989. Liu didn't have to look at the square to recall what it was like at the time. As a young intelligence officer, he had infiltrated the mass of protesters, initially reporting on discussions among their leaders and later targeting ringleaders who were then taken out by army marksmen.

After a full minute, Yao wheeled around and said, "Let's hope you succeeded in squelching the movement in Hong Kong."

"I believe I did."

Yao returned to his chair. He was staring hard at Liu. "Now tell me why I never received the Pentagon's Five Year Plan. That's what I most wanted and what you promised."

Liu knew Yao well enough to realize that being argumentative or showing anger would not only get him fired from his job, but tossed into prison. So he grabbed the sides of his chair to calm himself before replying, "We were on the verge of obtaining the plan when Senator Jasper was murdered. He was jogging near his home in Washington when he was targeted by robbers. It was a random act of violence."

"Humph."

Liu wondered what that meant. Yao couldn't possibly know about Liu's involvement in Jasper's murder. It was unlikely that the ambassador in Washington would have told Yao after Liu had threatened to kill the ambassador's child, a daughter living in Paris, if he did. The only other person who knew about it was Xiang, and he would not have been able to get access to the president to tell him anyway.

Liu decided not to show weakness. Instead, he'd bull ahead. "Jasper's murder is an example of the rampant crime in the United States, of their lawlessness."

"Failure is still failure," frowned Yao. "Excuses won't be tolerated."

Liu felt perspiration soaking his shirt under the arms. "Following the death of Senator Jasper, our primary American asset," Liu said, "I developed a plan for a new operation entitled 'New World Order.'"

Yao sat up straight, his eyes boring into Liu. The spymaster clearly had the president's attention. "Tell me about it," he commanded.

"Since the end of the Second World War, the United States has shaped and dominated the world order—both economically and militarily," Liu began. "The Americans dictated the course of events. After more than seventy years, that order is in tatters and its architect, the United States, is in decline. During this same period, our great nation has recovered from its century of humiliation at the hands of the Western nations. We are now prepared to challenge the United States. The time has come to create a new world order with China in control. We will wrest dominance from the Americans."

"Those platitudes all sound good," said Yao, "but how do you propose to do that?"

"I have in mind a two-step process. First, we confront and weaken America's presence in East Asia. Second, we negotiate with them as equals and reach an agreement on a new world order."

"And you think they will be willing to do that?"

"At the end of the Second World War, at Yalta, the United States reached that type of agreement with Russia, ceding control over Eastern and Central Europe. Then the US was invincible. Now they are weary as a nation."

Liu watched as Yao closed his eyes and stroked his chin. Liu thought he looked intrigued by the proposal.

When Yao opened his eyes, he said, "Our chances of success will be much better if we have a top American official working with us."

Liu was thrilled to hear Yao's words. "Precisely," he agreed. "I have already arranged that."

"How much did you have to pay the American to come over to our side?" Yao asked.

"Nothing. For him it is a matter of principle."

"I prefer that," approved Yao. "Those who sell out for money can easily be turned by a higher bidder. How soon will you begin?"

"It would be better to wait a month," said Liu cautiously. "Let the dust clear from our Jasper operation. Also, I want to find the right opportunity."

"As you wish, Minister Liu. You have the most at stake. I will not tolerate another failure on your part."

Yao's words jolted Liu, but he showed no emotion. Instead, he fired back, "Operation New World Order *will* succeed."

PART I

January, One Month Later

Bethesda, Maryland

Kelly Cameron assembled her team in a conference room in Walter Reed Hospital for a final prep session. It was fifteen minutes before ten o'clock on a blustery, rainy evening. The twenty were all, with the exception of Kelly, battle-hardened from the wars in Iraq and Afghanistan.

The twenty members of her team, sixteen men and four women, were in military dress so they wouldn't stand out in the military hospital—all except Kelly, who was wearing a black wool pantsuit. They were all members of an elite new FBI counterterrorism unit, AT-1.

Kelly was worried their operation would fail. And she had a lot riding on this operation. Even before she had planned it, her position had been precarious. Many in the FBI had criticized Director Forester for naming Kelly—a woman, and only thirty-five—as the chief of AT-1. Senator Dorsey's subcommittee on terrorism in the United States, she learned later, had put the FBI director through a grueling interrogation in a closed-door session over the appointment. Other top FBI officials had criticized it in the press while withholding their names. Several articles appeared in the *Washington Post* beginning with the words: "Unnamed sources in the FBI have stated that . . ." But Forester hung tough.

Now it was showtime. Racing through Kelly's mind were the things that could go wrong. Ten days ago, a CIA mole planted in Iraq had forwarded information to his handler in Baghdad: ISIS is planning an attack on Walter Reed at 2 a.m. in ten days. That was a little over four hours from now. The informant didn't know how many terrorists would be taking part, or whether they would be hitting the hospital by air or land. What he did report was that the terrorists wanted maximum publicity with the attack. They intended to show that the United States couldn't even protect its own wounded military personnel. The CIA was convinced the intel was reliable.

Forester had put Kelly in charge of the FBI's effort to stop the attack. For the last ten days, working almost around the clock, she had directed an intense search of the Washington area to locate the attackers. But that had turned up nothing.

She had then coordinated with the Department of Defense to have the Air Force position planes above Washington. They had been in place since eight that evening. Others were on the ground at Andrews Air Force Base. Also at Andrews, DOD had established a control center for a Patriot system to thwart a missile attack.

That left only defense from a land attack, the hardest to cover. Walter Reed was on a 110-acre campus that had previously been the Bethesda Naval Hospital before the US government had shuttered and relocated the original Walter Reed on 16th Street in Washington. The hospital was a nightmare to defend. It was in a residential area in close proximity to shops and restaurants in the booming upscale Washington suburb of Bethesda, Maryland. The hospital complex had five different gates. Two of them were along Rockville Pike, one of the major north-south corridors outside the city of Washington.

As soon as she had gotten the assignment, Kelly had decided not to publicize the tip the CIA had received about the attack. It wasn't simply to prevent panic and hysteria in the area. Rather, Kelly had concluded if the terrorists knew the FBI was aware of their target and time of attack, they might shift and hit another government installation in the Washington area at a different time. "As long as we know, and they don't know that we know, we'll have the element of surprise." Forester had agreed. However, that also meant Kelly had to keep the size of her force small. Otherwise, it would look as though something big were going down, and the media would pick up on it.

If the attack were coming on the ground, Kelly reasoned, it would most likely be with a powerful car bomb in a vehicle driven by a suicide bomber. The driver's objective would be to get close enough to one of the buildings with patients.

Following that judgment, she stationed four of her troops at each of the five Walter Reed gates. Two were in each of the gatehouses, one was on the road leading into the gatehouse, and the fourth was on the hospital grounds ten yards inside the gate. Kelly would be in the command center on the third floor of the tower, the largest patient building, located between gates one and two. She would be at a window with a view of both gates. All of her troops were armed and wearing Kevlar vests.

By eleven o'clock in the evening, Kelly's forces were in place. Director Forester called for a status report.

"We're all set," Kelly told him in a voice projecting confidence she didn't feel.

What made this operation especially risky was that Walter Reed was a functioning hospital. That meant patients and staff were arriving at all hours. They were used to seeing some security. Kelly didn't think what she had in place was enough to alarm anyone.

As the clock ticked down to 2 a.m., Kelly was standing at the third floor window, binoculars up to her eyes, her blonde hair pulled back in a ponytail. She felt nervous. What if she had made a tactical error by not having more troops? What if the terrorists sent enough people to overwhelm her meager forces?

Two o'clock came and went. No attack.

At 2:20 a.m., Kelly worried that they had been acting on misinformation, or that the perpetrators had gotten wind of the FBI's preparations. She decided all units would remain in place until 6 a.m. Then she would reassess.

Suddenly her phone rang. It was Captain Nelson in the gatehouse at gate one, the northernmost gate on Rockville Pike. She laid her phone down on the table and placed it in speaker mode. Through her binoculars, she looked at the gate. The rain was coming down in sheets. A black Range Rover was stopped at the gate, waiting to enter.

"Yes, Captain," she said.

"A staff physician, Colonel Ahmed Massoudi, is here," Nelson replied in his Alabama accent. "His ID seems in order. Photo matches. Should I pass him through?"

"Hold him until you hear back from me," she snapped. Gabriella, one of the Walter Reed administrative staff was in the room with Kelly. She asked Gabriella about Dr. Massoudi.

"He's in orthopedics. Been on the staff for at least five years."

"Dial his home phone and ask for him."

While Gabriella complied, Kelly, pressing the binoculars close against her face, kept her eyes riveted on gate one.

Thirty seconds later, Gabriella said, "He answered." Her voice quavered. "I just woke him."

Kelly's whole body tensed. She shouted to Nelson on the phone, "He's our man. Arrest him and—"

Kelly didn't have a chance to finish her sentence. Shots were being fired from the Range Rover at the two men in the gatehouse. The man pretending to be Dr. Massoudi smashed through the wooden gate and drove inside the hospital complex.

Kelly bolted toward an inside staircase. Glock pistol in hand, she tore down the stairs. When she reached the ground, she stepped outside into the hard, cold rain. All of her senses were operating at maximum capacity. She was taut, but totally in control. She saw the Range Rover stopped ten yards from the tower. Standing between the vehicle and the building was Lieutenant Dietz, his automatic weapon raised, shouting, "Out of the vehicle now."

The driver got out with the engine still running and fired two shots, taking down Dietz. Seemingly unaware of Kelly's presence, he placed his pistol on the roof of the Range Rover. Moving rapidly, he grabbed a brick from the back seat of the car. Then he stood up and yanked a phone from his pocket. He was holding it in his left hand.

My God, he's planning to put the brick on the gas pedal and ram the vehicle into the tower to detonate a car bomb, Kelly realized.

Drenched, with water running down her face, she raised her gun and shouted, "Drop the phone."

With his right hand, the man grabbed the gun from the roof of the vehicle and aimed at Kelly while making a sudden move to the right.

Before he had a chance to pull the trigger, she fired. As her shot struck him, he fired back. She hit the ground and the bullet flew over her head. From the wet pavement, she watched him crumple to the concrete.

Kelly sprang to her feet and called for emergency medical personnel as bomb experts descended on the Range Rover.

An hour later, she had the verdict. Three of her men, Lieutenant Dietz and the two in gatehouse one, had been wounded. Two were in surgery, but all would live. The driver of the Range Rover was dead. The vehicle had been loaded with a massive bomb that would have done tremendous damage to the hospital.

For Kelly, the operation had been a success. Yet she was kicking herself. The terrorist might have moved suddenly, but she still should have aimed better. She shouldn't have killed him. Alive, he might have yielded valuable information. Dead, he was worthless.

Kelly called Director Forester to report what happened.

"Great job," he told her. "Now I want you to go home. I have a clean-up crew coming on the scene."

"But . . ."

"But, nothing. Go now. That's an order."

*   *   *

Kelly's house was a mile and a half from Walter Reed in a subdivision off Old Georgetown Road. She quietly opened the door to the dark and silent house. That was good. It meant her daughter, Julie, and Luisa, the housekeeper who doubled as a nanny, were sleeping.

She showered, put on a white terrycloth robe, and went into Julie's room. Sitting in a rocker, she watched her eight-year-old daughter sleeping, her beautiful face partially covered by long blond hair, the same color as Kelly's own. Next to her head on the pillow was the American Girl doll that Kelly's father had given Julie for her eighth birthday a month previously.

Kelly began shaking, her teeth chattering. She pulled the robe tightly around herself. The adrenalin she had been running on was gone, leaving her to confront the stark realization that she had been seconds from death. And then what for Julie? The girl's father, Jason Ryan, her husband until their divorce last September, would take care of Julie, but Kelly would never see her grow up, never be a part of her life. And Jason would constantly remind Julie: Your mother always put her career first.

Their breakup had been amicable. Jason had been a Washington lawyer, a workaholic on a high-pressure treadmill in the Washington office of a New York-based international law firm, who suddenly concluded he didn't want the rat race any longer. He decided to move to rural Maine to become a farmer. Kelly refused to go. She argued that Julie should have the opportunities an education in Montgomery County, Maryland, provided. But deep down, while her protests were focused on Julie, she realized the truth, which Jason put into words: "Your work comes first. You won't leave your job at the FBI."

They didn't have a custody battle. Self-centered Jason, who never had much interest in being a father or in Julie, was happy to leave her with Kelly. They agreed Julie would spend August each summer in Maine "if it was convenient" for Julie and for Jason. Kelly was convinced that when August came, Jason would decline to take Julie for the month. This suited Kelly just fine. She loved having her daughter around.

Kelly was happy to be rid of Jason. She was a rising star in the bureau, and she loved her work. More than that, she wanted to help her country. Kelly had been a college freshman at Carnegie Mellon at the time of 9/11. As she had watched mobs in Arab capitals cheering on television, she vowed to go into law enforcement to stop similar attacks from happening again. When she had graduated from Carnegie Mellon in computers and management, she had turned down high-paying offers from industry to join the FBI. She wanted to help make the country a safer place. Kelly was also determined to make her mark. She wanted her stay on this earth to mean something, to make a difference in the world.

Thinking about her time at Carnegie Mellon drove home for Kelly that she had never loved Jason. Love was what she had felt for Xiang when they had both been juniors, and she had fallen wildly in love with him. Originally from Shanghai, Xiang had moved to the States for college, where he had majored in econ and management. Even after fifteen years, it was still painful for Kelly to recall Xiang. She had never been in love before, and she had been crazy about him. She knew he had felt the same way about her.

Xiang told her he intended to stay in the United States following graduation. When they finished college, they had planned to get married. Her parents liked Xiang and gave their approval. For the summer before their senior year, Kelly and Xiang had lined up jobs in New York and an apartment in Chelsea. They were planning to live together until they got married. Kelly signed leases for an apartment in New York for the summer, and one in Pittsburgh for their senior year. She started her summer job with a financial security firm while Xiang went to China to visit his parents for a week before heading to New York.

But Xiang did not return to New York. He called and told her his plans had changed. "It would be best if we ended our relationship," he had said. That was it. No explanation. Nothing. Just like that.

Kelly couldn't believe it. "Is it something I did?" she had asked.

"No, it's what I have to do," he had told her.

It was a peculiar comment. She had decided his parents must not want their son to marry an American. She didn't know much about Chinese culture or Xiang's relationship with his parents. She guessed that's the way it was, and there was nothing she could do about it. Her father had taken care of the leases, no doubt paying off the landlords. It was rough for her for a while, but she made up her mind to get over it. Back at CMU in the fall, when she passed Xiang on campus, neither spoke to the other. Fortunately, they didn't have any classes together. As far as she was concerned, Xiang didn't exist.

Since graduation, she had seen Xiang only once. The previous November, they had met each other by chance one evening at a Washington restaurant. She was finishing dinner with an FBI colleague when she spotted Xiang, dining alone, across the room. She decided to show him how well she was doing. With that in mind, she went over to say hello, mentioning her wonderful career. He explained he was now assistant economic attaché at the Chinese embassy, and not married. She had hoped he would call so she could enjoy turning him down; he never did.

She didn't want to think about Xiang anymore. It was time to get a couple hours of sleep. Before climbing into bed, she checked her iPad. She saw a new email from Charles Cameron, her father. "From the bits of news I'm getting, looks as if you scored a big success tonight. We can talk later, but if you see this message, please let me know you're okay."

She replied, "Couldn't be better. Will call you in a few hours."

*   *   *

Kelly was up at seven. She wanted to have breakfast with Julie and walk her to the neighborhood public school. Rain was smacking against the bedroom windows as she grabbed a terrycloth bathrobe, tucked her cell phone in the pocket, and went downstairs.

When she reached the kitchen, Luisa was pouring milk into a glass. Julie, who was sitting at the table, was angry. "I don't like cornflakes," she sulked. "I want Honey Nut Cheerios."

"But we don't have any, Julie," Luisa said. "You finished them yesterday."

"But I want Honey Nut Cheerios."

"Okay, Julie," Kelly said, taking charge. "That's enough. I'll get some today. This morning, we're eating cornflakes."

"They're disgusting," Julie retorted.

"One day won't kill you," said Kelly. "No more arguing."

"Okay, Mom," Julie said reluctantly.

Kelly poured herself a cup of coffee. It tasted wonderful. She recalled one of her mentors in training at Quantico telling her, "When you escape a near miss with death, everything in life seems better."

The cell phone in the pocket of her robe rang. It was Forester.

"How soon can you get down to my office?" he asked.

"I'll leave the house now. What's up?"

"Better if we talk in person." His voice was grim. She wondered what had happened.

After putting the phone back in her pocket, she turned to Julie. "I have to go to the office. Luisa will walk you to school."

"Okay." Her daughter sounded resigned. This happened more days than Kelly liked to admit.

"Make sure you wear your Barbie boots and matching raincoat," Kelly instructed.

"They make me look like a baby," Julie groaned.

"We'll get you new ones, but today you have to wear them."

Kelly had meant to take Julie shopping for a new rain outfit weeks ago; somehow that had slipped through the cracks.

Washington

Forester was alone in his office. Kelly walked in and took the single chair in front of his desk. The director had thick, wavy, gray hair and a patrician look befitting the scion of one of Indiana's wealthiest families. He had been a federal district judge in Indiana before becoming the director of the FBI.

"Sorry to drag you in here so early after last night," the director said.

"What happened?" she asked.

"I received a call from Senator Dorsey from Texas who heads up the intelligence subcommittee on terrorism. The senator is either angry or he's posturing about what happened last night. I never know with him."

"What's his beef?" Kelly asked.

"He says we had plenty of notice about the attack," Forester replied. "We should have caught this terrorist before he ever got to Walter Reed."

"We used all of our resources in the search."

"I told him that, which didn't satisfy him, of course. And that's not all."

"What else?" Kelly asked.

"He says you should never have killed the terrorist. That was a huge mistake. If we had been able to interrogate him, we could have learned enough to stop future attacks."

"I wasn't trying to kill him," Kelly explained. "I was aiming for his shoulder. As I fired, he darted to the right."

"That's good to hear," Forester remarked. "I didn't realize that, but I reminded Dorsey you were operating in a blinding rainstorm with the lives of hundreds of wounded soldiers, as well as your own, on the line. The key fact is that you stopped the attack. And let's be realistic. I told Dorsey that with the new rules prohibiting enhanced interrogating techniques, none of these terrorists talk any longer anyway."

"How did Dorsey react?"

"He dismissed what I said."

Kelly had a sickening feeling in her stomach. The senator had been opposed to Forester giving her the job from the get-go. She wondered what action Dorsey would take.

As if reading her mind, Forester added, "Dorsey is planning to convene a closed-door hearing of his subcommittee tomorrow. He wants you to testify. I insisted on being in the room. Dorsey agreed, but you will have to be alone at the witness table."

Kelly's anxiety level was rising. "I guess Dorsey can do whatever he wants."

"Unfortunately, that's how our system works," Forester replied. "Have you ever appeared before a congressional committee?"

She shook her head. "Nope."

"I'll get the lawyers in the general counsel's office here to prep you. No need to worry. You'll do fine."

Leaving Forester's office, Kelly was wobbling on her feet. The only job she had ever wanted was with the FBI. Until this, she had a meteoric rise; now she saw it all unraveling. It was so unfair.

Hong Kong

Andrew Martin sipped champagne in the first-class cabin of an Air China plane en route from Washington to Hong Kong. He thought about the phone call he had received earlier that day from the Chinese ambassador to Washington. It was morning and Martin had been in his office.

"There is an emerging crisis in Hong Kong," the ambassador had said. "Justice Minister Jiang is there now, and he wants to talk with you. Your flight leaves at five o'clock this afternoon."

Martin had gulped hard. He not only had a full day of meetings and calls scheduled for that day and the next couple of days following, but as one of Washington's most powerful lawyers, he wasn't used to being yanked around on short notice.

To be sure, the Chinese government was a client of Martin's, and for the last five years had paid Martin's firm a one-million-dollar retainer. But at the top level of Washington law practice where Martin operated, one million dollars in fees meant very little. Martin went out of his way to provide the highest level of service for clients who paid at least ten million a year. Had this been any other client calling, Martin would have told him, "Sorry, I can't come today. Let's set a video conference call." However, he couldn't do that with the Chinese government. In advancing his own interests while serving them in the

Jasper affair, Martin had barely escaped with his career intact. He had to find out what they wanted. This might be a follow-up to those unfortunate events.

Martin scooped up a few nuts from the bowl on his tray. He was pleased at how well he had survived professionally after the fallout from the Jasper affair. Sure, it would have been a great honor to be named as chief justice of the Supreme Court, but Martin told himself that he would have been bored after a couple of years stuck in that ivory tower anyway. After all, wasn't that why Arthur Goldberg resigned, to get back into the Washington action?

There were a couple of clients who had left Martin because they found his conduct in the Jasper affair reprehensible, all based upon that scurrilous article Allison Boyd had concocted, but they were a distinct minority. He hung tough, telling everyone in an indignant voice, "I didn't do anything wrong, I tried to help a friend and I got screwed. When I lent my house in Anguilla to Senator Jasper, I had no idea he was taking his mistress. And I certainly can't be blamed for her death."

In a matter of days the Jasper affair, as it had been dubbed, was old news. New scandals hit the press daily, confirming how quickly current events become ancient history in Washington. What did endure, however, was Martin's reputation. He was still "the lawyer to hire" for clients with difficult Washington legal problems. Martin always got results, whether in the courtroom, the board room, before an administrative agency, or behind the closed door of a congressional office. The fees were still steadily rolling in for Martin.

What had changed, however, was his personal life. One evening, he and Francis had been having dinner alone at their home on Foxhall Road, eating a fabulous grilled steak and reaching the end of a 1990 Haut-Brion after finishing most of a bottle of Taittinger. Martin had become loquacious, figuring he could confide in his wife of thirty-five years everything he had done in the Jasper affair that had not come out in the media. Martin was actually proud that he had emerged unscathed, and he was boasting as he told Francis about it.

Big mistake. Francis was appalled and outraged. That evening she had slept in the guest room. The next day she took a leave of absence from her music teaching job and went to live with one of their daughters in San Diego. Martin missed her, but he'd be damned if he'd go out to California, or even make a call to get her back. So for the last six weeks he and Francis hadn't spoken, and he lived alone in their large house. Nothing he could do about it now, he thought. He had to put Francis out of his mind and concentrate on what could be a difficult meeting tomorrow.

The flight attendant came by and offered to refill Martin's champagne glass but he declined, trying to minimize his alcohol intake. He wanted his mind to be sharp. Jiang and his colleagues were tough negotiators.

*   *   *

When Martin arrived at the airport in Hong Kong, a young woman dressed smartly in a black suit with a short skirt and holding a Peninsula Hotel sign that conspicuously omitted his name approached him at the passenger exit.

"Andrew Martin," she said softly.

"How did you know?" he asked.

"You look like your picture."

She escorted him to a Rolls-Royce waiting at the curb. It was a cloudy day, the air heavy and the humidity stifling. Martin hadn't been in Hong Kong since the Chinese took over control from the British. As the driver navigated the heavy traffic with honking horns, pedestrians in the streets, and vendors along the sides of the road, Martin looked for changes in the city. His recollection from his last visit was fuzzy. Superficially, he couldn't see much difference, but he suspected the real changes were deeper, in the political order. Those would be harder to discern.

In front of the hotel, a white-gloved doorman led him inside the lobby with its high, gilded ceiling.

"We have a suite reserved for you on the thirtieth floor of our tower. Room 3000," the front office manager told Martin in a British accent. "You'll have an excellent view of the harbor. Is that acceptable?"

Martin felt like an honored guest. "I'm sure it will be fine."

"Outstanding. Now can I help you with restaurant reservations this evening?"

"I'm by myself. I haven't made any plans."

"May I suggest our Felix Restaurant on the top floor of the tower? The food has won awards and the view is outstanding. It's progressive European cuisine."

Martin had no idea what in the hell progressive European cuisine was, but he guessed the food would be quite good. He generally preferred going out, rather than room service, even when traveling alone on business.

"Please reserve a table," Martin requested. "I should be there in about half an hour."

As soon as he stepped off the elevator, a bellman following close behind him, he was greeted by a butler who accompanied him to the suite. He offered to unpack for Martin, but Martin declined, thanking him and waving him away.

After a long, rejuvenating shower, Martin dressed for dinner. When he reached Felix, the maître d' led him to a table by the window with an incredible view of the harbor and thousands of little lights. The streets were still swarming with people. The dining room was about half full, the patrons equally divided between Chinese and Westerners. A combo was playing "New York, New York," the female vocalist singing, "If I can make it there, I'll make it anywhere . . ."

Mindful of his resolution to cut down on alcohol, Martin resisted the temptation to order a scotch. A waiter left the menu and wine list, but Martin didn't open either. He was feeling anxiety about his meeting with Jiang tomorrow. What would the minister of justice ask him to do?

He had already taken some terrible actions to conceal Chinese involvement in Senator Jasper's death. Having considered himself a patriotic American, Martin now regretted those earlier steps. Notwithstanding his effort at rationalization, he realized there was a fine line between legal representation of a foreign nation and espionage against the United States. Unfortunately, he had crossed that line. Martin couldn't undo what he had already done, but he could resolve to change his behavior. He would refuse to take any additional actions that were disloyal to the United States. And he would be firm with Jiang, regardless of the personal consequences.

Deep in thought, Martin felt a tapping on his shoulder. He looked up to see the waiter holding a glass of champagne.

"One of our guests," said the waiter, "asked me to deliver this to you." He pointed to a woman sitting alone three tables away near the window. She was a strikingly beautiful Chinese woman, about thirty, Martin guessed, close to the age of his daughters. She was wearing a tight-fitting, simple black dress and sipping champagne. When Martin looked her way, she smiled at him. For an instant, he thought about his alcohol resolution, then he decided every rule permitted exceptions. So he thanked the waiter and asked him to leave the champagne.

Martin stood up, glass in hand, and walked over to her table.

"That was very nice of you," he said.

"Well, you looked so serious and deep in thought, I figured you could use some cheering up."

"I did a lot of flying today," he replied. "That's never much fun."

She raised her glass. "To good times."

They both sipped.

"I feel better already," he said. "My name's Andrew Martin."

"Huan Ji," she replied, smiling and showing perfect white teeth.

"Would you like to join me for dinner?" Martin asked.

"I would love that. Your table or mine?" She laughed.

"Well I'm already here, so . . ."

Martin sat down across from her.

"Are you in Hong Kong on business?" she asked.

"Yes, I'm a lawyer from Washington. And you?"

"I'm a writer from Shanghai en route to the United States to do some research for a novel. I wanted to stop here for a few days to observe the protests. I may write about them at some point."

"Protests?" Martin asked.

"The pro-democracy movement in Hong Kong wants to have open and free elections to pick their own leaders," Huan Ji replied. "The monsters in Beijing are determined to block them. Today, it was peaceful. Tomorrow is unclear, but I can't afford to change my plane ticket so I'm flying out of here in the morning."

"Where are you going in the US?"

"New York, San Francisco, and probably Washington."

He noticed her English was spoken with a British accent. "Were you educated in England?" he asked.

"Oxford, with a degree in world literature."

"Really? I went to Oxford myself. Queen's College."

"I was at Magdalene," she said.

"We must have just missed each other," he joked. "I'm kidding, please don't ask when I was there."

"Before or after the Great War?" she quipped.

"Very funny."

The waiter handed Martin a menu and a wine list. He noticed Huan already had a menu open on the table in front of her.

"Have you decided what you want?" Martin asked.

"That's a fairly nebulous question," she replied.

"I meant to eat."

"Oh, actually, yes. Mixed seafood salad, and they have the most incredible duck, carved tableside."

"I'll have the same," Martin said.

"Wine?" the waiter asked.

Martin looked at Huan.

"I'm partial to French and Italian reds," she said.

"Then that'll be easy." He took a quick look at the wine list and selected a 2005 Domaine Leroy Chambolle-Musigny.

"You obviously know something about wine."

He laughed. "Just a little bit. I think you'll like this one. Madame Leroy is an incredible winemaker."

"Wasn't she the winemaker at DRC?"

Martin was surprised Huan knew that. "I'm not the only one who knows more than a little about wine," he remarked. "Have you written other novels?"

"This will be my first," she replied. "My protagonist is a young Chinese man named Wu. He grew up in Shanghai, was a brilliant student in math and computers. After graduation from college he works with a high-tech outfit in Shanghai. But he finds life in China too limiting—there are too many people and not enough freedom under the repressive government. So he decides to move to the United States."

Huan paused as the waiter brought the wine. Martin asked her to taste it. As she took a sip she smiled with pleasure. "Oh my. This is good."

The seafood salads soon followed, and as they ate, she resumed talking about her novel.

"Well, anyhow, Wu goes to Silicon Valley to work for a high-tech outfit, but he finds the people narrow-minded. A bunch of technocentric geeks. Then a Wall Street firm offers him a large bonus to work for an investment banking firm where computer trading is driving profits. So he moves to New York."

"What about his love life?" Martin asked.

"In California he only has awkward one-night stands. In New York he meets a colleague at his firm who's a rising star. She's a farm girl from Iowa. They have incredible sex, eat at the best restaurants, front row seats for Broadway shows and sports events, and . . ." Huan trailed off. "Hey, enough about my novel. I want to know about you."

"First, tell me where you're going with this," Martin said, intrigued by her story.

"Well, despite the money, the sex, his freedom and lavish lifestyle," Huan continued, "Wu isn't happy in the US. He feels that America, like England a hundred and fifty years ago, is an empire in decline. He also feels like a fish out of water. So eventually he goes back to Shanghai."

As the duck arrived, she repeated her question. "Now tell me about yourself, Andrew."

She seemed genuinely interested, he thought. "I'm the managing partner of a large Washington-based international law firm, Martin and Glass," he replied.

"You started it?" she asked.

"I did."

"Are you married?"

When Francis had left, he had taken off his wedding ring and tossed it into a drawer.

"Divorced," he said. Though that wasn't accurate, it was how he felt. "Things just didn't work out."

"Sorry to hear that," she said sympathetically.

"What about you?" Martin asked.

"I never met the right man," she replied with a smile.

After they had finished their duck, the vocalist was singing "That's Amore."

"Would you like to dance?" she asked.

"I'm afraid I've never done much dancing," Martin answered.

"I'm sure you'll be just fine," she replied, standing up and moving toward the small wooden floor in front of the combo. For a moment, Martin hesitated. She obviously expected him to follow. Oh, what the hell, he thought. He stood up and fell in behind her.

As Martin held Huan and they moved around the floor, an expression used by one of his tennis buddies at Kenwood Country Club came into his mind. "Age inappropriate." This described Martin with Huan, he thought, but so what? He was enjoying himself. Huan was intelligent and fun to talk with. And that wasn't all. Huan was incredibly sexy. As he held her close, he felt himself becoming aroused.

When they returned to the table, the duck was cleared. The waiter had left dessert menus. They both glanced at them.

"See something you like?" Martin asked.

"I have a better idea," said Huan.

"What's that?"

"Your room or mine?" she asked, laughing.

For an instant, Martin didn't know what to say. Through thirty-five years of marriage, he had never been with another woman. Also, from the time the Jasper affair began until Francis had left, they hadn't had sex. The couple of times they had tried, he couldn't perform. Going off with Huan now seemed like a disastrous and humiliating way to end what had been an enjoyable evening.

Without waiting for him to respond, she signaled the waiter. "We'll have the check, please."

When it arrived, she suggested they split it. Martin shook his head, snatched it from the table, and signed it to his room. When he had finished, she stood up and took his hand. In the elevator he pressed 30, then led the way down the hall to his room.

Once they were inside the living room of the suite, Martin asked, "Would you like a drink? I'm sure they have cognac, armagnac, and anything else you might like in the minibar."

She walked over, loosened Martin's tie, and leaned up to kiss him, leaving no question of what she had in mind.

He pulled away. "Listen, Huan, you're a wonderful person and I really like you, but I have to tell you something."

She looked alarmed. "What's that?"

"This may not be a good idea," he said.

"Why not?"

He was embarrassed. "Well, sometimes I've had trouble becoming aroused."

"I don't mind," she reassured him. "I give an incredible massage. I'd like to do that for you. Just relax and enjoy the massage. Don't think about anything else, turn your mind off. After I'm finished, I'll leave. So you don't have to worry or stress about anything else. How's that?"

"Sounds good," Martin said, sounding relieved.

"Let's go into the bedroom," she suggested.

While Martin undressed, he watched her take off her dress and hang it up. He stared at her in her white silk bra and panties, at her shapely legs. She was gorgeous, and even more beautiful when she took off her underwear. Her breasts were full and round and she had a thick brown bush between her legs. She went into the bathroom and emerged with a jar of body lotion and a hand towel, which she tossed on an end table.

"Okay, mister important Washington lawyer, are you willing to put me in charge?" she said.

"Sure. Anything you want."

"Good. Then lie down on the bed on your front. Just relax and enjoy yourself."

Martin complied, stretching out on his stomach. She crouched alongside him, rubbing lotion into his neck, shoulders, and back. Her hands felt incredibly good, and all of the tension drained from his body.

"That feels great," he said.

"You haven't felt anything yet."

She massaged the backs of his legs, starting from below the knee. Gradually, she worked her way up to his thighs and then his buttocks. His legs were spread, and she reached between them, stroking and caressing his balls. As she did, he felt his cock stiffening. She reached underneath and played with that as well.

"Time to flip over," she said.

As Martin did, he was astounded to see the size of his erection. He couldn't remember it ever being that hard. "Come on top," he said, desperately wanting to slip it inside of her.

"Nope. Remember, you said I could be in charge."

Martin had no idea what she would do next, but he didn't have to wait long to find out. She slid down and began licking the sides of his shaft. He couldn't believe how good that felt. Francis had never wanted to perform oral sex on him. Then she took his hard cock in her mouth. As she sucked, he felt an orgasm approaching, but she clutched his shaft at the bottom to keep him from coming. Finally, she climbed on top and slid him inside her. In a matter of seconds he closed his eyes, feeling the ecstasy of release. When he opened them, she was smiling at him.

"Did you like that?" she asked.

"It was amazing. But I don't think it was much pleasure for you."

"Wait," she smiled. "The night is still young. Let's take a shower."

The huge marble bathroom had a large shower with a beige marble bench in one corner. The shower could easily have held six people. Huan went in first and adjusted the water temperature, then Martin followed. He stood under the water, letting it run down his head and face. He felt marvelous.

She turned to Martin and began soaping him, running her fingers over his body. As she reached his genitalia, his penis was stiffening again. Martin couldn't believe it. Not since he was thirty had he been able to have an erection so soon after sex. She really was something.

She put down the soap, faced him, and put her arms around him. He held her tight, the water running over both of them.

"Kiss me," she said.

He gave her a long kiss, his tongue insinuating itself into her mouth. She reached down and took his hard cock in her hand, then led him to the bench. Sitting down, she spread her legs, opening her gorgeous bush to him.

"Make love to me," she said. "Now. Hard."

Martin had a bad knee from sports, and for an instant he felt a jolt of pain, but he shrugged it off. Crouching in front of her, he penetrated her, thrusting back and forth.

"Yes . . ." she cried out. "Yes! That feels so good . . . harder . . . harder!"

He complied and a few moments later they came together. Breathing heavily, he collapsed next to her on the bench.

Half an hour later, she was dressed and ready to leave.

"When's your plane?" Martin asked.

"Ten in the morning," she replied. "I'll sleep all the way to New York."

"Did you tell me at dinner you might be coming to Washington on your visit to the US?" he asked.

"That's my plan."

"Well, you better let me know when. I'd like to see you there."

She smiled, and they exchanged contact info.

At the door, he kissed her. "Thank you," he said.

"No, thank you. I'm so happy I was in that dining room when you arrived. You don't look much like the sad and worried man I sent the champagne to."

"I don't feel like him either," said Martin.

With her hand on the doorknob, she said, "Listen Andrew, I don't know where in Hong Kong you're going tomorrow, but be careful. Some of the protest leaders I spoke to today are planning to confront the regime more aggressively. If it turns violent, the police and army will do whatever it takes to crush them. Some of the top leaders have come here from Beijing. So watch your step."

*   *   *

At breakfast, Martin turned on CNN to check on the protests, but there was no news. Not surprising. The regime must have blacked it out.

On the half-hour car ride to his meeting with Jiang, Martin constantly looked out of the tinted windows, searching for some sign of the protests. He didn't see a thing. Hong Kong, or at least this part of it, seemed to be business as usual. It was just another frenetic day in one of the world's most bustling cities.

The car pulled up in front of a nondescript, ten-story, gray stone structure. There were no signs on the building, and six armed soldiers brandishing automatic weapons were standing at the top of four concrete stairs. Inside, a receptionist with heavy, brown-framed glasses wearing a short tan skirt and matching tight sweater, led Martin into a conference room on the top floor with a view of the harbor. In halting English, she offered Martin coffee, which he accepted.

In their three previous meetings, Jiang had always kept Martin waiting—at least for half an hour. Over the years, Martin had been subjected to similar treatment by various corporate executives and government officials around the world. It was their way of showing they were in charge. To Martin, it made them seem petty and insecure.

Today, there was no waiting. As soon as Martin moved away from the window and took a sip of his coffee, Jiang entered the room carrying a coffee mug of his own. In a country where height mattered, Jiang was fortunate. He was six foot two and had a large frame.

Jiang was smiling, which worried Martin. He'd never seen the somber looking Jiang smile before.

"I appreciate your coming on short notice," Jiang said, gesturing to the table. They both sat down.

"The Chinese government has been a valuable client for five years," said Martin. "I'm grateful for that."

"Your work for the People's Republic of China is something I want to talk to you about," said Jiang. He paused for a moment.

Waiting for him to continue, Martin tried not to appear apprehensive. He wondered how much, if anything, Jiang knew about the Chinese involvement in Jasper's death and what Martin had done.

As if reading his mind, Jiang said, "I have been informed by our ambassador in Washington that you were very helpful in connection with that unfortunate business involving Senator Jasper. I'm well aware your actions have had adverse consequences for you."

"It was a complicated matter," Martin replied. "The senator was my good friend, or at least I thought so when the incident began. His behavior created a regrettable situation for all of us, and I made certain decisions that in retrospect I should not have made. However, that is all water over the dam now, as we say in the United States."

Jiang laughed. "In Boston, when I was at Harvard Law School, they referred to it as water under the bridge."

Martin tried to force a laugh. "Well, they have lots of bridges in Boston."

"Did you ever row on the Charles?" Jiang asked.

"Can't say I did."

"Oh, that's right, you went to that other law school in New Haven. Well regardless, the US government is not pursuing the Jasper murder. You used your relationships with Jane Prosser and George Wilkins to convince them to halt their investigation. You made it go away.

You fixed it. Is that an appropriate word for describing what a powerful Washington lawyer does?"

Martin frowned. "Some people use that word," he said. "I've never liked it."

"Well, regardless of how we describe it," said Jiang, "my government is extremely pleased by what you did. I've arranged for your firm to receive a one-million-dollar success fee. It will be sent by wire transfer today."

Martin was floored. Clients rarely offered voluntary additional payments as success fees. "Thank you very much."

"I presume you're planning to stay at the law firm?"

"For sure," said Martin. "I'm quite happy at Martin and Glass."

"I'm glad to hear you are pleased with your current situation," Jiang remarked, "because I would like to change our relationship."

Well here it was. The reason for the meeting. "Change it how?" Martin asked.

"For the last five years, we have had a one million dollar per year retainer with your firm."

"That's right," Martin agreed.

"The work has been excellent. However, it has been confined to the United States."

"Correct."

"Your firm has offices elsewhere in the world," Jiang noted.

"In Europe and Asia," Martin confirmed.

"We want to expand your firm's representation to include work throughout the world. Martin and Glass would become the primary law firm worldwide for the People's Republic of China. And we would increase the annual retainer to ten million dollars. Is this something you would be willing to do?"

"Of course. We will do all of your work at a high level of quality."

"There is one condition," said Jiang.

Martin was concerned. Conditions on representation were generally troublesome.

"You must remain at the firm and in charge of this representation," Jiang continued. "That means no retirement or pursuit of other opportunities for at least three years."

"That won't be a problem," Martin replied. "The law firm is my life, I have no plans to leave."

"Excellent."

While Jiang paused to sip his coffee, Martin thought about what he had heard. Jiang's words didn't make sense. There couldn't be nine million dollars' worth of work that Martin's firm could do outside of the United States. This new arrangement involved something more that Jiang was not telling him. Martin remained still, waiting for the other shoe to drop.

Jiang cleared his throat, then continued, "Legal assignments will be given to you from time to time by various people in the Chinese government, including our ambassador in Washington."

"That's fine with me," said Martin. "You may distribute my contact info to your officials as you see fit."

"One other matter. Before you return to the US, I would like you to meet Liu Guan, our minister of state security, who is here in Hong Kong with me. He has an assignment for you."

Martin gulped hard. His euphoria was fading fast. He had never met Liu, but he knew of Liu's reputation. The man was hard and cruel, someone who took no prisoners. Also, Liu was known to be a hardliner in terms of Chinese relations with the United States. Aware that Liu's agency, MSS, the Ministry of State Security, was China's premier intelligence agency, Martin was concerned about the assignment Liu would be giving him. He was worried that what the Chinese were looking for was Martin's involvement in espionage directed against the United States. If that was the case, he would turn down the ten-million-dollar retainer. He had no intention of making this Faustian bargain. And Liu couldn't compel him to do it. But did he need to clarify that with Jiang?

Martin decided not to say anything to Jiang. Perhaps he was being too pessimistic in his assessment. He would hear what Liu wanted first. Over his long legal career, Martin had held many difficult discussions with presidents and prime ministers, kings, and corporate leaders. He would know how to push back with Liu if he had to.

"When would you like me to meet with Liu?" he asked.

"I'm leaving now," said Jiang. "He'll be here shortly."

Ten minutes later, Liu entered the room. The spymaster had a jowly face, pencil-thin mustache, and his lips were pressed tightly together. He was wearing narrow, wire-framed glasses below thinning black hair that was parted in the center. Behind those glasses were hard, cruel eyes.

Liu sat across the table from Martin and lit a foul-smelling cigarette. He held out the pack to Martin, who shook his head.

"I appreciate your coming to Hong Kong," Liu said. "I am involved here in dealing with protests against the government. The protesters are unfortunately being supported by the Japanese government. This is a complex situation. If Tokyo does not stop meddling in our internal affairs, they will have a heavy price to pay. And I hope your President Braddock will not support the protesters."

Martin was glad Huan had briefed him about the protests. "I have no idea what Braddock will do," he replied. "I have had my own issues with the American president."

"I understand that from our ambassador in Washington. This is part of my reason for wanting to see you."

"I don't understand."

Liu paused to blow circles of smoke into the air. Then he said, "You should know that I supported Jiang, our justice minister, in his proposal to expand your retention agreement. Our ambassador in Washington informed me of everything you did for us in connection with the Jasper affair. You are well-versed in the ways of your government."

"I have been in Washington a long time," Martin said guardedly.

"Senator Jasper was a good friend of yours," Liu remarked.

"Since college. We were roommates at Yale. I advised him in his campaigns."

"He was a fool, letting that woman Vanessa Boyd bring him down."

Martin had no intention of defending Jasper, who had turned on him despite his efforts to help. On the other hand, Liu was far from blameless. Martin didn't dare say that directly, but he did hint at it.

"Mistakes were made by many in that matter." Then, frightened by the menacing scowl that appeared on Liu's face, Martin added, "I meant by me as well as Jasper. I should not have made that call."

Liu snarled, but didn't pursue it. "As a part of your work under the expanded retainer," he said, "I have a Washington project for you."

"What's that?"

"From time to time, an official in the American government will be delivering materials in a sealed envelope to you in your office. Each time you receive an envelope, I would like you to call a man named Xiang. He's the assistant economic attaché at our embassy in Washington. Ask him to come to your office for a meeting. You will then hand over the sealed envelope to him. That's all."

"Who's the American official?"

"In good time, I will tell you."

This was precisely what Martin feared. "You want me to commit espionage? To be a traitor to my country?"

Liu shrugged. He put out his cigarette and lit another, a tiny smile appearing beneath his mustache. "I merely want you to be a conduit passing information among friends. You will have no idea what's in the sealed envelopes. There will be no risk to you. As an influential Washington lawyer, it will be natural for you to meet with the American official. As the lawyer for the People's Republic of China with a ten-million-dollar retainer, it will be natural for you to meet with the assistant economic attaché from our embassy. None of this will seem out of the ordinary for a powerful Washington lawyer. No one could possibly become suspicious—or even raise a question."

"It will still be espionage. We have an American expression: A rose by any other name is still a rose."

"Don't be ridiculous," said Liu. "You won't be planting documents under a park bench, in the hollow of a tree, or anything like that."

Liu said it smoothly, but it didn't alleviate Martin's concerns. "I didn't realize that espionage was part of my arrangement."

The phone on Liu's desk rang. He picked it up. Martin couldn't understand what Liu was saying in Chinese, but the spymaster looked increasingly angry and agitated. Finally, he pounded his fist on the desk and shouted out what sounded like orders. Then he put down the phone and looked at Martin.

"For days I've tried to be reasonable with those protesters," Liu said. "I will not turn over Hong Kong to them. The time has come to show them we're serious. I've told my people to crush the protestors, to do whatever it takes, using the army and starting with tear gas and water hoses. After that, rubber bullets and even live ammunition if necessary."

Listening to Liu, Martin became more apprehensive.

"Let's return to your situation," Liu said. "If you want to cancel the ten-million-dollar retainer I'm sure the justice minister will understand."

Martin was rapidly coming to the conclusion that the ten-million-dollar retainer wasn't worth what he was being asked to do. And Liu was terrifying. He would do better to walk away and sever his relationship with the government of China entirely.

"I'm no spy," Martin said boldly as he stood up, signaling that the meeting was over.

Liu remained seated. "Before you get too carried away with self-righteousness, Mr. Martin, let me remind you that you presented a patently false story to Secretary of State Prosser to persuade her to have the Washington police close out a murder investigation. Also, as a result of your concealment of a certain CD, Senator Jasper was killed. I am no American legal expert, however our justice minister, who was educated at Harvard Law School, has informed me that you could be charged as an accessory to murder if these facts become known to Arthur Larkin, your attorney general."

Martin collapsed back into his chair. What Liu said was accurate, but Martin's objective hadn't been to aid the Chinese government. Still, he realized his actions could be misunderstood, viewed as improper, even as espionage and accessory to murder.

"Yes, I did those things," Martin replied firmly. "And your government benefitted enormously."

"I'm not sure we did. In any event, that's not the point."

"What *is* the point?" Martin asked.

For a full minute, Liu, his eyes boring in on Martin, didn't respond. Then in a sharp voice, he said, "I'm prepared to have our ambassador in Washington disclose all of these facts to your secretary of state and attorney general. Prior to that disclosure, the people involved from our embassy who have diplomatic immunity will fly back to China. You alone will be in Washington to face the criminal charges. And I am certain they will reach out to Allison Boyd. No doubt Allison will be happy to confirm your improper and illegal acts."

Liu's words cut through Martin like a machete. The spymaster gave Martin a sinister smile before continuing. "Since you're fond of

American expressions, here's another one I've learned: I have you over a barrel. That's appropriate for this situation, isn't it?"

When Martin didn't respond, Liu leaned across the table and said, "Either you do what I ask, or I will break you, Andrew Martin."

Martin did not want to do Liu's bidding. Desperately, he tried to find a way out of this dilemma. But he couldn't. His prior behavior left him no choice.

One thought kept him going: *I'll never get caught.*

*   *   *

On the long plane ride from Hong Kong to Washington with a stopover in Tokyo, Martin hashed and rehashed in his mind his disconcerting conversation with Liu. The Chinese spymaster was shrewd. Thanks to Martin's error of judgment, or stupidity, in trying to help cover up what happened to Jasper in Anguilla, he had made himself vulnerable to Liu's blackmail. Now Martin had no choice—he had to do what Liu wanted. If he didn't, he would face more disgrace and possible disbarment.

Once more, Martin considered his other options. He could talk to Arthur and try to cut a deal for immunity with the attorney general. The problem with that was Arthur was already angry with Martin for not leveling with him earlier. Arthur was fiercely competitive, hated losing or looking bad, and was vindictive. Arthur would spurn Martin's offer. Martin had no doubt the AG would then charge him with being an accessory to Jasper's murder. Allison would make the government's case. That was the result Martin reached each time he analyzed the issue.

Unfortunately, he didn't have anyone with whom he could discuss it. Until Francis had left, through their thirty-five years of marriage, he had always discussed hard issues with her. Of course, he could call Francis and ask her to come back, or even go to California to see her, but his pride precluded that. She had left and he'd be damned if he'd beg her to return.

Thinking about Francis, Martin focused on Huan and their night together. That had been great fun and reinforcement for his virility. No use kidding himself, however, it was still a one-night stand. Sure, they had exchanged contact information, but that was something he had done with hundreds of business people over the years and nothing ever came of it. He tossed their cards into a desk drawer at the office or at home. That's what Huan would do with his contact info. Their parting words had been the equivalent of, "Let's do lunch."

Martin chided himself for continuing to rehash his decision to do Liu's bidding. That wasn't how he had ever operated. He was always a compartmentalize and move on type of person. This time, the enormity of what he was doing and the risks he was facing made that difficult. Still, he had to stop second-guessing. Fortunately, Liu had structured the operation in a way to minimize the chances of Martin getting caught. Now he had to play the hand he had been dealt with strength and self-confidence.

By the time the plane touched down at Dulles Airport, Martin was ready to do that.

I'll never get caught, he told himself again.

Chevy Chase, Maryland

Kelly's head was spinning. Starting at two that afternoon and continuing until five, she had been stuck in a windowless conference room at FBI headquarters with three of the bureau's lawyers. Their mission was to prepare her for tomorrow morning's testimony before Senator Dorsey's subcommittee.

Until that afternoon, she had thought it would be a relatively simple matter to tell Dorsey and the subcommittee about the FBI's effort to locate the terrorists and what happened at Walter Reed. Not so, they explained. "Each answer you give must be carefully thought out, both because of its implications for you and also how it will reflect on the bureau. You don't want to end up with personal liability, and you don't want the bureau to appear incompetent. You must be polite and contrite—always respectful."

They took turns firing questions at her. Then they analyzed each answer, telling her how it could be improved. By the end of the session, she decided that she hated all nitpicking lawyers; she wanted to scream.

As they were breaking up, perhaps guessing what Kelly was thinking, one of the lawyers said, "You'll be grateful to us tomorrow at this time."

She wanted to say, "I doubt that." Instead, she forced a smile and politely replied, "Thank you for your time."

Luisa wanted to meet friends that evening, so Kelly had arranged for Luisa to drop Julie at her father's house in Chevy Chase. The three of them would have dinner there. Driving to her father's house, Kelly thought about how lucky she was to have him as a sounding board and to help her with Julie.

He still lived in the red brick Georgian on Leland Street—the house in which Kelly had grown up. Before she was born, her father had selected the location because it was between CIA headquarters in Langley and his parents' home in an upscale Baltimore suburb. His wife, Kelly's mother, who was from a small town in Ohio, had no real say in that decision or in any of the other decisions in her forty years of marriage to Charles Cameron. Kelly was convinced her dad never fully appreciated her mother and all she did for him until she died of ovarian cancer two years ago.

That had been an enormous loss for Kelly, an only child. She and her mother had enjoyed a close relationship, forged during her early years when her dad had been away, out of the country for weeks or months at a time. Her mother simply told her he was away on "business," but he was unable even to communicate by phone with them during these absences.

Suddenly, he stopped doing that "business." Her father then began to work for his father's candy company, headquartered in Baltimore. No explanations were given to Kelly by her mother or father. At the time, she didn't understand what had happened. He had made a 180-degree turn and never seemed to look back.

It wasn't until Kelly was a senior in high school that her father told her about "the business" he had been doing before he switched to the candy company. He explained that he had been with the CIA. It was the last years of the Cold War, and his job had been running operations to smuggle scientists and others of "high value" to the United States out of East Germany and other countries behind the Iron Curtain.

An operation, his final one, had been compromised, and he took a bullet in the leg while covering the successful escape of a high-level nuclear scientist. Surgeons saved the leg and ultimately he made a complete recovery, but they told him that would take time and for a while he would have a limp, confining him to a desk job at Langley. He told Kelly that he couldn't endure that, so he had quit the agency and joined his father in operating the candy manufacturing business that had been in the family for three generations. Kelly viewed what he had done with pride. It became a major factor in her decision to join the FBI.

Shortly after Kelly's mother died, Hershey bought the candy company. Kelly thought her dad would go nuts with nothing to do, but he proved her wrong. He traveled, read incessantly about geopolitical affairs, and advised Kelly on her career. He told her he'd be happy to discuss work issues with her. With his experience, she appreciated it. Though it violated FBI rules, she never hesitated to talk to him, both about her cases and about the Washington bureaucracy. After all, he had once had clearance for top secret matters when he had been with the CIA.

When Kelly's marriage broke up, her father stepped in and helped fill the void for Julie. This surprised Kelly, who had always resented that he wasn't there for her when she had been growing up. When she saw the close bond that Julie and "Grandpa" formed, and how much it meant to Julie, Kelly was willing to put aside her own grievances.

As Kelly let herself in to her father's house, she found him and Julie playing a computer game, competing with each other to see who could blast the most fast-moving enemy aircraft out of the sky. It wasn't Kelly's favorite game for her eight-year-old daughter, but her dad always brushed aside her concerns and told her, "It'll improve her hand-eye coordination."

As soon as he saw Kelly, he said, "Okay, kiddo, game's over. Time to do your homework."

"One more game," Julie pleaded.

"No more. Your mom and I have to make dinner."

"She can do it herself."

"No fresh talk," he reprimanded as he turned off the computer.

Julie went upstairs to her room, the room she used when staying at her grandpa's house—the room that had once been Kelly's.

Once they were in the kitchen, her dad said, "I'm grilling salmon. You want a beer first?"

"Sure," Kelly replied.

He opened two bottles of his favorite craft beer, handed her one, and led the way to the den.

"Don't you have to get dinner ready?" she asked.

"It can wait. I want to hear how it went this afternoon."

"They grilled me. I hate lawyers."

He laughed. "I'm right with you there. Especially ones who work for the FBI or CIA."

She raised the bottle and took a sip. "I'm scared about tomorrow," she admitted.

"You're right to be worried, but you shouldn't be scared. That's what you feel when somebody's pointing a gun at you."

"I'll be a fish out of water in that damn Senate hearing room."

"That's ridiculous," he said. "You did an outstanding and heroic job. You saved hundreds of lives. You've got nothing to be ashamed of. Blowhards like Dorsey get their rocks off going after courageous public servants."

"It just seems so unfair."

"Of course it is. Dorsey is being ludicrous. You risked your life for this country."

"I'd like to tell him that," said Kelly.

"You can't in so many words, but you can be bold and aggressive with the senators. Not defensive; but proud of what you did. If they push, you push back—hard."

Her dad's advice was diametrically opposed to the bureau's lawyers, who told her to be "polite and contrite—always respectful."

She didn't know what to do.

Washington

At ten minutes to ten the next morning, Kelly took a seat at the table in front of a raised stand with six empty chairs and name tags—one for each member of the subcommittee. The only other people in the room were Forester, sitting behind Kelly in the first row of the gallery, and a court reporter transcribing the proceedings at a desk off to one side

The room was warm. Kelly poured a glass of water from the pitcher on her table, but cautioned herself against drinking too much. She wanted to get this over with as soon as possible, and not have to ask for a bathroom break, which would extend the hearing.

All six members of the subcommittee filed in. Dorsey led the way with his protruding stomach and a surly look while the others followed joking and laughing. The clerk administered the oath to Kelly. Then Dorsey, a former Houston prosecutor, began the questioning. He took her through her investigation to locate the terrorist, each lead she had, and how it had been pursued. At every stage, he asked: Couldn't you have also done this, or couldn't you have also done that? Most were absurd suggestions, but she remained polite and contrite.

Dorsey said, "The terrorist could have given us valuable information. Why did you kill him?"

"I only intended to wound him by shooting him in the shoulder," she said, attempting to sound respectful.

"Do you consider yourself a good marksman, Ms. Cameron?"

"I have scored very well in all FBI tests."

"Answer my question," he snapped.

"Yes, I do."

"What was your distance from the terrorist?"

"Approximately twenty yards," she replied.

"And at that distance you didn't just wound him, you killed him. I'd say you need more time at the shooting range. Or maybe you were so angry at what this man was trying to do that you wanted to kill him? You can admit that to us."

"That was not my intention, Senator Dorsey."

"You are under oath. Is that still your answer?"

"Yes it is."

"Then are you just a bad shot, Ms. Cameron?" he pressed.

This was too much for Kelly. She was tired of polite and contrite. She decided to follow her father's advice.

"Listen, Senator Dorsey, it was raining hard and it was dark," she said, raising her voice with emotion. "I had a good aim at the terrorist's shoulder, but at the last second he moved. Had he not moved, the bullet would have hit its mark. He was aiming at me and I fired only an instant before he did. Had I not hit him, his car bomb would have exploded and hundreds of our wounded and recovering soldiers would have been killed."

From her research, she knew that Dorsey had never been in the military or law enforcement, so she added, "Have you ever been face-to-face with an armed enemy combatant? Do you have any idea what it's like? My first objective was to save the lives of those wounded veterans in the hospital. I did that, and I'm damn proud of it, Senator."

Dorsey didn't respond. After that the others tossed her a few softball questions, and the hearing ended.

Kelly and Forester climbed into the car waiting for them in front of the Hart Senate Office Building.

"You did an outstanding job," Forester said. "I was very proud of how you handled yourself."

"Thank you, sir," Kelly replied.

"Can you join me for lunch?"

"I'd be happy to."

Back at the bureau, they went to the director's private dining room and Forester ordered a shrimp salad and iced tea. Kelly did the same.

"Dorsey is a despicable individual," Forester said.

"You won't get an argument from me on that," Kelly replied.

"Unfortunately, I have to work with him." Forester paused, then said, "I'm giving you a new assignment."

Kelly was flabbergasted. "But I like this counterterrorism job. I haven't been in it that long. And I believe I'm making a contribution."

"You're doing a first-rate job," Forester agreed. "However, I have something more important for you."

"What could be more important that stopping terrorists?" she asked.

Forester paused to take a bite of his salad. Then he said, "This country is locked in an existential battle with China. They pose as great a threat to the United States as Russia did during the Cold War. Moreover, they have adapted the KGB playbook. Chinese intelligence under MSS head Liu Guan is planning elaborate spy operations inside the US. I want you to be in charge of a new unit I'm creating in the bureau to counter Chinese espionage. This will be a promotion for you, accompanied by a pay increase. And you will report directly to me."

Forester's words hit Kelly hard. She didn't believe for a second that this was really a promotion. She was sure she was being tossed under the bus to placate Senator Dorsey. His subcommittee only dealt with terrorists, not Chinese espionage. He wouldn't have oversight in her new assignment.

"But I now have so much knowledge about terrorism," she protested.

"You're a quick study, you'll get up to speed fast on the Chinese issues."

"I don't know anything about China or its spying."

"Aren't you forgetting something?" Forester pointed out.

"What's that?" Kelly asked.

"You were the one who established that the Chinese were responsible for Senator Jasper's murder last November before I gave you the terrorism job."

"That didn't do any good." She sounded bitter. "The White House shut down my investigation before I even had a chance to identify the individuals involved."

Forester took a sip of his iced tea. "It's unfortunate that President Braddock listened to Wilkins, his national security advisor, and that Wilkins was able to convince him that national security issues with China overrode your murder investigation."

Kelly was feeling frustrated. That morning it had been politics with that blowhard senator, now it was the president's national security advisor. Was there any way that people in law enforcement in Washington could do their jobs?

"In your new job," Forester continued, "you'll need some legal support from the Department of Justice. Arthur Larkin, the attorney general, has designated Paul Maltoni, one of his lawyers, to provide it. Maltoni will call you in the next day or so."

Great, just what I want, Kelly thought to herself, time with a Washington lawyer. But there was no use arguing any further with Forester over the job shift. It was a done deal.

"I understand," she said as she rose from the table.

"One other thing," Forester added. "I don't intend to make any announcements about your new position or put it on the bureau's website. I will only tell top officials in the bureau and defense agencies, so please keep this confidential."

*   *   *

Running after eating was a dumb thing to do, but Kelly didn't care. Needing some release from everything that had happened that day, though it was twenty-eight degrees and windy, Kelly changed into running clothes. She left the FBI building and ran along the mall, heading in the direction of the Lincoln Memorial. She was angry about being sacked from her counterterrorism job. It was all so unfair. Besides, what was the new China espionage job? It sounded like a dead end.

Face it, she told herself, her FBI career was over. She should quit and do something else. If her dad hadn't sold the candy company, she could go to work with him. Maybe she'd go to business school and join the private sector. That sounded like a good idea. She'd tell her dad tonight.

As she reached the Lincoln Memorial and turned around, she changed her mind. She was no quitter. The reality was that Forester had to move her from the counterterrorism job to placate Dorsey. This was Washington 101. Besides, it would have been a problem for her to remain in counterterrorism. Dorsey would have made her life miserable.

She was convinced that Forester still had confidence in her. He was giving her a chance to redeem herself and to get her career back on track. But she could only accomplish that if she did an outstanding job in her new position.

She had an opportunity to save her career and her pride. And she would do everything within her power to do so.

*   *   *

General Darrell Cartwright was on the edge of his seat, leaning forward close to the railing in the box as he watched the Washington Capitals and the Los Angeles Kings on the ice in the Verizon Center.

"Go Caps, go!" he yelled.

Cartwright loved hockey. Growing up in Oconto Falls, Wisconsin, he learned to skate before he could walk. Even in grade school, his body, which ultimately grew to six foot six and two hundred and ten pounds, had begun to fill out. He was willing, even eager, to use that powerful body to blast an opponent on the ice.

Cartwright starred on the hockey team at the Air Force Academy, though that never interfered with his academic performance. He graduated first in his class, which led to a two-year graduate degree at the Woodrow Wilson School at Princeton, before heading off to the Middle East to fly bombers.

Cartwright had been transferred to Air Force headquarters at the Pentagon three years previously, a year before being named chairman of the Joint Chiefs, the country's highest ranking military official, by President Braddock. He immediately bought a box for Caps season tickets. Often, he used it to entertain other officers and civilian friends. And his wife, Sally, had been an avid fan as well up until her sudden death from a brain aneurysm a year ago.

That evening it was only Captain Mallory, Cartwright's personal aide and pilot, in the box with the general. They were both in their Air Force uniforms.

The Caps were on a power play. Ovechkin was racing down the side of the rink, the puck held to his stick as if by some magic force. When he was close enough, he pulled his stick back, lashed it forward, and propelled the puck at the upper right hand corner of the net. The Kings' goalie couldn't react in time. The red light went on and the announcer screamed, "Goal." The crowd was on its feet yelling.

Cartwright jumped up, with Mallory next to him. They were watching the replay on the video screen above center ice when an usher walked into the box and said, "General Cartwright?"

Cartwright wheeled around. "Yes, I'm General Cartwright."

The usher reached out and handed him a sealed envelope. Cartwright opened it, pulled out a handwritten note, and read: "Box 120." That was all that was on the note. Cartwright had no idea what it meant, but it was so mysterious that he was curious to find out. He told Mallory that he had to go to the men's room and exited the box. In the corridor, he looked at a sign on the wall. Box 120 was to the left. Cartwright followed the signs until he came to the box.

At Box 120, he opened the door and glanced inside. A single figure, Carl Dickerson, was alone in the box, standing at the bar in the back. Cartwright marveled at how good the tall, thin billionaire businessman looked for seventy-five years. He had a ruddy complexion, no doubt from spending time on his yacht in Saint-Tropez in the summer and the British Virgin Islands in the winter. Cartwright knew from press profiles that Dickerson ran five mornings a week and could press two hundred pounds. He either had a full head of hair or the best damn toupee Cartwright had ever seen.

Based in Los Angeles, Dickerson operated hotels and casinos throughout the world and was one of the largest importers of European luxury goods into Asia and Latin America. Cartwright had met Dickerson two months earlier at a gathering of West Coast top industrialists at Rancho Valencia Resort north of La Jolla. Cartwright had been the main speaker at their banquet, discussing American foreign policy. The conference organizers had promised Cartwright his speech would be off the record, so he had spoken frankly.

Cartwright's thesis was that American foreign policy was a disaster. Since the end of the Cold War and the fall of the Berlin Wall, the United States had never had a coherent foreign policy. Both Republican and Democratic administrations had lurched from crisis to crisis, being buffeted by changes in the world. The United States was still the most powerful nation, but had stopped being a master of its own destiny. Following his speech, he and Dickerson had spoken for a few minutes. He remembered Dickerson being very complimentary at the time.

Now Dickerson came forward and shook Cartwright's hand. "We met at Rancho Valencia in November at the West Coast industrialist conference."

"I recall very well," Cartwright nodded.

"I read you were a hockey fan and had a box," said Dickerson. "I happened to be in town and came to see the Kings."

"You're a part owner of the team, as I recall," Cartwright remarked.

"That's right. I was hoping you'd be here; I wanted to talk to you. Would you like a drink?"

"Thanks, I can fix one."

Cartwright poured some 12 year old Macallan over ice and grabbed a handful of cashews from a silver bowl. Never one for small talk, he said, "What's on your mind?"

Dickerson pointed to a round table and they sat down across from each other.

"I was impressed with what you said at Rancho Valencia," Dickerson began, "that it's impossible for the US to be the world's policeman."

"That's part of it," agreed Cartwright. "Even more than that, we simply don't have any meaningful foreign policy."

"Agreed. I was also impressed by the talk you gave at West Point in November."

In surprise, Cartwright pulled back. "You were there?"

"I read a transcript of the talk."

"It was never published."

"I have friends who know people at West Point."

Cartwright sipped his drink, anxious to hear what Dickerson had to say.

"Braddock is a disgrace," Dickerson said. "He's weak and gutless. As you said at Rancho Valencia, the US has no foreign policy. Even on domestic issues, Braddock is in over his head. I realize he's your commander in chief, but still . . ."

Cartwright smiled.

"You can speak frankly," Dickerson added. "Nothing said here leaves this room."

Cartwright believed him, so he responded, "Thoughts like yours about Braddock have crossed my mind."

"We can't let Braddock be reelected in November," said Dickerson.

"But if the Republicans don't get together behind an electable candidate, that's exactly what will happen," noted Cartwright.

"I'll do what it takes to prevent that from happening."

"You no doubt have a candidate in mind?"

"We have some mutual friends," Dickerson began. "They asked me to make a proposition to you. If you declare as a Republican candidate, I promise you will have an unlimited war chest. My money and what I can raise via super PACs. All perfectly legal. With enough money, you'll get the Republican nomination and you'll defeat Braddock in November."

Cartwright swished the scotch around in his glass. "You're serious."

"I don't joke about something this critical."

"It's too late for me to enter the race. Twelve candidates have been at this for months."

"And none of the twelve enjoys broad public support."

"The people would never vote for a general," said Cartwright, shaking his head.

"They voted for Washington and Eisenhower," Dickerson pointed out.

"You omitted Grant."

Dickerson laughed. "For good reason. Nobody would ever think you had anything in common with that horror. So far, you haven't given me a convincing reason for not running."

"Politics is a dirty business," Cartwright observed.

Dickerson laughed. "Unlike warfare."

"Fair point."

"You know damn well the two essential ingredients a presidential candidate needs are charisma and money," Dickerson continued. "You have the first. I'm prepared to give you the second. You happen to have good ideas, which means a lot to me, though most people won't care about that. If you appear on a debate stage with Braddock, you'll crush him."

For a full minute, Cartwright thought about what Dickerson had told him, then he said, "I'm flattered, but I'm a military man, not a politician."

Dickerson didn't flinch; he didn't argue. He reached into his pocket and pulled out a card. "This has all of my contact info," he said. "My offer will remain open until the Republican convention in August. On the other hand, the longer you wait, the harder it will be to pry the nomination away from one of those twelve lightweights."

Cartwright slipped the card into his pocket. "I'm a military man, not a politician," he repeated politely but firmly. Then he put down his glass and left the box.

Walking along the corridor, Cartwright replayed in his mind the conversation with Dickerson. With the money he had been promised, he believed he could get the Republican nomination, and he could defeat Braddock in November. Nevertheless, jumping in now would be a mistake. He needed the right opportunity. Cartwright was a patient man, a quality that had served him well as a fighter pilot. Always pick the right moment to act.

*   *   *

Good for you, Kelly Cameron, Paul Maltoni thought as he read her statements to the blustering Senator Dorsey who loved exerting his power. She had definitely put him in his place.

The transcript from yesterday's hearing had arrived in Paul's office at the Department of Justice a short while ago, and he had dropped what he was doing to read it.

As he perused the file, the telephone rang. It was Helen, Attorney General Arthur Larkin's secretary. "Paul, he wants to talk to you now," she said.

"I'm on my way."

Paul climbed the stairs from the third floor to the fifth where the AG's corner office was located.

When Paul arrived, Helen said, "He's on the phone. I think you should hold here. You want coffee or water?"

"Thanks, I'm fine," he replied. Hurry up and wait, Paul thought. It was always like that with the AG.

As he sat down, Paul thought about how much his life had changed in the last two months. At the beginning of November, he had been an eighth year associate at the prestigious Washington law firm Martin and Glass. He had been working for the two most powerful partners, Martin and Jenson, and had been on track to become a partner with a million-dollar-plus income per year for decades. At the time, he had held incredible admiration for Martin.

All that had changed once he saw how despicably his demigod had behaved in the Jasper matter. Paul had quit the firm and taken a job as a trial lawyer in the civil division of the Justice Department. He was convinced he would love the job because he would be trying cases. But he wasn't there long enough to confirm that conviction. After Paul had negotiated a huge settlement for the United States, Arthur, who knew Paul from his days as Martin's assistant, tapped Paul to be the head of the US government's national security legal support group.

"You're wasting your time trying cases," Arthur had said. "Anybody can try cases. I want you to do something important for your country."

Paul had misgivings, fearing he would end up spending his time in endless, boring meetings rather than in court, which was what he wanted to do. However, he couldn't say no to the attorney general of the United States, and Arthur would never have accepted no for an answer anyway. Fortunately, Paul's concerns proved to be unfounded. To be sure, there were lots of meetings, and not all of them were exciting. On the other hand, he loved being at the center of the US government's effort to deal with security issues for the country.

In the past few weeks, Paul had been called upon to draw the line between Americans' personal freedoms and the efforts of the FBI, Homeland Security, and the Pentagon to keep the country safe. How to avoid another 9/11 without trampling on individual liberties was a constant challenge, and Paul often had a critical say on these issues. His job also brought him into close contact with the gruff Arthur. He had grown fond of Arthur, who was always available when Paul needed him, even if that meant lots of waiting on Paul's end.

For Paul, this was a new field. Though Arthur told him, "You're smart. You'll figure it out," in fact he spent long hours every night reading endless books and articles on the subject. He didn't have to worry about it interfering with his social life because Paul, who had never been married, didn't have one. His sister, studying for a PhD in psychology at Columbia, was constantly inviting him to New York to fix him up with friends. Paul regularly told her, "Maybe next month. Right now I'm too busy."

The buzzer rang on Helen's desk. She pointed to the closed door and Paul entered the inner sanctum. Sitting behind his desk, the AG was looking like his usual disheveled self. He was five foot six and pear-shaped, with thin, gray hair ruffled and out of place. He was wearing a white shirt, tie loosened at the neck, and red suspenders, but no jacket.

"You wanted to see me, Mr. Larkin," said Paul.

"Don't call me that. It's Arthur," he said in his usual gruff way. "And not Art."

"Yes, sir."

While snapping his suspenders, Arthur moved across the room to the conference table, then they both sat down.

"I'm adding a new assignment to your workload, Maltoni," he said.

"What's that?" Paul asked.

"The Chinese have revved up their spying in the US. In response, the FBI has set up a unit to deal with it, and I want you to provide them with legal support."

"Sure, I'd be happy to."

"Forester put one of his people, Kelly Cameron, in charge. Jim's high on her. I want you to call her and get started. Helen will forward her contact info to you."

"She's the one who killed the terrorist at Walter Reed," Paul remarked. "I was just reading her testimony before Dorsey's subcommittee."

Arthur smiled. "I had lunch yesterday up on the Hill. I don't know what that girl did, but people were talking about her. They said she stood up to that bully Dorsey and kicked his butt. Would you agree?"

"That's a fair description."

"Good, Dorsey deserved it. So call her and help her out."

As Paul walked back to his office, reverberating in his brain were Arthur's words, "The Chinese have revved up their spying in the US."

As soon as he heard that, he immediately thought of his one-time lover, Vanessa Boyd, and her sister, Allison. When Paul had helped Allison nail Senator Jasper for her sister's death, Allison had been attacked and chased by Chinese men. Paul didn't know if they had any connection with the Chinese government, and she had refused to give Paul any details. Still, it seemed to him there had to be a relationship. Vanessa had been a staff member on the Senate Armed Services Committee and her lover, Senator Jasper, had been the chairman.

Now that his work included Chinese espionage issues, Paul decided he should press Allison to tell him what had happened. His motives weren't purely work related—he really liked Allison and he wanted to develop a romantic relationship with her.

Paul thought about the last time he had seen Allison. It had been in early December after he had quit his job at Andrew Martin's law firm and before he had started at the Department of Justice. He had flown to Israel to visit her on the archeology dig she was directing. At the time he had tried to start a romance with her, but hadn't been successful.

Now that he would be working with Kelly on China matters, it would make sense for him to see Allison again. She might be able to tell him about any Chinese government involvement in the case with Vanessa. Besides, he wanted to make another stab at a romantic relationship. He wasn't willing to go to Israel again, but he knew that as a professor at Brown, she returned to the States from time to time.

Back at his office, he emailed Allison to ask if she had any plans to come to the US. She replied immediately. The email read: "I am presenting a paper at the American Archeology Association in Washington in April. I should have time on Monday the 22nd. Can we have lunch?"

He replied, "Lunch would be great. Central at 12:30." He was pleased she wanted to see him. Perhaps after being stuck in Israel for so long, she might be more interested.

After emailing Allison, he decided to call Kelly. When she answered, he began, "I'm Paul Maltoni and I have been assigned—"

"To be my lawyer and keep me out of trouble," Kelly cut in.

"That's right," said Paul. "Can I come by to meet my client?"

"When would you like to do that? I'm flying to San Fran in the morning."

"How about right now?"

"Great, I'm in main FBI. Check in at the desk and they'll send you up."

As Paul crossed Pennsylvania Avenue, he considered whether he should tell Kelly about Allison and the possible involvement of Chinese intelligence in the Jasper affair. He decided not to until he learned more from Allison. The information he now had was so sketchy and speculative that he'd seem like an idiot for not knowing more, and he wanted to get off on the right foot with Kelly.

*   *   *

Paul liked Kelly the minute he sat down across her desk and she said, "I have no idea what the hell I'm doing in this China espionage job, but I intend to get up to speed. So you'll have to bear with me, Counselor."

Paul laughed and said, "We'll learn together. I've never even been to China. I can barely find it on a map."

"Don't bs me," Kelly replied. "Every Yalie knows a lot about China."

"Somebody did their homework. But I've heard you've been busy the last couple of days. Word around town is that you kicked some serious butt up on the Hill yesterday."

Kelly seemed startled. "You heard that?"

"Arthur Larkin did when he was up there for lunch. Me, I just read the transcript."

"Will you send me a copy?" she asked.

"Sure, you're my client. Do you need anything else now?" Paul inquired.

"Not yet. I'm flying to San Francisco in the morning. A branch office of the bureau out there has been chasing Chinese spies for a number of years."

"I imagine they'll be happy to meet their new boss," he commented.

"That's what's been worrying me," Kelly scowled. "You didn't have to say it."

Paul glanced at his watch. It was close to five thirty. "You have time for a drink?" he asked.

"I'll take a rain check. I'm coming back on the redeye tomorrow so I want to get home for dinner tonight with my daughter. Then I have to set her up for an overnight with her grandfather. It goes with being a single mom. Thanks for coming," she added. "We'll talk next week."

*   *   *

"Minister Liu wants to talk to you," Wu, the director of security at the Chinese embassy in Washington, said to Xiang. "Come with me."

Xiang was led by one of the security men at the Chinese embassy to a windowless conference room in the basement. There, a red phone was waiting for him on an old wooden table, which the embassy's high-tech people were convinced was a secure hookup with one of Liu's phones.

It wasn't the physical surroundings that frightened Xiang. It was Minister Liu. Xiang dreaded phone calls from Liu. He had been terrified of the spymaster from the time he had recruited Xiang back when he was beginning his last year of high school in Shanghai.

Recruited was the wrong word, Xiang realized as he rode in the elevator with the security guard. Drafted was much more accurate. Xiang had been an outstanding student—the top of his class, and planning to go to the University of Beijing the following year. That was eighteen years ago.

Without notice, he had been picked up on the street in Shanghai and driven in an unmarked car to Liu's branch office in Shanghai. There Liu told him he would be going to college in the US, and that he would apply to Stanford, University of Illinois, and Carnegie Mellon. He would be allowed to select among the ones that admitted him and all expenses would be paid by the state.

"Can I ask the point of this?" Xiang had said.

"We want you to learn everything you can about the United States. After graduation, you will be of value to the People's Republic of China."

Xiang didn't like the orders he was receiving. Four years at a top American University seemed exciting for the son of a peasant farmer from Western China, but mortgaging his life to the state was too high a price to pay.

"I have to think about it," he had said.

"Your parents will be very pleased when you do this. It will provide them with an opportunity for a better life."

Xiang was knowledgeable about how the government operated since Mao, and quickly understood what Liu was telling him. His parents were being held hostage to ensure his compliance with Liu's wishes. Later, Xiang had been admitted to all three American universities. He had selected Carnegie Mellon.

After the security guard deposited Xiang in the basement conference room, he withdrew, locking the door from the outside. Though it was no more than sixty-five degrees, perspiration dotted Xiang's forehead and his shirt was damp under the arms.

Waiting for the red phone on the table to ring, Xiang recalled his last conversation with Liu a week ago. The spymaster had told him that he would have a critical role to play in a new operation: New World Order.

From time to time he would be summoned to the office of Andrew Martin, a prominent Washington lawyer, on Pennsylvania Avenue. There, Martin would personally deliver a sealed envelope to him. His orders were to put the envelope into another envelope with Minister Liu's name on the front. That would then go into the diplomatic pouch for shipment to Beijing. In no event should he open the envelope from Martin.

Xiang had been frightened by the whole process. He thought it likely that when he left Martin's office, which was only two blocks from the FBI headquarters and across the street from the Department of Justice, with an envelope containing military secrets, FBI agents would swoop down and arrest him.

With his diplomatic immunity, they wouldn't hold him or convict him of a crime. However, they could expel him from the United States. Liu would no doubt blame him for the destruction of his New World Order operation. That would mean punishment, not only for Xiang, but for his parents. Liu had set them up in a comfortable Beijing apartment and paid them a cash stipend for their son's valuable work for the state. They were already in a vulnerable position.

The phone rang. Xiang picked it up, his hand moist. "Xiang here," he said.

"You are a miserable failure," came Liu's voice over the receiver. "A worthless piece of shit."

"Wha . . . what did I do?"

"The FBI has set up a new section to deal with Chinese espionage. I'm in Beijing, but I've managed to learn about it. You're in Washington, and you didn't even know about it, did you?"

"No, sir," said Xiang, chagrined.

"That is your job," Liu seethed. "To learn about matters like this and immediately inform me."

"I'm sorry, I . . ." Xiang faltered.

"You realize of course this could disrupt our Operation New World Order. We can't let that happen."

"No, sir. We won't."

"The FBI has placed Kelly Cameron in charge of this new section. I'm sure you remember your old girlfriend from college."

Xiang's blood ran cold. "Yes, sir, I do."

"That relationship could be an advantage for us," said Liu. "I want you to rekindle your romantic relationship with Kelly Cameron and find out what she is doing in this new job. Are you man enough to do that?"

"I can try."

"I don't want you to try, I want you to do it."

"Yes, sir."

"And one other thing. If Kelly Cameron gets close enough to critical information relating to New World Order, I want you to kill her. Can you do that?"

Liu's words hit Xiang hard. He opened his mouth to speak. Nothing came out.

"Well?" Liu asked.

"Yes, sir," said Xiang.

"And keep me informed with periodic reports," Liu added.

Then the phone went dead.

Xiang realized he should walk over to the locked door and knock so he could be let out, but he couldn't move.

He sat there, staring at the dead phone. He was in a terrible situation. He had never stopped loving Kelly Cameron. What in the world was he going to do?

San Francisco and Chevy Chase, Maryland

Kelly was expecting a difficult meeting with Timothy Brock, but it ended up being even worse than she had anticipated. Before boarding the plane that morning at Dulles Airport, she had read the email that Forester had sent to Brock:

> "I'm aware that Kelly Cameron is coming out to meet with you today. I trust that you will have a full and open discussion with her about the fine work your office has been doing."

On the airplane, Kelly tried to imagine how Brock felt when he received this email. He was fifty years old, having spent his entire career as an FBI agent, following four years at USC where he had been an all-American halfback, and three at UCLA Law. For the last ten years, Brock had headed up a special FBI unit devoted to Chinese spying. Their work had led to some high-profile arrests, most notably of two Chinese American scientists who worked at Lawrence Livermore Labs.

When the director had established a section at headquarters devoted to Chinese espionage, Brock must have viewed himself as the logical choice to head up the section. But Brock was passed over in favor of a woman fifteen years his junior who knew absolutely nothing about China.

In a call the previous afternoon when Kelly had told Forester she was flying to San Francisco to meet with Brock, he had said, "I've never been impressed with Brock. I think he's taking credit for the efforts of his subordinates. And there was evidence a couple years ago that he was having an affair with a Chinese American woman on Beijing's payroll—the old honey trap. We didn't have enough evidence to justify disciplinary action, but it raised red flags. So proceed accordingly."

Now they were in a conference at the FBI's San Francisco field office. Their meeting had been scheduled for 1:00 p.m., however Brock didn't return from lunch until 1:45. His secretary, Carol, had left Kelly in the conference room alone. She spent the time returning emails and reading a book about Chinese intelligence activities in the United States.

On his arrival, Brock didn't apologize. "I was meeting with a source," he said. "She was loquacious. I didn't want to stop her from talking."

Brock's hair was slicked down and he had a freshly clean look. She wondered if he was late because he'd been having sex and then showered.

"I would like to get information on your current active cases," Kelly said.

Brock picked up the phone, "Carol, bring me the files on the table in my office."

Moments later, Carol wheeled in a cart with about twenty red file folders.

"These are all the cases," Brock said.

"Can you give me a summary of each and their current status?" Kelly requested.

He waved his hand toward the cart. "The best approach would be for you to review the files yourself."

Kelly was struggling to keep her anger in check. "Listen, Timothy, we're on the same team here."

"Of course," he said. "I just have too much to do to babysit you on this." With that, he stood up and left the room.

Kelly was ready to scream. As she picked up a couple files and leafed through them, she realized that the other six agents in the office had the lead on each case. Fortunately, five were in the office that afternoon. She spoke with each of them and they were delighted to fill her in on the details of their cases.

She met with them one at a time, taking copious notes, until a little past eight in the evening. The last was Gerald Corbin, a thirtysomething with a blonde crew cut. He offered to take her to dinner before she left for the airport.

They went to a small trattoria nearby, where the host seated them at a quiet corner booth. When the pasta they ordered had arrived, Kelly asked Gerald, who had been working in the Chinese espionage unit for eight years, to sum up what he had learned there.

In a soft voice with a Georgia drawl, he told her, "Liu Guan, the MSS minster, is a formidable adversary. Liu will do anything to gain information about our military secrets and technology. He must have a former KGB mentor because he is following their playbook. And one other thing," he paused to take a bite of his pasta.

"What's that?" Kelly asked, on the edge of her chair.

"Liu is not only brilliant and cunning, but he's totally immoral. A real mean son of a bitch. The man would kill his own mother if it helped him obtain information. If you ever go head to head with Liu, I'd advise you to sleep with a gun next to your bed at night."

After dinner Gerald drove her to the airport. The FBI didn't pay for business class, and Kelly had only bought her ticket a day ahead; that meant a middle seat in the back of economy. Sleeping on the plane was impossible. When they arrived at Dulles Airport at six in the morning, Kelly went home to shower and sleep for a couple of hours before picking up Julie at her dad's house.

It was a little after ten o'clock when Kelly got there. Her father and Julie were in the kitchen eating breakfast. Kelly looked surprised.

"We had a late night, Mom," Julie explained.

"Really, doing what?"

"Grandpa took me to the Caps game and it went into overtime. There was a shootout. Do you know what a shootout is?"

"Yes, I know what a shootout is," said Kelly.

"Then we got ice cream. So we didn't get home until . . ."

"A little past nine," Kelly's dad chimed in.

"No, Grandpa, it was eleven thirty," corrected Julie. "But the Caps won."

Kelly was glad that Julie sounded so excited. "Okay," she smiled. "Put your dishes in the dishwasher and pack up your things."

When Julie had gone upstairs, Kelly's dad asked, "What happened in San Francisco?"

"The head of the office was a total asshole," Kelly replied. "He's pissed because I got the job instead of him."

"Big surprise there."

"The other agents were very helpful."

"You want some coffee?" he asked.

"I can get it." She yawned and poured herself a cup. "I promised to take Julie to the Spy Museum today. You want to come with us?"

He shook his head. "No way. I love that place, it's a wonderful museum, but too authentic on Cold War stuff. It's a part of my life I left behind and don't want to relive it. Besides, you and Julie should have some time alone. She's a great kid, and intelligent to boot. She told me the Caps coach should never have changed goalies in the third period, and she was right. The new one let the Penguins tie the match."

Kelly laughed. "She'll have a great career in hockey one day."

"You think that's worse than what I did and you do?"

"At least nobody's shooting at you," Kelly agreed.

Julie came into the kitchen carrying her backpack. "Who's shooting at you, Mom?" she asked.

"We're talking about hockey players shooting pucks," Kelly said.

"Yeah, right," Julie rolled her eyes as her grandfather smiled.

"Now kiss Grandpa goodbye and say thank you," Kelly said. "Then let's go."

Washington

Kelly knew one of the managers at the Spy Museum, and had used that relationship to arrange a VIP tour for her and Julie. Midway through the tour, Kelly and Julie saw a video clip from the Cold War. In West Berlin, American agents were opening the trunk of a Trabant, a small green East German car. Two men and two women climbed out of the trunk. Another American agent then came on the scene and greeted the fugitives.

"Hey, that's Grandpa," Julie cried out.

And she was right. Kelly realized that Charles Cameron, the cold warrior, had been captured by the camera. She wondered whether he knew about the video being shown here.

After they finished the tour, Kelly bought Julie some spy paraphernalia at the gift shop. Then she said, "Okay, time for lunch."

"Can we have pizza?" Julie asked.

"Sure."

They got back into the car. Kelly decided they would go to Alta Strada, so she drove north and east, crisscrossing streets until she reached K Street. Then she turned right. From time to time, she looked into the rearview mirror. A gray Lexus, with plates DPL 6279, seemed to be following her. You're tired from the long flight, she told herself. Don't get paranoid.

Feeling the effects of her late night, Julie had gone to sleep in the back. Kelly reached across the front, moving her bag close in case she had to go for her gun.

Once they reached the restaurant, Kelly asked the maître d' to seat them in a booth along the side wall. From there, she would have a view of the front door and the entire restaurant—just in case.

As Kelly was glancing at the menu, Julie made her position known. "Pizza with tomato and cheese! No peppers or mushrooms or olives. Yuck. They're disgusting!"

Through the corner of her eye, Kelly saw a Chinese man walk into the restaurant. She clutched her bag tightly. Then she froze. It was Xiang! This couldn't be a chance meeting, Xiang must have been the one following her. Confirming her suspicions, he headed straight for her table.

"Kelly Cameron," he said. "What a coincidence. I just came in to pick up a pizza to take out."

No way, she thought. After all these years, why was he reaching out to her? She knew Xiang worked at the Chinese embassy. Could he be a spy? Were the Chinese aware that she had been appointed to head up a section investigating Chinese espionage? Perhaps his superiors were familiar with their prior relationship and were using that to gain information about her latest assignment.

Kelly wanted to know the answer to all of these questions, so she decided to act friendly and let Xiang talk. There was no risk doing that in the middle of a restaurant, she reasoned.

"This is my daughter, Julie," said Kelly. "We're just about to order a pizza. Would you like to join us?"

Xiang seemed nervous. "I don't want to impose," he said.

"Not at all," Kelly insisted.

Xiang sat down and Kelly ordered a margherita pizza from the waiter.

Julie, who had been learning about China in school, had lots of questions for Xiang, all of which he deftly answered.

Then she looked him squarely in the eye and asked, "How'd you get that scar on your left cheek?"

"Julie," Kelly said. "We don't ask people personal questions."

"It's okay," Xiang replied. "When I was a boy, I was doing very well in school. Because of that, some other boys didn't like me. They burned me with a piece of hot coal."

"Did it hurt?" Julie asked.

As the pizza arrived Kelly said, "Okay, Julie, that's enough."

When they had finished eating, Kelly pointed to the open kitchen and told Julie, "You see that tall man in the chef's uniform?"

"Yeah."

"He's the chef. If you go over and ask him, I'll bet he'll let you watch them make the pizza."

"Really?" asked Julie, scooting out of her chair and heading to the open kitchen with its large oven.

"She's a smart kid," Xiang said.

Kelly ignored his comment. "Are you driving a gray Lexus with plates DPL 6279?"

Xiang looked alarmed. "Yes. Why do you want to know?"

"You were following me to the restaurant."

"How do you know that?"

"It's my job. Tell me why."

Xiang took a deep breath and exhaled. "Listen, Kelly, I've never forgotten about you. The truth is, I've never loved anyone else. We really had something special."

"Then why'd you destroy it?" Kelly asked.

"There were some things I couldn't help."

"What things?"

"I can't tell you. They're over now."

"And you expect me to take your word for that with no explanation? That's insulting."

"After our chance meeting in November, I was sorry I didn't call you," Xiang explained. "I wanted to see you again and hopefully make a date with you for dinner."

"Then why didn't you call?" Kelly persisted.

"I was afraid you'd turn me down. But I thought if we spent a little time together like this, you might be willing to give me a chance. I've always regretted breaking up with you in college."

Kelly doubted Xiang was telling the truth and that he was here due to his romantic feelings. Even if that were the case, she was determined to slap him down for what he had done to her fifteen years ago. Let him feel rejection this time.

"Stalking me is not a good way to rekindle a relationship," she countered harshly.

"That's true," Xiang nodded. "I'm sorry if I frightened you." He reached for her hand on the table. As soon as he made contact, she pulled away.

"Listen, Xiang, we did have something special when we were at CMU. As I said, you destroyed it. Besides, that was a long time ago and I have no interest in rekindling it. Zero. Do you understand?"

He nodded. "Now that I've messed this up today, I'd like to start over. Can we have dinner together sometime? Just the two of us."

She glared at him. "You're not listening to me. The answer is no. That's N and O." She felt better saying it. "Do you understand?"

He nodded again. Then he took a pen and piece of paper out of his pocket. He wrote down a number and handed the paper to her. "It's my private cell phone," he said. "Nobody at the embassy knows about it. If you change your mind, please call me."

He reached into his pocket, took out some cash, and placed it on the table. "I want to pay for my share of lunch. I don't want to create any problems for you."

"Forget it," said Kelly. "Keep your money. Just leave me alone."

Watching Xiang walk away from the table, Kelly recalled why she had loved him so much her junior year at CMU. She had been a virgin when they began dating. He had professed to being one as well, though she was never sure whether she believed him or not. They had enjoyed the most incredible sex together. Thinking about it sent a chill up and down her spine. She had never felt the same pleasure with any other man. In bed, he always cared about her, not just himself, driving her to one climax after another.

But it was more than just sex. He was very bright, the only man she'd ever met who was smarter than she was. Yet, he didn't resent her intelligence, unlike some of the boys she had dated in high school. He was hardworking and ambitious, with dreams of making a good life for himself and his family. Thoughtful and caring, he was interested in her and everything she did. And he loved his parents, becoming emotional whenever he spoke of them. He had planned to bring them to the United States where they could have a better life.

Most of all, they had always had fun together. They had run in Schenley Park. Xiang was passionate about American movies. Even with their studies, they had made time to see every interesting new release. Then afterwards, Xiang had always found new little ethnic restaurants to try.

All of that was so long ago—almost half of her life. Even if he was being sincere now, he didn't seem like the same person she had known. That Xiang had been relaxed and easygoing. He had always looking for the humorous side of what was happening. This Xiang was tense and pressing. He acted as though he had been ordered to make a date with her. She had no interest in seeing Xiang again.

Kelly signaled the waiter, who brought her check. Once she handed him her credit card, Julie returned to the table.

"What happened to that Chinese man?" she asked.

"He had to leave."

"He's a spy," Julie announced.

Kelly was dumbfounded. She knew her daughter was smart, but she never expected this. "Where did you get that?" she asked.

"He seemed like it," said Julie simply.

"You spent too much time at the Spy Museum today. He's a friend of mine from college."

"Okay, if you say so."

That was one of Julie's sassy expressions that Kelly had asked her not to use. Today, she didn't correct her.

While signing the credit card receipt, Kelly thought about Julie's conclusion that Xiang was a spy. Her discussion with Xiang hadn't told her a damn thing about his true motives, but she was convinced it wasn't romantic, as he had claimed. Assistant economic attaché was a perfect cover for an intelligence agent. The Chinese government must have found out she was heading up a new section dealing with Chinese espionage. Then they must have sent Xiang to spy on her, taking advantage of their prior relationship.

That conclusion was very troubling. She had only been appointed to her new job a couple days ago, and it hadn't been announced to the media or put on the bureau's website. Forester told her that he was disclosing it only to top officials in the FBI and government defense agencies. Yet, the Chinese knew about it. That meant there was a mole near the top of the government.

Her first instinct was to report all of this to Forester, but then she reconsidered. Once the director knew about her former relationship with Xiang and his attempt to make use of it, she was afraid Forester would yank her from her new job to avoid what a congressional committee could later claim was a conflict of interest. If she lost her job that way, her FBI career really would be over. Her next assignment would be reading and filing documents in one of the bureau's field offices—if she was lucky. She couldn't let that happen.

Kelly decided she would tough it out. Remembering what Gerald Corbin had told her in San Francisco, she would sleep with her Glock pistol next to her at night.

She was also convinced of something else. She hadn't seen the last of Xiang.

*   *   *

Leaving the restaurant and driving back to the Chinese embassy, Xiang felt miserable. Kelly was the only woman he had ever loved, and being with her today convinced him that he still loved her. He tried to imagine how different his life would be if he had not broken up with her.

They would have gotten married and lived in Washington or New York, where he would have a career in finance while she would have gone into law enforcement. They would have a house in the suburbs and a couple of children—a daughter like Julie, who was intelligent and articulate. But more than all that, he would be different. With Kelly, he always had fun. She was so smart. They discussed, and sometimes argued about, books and movies. And they had always tried new things together.

Thinking about it made him feel depressed. He had never wanted to break up with her. That June fifteen years ago, right before he was supposed to move in with Kelly, Xiang had flown home to China to visit his parents. Five minutes after he got to their apartment in Beijing, Liu had called his cell phone and said, "Two of my men are waiting out front. They will bring you to me."

Xiang had quickly invented a story so he wouldn't worry his parents when he left the apartment.

When Xiang had shown up at the meeting, Liu had looked angry, and there was a gun on the desk in front of him.

"You are on the verge of betraying me and your country," Liu had told Xiang.

"I don't understand."

"Don't lie to me. I've been informed that you plan to marry a woman named Kelly Cameron and remain in the United States, wiping out my investment in you and betraying your country."

Xiang had been stunned. How in the world did Liu know this? He must have had someone spying on Xiang. There was no point arguing with Liu.

"Do you deny it?" Liu asked.

"No, sir."

"When you get back to the US, I want you to terminate your relationship with this blonde devil. Do not give her any explanation. Do you understand?"

"Yes, sir," he had replied weakly.

"Louder."

"Yes, sir," said Xiang more firmly.

"And one other thing." Liu picked up the gun and held it in the palm of his hand. "If you ever think about betraying me again by maintaining your relationship with this woman, never forget that I will know what you are doing. Your parents are still here in China under my control. Am I making myself clear?"

Xiang had no doubt that if he continued his relationship with Kelly, Liu would kill his parents. When he returned to the US, he broke up with Kelly. He had felt as if there were no other choice. And he didn't dare tell her why. If Liu ever found out that Xiang had disobeyed his orders, it would mean death for Xiang's parents. A part of Xiang had died that day.

Again, he tried to imagine what his life would have been like if he hadn't done Liu's bidding and broken up with Kelly. Stop it, he told himself. Forget about Kelly and move on with your life. But that wasn't possible. Suddenly she was back in his life again.

But now that Kelly refused even to have dinner with him, Xiang had another problem. If he told Liu this was the situation, Liu would find a way to obtain information about what Kelly was doing. Knowing Liu, Xiang's guess was that the spymaster would move against Kelly's daughter, Julie. Liu was a monster, and Julie was the obvious pressure point to use against Kelly. Xiang couldn't let that happen, he had to protect Kelly and Julie. He could do that by pretending to see Kelly from time to time and filing bogus reports with Liu, explaining that it would take time for him to develop their relationship sufficiently to obtain useful information about her work.

Xiang was confident he could pull that off for several months. Certainly until April. And after that? He didn't know what he'd do.

PART II

April, Three Months Later

Bethesda and Washington

At five thirty in the morning, Kelly Cameron was averaging a seven-minute mile on a treadmill in the first-floor study of her Bethesda house. Most mornings Kelly ran outside, but she hated running in the rain. That morning a nor'easter was pounding the region with heavy downpours and high winds.

Except for the rain smacking against the windows in sheets, the house was quiet. Julie and Luisa were still asleep upstairs. A television tuned to CNN rested on the shelf in a cabinet in front of Kelly. She was half watching and listening to CNN while thinking about a new sting operation being launched by the San Francisco office. They wanted to catch an engineer at a Silicon Valley high-tech firm believed to be assisting the Chinese in hacking into the computers of US financial firms.

Suddenly, she heard the CNN reporter say, "War with China narrowly averted."

My God, Kelly thought. She anxiously tuned in to hear what was coming next. The television showed an aerial photo of clumps of rocks in a body of water.

"In the past few days, the rhetoric between China and Japan has escalated over these disputed islands," the reporter continued. "Today, it reached a breaking point with China attacking and shooting down two Japanese Self-Defense Force aircraft. Japan invoked its treaty with the United States and called for US assistance. In response, the United States launched several planes from a nearby aircraft carrier to confront the Chinese planes. However, at the last second, the US planes veered away and returned to the aircraft carrier. China is now claiming control of the disputed islands."

Next, CNN cut to Tokyo where Japanese prime minister Nakamura, standing in front of a cluster of microphones, angrily asserted, "I am extremely disappointed that President Braddock did not honor his country's treaty obligations to Japan and permitted this unlawful Chinese action to go unchecked."

This was followed by a shot of CNN's White House correspondent standing on Pennsylvania Avenue, microphone in hand, reporting, "We're still waiting for a statement from President Braddock on this Chinese aggression."

"Meantime," the CNN anchor continued, "in Baghdad, Sunnis and Shiites continue to battle."

Kelly wasn't listening any longer. Her mind was stuck on what had occurred in the East China Sea. Ever since she had started her new job and learned more about China, she had expected China and Japan to square off over these islands sooner or later. If in fact China had attacked, as CNN reported, then she was surprised Braddock hadn't responded with force. On the other hand, it seemed crazy to start a war with the second most powerful country in the world over a couple of piles of rock. The whole business was so complicated.

She heard her phone ringing from a holder hooked to the treadmill. Without breaking stride, Kelly brushed back the blond hair that had fallen into her face and grabbed the phone. From the caller ID she saw it was Forester. She cut her speed as she answered.

"Kelly here."

"It's Jim Forester. I want you to attend a White House meeting with me this morning."

"Yes, sir. What time?"

"I'm leaving my house in Potomac in a few minutes. I'll have my driver swing by and pick you up. Should be about fifteen minutes from now."

Kelly didn't have to ask Forester the subject of the meeting. It had to be the confrontation in the East China Sea.

Phone in hand, Kelly raced upstairs. She had to shower and dress quickly. By the time she finished, Luisa was up. Kelly explained that she would be leaving early again, and that she needed Luisa to walk Julie to school.

Kelly decided to wear a navy suit and powder blue blouse, wanting to look professional and businesslike. She tucked her gun and FBI badge into her bag, put on her navy raincoat, and went to wait in the living room, looking out of the window and watching for Forester to arrive. When she saw his black Lincoln pull up, she grabbed an umbrella and made a dash for the car.

Forester was alone in the back seat and the glass partition that walled off the driver was raised. As the car pulled away from the curb, Kelly noticed the grim, intense look on the director's face.

"Have you heard what happened with China?" he asked.

"Only what was on CNN."

"Their information is accurate. A little while ago, President Braddock called and told me about it in summary form. He set a meeting in the White House situation room thirty minutes from now. This incident has an espionage component, so I think you had better be there."

"Do you know who else will be attending?" Kelly inquired.

"Braddock told me Chad Vernon, his chief of staff, would email and let me know." Forester removed an iPad from his briefcase, looked at it briefly, and said, "Besides the president, George Wilkins, his national security advisor, Arthur Larkin, the attorney general, Paul Maltoni, Justice Department lawyer whom you know, and somebody from the CIA. Director Harrison is in Pakistan, so he's sending a rep."

Kelly had expected General Cartwright to also be there. He was, after all, the chairman of the Joint Chiefs, and they would be discussing military events. She guessed there must have been a disagreement between Braddock and Cartwright. Perhaps the general had been in favor of attacking the Chinese planes and Braddock had disagreed.

They were stalled in heavy traffic on the Beltway, but that was par for the course on a rainy day in the Washington metro area. Forester looked anxiously at his watch as the Lincoln began moving again.

With Forester deep in thought and silent, Kelly recalled her one previous meeting with President Braddock. He obviously didn't share Senator Dorsey's view of the Walter Reed incident. Three weeks after it occurred, he had invited her and the twenty members of her unit—two still in wheelchairs—to the White House along with their family members. Kelly had brought her dad and Julie. On an unseasonably warm day in the rose garden, the president had presented all twenty-one of them with gold medals, "as a symbol of our nation's gratitude."

The president met so many people every day, she wondered if he'd even remember her.

*   *   *

Walking into the White House Situation Room behind Forester, Kelly was amazed by what she saw. This was no ordinary conference room. The 550 square foot space in the basement of the west wing of the White House was an intelligence management center equipped with secure, advanced communications equipment, including half a dozen viewing screens. The president could conduct high-level briefings with officials at remote locations. He could also maintain command of US forces around the world.

As they entered the room, Chad Vernon, the chief of staff, said, "Now that everyone's here, I'll get President Braddock."

After Vernon left, Kelly looked around the room at the others milling around and talking. Though she had never met Arthur Larkin or George Wilkins, she recognized them from their photographs. Off to one side she saw Paul Maltoni with his unruly black hair, wrinkled suit, and off-center tie. He was talking with an African American man in his thirties, who was wearing a perfectly pressed charcoal gray suit.

She went over and said hello to Paul. The other man held out his hand. "Lance Farrell, CIA," he said. As she shook his hand, Braddock entered the room, followed closely by Vernon. He walked over to the three of them.

"Good to see you again, Kelly," the president said. "How long has it been since the Walter Reed ceremony?"

"Seventy-six days, but who's counting," Kelly quipped.

The others laughed. Then Paul and Lance introduced themselves.

"I'm a stand in for DCI Harrison," Farrell said.

"Yes. I know he's in Pakistan," replied the president. "Good to have you. Okay, let's get down to business."

Everyone took a seat around the large table.

"As you are aware," Braddock said in a gravelly voice—Kelly wondered if it was from talking so much—"approximately eight hours ago, I made a decision not to engage Chinese war planes over the East China Sea. That decision was made in this room. Those present were George," he pointed to George Wilkins, "Chad," he pointed to Chad Vernon, "and General Cartwright."

"Three hours later," the president's voice now quavered with emotion, "I received a call from Japanese prime minister Nakamura. In that call, Nakamura expressed outrage that the US did not respond to the Chinese military offensive. He claimed that our failure to act was a violation of our treaty commitments to Japan. I had been expecting that call. Then Nakamura went on to say that the US had never had any intention of countering the Chinese planes, and that the Chinese knew that. I was flabbergasted by his accusation, and pressed him for evidence in support."

Braddock paused for a moment and took a sip of water. Kelly saw that everyone's eyes were squarely on Braddock, waiting to hear what he would say next.

"Nakamura explained that they have sophisticated listening equipment that enables their pilots to pick up conversations from planes in the area. Utilizing it, a Japanese pilot who is fluent in Mandarin overheard a conversation between two Chinese pilots. One told the other, 'You don't have to worry, I know the Americans will never attack.' From this, Nakamura concluded that prior to this incident, the US had decided not to respond militarily, and that this US decision had been leaked to the Chinese."

Arthur Larkin sprang to his feet. The former New York trial lawyer said, "That's a ridiculous inference, the Chinese pilots were just guessing what we would do."

Braddock looked at Arthur. "That's what I told Prime Minister Nakamura," he said. "His response was that his pilot had recorded the conversation between the two Chinese pilots. The nuances and inflection support Nakamura's interpretation. I asked him to send me the recording electronically, which he did. I turned that over to George."

"And?" Arthur asked. Everyone was looking at George Wilkins.

"We had our Mandarin experts analyze it," the national security adviser said. "They agree with the Japanese interpretation."

"In other words," the president responded, "the Chinese knew I had made a prior decision not to attack Chinese planes if a battle erupted over these islands. I simply didn't think a couple of clumps of rock justified going to war with the second most powerful military in the world."

"When did you make this decision?" Arthur asked.

"At Camp David about two weeks ago when we had a review of our Asian policy."

Arthur was pacing in his courtroom demeanor. "Who was present for that discussion?"

Wilkins responded, "Twelve top officials in the administration. I was one of them."

"So, we have a Chinese spy at the top of our government," Arthur said, "someone who relayed your decision to the Chinese."

Kelly thought about Xiang approaching her at the restaurant in January. Did that same spy inform the Chinese about her appointment as head of the FBI section dealing with Chinese espionage?

Braddock looked grim. "You have a succinct way of expressing yourself, Arthur, and quickly cutting to the heart of the matter."

"What other explanation is there?" Arthur asked.

"I didn't want to believe that," the president replied. "It seemed too horrible to contemplate."

"What other explanation is there?" Arthur repeated.

"I can't think of another."

"Well, that's what we have." Arthur pointed to Farrell. "Would you spooks prefer the word mole?"

"Doesn't matter what you call it," Farrell replied, "we have a problem."

Braddock picked up the discussion, "And we're going to find out who it is. I'm appointing a task force whose existence will be kept secret. The members of the task force will be George Wilkins, Lance Farrell, Kelly Cameron, and Paul Maltoni, who Arthur selected. Besides George, I expect the rest of you to make this your top priority, dropping everything else you're doing. Nothing is more important for our country right now."

"I will serve as chairman," Wilkins said.

As soon as the words were out of Wilkins' mouth, Arthur pounced, "I don't think so. This is a law enforcement matter. Paul Maltoni should be chairman. He'll report directly to me."

Wilkins shot a surly look at Arthur. "With all due respect, Arthur, what's Maltoni know about China? Has he even been there?"

"That's irrelevant," Arthur fired back. "The spy is here in Washington. Besides, let's face it, George, you've spent a lot of time in Beijing. That's a liability. It could affect your objectivity."

Wilkins reddened. "I resent that. What are you insinuating?" he said, raising his voice.

"I'm merely stating a fact."

Kelly was astounded at the animosity between the two men. They had obviously clashed in the past. She wondered how Braddock would resolve this.

The president tapped his water glass on the table. "Okay, okay, that's enough. The round's over. Both of you return to your corners."

Chad Vernon laughed, but no one joined him.

"All right, here's what we're going to do," Braddock said. "Kelly, you'll be chairman of the task force."

Wilkins butted in, "You're putting *her* in charge?" The disbelief was evident in his voice.

"That's right," said Braddock. "I am." He turned to Kelly. "It's your reward for doing an outstanding job at Walter Reed." He smiled. "No good deed goes unpunished. You'll keep Director Forester informed at all times. Jim, you'll keep me in the loop," he added, turning to Forester.

"Yes, Mr. President," Forester said.

Kelly was flattered. The assignment the president had just given her was huge. But her enthusiasm was dampened by Wilkins being a member of the task force. Commanding the national security advisor was certain to be a challenge.

As the meeting was breaking up, Kelly pulled Wilkins, Farrell, and Maltoni into a corner. "Let's start with a noon meeting at the FBI today," she said. "I'll order lunch to one of the conference rooms."

The others agreed to be there. Farrell and Maltoni sounded eager to work with her, but Wilkins looked unhappy and immediately left the room.

As Kelly was gathering up her papers, she overheard Arthur talking to Paul. "Don't take any crap from Wilkins. You know what I mean?"

"Yes, sir. I do," nodded Paul.

"I don't trust that SOB."

"You think he's the Chinese mole?" Paul sounded alarmed.

"I never said that. What I have seen is that he's always sucking up to Beijing. That may just be his idea of how to conduct foreign policy. At any rate, I want you to keep me closely informed."

"Yes, sir. I'll do that."

"And don't fuck this up," Arthur added.

This should be quite an assignment, Kelly thought to herself.

She laid out a course for the rest of her morning as she headed back to her office. For the next few hours she would close her office door and give herself a crash course on the disputed islands. She would also pull up and study the bios of Wilkins and Farrell. She particularly wanted to understand what game Wilkins was playing.

*   *   *

As he knotted a red Hermes tie in the bedroom of his Foxhall Road house, Andrew Martin thought about how much his life had changed in the last two months.

It had all started with a phone ringing in his office on a Friday afternoon. As usual, he had let his secretary, Alice, pick it up. A few seconds later, she buzzed him on the intercom. "It's a woman by the name of Huan Ji."

Martin's mind flashed to that great evening in Hong Kong a month earlier. "Thanks. I'll take the call," he said. He picked up the phone. "Hi, Huan, how are you?"

"Great, I'm in New York," she said.

"You enjoying the city?"

"Absolutely. I was planning to come to Washington next Monday to do some research on the Securities and Exchange Commission for my book."

"That's great. Would you like to have dinner with me Monday evening? I'm a member of the Cosmos Club. It's a very international place. I think you'd like it."

"Sounds wonderful," she said. "I have a question for you, by the way."

"Sure."

"Do you have any hotel recommendations? Something in a good location and not too expensive would be ideal."

"You can stay with me," Martin said.

"I don't want to be an imposition," Huan said hesitantly.

"You won't be," Martin assured her. "I live alone in a large house. It'll be a pleasure having you." Will it ever, Martin thought.

"Well, thank you," she said. "My train gets into Washington at 4:45 Monday afternoon."

"Call me when you're about ten minutes from the station and I'll meet you out front. I'll be driving a green Jag convertible."

"I really appreciate it," she said before hanging up.

Martin put the phone down and leaned back in his chair, thinking: *What am I doing?* Over the years, he and Francis had laughed at men, their contemporaries, who had mistresses or second wives younger than their children. They looked foolish, like they thought they could turn back the clock, and often they were being taken advantage of financially.

What would happen if he walked into a Washington restaurant with Huan and saw people he knew? Would they have admiration for his sexual prowess or treat him as an object of ridicule? After a few minutes of thought, he decided he didn't care. The sex would be fun, and perhaps it would take his mind off the enormity of the crime he was committing in delivering those envelopes to Xiang. Despite his efforts at compartmentalizing, Martin couldn't stop worrying about the risks involved with the espionage he was committing for Liu.

One thought kept him going: *I'll never get caught.*

After picking Huan up at Union Station, he had brought her to his house and helped her carry her things up to a bedroom formerly used by one of his daughters.

"Why don't you get settled," he suggested. "We can head out around 7:30 for dinner."

"That sounds wonderful," she said with a smile.

"I'll be downstairs," he added. "If you need anything, just let me know."

Half an hour later, she had called to him, "Andrew, could you please come upstairs?"

To his surprise and amazement, when he reached the top of the stairs he saw her standing in the hallway, her hair still wet from the shower and with nothing on except a towel draped over her shoulders.

"Well, well," he said.

"You told me to call you if I needed something and I do," she said with a coy smile.

"I can't imagine what it is."

"Your bed or mine?" she laughed.

"Mine," said Martin. "It's larger."

And with that, they made love in the bed he had shared with Francis for thirty-five years of marriage.

The sex was wonderful, and later they had a great time at dinner, with Huan regaling him with her impressions and experiences in the United States. When they returned to his house, they made love again and fell asleep together. She had been there ever since.

The sex with her was great. She was intelligent and fun to be with. Besides that, having Huan in the house was very pleasant. She simplified his life. Not only was she a fabulous cook, but she shopped and did other errands while she worked on her novel. She was never demanding, and she never tried to dominate him.

From time to time, Martin became suspicious about Huan—not because of anything she did, but because of the circumstances behind their meeting and current arrangement. It seemed almost too perfect, like it had been planned: her meeting him in Hong Kong where she happened to be having dinner alone in his hotel, then her coming to Washington and virtually moving into his house. All this occurred at the same time he had been recruited by Liu and was passing envelopes to Xiang. Martin had never believed in coincidence. To him, a roulette ball landing on red eight times consecutively signified a crooked wheel. He wondered if Liu had sent her to watch him.

The previous week he had asked Huan how her novel was proceeding. She had told him about the places she was going for research and had given him the answers he would expect. He had then asked her if he could read what she had written. She had replied, "I would love you to, but I write in Chinese."

"Could you translate some for me?"

"I'm sorry, but I'm superstitious like many Chinese people. I never show my work to anyone until it's finished. I'm afraid it would jinx me."

After thinking about the issue, Martin had decided to brush aside his suspicions. He was gaining too much from the relationship. Perhaps she was working for Liu, but he didn't see how he could be hurt by her.

With his tie knotted exactly the way he liked, he headed down the stairs to the kitchen. The table was set with melon and berries, shredded wheat, skim milk, and homemade blueberry muffins. Everything Martin liked.

Once he had sat down at the table, Huan poured him a cup of coffee. The small television on the kitchen counter, which Francis had always hated, was on mute. The *Washington Post, New York Times,* and *Wall Street Journal* were on the table next to Martin's plate. He was glancing at the front page of the *Post* when something on the television screen caught his eye. As soon as he saw the words Chinese and East China Sea, he grabbed the remote.

Dale Hart, the president's press secretary, was conducting a press conference. He was standing at a lectern in a room filled with reporters.

"What we know," Hart said, "is that Chinese war planes attacked and destroyed Japanese planes in a battle over disputed islands in the East China Sea. That is the fact of what occurred."

A reporter shouted, "What response has President Braddock made?"

"Our planes flew close to the Chinese planes, but there was no engagement. We have filed a protest with Beijing."

"Don't we have treaty obligations that require us to come to the aid of Japan?" the reporter asked.

"All options are being considered," Hart replied.

That's certainly helpful, Martin thought. He looked across the table at Huan. She had a sad expression on her face. He imagined she must be worrying about her family in China. A war with the US would not be good for people in either country.

He tried to calm her anxiety. "The leaders in Beijing and Washington will find a way to resolve this peacefully. I'm confident of that," he said.

"The Tiananmen Square protests weren't resolved peacefully," said Huan, shaking her head. "My older brother was a student carrying banners there. That's all he did. He was killed when a tank fired at him and other students. It was murder, plain and simple. There was no effort at a peaceful resolution."

Before Martin had a chance to respond, the phone in his pocket rang. The caller's number was blocked. Martin answered.

"Andrew Martin here."

"Andrew, it's General Cartwright."

Though Martin knew Cartwright well enough to call him by his first name, doing so had never felt right. The man was a much decorated Air Force general and currently chairman of the Joint Chiefs, which made him the president's top military advisor. And in terms of his physical appearance, Cartwright was larger than life. Calling him anything other than General Cartwright seemed inappropriate.

"What's on your mind, General Cartwright?" Martin asked.

"Have you heard about the incident in the East China Sea?"

"I have. Something like this was inevitable."

"I couldn't agree more," said the general. "We have to talk. Can you join me for dinner this evening?"

"Sure."

"Great. Let's meet at eight o'clock at the Capital Grille on Pennsylvania Avenue."

Martin put down the phone and told Huan he would be out for dinner that evening.

"Don't worry about it, I'll be busy writing. That is as long as you're not meeting another woman," she added. "I would hate to lose you, Andrew."

As Martin drove to the office, Huan's final words reverberated in his mind. Even if she wasn't working for Liu, he wondered where their relationship was going. More importantly, what did Huan really want from him? A place to live, a man to take care of her, or did she have some other agenda?

Beijing

"We have a problem," General Piao, the head of the People's Liberation Army, said to Liu.

They were in Liu's office. As the general paused to clear his throat, Liu put out his cigarette and lit another. How could there be a problem, he wondered. Today was a glorious day for China. They had humiliated their archenemy Japan in the confrontation over the East China Sea, and the United States hadn't had the courage to intervene.

The general was stalling. It was obvious he didn't want to tell Liu.

"What problem?" the spymaster asked.

"Following the incident in the East China Sea," Piao continued, "we increased monitoring of conversations emanating from Japan. We picked up a conversation between Prime Minister Nakamura and President Braddock. In it, Nakamura reports on a conversation between two of our pilots in which they make it clear they knew the Americans would not attack."

"Meaning that the Americans are now aware we have a spy at a high level in their government."

"That's correct."

Liu was furious. He had given the information that the Americans would not intervene to General Piao with the express understanding it was to be acted upon but not repeated. "Didn't you tell your pilots what I told you? Under no circumstances were they to discuss this information."

The general looked pale. "Yes, sir, I did. There is no excuse for what happened."

"I want these two men punished."

"They've already been demoted. They'll never fly again."

Liu pounded his fist on the desk. "That's not enough. I want them imprisoned indefinitely. We must make an example of them. That's what happens when you disobey orders."

"But," the general began to protest, then apparently thought better of it. "I'll make sure they are imprisoned," he said.

When the general had left, Liu smoked two more cigarettes while trying to decide how to play his meeting with President Yao, which was scheduled to take place in an hour. The purpose of their meeting was to discuss the incident in the East China Sea. In reliance upon the information Liu had given Yao, that the Americans would not intervene, the Chinese president had ordered the attack on the Japanese. Liu should have been praised, since he had obtained that information as part of Operation New World Order, but Yao didn't give praise—or even thanks. Still, Liu knew the Chinese president was sure to be pleased. That would have made for a satisfactory meeting with Yao, but now there was this revelation from General Piao to contend with.

Liu wondered what he should do. Disclose this new information to Yao, or keep it to himself? With bad news, Liu's general rule was only to disclose it to the president if there was a good chance he would learn about it on his own, since then Liu would have to answer both for the mistake and his failure to disclose it.

In this situation, it was possible the American president would complain to Yao about the Chinese spying on the US. Then Liu would be in deep trouble. The spymaster decided he had no choice, he had to make the disclosure.

Liu was still cursing those two pilots half an hour later as he left his office for the meeting with Yao.

*   *   *

Liu and Yao were alone in Yao's office. The president was extremely pleased at how the incident had gone in the East China Sea. To celebrate, he poured glasses of an eighteen-year-old scotch for the two of them.

After taking a sip of his drink, Liu said, "We have a small complication." He then explained what General Piao had told him. As Liu spoke, Yao became so red in the face with anger that Liu thought he might have a heart attack.

"It's all your fault," Yao blurted out. "You didn't impress upon the military the importance of confidentiality."

Of course Yao's charge was ridiculous, but Liu saw no point in denying it. The president would never believe him, and arguing the issue might put Liu in prison along with the pilots. Instead, he tried to shift the discussion.

"It's immaterial that the Americans know we have a mole at the top of their government," said Liu.

"How can you possibly say that?" asked Yao. "They'll go on a witch hunt to discover who he is."

"They'll never find him," Liu said with confidence he didn't feel. "Now we move into the next phase of Operation New World Order, right on schedule."

"For your sake, I hope you are right."

"Don't worry, I am."

"Andrew Martin is your weak link," Yao remarked.

"Martin can't do us any damage. I have a way of controlling him."

"How?" Yao demanded to know.

Liu never liked disclosing any of his sources of information, but with Yao he had no choice.

Reluctantly, he said, "There is a woman watching Martin and reporting to me."

*   *   *

On the way back to his office, Liu thought about what President Yao had said. The Americans would go on a witch hunt to discover the mole in their government. Liu had to find out what they were doing, and fast.

By the time he reached his office, Liu had an idea. Undoubtedly, Kelly Cameron would be involved in this witch hunt. In view of her job at the FBI, she would have to be. And following Liu's orders, Xiang had been seeing Kelly every couple of weeks. Liu hadn't discussed with Xiang his relationship with Kelly, but he had read all of Xiang's reports. Xiang had said their relationship was gradually improving and romance was developing anew. So far Xiang hadn't gotten any useful information, but in his last report he predicted that he might get Kelly into bed with him soon. Then he would be able to obtain important information. When Liu had read that, he had been prepared to wait. All of that had now changed. He had to find out what was going on, and he had to find out now.

Liu called Wu, the director of security at the embassy in Washington, and ordered him to take Xiang to the basement room for a call.

Once he had Xiang on the line, Liu told him, "We believe the Americans are launching a major effort to identify a mole in their government. I want you to find out from Kelly Cameron what they are doing."

When Xiang didn't reply, Liu said, "Are you still there?"

"Yes, sir."

"I want you to obtain this information as soon as possible. It is critical. Do you understand?"

"Yes, sir."

"When is your next date with Kelly Cameron?"

"I'm not sure," Xiang sounded flustered.

"What do you mean you're not sure?"

"I have to call her and set it."

"Well, you better do it soon."

"Yes, sir."

"And you better obtain this information."

"Yes, sir. I will."

When Liu put down the phone, he was convinced from the sound of Xiang's voice that Xiang was lying or concealing something. He went back and reread all of Xiang's reports on his meetings with Kelly, which he hadn't read very carefully when he had received them. As he did, he became convinced they were bogus. They were all too general and didn't seem authentic. In view of how Xiang sounded today, Liu doubted whether he'd even had any dates with Kelly. Another possibility was that Xiang and Kelly were lovers again, and he refused to spy on her. Liu had to know for sure.

He called Wu back and instructed him to have embassy security people follow Xiang around the clock and immediately report back if he was with a blonde American woman. Liu would find out what Xiang was really doing. If he was deceiving Liu, the spymaster vowed to come down hard on him.

Washington

As noon approached, it was almost time for the task force meeting. Kelly summarized in her mind what she had learned in the last couple of hours.

These so-called islands in the East China Sea for which Japan and China had rival claims, were nothing more than clumps of rock in the ocean. They were neither inhabited nor habitable. To be sure, there might be oil and minerals under them, but the dispute over the islands themselves was a matter of patriotism and pride, as well as an effort to settle past scores and exploit antagonism and hatred between China and Japan. Kelly was no expert on foreign policy. To her, for the United States to be dragged into a war over these "islands" seemed ludicrous.

As for the other members of her task force, she had found out that George Wilkins had graduated with distinction from Georgetown's School of Foreign Service. Following graduation, he began as an intern at the National Security Council during the Carter administration. Whenever the Democrats were in the White House, Wilkins had a position in the NSC, gradually working himself up to the top position as the president's national security advisor under Braddock. When the Republicans were in, he joined prestigious foreign policy think tanks, including the Council on Foreign Relations and Brookings. During those off years, he wrote and spoke extensively.

Lance Farrell had been with the CIA from the time he had graduated from Cornell. He had received the agency's "outstanding young agent" award five years ago. Following that, he had been assigned to "special projects." Two years ago, he had been put through a crash course on China and was now a member of an elite CIA China policy team. Including Paul Maltoni, the three were a very talented group. For Kelly, being their chairman was a great honor.

All four arrived at noon at the FBI conference room. They ate sandwiches and made small talk until Kelly decided to get down to business.

"Tell us about the Camp David gathering," she said to Wilkins.

"Let me put Camp David into context," Wilkins said, putting his coffee cup down. "Following the February 28 summit meeting in Beijing, President Braddock conducted a full review of our Asia policy and decided to move more of our military forces to the area in a signal to our allies that we would not yield control of Asia and the Pacific to China. Then about three weeks ago, the rhetoric between Japan and China became more intense. It seemed likely there would be a military confrontation over the islands in the East China Sea. So two weeks ago, the president convened a high-level gathering at Camp David to discuss our response in the event of hostilities."

Paul, who was taking notes, looked up. "Who was there?" he asked.

Wilkins reached down to his briefcase on the floor, pulled out four sheets of paper, and gave them one each. "I thought you would want to know, so I made copies."

Kelly glanced over the list. It had all the people she would expect, including the president, vice president, the secretaries of state and defense, their deputies, Cartwright, as well as Wilkins and Vernon. Twelve altogether, including Wilkins, plus the president.

"How did the discussion go?" Kelly asked.

"Not at all the way I had expected," Wilkins replied.

"Meaning what?"

"President Braddock and the vice president were the only ones pushing for a military response."

"The two politicians," Farrell interjected.

"Correct," said Wilkins. "The rest of us were opposed. Being the only military man present, General Cartwright and his position in opposition to a military response carried a great deal of weight. We didn't think what was at stake, some meaningless clumps of rocks in the Pacific, justified the risk of war. Can I speak frankly?"

"Of course," Kelly responded. "Everything said here remains with us." She glanced at Paul and Farrell.

"Correct," they agreed.

"Okay," Wilkins continued. "What I want to say is, Braddock was more stubborn at Camp David than he usually is. Eventually, he retreated to an economic rather than a military response: sanctions against China in the event they attacked Japanese planes. Even that was strongly resisted by this group. They believed the sanctions would only hurt our economy. In the end, I think Braddock was sorry he had convened the group. After all, he's the president. He could have acted on his own."

Paul asked, "Was the decision not to respond to a Chinese attack over the islands memorialized in a written document?"

Wilkins again reached into his briefcase and pulled out copies of another sheet of paper. He distributed them.

Kelly studied the document. It was a single page memorandum entitled, "Camp David consensus."

"When was it prepared?" Paul asked.

"Before the gathering at Camp David broke up," Wilkins replied. "I drafted it and asked the president's secretary to type it."

"And were copies distributed to all those present?" Paul inquired.

"Exactly," nodded Wilkins.

"So this document could have been leaked to the Chinese?" Paul continued.

"The president is convinced, based upon his conversation with Prime Minister Nakamura, that this document was turned over to the Chinese. Or at least, its contents were leaked to them. I'm not sure he's right, however, we have to accept that."

Silence settled over the conference room as they studied the document.

"I have an idea," Kelly finally said. All eyes were on her. "Let's set up a sting. We'll prepare a new document, a phony presidential decision with the opposite policy. It will say: 'In view of what occurred today, I have changed my position. The next time there is an incident between China and Japan, the US will intervene on the side of Japan and attack Chinese forces.' The document will be marked with 'Classified. Highly Secret. No copies made. Do not take from your office.' We will distribute copies to all those who were at Camp David."

Paul asked, "How will we know if one of them violates those instructions?"

Farrell responded before Kelly had a chance. "We can insert on each document a concealed nano chip that will permit it to be tracked and which will establish whether a copy is made. Also, it will tell us if the document is photographed or removed from someone's office. In other words, we could track each document electronically. Is that what you had in mind, Kelly?"

"Precisely," she affirmed. "I've heard about the technology, but never used it."

"The CIA used it for an operation in Jordan," said Farrell. "It helped us catch a traitor in their government."

Kelly looked at Wilkins. "What do you think?" she asked him.

"I don't know. Lots could go wrong."

"It can't hurt to try," Paul said.

"What if the substance of the document is passed orally?" Wilkins asked.

"We'll be no worse off than we are now," Kelly replied. "Does anybody have any objections?"

"I don't like the idea," Wilkins said, "of treating the top officials of our government as spies."

"We're not doing that," Kelly insisted, "we simply want to identify the mole."

"If this illustrious group learned what we were doing or word gets into the press, we'd be crucified," said Wilkins.

Kelly held her ground. "I haven't heard another idea of how we should proceed."

Paul spoke up. "I'm in favor of Kelly's proposal."

"Let's do it," Farrell said, sounding excited. "We can prepare the document at Langley using our high-tech people."

"That's okay with me," Kelly replied. "I'll have to get Director Forester's approval." She looked at Wilkins. "Are you in with us, George?"

"I guess so, but I'll need the president's approval," he replied.

"Ditto for me with the AG," Paul said.

They decided to seek those approvals and confirm by email with a simple yes or no in case anyone hacked the emails.

The next step, Kelly told them, was to meet later that day at Langley to get started. The goal was to distribute the phony document the following morning.

An hour later, Kelly had Forester's approval. He liked the idea of the sting operation. "This is top priority," he told her. "Use my name to get access to any resources the bureau has."

She immediately accepted that offer, asking the head of the investigations branch to prepare personal profiles on all twelve of the participants at Camp David and to forward the profiles to her electronically.

While waiting for emails from the other members of the task force, Kelly called home to tell Luisa she wouldn't be back until quite late. Once again, she wouldn't be having dinner with Julie, or even putting her daughter to bed. When she spoke to Julie to explain, her daughter sounded resigned and asked if she could watch a video on her iPad, to which Kelly readily agreed. She considered telling Julie that she'd take her to the Nats game Saturday, but she decided she might have to work through the weekend on the project. She didn't want to make one more promise to Julie that she would have to break.

*   *   *

Andrew Martin left his Jaguar XK8 convertible, painted in British racing green, with Clyde, the parking attendant on Pennsylvania Avenue in front of the Capital Grille. He handed Clyde a twenty dollar bill, saying, "Take good care of my baby." Then with a swagger, he walked into the restaurant, passing sides of beef in a glass walled refrigerator and the wine lockers some of the regulars maintained. It was Thursday evening and the place was booming. The near deafening noise greeted Martin before he made it to the maître d's stand.

Jacinda immediately recognized him, "Evening, Mr. Martin. General Cartwright is at the bar."

She pointed to Martin's right. The area was crowded by mostly men, with the exception of a couple of busty blondes in short skirts. As Martin surveyed the scene, General Cartwright, standing near the bar with a glass in hand, stood out. Not just because he was wearing his blue Air Force general's uniform heavily adorned with medals, but because the tall, broad-chested Cartwright had a charisma and presence that drew eyes like a magnet. He was talking to a man in civilian clothes standing next to him. The general was speaking in his normal booming voice, talking about the threat the Russians posed to Central Europe. The bartender held out a drink to Cartwright. He drained his glass and swapped it for the new drink.

As Martin approached the bar, Cartwright pulled away from the other man. "Ah, Andrew, glad you could come. Let's go to the table."

Jacinda led the two of them through a throng of others waiting for tables, like Moses at the parting of the sea. She seated them in a booth for four along one wall. The aroma of steak and fries was in the air, the decibel and testosterone level high, and the lights dim as Washington power brokers conducted their business. Martin spotted Senator Kendall from Alabama across the room. The senator waved to Martin, who ignored him. Contrary to the sense of collegiality that was supposed to govern the Senate club, for years Kendall had done everything possible to undermine Senator Jasper from Colorado, who was then Martin's friend. About a week after Jasper's death, Martin had encountered Kendall in the corridor of the Hart Senate Office Building. Kendall had said,

"So sorry to hear about your friend and my beloved colleague. It's a shame his daddy never taught him to keep his pants zipped."

Martin had sneered at Kendall and replied, "With all the sleeping around you've done, publication of that incident must have struck terror into your heart."

Kendall had blushed and quickly walked away.

A waiter came over to Martin and Cartwright's table.

"I'm drinking scotch," Cartwright said. "You want one or should we start on wine?"

"Let's go for the wine," Martin replied.

"Pick a good Barolo," Cartwright requested.

"They have Vajra, an excellent producer."

"Okay with me. And let's order some dinner. I'm starving."

Cartwright ordered a salad and a 20-ounce porterhouse, while Martin selected a salad and small fillet. Since Huan had come to town, he had decided to shed a few pounds. She was a helluva lot younger and never tired in bed. He had to be in good shape to keep up.

As they waited for their wine to arrive, Martin was becoming increasingly curious as to why Cartwright wanted to have dinner with him this evening.

A few minutes later, after their salads and wine came, Cartwright leaned forward. In a soft voice, he said, "I've decided to challenge Braddock for the presidency. I wanted you to be the first to know."

The news startled Martin. The election was in November, seven months from now. Braddock, a Democrat, seemed a shoo-in for reelection. No Republican had gotten widespread support.

Martin and Cartwright had never before discussed presidential politics. "I assume you'll be trying for the Republican nomination," Martin said.

"That's right," confirmed Cartwright.

"Are you sure you want to do this?"

"You sound dubious. Why not?"

"Presidential campaigns put the candidate's life under a microscope," Martin pointed out.

"I can handle it."

"You don't have much time. The convention's in mid-August."

"That's plenty," Cartwright said confidently. "The primaries have left the field wide open with the existing candidates splitting the delegates.

Nobody is close to the number of votes needed to nominate. Several key primaries have not yet been held. So, bottom line, the party can easily coalesce around a new charismatic candidate, either prior to or at the convention."

Martin paused to sip his wine and ponder what he had just heard. He was enthusiastic about Cartwright running. He despised Braddock. Apart from his personal issues, he viewed Braddock as weak and a poor leader, and he thought others had to believe that as well. Cartwright could very well defeat Braddock.

The waiter cleared their salads, then brought out the steaks. Cartwright, who had been drinking wine like it was water, ordered another bottle.

"I'm telling you about my plan to run," Cartwright said, "because I want you to be my advisor during the campaign. You have the inside Washington knowledge and political savvy I need. Will you do it?"

"Aren't you worried I'll be a liability after my involvement in the Jasper affair?" Martin asked.

"That's old news. And at any rate, what'd you do? Lent your house in Anguilla to an old friend and tried to help him out when he told you some bimbo died."

"You're right, that is all I did."

"So I want your help," Cartwright continued. "Nobody knows Washington as well as you do, Andrew. Are you in?"

"For sure, all in," Martin replied, the enthusiasm evident in his voice. Martin loved the prospect of being back in the political action. And there was something else—if Cartwright were to capture the presidency, Martin could become his close advisor and confidante the way Clark Clifford, Abe Fortas, and other powerful Washington lawyers had been for past presidents. That was an ideal position. It didn't require Senate confirmation, and he would have a real say on critical domestic and foreign issues. That was power! At the same time, it would enable him to expand his law practice.

Martin raised his glass and Cartwright did the same.

"To victory in November," Cartwright said.

For several minutes they were silent as they ate their steaks. Then Martin said, "You realize you will have to resign from the Air Force in order to run."

Cartwright smiled and said, "You don't have to worry. I won't be in the military much longer."

It was a peculiar comment, but Martin didn't press him. "Money will be the key," Martin said. "You'll have to hit the ground running to raise money."

"I figured as much. I want to do this the right way. I've lined up a couple of squeaky clean Wall Street finance guys to head up my fundraising. However, I do need advice on one aspect of it."

"What's that?"

"I want to understand the laws related to campaign financing. I don't want to screw up there. Can you help me?"

"I only know the general concepts," said Martin. "One of my partners, Karen Miller, is an expert. I'll set up a meeting for you with her."

"Good."

When the waiter came to clear their main courses, Cartwright glanced at his watch. "Excuse me, I have to visit the restroom."

He swayed as he left the table and headed toward the bathroom on the other side of the bar. Martin looked at the wine remaining in the second bottle, thought about what he'd drunk, and decided that Cartwright, who began with at least a couple of scotches, had consumed a huge amount of alcohol. He was amazed Cartwright was still standing.

He followed Cartwright with his eyes as he walked past the bar. A few minutes later, he was coming from the other direction. He saw Cartwright stop at the bar and talk to someone seated there. When the man turned his head, Martin recognized Dale Scott, a political reporter for the *Wall Street Journal*.

Scott climbed off the barstool, grabbed his thin briefcase, and followed Cartwright to the table where he gave Martin a warm greeting. His paper had always treated Martin fairly. Martin reached out and shook his hand.

At Cartwright's urging, Scott sat down in the booth next to Martin across from Cartwright. When a waiter appeared, Cartwright, slurring his words, told him to bring another glass for the reporter.

Once the waiter had done so, Cartwright looked at Scott and said, "Today was a black day for the United States."

"You mean the incident in the East China Sea," Scott replied.

"That's right."

"Because we didn't come to aid of our ally and honor our treaty commitments?" he asked.

"That's only part of it," Cartwright continued. "At the critical moment when Braddock had to decide whether the US planes should attack the Chinese, he was worse than indecisive. He was shaking and perspiring, completely panicked at having to make the decision."

Martin turned sideways to look at the reporter, who seemed flabbergasted by what he was hearing.

"I assume you're telling me this privately, General. You don't want me to put it in tomorrow morning's newspaper."

Martin reached across the table and placed a hand on Cartwright's wrist. "That's right," Martin said.

Cartwright pulled his hand away. "You can print it," he said.

"Maybe we should discuss this by ourselves," Martin interjected.

"That's not necessary," Cartwright said. He turned back to Scott. "If you like, I'll give you some more details, including the setting in the Situation Room as background for your story."

Scott pulled out his iPad. "Okay if I take notes?" he asked.

"Sure."

Martin was astounded by Cartwright's behavior. He thought the general was being reckless, perhaps because he was drunk. Then, listening to Cartwright's clear and incisive recounting of events, Martin realized this must have all been a setup. Cartwright had asked Scott to come to the Capital Grille so he could give him the story. This had to be the launch of Cartwright's presidential campaign. Martin had no doubt Braddock would fire Cartwright as soon as he saw the *Wall Street Journal* article. That's why Cartwright had told Martin he wouldn't be in the military much longer.

Scott asked Cartwright, "You said Braddock was indecisive, shaking, and perspiring? That he was panicked by having to make a decision?"

"Yes, those were my words," Cartwright confirmed.

It promised to be a helluva campaign, Martin thought. Cartwright was going after the presidency like a military battle. He was determined to vanquish Braddock.

Washington and Saint Michaels, Maryland

Friday morning at seven o'clock, after five hours of sleep, Kelly drove into the garage underneath the FBI headquarters. The previous evening, once Wilkins and Maltoni had gotten approvals from Braddock and Larkin for the sting, all four of the task force members went to work with CIA technical personnel preparing the phony documents that would be distributed at ten that morning.

Wilkins had left at midnight when he received a call from Chad Vernon, the president's chief of staff, summoning him to the White House. "He didn't tell me what happened, just to come quick," he had said.

The others had kept going until they finished the job two hours later.

At 7:15 in the morning, Paul and Farrell joined Kelly in the conference room. A few minutes later, a grim-faced and weary looking Wilkins arrived.

"Any of you hear the news this morning?" Wilkins asked.

They all looked at him with puzzled expressions. Farrell replied, "Hey, we were at Langley until two o'clock. I was happy for a little peace and quiet in the car on the way in."

"Ditto for me," Paul said.

"And the same," Kelly added. "What happened?"

"General Cartwright gave an interview to Dale Scott at the *Journal* about yesterday's incident with China and Japan."

"What'd he say?" Kelly asked.

"That while in the Situation Room, Braddock was indecisive, 'shaking and perspiring.' Scott put those words in quote. Also that the president was panicked by having to make a decision."

"Were you in the Situation Room with Braddock?" Kelly asked. "Is that what happened?"

"Well, let's just say there was some indecisiveness on Braddock's part. Nevertheless, I definitely would not have used those words."

Kelly took that as confirmation of what Cartwright had said. "How's the president dealing with this?" she asked.

"Vernon told Scott it was all a pack of lies. We were up all night doing damage control with the Hill and media."

"What about Cartwright?" Paul asked.

"The president intends to fire him first thing this morning and tell him never to set foot in the Pentagon again. That'll be announced by Vernon at a press conference at nine this morning. Cartwright has called his own press conference for eleven. We have a real donnybrook."

"I don't think this should interfere with what we're doing," Kelly said.

"Agreed," Farrell responded. "If anything, it makes it more urgent to find the mole. As I was coming up in the elevator for this meeting, I received an email from the techies at Langley. They're on their way in with the phony documents, each in an envelope addressed to one of the twelve recipients. They'll also have the software to permit us to track the documents, which they'll show us how to operate it."

"All sounds good," Kelly said.

"Once you give me the green light," Wilkins said, "I'll get the twelve envelopes to Chad Vernon to be distributed by White House couriers. Actually, eleven now. No point giving me an envelope."

"What about Cartwright's envelope?" Paul asked. "We just heard he'll be out as chairman of the Joint Chiefs."

"Braddock intends to appoint Admiral Merriweather to succeed Cartwright as chairman of the Joint Chiefs on an interim basis," said Wilkins.

"Then no need to give General Cartwright an envelope," Kelly said. "He's no longer in the government. Nor Merriweather, since he wasn't at Camp David."

"Which means we have eleven possibilities," Farrell said. "Sorry, George, I included you by mistake. I should have said ten."

At 9:15 a.m., Wilkins stuffed the envelopes into his briefcase. "I'll make sure they're all delivered by noon."

"We'll be watching the monitors from that point on," Kelly said, "to see if any document is copied or moved out of the recipient's office."

Kelly arranged to have a television brought into the conference room. That way they could hear Cartwright's press conference.

Kelly turned it on a few minutes before eleven. She watched the general, dressed in a civilian suit and tie, walk over to a cluster of microphones at the bottom of the Capitol steps.

"Following my discharge by President Braddock," Cartwright began in a booming and self-confident voice, "several people, students of history, called to remind me of President Truman's discharge of General Douglas MacArthur, that great American war hero. I reminded them there was a basic difference in these two situations.

"MacArthur had a policy dispute with Truman over the conduct of the Korean War. Here, my concern is over presidential leadership, or more precisely, the lack thereof. I thought long and hard before I gave that interview to the *Wall Street Journal*. I believed last evening, and I still do, that the American people have a right to know how their president behaved at the time of a great crisis for the United States. I believe they have a right to know that he was indecisive and panicked at having to make a decision on the single most important foreign policy issue facing the United States—our relations with China.

"I realized, of course, that my disclosure of those facts would result in the end of my military service to this great country, which has meant more to me than anything else in life. I have also decided I should not—indeed cannot—limit myself to words. I am a man of action, as my Air Force record demonstrates. So I intend to seek the Republican nomination. In November, I will defeat Braddock when he seeks reelection. I will end the reign of this indecisive man. We need real leadership in the White House right now."

Cartwright paused, then added, "I'll be happy to take questions."

A reporter asked, "Do you have any regrets, General Cartwright, over what has transpired in the last couple of days?"

"Only that my wife Maureen could not be with me to share these momentous personal decisions. As many of you are aware, her passing was a huge personal loss. We had shared all of life's challenges and decisions."

"I'll bet," Kelly blurted at the screen. "Don't you love it when these guys throw in the little wife for sympathy and support?"

"It's worse than that," Farrell added. "Three years ago when Maureen was still alive, we had to cover up Cartwright's mess. We were aware that Cartwright was constantly picking up women, particularly when he traveled. It got him into trouble in Prague. Helena, a Russian woman he picked up, forwarded sensitive emails from the general's computer to her spymaster in Moscow. The Russians let us know they had the emails."

"Will that come up in the campaign?" Paul asked.

"Never. The director loves Cartwright. He buried it so deeply at Langley that it would take a bunker buster to unearth it."

"How do you know about it?" Kelly asked.

"The director sent me to Prague as his personal rep to do damage control, convincing the Czech government to expel Helena back to Russia, and, in return for lifting trade restrictions, to forget this ever happened. I get all the fun jobs."

Kelly looked at the television screen. Cartwright was merely repeating what he'd already said. She turned to the others and pointed to the screen. "You two had enough of this?"

"Any more and I'll throw up," Farrell declared.

"Wow. You're a cynic," Paul said.

"Not really," said Farrell with a shrug. "The good general wasn't even contrite when we were together in Prague. It was as if he had a God-given right to fuck whatever wore a skirt. He told me it was a shame Helena turned out to be 'tainted.' That was his word. He also told me she was one of the best lays he'd ever had."

"Careful now," Paul said. "You may be talking about our next president."

"In that respect, he won't be any worse than some of the others we've had."

Kelly ordered in sandwiches for the three of them while they concentrated on following the devices tracking the documents. By noon, all ten had been delivered. They ate lunch, followed by coffee, then more coffee. But nothing happened. None of the documents were moved; none copied.

At three o'clock, Wilkins returned and joined them in the conference room. He was constantly pacing, the least patient of the four. Probably because of the nature of his work, Kelly thought. She and Farrell spent a large part of their lives waiting for something to happen. This was standard operating procedure for them. Paul had his eyes closed. She couldn't tell whether he was resting or dozing.

Finally, at 4:40 in the afternoon, something did happen. Kelly noticed that the copy delivered to Owen Peterson, the deputy secretary of defense, was leaving his office in clear violation of the order stamped on the envelope. The document was moving along a corridor in the Pentagon. She pointed this out to the others.

"Maybe he can't read," Farrell said.

Nobody laughed.

The document went down the elevator and out into the Pentagon parking lot. Kelly had FBI agents stationed in the vicinity of the parked cars of all ten of the people who had received the document.

One reported that Peterson was clutching his briefcase with the document as he walked across the Pentagon parking lot to his car. The briefcase went into the backseat of his gray BMW sedan. When the car pulled out of the parking lot, an FBI car was moving as well in a loose tail. No need to worry about losing the BMW, since they had tracking on the document.

While Kelly followed Peterson's document, Paul and Farrell kept checking the other nine copies. There was no movement on any of them.

"What do we know about Peterson?" Paul asked.

With one eye on the computer screen tracking the document, Kelly pulled up Peterson's bio, which the bureau's investigation unit had prepared.

"Peterson's fifty-two," she said. "Until two years ago, he worked for an aerospace company in a variety of executive positions. Then he became deputy secretary of defense. Married once, divorced four years ago. One child living in Seattle. Primary residence is McLean, with a second home in Saint Michaels on the Eastern shore. That's the bare-bones bio I asked our investigators to prepare on all the Camp David attendees. Now that we're focused on Peterson, I'll ask them to do a full workup."

The BMW turned onto the Beltway heading into Maryland. When he exited for Route 50, east toward the Bay Bridge, Farrell said, "It's Friday afternoon. Our target's off for a weekend at his country house."

"Where he may be meeting his Chinese contact," Wilkins said, "to turn over the document."

"Have any of the other documents been moved?" Kelly asked.

"Negative," Farrell said.

Kelly was beginning to think Peterson was the mole. She made a quick decision. "The tracking devices have enough range that we can follow the other documents from the road. We have to go to Saint Michaels ourselves."

"For a weekend in the country," Paul sang from the Stephen Sondheim musical *A Little Night Music*.

"I can't leave town," Wilkins said, "since Braddock's here."

"We'll keep you informed," Kelly told him. Then she called the bureau's travel office to handle reservations and logistics. After that she pulled up Peterson's house on a map on her iPad. It was isolated on a sliver of land jutting into the water.

There were two agents in the car tailing the gray BMW. She arranged for four other agents to join them in Saint Michaels. She wanted to have a stakeout on Peterson and his house around the clock.

"I'll set up electronic surveillance on Peterson's house," she told Paul and Farrell. "All phones and emails."

"We'll need a court order," Paul said.

Kelly and Farrell looked at him as if he were from Mars.

"No really, we need it," Paul insisted.

"How soon can you get it?" Kelly asked.

"An hour or so."

"Okay. Go get it. Farrell and I will head to Saint Michaels. You can join us there."

Kelly and Farrell were excited as they climbed into an FBI car, a GM SUV, a few minutes later. Both believed the sting was working; that Peterson was their man.

Farrell drove with Kelly in the passenger seat beside him. Unwilling to wait for Paul to get his court order, she was arranging electronic surveillance on Peterson's house. They would be able to listen in on any calls Peterson made or received on cell phones and landlines. They would also be able to pick up any emails he sent or received, and they would have enough agents in the area to follow him if he left his house. Additionally, she would be able to call in a drone for air surveillance.

When they were on Route 50, they received a report from the unit trailing the gray BMW. Peterson had stopped at a supermarket on Route 33 on the outskirts of Saint Michaels. He had bought groceries, then driven on to his house.

Kelly doubted if Peterson's rendezvous with his Chinese handler would occur that evening. By the time they reached the small hotel where they'd be staying, ten miles outside of Saint Michaels, Paul called to say he had the court order. "I'm on my way."

When Paul arrived, the three of them had dinner in the hotel dining room. Midway through the main course, Kelly received a call from Agent Rolfe in charge of the unit watching Peterson's house. "The house has gone dark," he reported

They all relaxed. Nothing else would happen that night. The wine began flowing freely.

During dessert, Farrell said to Kelly, "I've been meaning to ask, are you related to Charles Cameron?"

"He's my father," she replied. "Why?"

"He's an iconic figure at the agency. He was responsible for getting more people across the wall than anyone else. He did incredible work. It's a shame his career ended the way it did."

"You mean with him being wounded in the leg?"

Farrell paused to take a sip of wine. "Yeah. The whole Fritz Helfund business was so unfortunate. Your dad was a true successor to Wild Bill Donovan. Unfortunately, there's nobody around these days even remotely like him," Farrell said with admiration. "When the seventh floor at Langley decided to sack your father, there was a huge outcry among the people in the field and in the Russian section. They were furious. Charles Cameron was their hero. But they couldn't do a damn thing to get his firing reversed. You know how those things go."

Kelly was too startled to respond. Farrell's story was so different from what her father had told her. The story she had grown up hearing was that in his last operation, her father had gotten a valuable German scientist safely out of Germany. The operation had ended successfully, but he had been wounded, so he had been offered a desk job at Langley, which he had then turned down.

Farrell must be wrong, she thought, but how could he make such a mistake? Or had people at Langley generated false stories about her father to advance their own interests? She wondered. She had to find out what had happened.

"Is this Fritz Helfund incident and my father's involvement written up and maintained in the archives at Langley?" she asked Farrell.

"I imagine so. Would you like to read it?"

"Sure."

"All our stuff is now electronic. I'll try to find it and send it to you Monday."

*   *   *

"Your press conference was excellent," Martin told Cartwright. It was Saturday morning and they were in Martin's office.

Cartwright was smiling. "I've been very pleased with the response," he said. "Emails from Republicans around the country and lots of wealthy people who want to jump on my bandwagon."

"What can I do to help?"

"I need your intelligence. I want you to develop a brain trust for me, a cadre of outstanding policy wonks and lawyers who can develop a steady stream of issue papers you'll edit and convert into speeches for me."

"I'd be happy to do that." Martin had enough relationships among Washington hands in think tanks and consulting firms to assemble a group like that for Cartwright. Many of them had formerly been in positions of power. Almost always, they were itching to get back into the game, but that meant finding a horse to ride in on. The revolving door in Washington never stopped turning.

"I know the foreign policy area," Cartwright said, "and I'll add my own personal touches to speeches there, but I'm weak on domestic issues."

"I understand. Who will be managing your money?"

"Ted Chase in New York. He used to be at Goldman. I figure Braddock's people will be gunning for me. If I make a slip, they'll pounce. That's why I wanted to meet with you and your election finance expert."

"That's my partner, Karen Miller."

"Yeah. I want to understand the rules myself, at least the broad outline."

"Very wise," agreed Martin. "Karen is here and available. She can give you a quick primer."

While Martin called Miller, Cartwright refilled his coffee cup from a silver thermos on a credenza.

Karen Miller entered the room. She was in her mid-forties, five foot four and stocky, wearing a black pantsuit. She had scratches on her face, and her right foot and ankle were in a medical boot.

"What happened to you?" Martin asked.

"I tried to keep up with my teenage son on a mountain bike," she replied. "I think I'll stick to golf next time."

"You'll have to watch out for uneven patches in the fairway," Martin quipped.

"Thank you, Andrew."

When the three of them had sat down at the conference table, Miller said, "Okay, how can I help?"

"Could you give General Cartwright a broad overview of the laws relating to election financing?" Martin said.

"Sure, I'd be happy to."

Cartwright pulled over a legal pad resting on the table and removed a pen from his pocket, ready to take notes.

Miller was looking at the general. "I'll focus on presidential elections, because I assume that's what you want to hear about," she said.

"That's right," the general agreed.

"Let's start with the proposition that money is the key to winning a presidential election. Make no mistake about it, it is."

"I figured as much."

"This whole area has exploded in the last several years with decisions by the Supreme Court. As matters now stand, an American citizen can give unlimited funds to a Super PAC to finance advertising for a candidate. This result is based on the free speech amendment to the Constitution."

"They can't give directly to the candidate?"

"Correct," Miller confirmed. "The Super PAC funds advertising. There are no limits on the amount contributed. So if you have one or more supporters with vast resources and they really want to help you, the sky is the limit on how much advertising your campaign can do. And a number of studies have shown a direct correlation between the amount of advertising and voter support. It's all about name recognition and perceptions. Do you have any supporters with megabucks who want to use them for your campaign?"

Cartwright didn't respond. He looked at Martin.

"You can talk freely with Karen," Martin said. "This is a privileged conversation. Karen is very discrete. Besides, if she ever said a word to anyone, I'd break her other leg."

They all laughed.

Cartwright nodded and said, "So far, one. Carl Dickerson."

"You only need one like Dickerson," Martin said. "Forbes listed him as one of the twenty wealthiest people in the world."

"How did he make his money?" Miller asked.

Martin replied, "Hotels and casinos around the world, particularly in Asia. Also he's a major importer into the Asian market of luxury goods representing European producers of apparel, wine, and other high-end items. With his contacts, he provides them access to markets difficult to penetrate. In return for that, he gets a cut of what they sell. Dickerson is based in LA. I visited him in his Beverly Hills office a few years ago to make a pitch to get some of his legal business. Unfortunately, one of the big LA firms has a lock on it."

Miller looked worried. "We have to be careful. We could have a problem."

"What's that?" Cartwright asked.

"The law prohibits contributions by foreign entities. The idea is that foreign governments and entities shouldn't influence an American election."

"But Dickerson is an American citizen," said Cartwright.

"Whose income is derived substantially or primarily from foreign operations, based on what Andrew said. And probably many of those are in China," Miller pointed out.

"Nevertheless," Martin said, "there's a simple solution. Make sure all the political contributions come from Dickerson's personal accounts, nothing from his businesses. What do you think, Karen?"

"That should work," she replied. "If you'd like, put me in touch with Dickerson's lawyers. I'll make sure we set it up so we don't have a problem."

Martin agreed to do that.

Cartwright was very pleased. He'd have unlimited money for advertising, and it would all be perfectly legal.

"What about your own money," Miller asked, "are you planning to invest some of that on the campaign?"

"I spent my whole life in the military and my dad was a mechanic at a pulp mill in Oconto Falls, Wisconsin. I don't have anything to invest."

"Do you have any offshore accounts?" she asked.

Cartwright looked irate.

"Sorry, I had to ask," Miller said.

"The answer is no."

When the meeting broke up and Cartwright left, Martin went back to his office. He leaned back in his chair, closed his eyes, and thought about what he had learned that morning.

Dickerson was funding Cartwright's campaign. And as Karen had said, a huge amount of his income was derived from business operations in China. Martin wondered whether Dickerson on his own had stepped forward to fund Cartwright. Or had he been pushed to do it in order to preserve and enhance his Chinese operations. Perhaps another move by the spymaster Liu?

In addition to everything else he was doing, could Liu be manipulating the American presidential election?

Saint Michaels, Maryland

"Target is on the move," Kelly heard from Agent Rolfe on her phone. It was eleven o'clock on a bright, sunny Saturday morning. "Peterson is on foot, dressed in khaki shorts and a navy polo, walking along the narrow road that follows the water," Rolfe reported.

Kelly, Paul, and Farrell were in the living room of her suite, which had become their war room. She pulled up an aerial photo of the area and zoomed in on the road. It was deserted and had lots of turnoffs, some concealed by trees and thick vegetation, perfect for a clandestine encounter. Even though the tracking device showed the document had been left in the house, Kelly thought this might be it. Peterson could provide the contents of the document orally to his handler.

Kelly called for a drone to give them air surveillance. Moments later, unseen from the ground, it was following Peterson and sending images to her computer. Peterson walked for nearly an hour, making a large loop and returning to his house. He didn't meet anyone. Perhaps, that was just an effort by Peterson to see if he was being followed, Kelly thought.

He went back into his house, then emerged a few minutes later carrying a small leather case, and got into his car. The document was still in the house.

They tracked him into the shopping and restaurant area of Saint Michaels, a very upscale town. It was frequented by the rich and famous from Washington and elsewhere who had expensive homes along this gold coast of what was known as the Eastern Shore.

Peterson went into a bookstore, an agent following at a distance. Rolfe reported that he had brief conversations with two women, just greetings, then bought newspapers and a couple of books. He walked along the main street, then stopped for lunch, eating alone at a small café and speaking only to the waiter. Afterwards he drove home.

When he turned on the television and settled in to watch the Nats game, Kelly became convinced nothing would happen that day. She told Paul and Farrell and they agreed.

Kelly had people following the locations of the nine other documents back at FBI headquarters. They confirmed that none had moved.

At 2:30 p.m., Farrell's phone rang. She heard him say, "Yes, sir. I'm in Saint Michaels now with people from the task force. I'll get there as soon as possible.

When he put down the phone, he told Kelly, "CIA Director Harrison has returned from Pakistan. He wants an immediate briefing on what we've been doing. I have to go."

"Don't worry, Paul and I can handle it here," she said. "Take my FBI car. Paul has another car to drive me back into the city. No need for you to come back tomorrow if we're still here. I'll give you a report."

Once Farrell left, Kelly told Paul, "We'll probably be here overnight again. We should go into town and buy some things. Clothes, toiletries, whatever. We'll take turns and communicate by phone if anything happens."

"Good idea," he said. "You go first."

Kelly drove into Saint Michaels and parked on the main shopping street. As she was preparing to get out of the car, she thought about Julie, left alone for the weekend with Luisa. Her daughter was growing up fast, and instead of spending time with her, Kelly was in Saint Michaels on a stakeout. She couldn't help that and Julie was accepting, but she still felt sad and guilty about it.

She was convinced she wouldn't make it home that evening. One likely scenario was Peterson would meet his handler tomorrow. That meant another day in Saint Michaels. But she had to do something for Julie. The Nationals were playing at home, and Julie loved going to sports events with her grandfather. She reached for the phone to call her dad when she recalled what Farrell had told her about his separation from the CIA. He might have been lying to her all these years. Hold on a minute, she cautioned herself. Until she read the CIA file, she shouldn't act as if he were guilty.

When Kelly's dad answered, she said, "I need a favor."

"The answer's yes," he said. "Of course, I'd like to take Julie to the baseball game tomorrow."

"How'd you know?" Kelly asked.

"Well when you told me you were heading up a task force, I figured this weekend might be busy for you. Let her stay here tonight."

"That would be great. Thanks, Dad. I really appreciate it."

"You want me to call her or you want to?"

"I'll call now. You call in ten minutes."

"Will do. Hope it's going well."

"Nothing yet."

"Sorry to hear that."

Kelly called home and Luisa gave the phone to Julie. She heard Kelly's voice, and said, "Hi, Mommy." She sounded sad. "When will you be home?"

"Not today, honey, but I have a surprise for you."

"What's that?" Julie asked warily.

"You can go to Grandpa's house tonight and he'll take you to the Nats game tomorrow."

"Wow! And can I get a new cap?" asked Julie, perking up. "I lost my other one."

"You'll have to ask Grandpa. I'm sure he'll buy you one."

Kelly felt better when she hung up the phone. In town, she stopped in a pharmacy to get cosmetics. Tired of wearing the same slacks and blouse, she saw a chic looking boutique and glanced in the window.

If she was correct about Peterson not meeting his handler until tomorrow, she'd be having dinner alone with Paul that evening. She found him attractive. She thought about her ex, Jason, another

Washington lawyer. She hadn't been wildly in love with him when they married, but she had enjoyed spending time with him. Then he'd changed, becoming totally indifferent to her and even Julie. Initially, she thought he had another woman, but eventually she realized that the law firm, a jealous mistress, had taken over his life. He was a transaction lawyer who worked incessantly. Deals were all he thought about until he snapped, "I hate my life here at the law firm, he told her. I'm going to Maine to farm." And that was the end of their marriage.

Paul had some similarities with Jason. He, too, had quit his law firm. She wondered how Paul would be as a lover. Then she stopped herself. While she had enjoyed a number of brief relationships since her divorce, she had made a rule against dating anyone she worked with. On the other hand, Paul wasn't with the FBI. They were only doing this one project together.

She went inside the shop. With the assistance of a helpful clerk, a young woman from Philadelphia, she bought a new powder blue cotton blouse to go with her slacks for daytime. For later that evening, she settled on a fitted black skirt and a cream silk blouse. As she looked in the mirror, she unbuttoned the top button on the blouse. She was keeping all options open, she thought.

*   *   *

After the Nats game ended, Peterson took another walk. Then he had dinner at home, grilling a steak in the back. Watching him through binoculars, Rolfe reported, "He's drinking Château Cheval Blanc with his steak."

"Doesn't tell me anything," Kelly said. "I grew up with a beer-drinking dad."

"I'm jealous," Paul interjected. "It's an excellent Bordeaux from Saint-Émilion. Depending on the year, it'll cost several hundred dollars or more. It means our friend has expensive taste and the money to satisfy it."

"I'm glad one of us knows something about wine," Kelly said.

While Peterson ate dinner, Kelly noticed that her investigators at the FBI had forwarded the detailed write-up on Peterson. She sent it to Paul's iPad so they could both read it.

Peterson had grown up in the LA area, where his father had been a high-ranking exec in an aerospace company. After graduating from Stanford, Peterson enlisted in the Air Force, became a fighter pilot, and flew in the first Gulf War. Following his father's death from a sudden heart attack, he left the Air Force and joined another large aerospace company. There he had a meteoric rise to the number two job. When the top position became available, he was passed over. Peterson went into the government in his current post, even though he was a Republican.

Besides his two homes, Peterson had about twenty million dollars in assets, most of it in blind stock trusts he established when he had gone into the government.

Paul finished reading and said to Kelly, "He can clearly afford the Cheval Blanc with his steak."

"Listen, Paul," said Kelly, "this is making me hungry. How about you and I clean up and have some dinner ourselves?"

"Good idea. Also we have to get out of this hotel or we'll go stir crazy. When I went shopping, I found what looked like a good little restaurant in town. They're holding a table for us. We'll keep our phones on. Rolfe can call us if anything happens. Then we'll hot foot it back here."

*   *   *

The restaurant was called Talbots. It was dimly lit and crowded with an upscale clientele. The hostess led them to a quiet table in the corner. Kelly was impressed at how smoothly Paul had arranged this.

When he had picked her up in her hotel room, he had said, "You look terrific." Tonight definitely had possibilities. She was glad she had straightened up her bedroom. Just in case.

I am off duty tonight, she told herself. Well, almost. She took her cell phone out of her bag and placed it on the table. If she were wrong about Peterson meeting his handler that evening, she didn't want to miss Rolfe's call.

The waiter came by their table, left two menus and a wine list, and asked, "What would you like to drink?"

Paul looked at Kelly.

"Pick a red wine," she said. "You're the expert. Whatever you'd like."

While the waiter was standing there, he glanced at the wine list and selected a Morey-Saint-Denis.

"What's that?" she asked.

"It's not Cheval Blanc, but it's a very soft, drinkable Burgundy. Velvety. Feminine."

"Sexist," she retorted.

He laughed.

After the waiter returned with the wine and Paul had her taste it, she had to admit it was the best wine she'd ever had.

"What do you think?" he asked.

"Definitely feminine," she replied.

"Touché."

Then they both ordered steamed mussels to start. Kelly selected the duck with orange sauce for her main course, while Paul opted for the tenderloin with cognac sauce.

"When we first met, you told me you were a single mom with a daughter," said Paul. "How old is she?"

"Julie's eight. A good kid, but definitely a handful."

"Must be tough raising her alone while you're doing this job."

"I've been managing since Julie's father and I divorced last year."

"Sorry to hear that," said Paul.

"It was amicable. Or, about as amicable as it could be. Fortunately, I have a great housekeeper and my dad's a widower who lives nearby. He helps out."

"The former CIA icon Farrell was talking about last evening."

Yeah, the same man who may have lied to me my whole life, Kelly thought. "He's the one," she said aloud.

Paul had given her the perfect opening. She waited until the mussels came to ask, "What about you? Married? Any children?"

Dodging her question, he raised his glass. She did the same.

"To our success this weekend," he said.

"I'll drink to that."

Her question was still hanging in the air. Paul ate a couple of mussels before responding.

"Never been married, and no children," he said with ambivalence.

"But?"

"It's a long story. You don't want to know."

"We have nothing but time this evening. I doubt if anything will happen."

"There was someone. A Hill staffer. A former runway model. I was very much in love with her. I thought we'd get married. Then bam, she broke it off with me about a year ago. I guess I haven't gotten over her."

"I'm sorry to hear that," said Kelly. "Could you make another try? Maybe she's had a change of heart."

He sighed deeply. "It's too late now, she passed away recently."

"Oh my, I'm so sorry. What happened?"

"Actually, I'm sure you read about it in the *Post*. Her name was Vanessa Boyd . . ."

Astounded, Kelly interrupted him. "Wait a minute. This is the woman Senator Jasper went to Anguilla with?"

"So you did read about it."

"It's more than that, Paul." They were far enough from the next table that they couldn't be overheard. Still, she lowered her voice to a whisper. "Last November, I was in charge of the investigation into Senator Jasper's death. I established that the Chinese government was responsible for Jasper's murder, but before I could identify the individuals involved, Wilkins convinced Braddock that national security considerations trumped my murder investigation. I was ordered by Forester to shut it down. Now I'm wondering whether the same person in Beijing who was responsible for Jasper's murder is now running the mole in our government. If we could find out about Jasper's murder, that might lead us to the mole. So we definitely have to talk about this."

Paul leaned forward. "What can I tell you?"

"Were you involved in establishing that Jasper killed Vanessa and leaking that to the *Post*? They refused to identify their source."

"Allison Boyd, Vanessa's twin sister, leaked it to the *Post*. I helped her identify Jasper as the man who went to Anguilla with her sister. The bastard drowned her, then took off, helped by his good buddy, and my former boss, Andrew Martin."

"What about Jasper's murder?" Kelly asked.

"I don't know anything about that. Allison did, but she refused to confide in me. I do know that Allison was attacked a couple of times by Chinese men while she was in Washington."

"That means Allison is the key. As I recall from my investigation, she's an archeology professor at Brown. At the time she was off on a dig in Israel, so I never had a chance to meet with her before I was shut down. Can you arrange for us to talk to Allison?"

"That'll be a challenge." He sounded troubled.

"Why? Is she still in Israel?"

"She's in the US now. On Monday she's coming to Washington to present an archeology paper. We're scheduled for lunch Monday."

"So what's the problem?"

"Not surprisingly, Allison was very scared from everything that happened," Paul explained. "She's also strong-willed. In the past, she refused to talk about it. And we can't compel her to talk to us."

"I have some confidence in you, Paul. Why don't you have lunch with her alone, then afterwards we can meet with her."

Paul didn't respond. He was looking down at the table, and appeared to be deep in thought. As Kelly finished her mussels, she wondered whether he was in love with Allison now that her twin Vanessa was dead.

By the time the main courses came, Paul looked up. "I'll do my best to get Allison to talk to us about what happened," he said. "But it has to be just the three of us Monday afternoon. We have to leave out Wilkins and Farrell."

"Agreed," said Kelly. "Wilkins would make her clam up. And bringing in the CIA might freak her out."

Paul then changed the subject and asked Kelly how she got into law enforcement. She told him that her dad's CIA background was a major factor, and that she had wanted to do some good for the country after 9/11. Paul was easy to talk with, and she enjoyed being with him. From time to time, she glanced at the silent phone.

For dessert, they shared a wonderful profiterole with hot chocolate sauce poured on top. After that, they drank espresso. When she put her cup down, her hand was resting on the table. Paul reached across the table and placed his hand on top of hers. The signal was clear.

She recalled her thoughts from that afternoon. Paul was a wonderful man. Hopping into bed with him back at the hotel would probably be fun. However, she had learned two facts at dinner that turned her against the idea. He was still hung up on Vanessa, and maybe even

Allison, now that Vanessa was dead. And even more critical, in view of his relationship with Allison, he was a witness in the Jasper murder case. Getting involved with Paul personally would destroy her objectivity and compromise her investigation, and she wasn't willing to do that. Jason had been right, her work always did come first.

She pulled her hand away. "Listen, Paul, I really like you."

"But."

"I have a rule against getting involved personally with men I work with. I think you can understand that."

"Of course." He smiled. "I don't have to like it. However, I can understand it. Besides, I guess we could both use a good night's sleep. Tomorrow could be a big day for us in Saint Michaels."

*   *   *

Sunday was another gorgeous spring day on the Eastern Shore of Maryland with lots of bright sunshine. Rolfe reported to Kelly that after Peterson ate breakfast, he headed toward the dock in the back of the house and his catamaran. With a light but persistent wind, it would be ideal for sailing on Chesapeake Bay.

The bay would also be the perfect place for Peterson to meet his handler and pass along the new decision made by the president. The document was still in his house. Kelly wondered if Peterson was aware of the surveillance and, as a result, had found a way to arrange an encounter on the water. Or maybe he had set it up on Friday before leaving for Saint Michaels.

Regardless, they now had a hellish problem with surveillance. Being so close to the Naval Academy, Kelly was able to arrange a couple of fast boats that could be in the vicinity and move in if Peterson had a rendezvous with another boat. She also had air surveillance through which they were receiving a steady stream of reports on Peterson's activities.

For three hours, Peterson sailed without hooking up with another boat. Then he headed into shore and docked next to The Narrows restaurant in Grasonville.

From one of the boats on the water, Kelly got the report, "Peterson has tied up. He's going inside the restaurant. We're watching him with binoculars. Unless he has his meeting on the restaurant deck, it will be impossible to see him. It would take too long for Rolfe and his people to drive to the restaurant. What do you want us to do?"

Damn, damn, Kelly thought. She had tried to consider every possibility, and she had overlooked this. Despite all of their good work, Peterson had outsmarted them. He could be meeting his handler inside the restaurant. They'd never know about it.

An hour later, he got back into his boat and sailed home.

After another couple hours, Rolfe reported, "He's back in his house. Appears to be packing. Probably to drive home to McLean."

Kelly made a decision. She told Paul, "I want to confront Peterson before he leaves. You'll take the lead in interrogating him. You okay with that?"

"Absolutely."

She called Forester for approval, quickly telling him what had happened.

"What's your gut telling you?" he asked.

"He's the man."

"Then go for it."

They arrived in front of Peterson's house in two cars. Kelly and Paul in one; Rolfe and another agent in the second.

Peterson was loading a wheelie suitcase into his trunk. Kelly and Paul sprang out of their car. Kelly was wearing her suit jacket unbuttoned, exposing the gun holstered to her chest.

She held out her ID, "Mr. Peterson, I'm Kelly Cameron. FBI. This is Paul Maltoni from the DOJ. We want to talk to you."

Paul pulled his ID from his wallet.

Peterson looked stunned. "What is this about?"

"Can we go inside?"

"Sure."

They walked into the living room.

"You want to sit down, Mr. Peterson," Paul said.

"No, I don't want to sit down. I want to know why the hell you people are bothering me."

"On Friday," Paul said, "you were given a classified, top secret document with a decision from the president relating to Asian policy.

That document clearly stated that it was not to be taken from your office. You violated that directive."

"How do you know that?"

Paul glanced at Kelly who nodded.

"Because," Paul said, "it contained a nano chip which permitted us to follow it. The document's in your briefcase on the desk." Paul pointed to a brown Berluti bag.

"Did it ever occur to you I was busy on Friday? I loaded it in my bag with other papers to read over the weekend."

"And did it occur to you that you were violating US law by disregarding the instructions on this classified document?" Paul countered.

Peterson looked away. "Who gives a shit about stuff like that? Since you geniuses were tracking the document, you know it never left this house all weekend. And since you were no doubt watching the house, you're aware no one came here."

Paul moved in close to Peterson. "You could have passed its contents to someone when you stopped at The Narrows restaurant a little while ago."

Peterson's face was red. "You bastards were following me on the bay? Those naval ships were yours," he added with sudden realization.

"That's right."

"Call the restaurant," Peterson said, sounding irate. "Talk to Gloria, the manager. She'll tell you I ate alone. While you're at it, ask her to check the men's room. Have her look inside the toilet to make sure I didn't leave a note there for my handler. You guys are so far off the mark it makes me sick." Peterson shook his head in dismay. Then he sat down in a leather chair, pointing to the sofa. Kelly and Paul sat as well.

"Okay, I figured out what this is about," he said, pointing to Kelly. "The president must have decided the Chinese were able to make fools out of us in that encounter with the Japanese because they had a mole in the US government who told them about the Camp David decision. So you geniuses decided to set up a sting operation."

Paul looked at Kelly. "We can't comment on that."

"No, of course not," said Peterson.

"When you were at Camp David," Kelly said, "you went along with the decision not to confront the Chinese, didn't you?"

"So what? That doesn't make me a Chinese spy. Everyone else did as well. Only Braddock was pushing for military engagement. Then he finally backed off. The idea of going to war over those stupid pieces of rock is preposterous."

Paul interjected, "Suppose I told you we have irrefutable evidence that the Camp David decision was passed to the Chinese. What do you think of that?"

"Anything's possible. But knowing the people at Camp David, I would scrutinize your evidence a little closer."

"It's clear," Kelly said.

Peterson put his hand up to his chin and shook his head. "I hope to hell the real spy didn't pass along this document to the Chinese while you were wasting your time following me around Saint Michaels. Now get out of my house so I can get on the road and beat some of the Sunday traffic."

"We could arrest you," Kelly said.

"For what?"

"Violating the instructions on a classified document."

Peterson laughed. "Get real. If you morons did that, you'd be looking for new jobs tomorrow morning. Whatever support you had from Director Forester and the AG for your antics here would vanish faster than an ice cube in Palm Springs on a summer day." Peterson paused, then added, "Even if you don't arrest me, I intend to have your ass fired, Kelly Cameron, for what you pulled on me."

Kelly was confident Forester would back her. He had approved the operation.

"Be my guest," she said. "You have Director Forester's number?"

Peterson stood up, walked over to his briefcase, and picked it up. "Now get out. I have to lock up. Unless you want to stay and search the house. Then you can lock up without me. And by the way the password to my computer is 'top gun' if you want to read my emails. But I imagine you already have, all without a warrant, no doubt."

"We have a warrant," Paul said.

Peterson shook his head again. "I can't even imagine how much taxpayer money you clowns wasted on this operation. Now get out," he repeated.

Paul didn't wait for Kelly to respond. He said, "We're leaving."

She didn't argue. He was the lawyer, and he had decided they couldn't charge Peterson without looking ridiculous.

As they stood in the driveway, watching Peterson pull away, Paul said, "I believe him. He's not our mole."

"I do as well," said Kelly. "I just want to check on what Peterson told us."

They drove to The Narrows restaurant, where Gloria confirmed Peterson's story. He had eaten alone, and to her knowledge, he hadn't spoken with anyone. He had also used the bathroom, so they checked it, including the toilet tank, but there was nothing there.

Back in the car, she called Forester and gave him a report. The director was supportive. Then she called Farrell.

"You did the right thing," he said.

"We'll talk tomorrow," said Kelly. "By then, I'll have a proposal for our next move."

Wilkins had a different reaction. "You shouldn't have confronted Peterson. He might have been planning a rendezvous with his handler on Monday in Washington."

"We don't believe he's the mole."

"Let's not jump to that conclusion. It's too early to shut down your surveillance on Peterson."

"I was planning to do that," said Kelly.

"It's your call, but I think you should reconsider," urged Wilkins. "Give it a while longer."

Feeling vulnerable from everything that had happened, Kelly decided to back down. "Fair enough. We'll maintain surveillance on Peterson in Washington as well as taps on his phone lines, and we'll continue to monitor his cell phone calls and emails."

"Okay. That's good."

Kelly was confident it would be a waste of time and resources. Still, it was worth doing to placate Wilkins.

Paul drove her back to Washington. In the car, she checked on the monitors covering the other nine documents. None had moved or been copied.

"We're at a dead end on the sting," she said grimly. She thought about her conversation with Paul the previous evening and his Monday lunch with Allison. Right now, Allison was their best hope.

Chevy Chase, Maryland

Kelly had Paul drop her at her dad's house in Chevy Chase. She would pick up Julie and take her home in one of her dad's cars. As she walked up the stairs to the house, she recalled what Farrell had said about the Fritz Helfund matter. She was tempted to raise it with her father, but ultimately she decided against it. She couldn't do that until she had read the CIA file. For now, she had to pretend Farrell hadn't said anything.

She walked into the house and looked in the study. Julie was engrossed in building a gigantic Lego house her grandfather had bought her and barely said hello.

When they went into the kitchen, her dad said, "You look like you lost your best friend."

"Tough day in the salt mines," sighed Kelly.

He took a couple of beers from the refrigerator and handed her one. "Let's go outside," he suggested. "You can tell me about it."

Kelly laid out the whole story of her weekend on the Eastern Shore. At the end, she said, "I think I screwed up."

"I don't get that from what you said," her dad remarked. "Peterson moved the document in violation of a presidential directive. You acted appropriately. Despite all of your efforts, Peterson may have learned of your surveillance. He could still be the mole."

"That's what Wilkins thinks."

"From what I've heard, I don't trust that bastard."

"Peterson?"

"No, Wilkins. He could want you to keep focused on Peterson to divert your attention."

"You think he's the mole?"

"Perhaps. That's not what I'm staying, however."

"What are you saying?"

"Wilkins always has his own agenda."

"Thanks for your support, Dad, but I still think I screwed up."

"Doesn't sound so bad to me. For starters, nobody died. That's how I define a failed operation: when I lost somebody, one of our friends or allies."

Kelly thought about what Farrell had told her Friday evening. Had Fritz Helfund died in her father's last operation in Berlin? She was dreading what the CIA file would show, but she didn't say any of this. Instead, she listened as he continued lending support.

"Besides," he added, "Forester will back you over this. At least I hope so. If he does, you're in good shape. The question is, what's your next move? You better decide on it before your meet with Forester."

She told him about Allison

"Allison could be critical," he said.

"I hope so. I definitely need a break."

Washington

When Kelly arrived at her office Monday at eight, the message light was flashing on her office phone.

Pressing the play button, she heard, "This is Harriett Barton, director of internal investigations, extension 7800. Please call me immediately."

Kelly had never met Harriett Barton, but Rolfe had called her "a bitch on wheels." And she sounded ominous on the voicemail.

Kelly called back. "This is Kelly Cameron."

"Come to my office right now. 6100."

"I'll be there."

Climbing the internal staircase, Kelly wondered with trepidation what this was about.

As soon as she walked into the office, Harriett, heavyset, in her fifties, with a bad complexion and stringy brown hair, stood up behind her desk.

"Kelly Cameron?" she said.

"Yes, ma'am."

"Turn in your badge and gun."

Kelly couldn't believe what she had just heard. There must be a mistake. But she had to comply. She placed them on the desk.

"Can I ask what this is about?" she asked.

"Owen Peterson, deputy secretary of defense, has filed a complaint against you. Following our normal protocols, you will be placed on administrative leave until the complaint is resolved."

"What does he claim I did?" asked Kelly.

"Unjustified surveillance and harassment."

"That's ridiculous. Everything I did was authorized by Director Forester."

"You'll have an opportunity to explain that to the administrative law judge at your hearing."

"Are you joking?"

"Do I look like a person who makes jokes about matters like this?"

"No ma'am, you don't."

"Your hearing will be sometime next week. Until then, you may come into the office, but you cannot work on any active matters."

"I'm in the middle of an important task force investigation."

"Someone will have to relieve you."

Kelly was panicked. For sure, her FBI career was now over. In a daze, she left Harriett's office and went right to Forester to explain what happened.

Outraged, the director called Harriett and put it on the speaker phone. "You have no business suspending Kelly Cameron," he said. "Everything she did was authorized by me."

"I'm following normal protocol when a complaint is filed by a high-ranking federal official."

"And I'm overruling you. Now bring her badge and gun back to her office ASAP."

Kelly was so relieved she nearly jumped up and down for joy.

"By acting this way, you're compromising my independence and the integrity of the FBI," Harriett shouted.

"Don't you raise your voice with me," said Forester. "I'm the director of this organization."

"If you persist in this, I will not be able to do my job. I'll be forced to resign."

"That'll be your decision."

Harriett slammed down the phone.

Forester muttered, "What a troublemaker."

"I'm sorry to cause you this headache," Kelly said as he turned to look at her.

"You were just doing your job. I approved everything you did. Now forget about this bureaucratic nonsense and tell me what your next move is."

She explained the possible connection between Jasper's murder and the mole in the US government. "Both could be part of a single operation being run in Beijing, or two related operations directed by Liu, their director of intelligence. We have a possible witness, Allison Boyd, who could blow both wide open if she's willing to talk to us."

"Anything I can do to help?"

"I think we have a shot. Paul Maltoni is having lunch with her. The goal is for the two of us to meet with her this afternoon."

Forester's face lit up. "If she's willing to tell you what she knows, that would be good news. Keep me informed."

When Kelly returned to her office, she saw her gun and badge on her desk. There was no note from Harriett.

She booted up her computer. Farrell had forwarded a document from the CIA archives entitled "Record of Decision in the Matter of Charles Cameron."

With apprehension, she began reading.

"This decision is submitted by Daniel Lynn on behalf of himself, Brian Penn, and Corey Michaels, the three of us having presided at the disciplinary hearing of Charles Cameron.

"At the outset, we take notice of the laudatory work Charles Cameron has done for the CIA during his eighteen years of service His successes have been numerous and significant. Both the agency and the United States owe an enormous debt of gratitude to Charles Cameron.

"However, Cameron's behavior in the matter of Dr. Fritz Helfund was reprehensible. Charles Cameron proposed a daring plan to rescue Dr. Helfund, an extremely valuable German physicist, and get him across the border. Initially, that plan was approved by the director of special operations. It called for Charles Cameron to remain in West Berlin and be there to greet Dr. Helfund on his arrival in the West.

"When the director of special operations received information establishing that Dr. Helfund's rescue mission had been compromised, and that the Stasi had learned of it, he directed Charles Cameron to abort the operation. Cameron not only persisted in implementing the operation, but he went into East Berlin himself to rescue Dr. Helfund. Cameron was wounded in the leg and narrowly escaped with his life. Dr. Helfund was shot and killed by Stasi agents.

"For this insubordination and reckless failure to follow orders, it is our decision that, notwithstanding Cameron's prior exemplary record, Cameron should be dishonorably dismissed from the CIA and should not receive a pension or any other benefits. It is important to set an example for other field agents."

The words in the decision hit Kelly like a bolt of lightning. She read it a second time. It was a tremendous blow, to come face-to-face with the lies of her father. From the little she knew, she couldn't judge whether he had acted recklessly in disregarding the orders of his supervisors. Langley wasn't always right, and her father had been on the scene. Perhaps the risks were justified. He had put his own life on the line, after all.

That wasn't what was devastating for Kelly. Rather it was the blatant lies he had told her for so many years. Why? Was he ashamed of what he'd done? Did he think she would lose respect for him? And how many other lies had he told her over the years? Kelly now had to face the question of what to do about his lies. At first, she thought she would confront him, but as she thought about it further, she asked herself: why do that?

Her father would never be contrite. The only thing she would accomplish would be to wreck their relationship. And the reality was that she needed her father too much. She needed him as a sounding board, particularly now that she no longer had her husband. And she needed him for Julie. Not just to help care for his granddaughter when Kelly was in a crisis at work, which was often these days, but more importantly because besides Kelly, her father was the only family member Julie had. Kelly couldn't possibly rip that away from her daughter.

All of those factors made perfectly good sense, but they didn't carry the day. Her visceral reaction prevailed. She would confront him. She had to confront him.

*   *   *

"You look great," Paul told Allison as she walked over to his table at Central and he stood up to greet her.

He kissed her once on each cheek. She was suntanned and dressed in a pink V-neck sweater and fitted jeans that showed off her shapely legs.

She had sunglasses perched on top of her brown hair and was wearing tiny turquois earrings. She looked more like a tourist in Washington than an archeology professor who had come to deliver an erudite paper at a gathering of her peers.

For lunch, they both had the delicious lobster burger and fries with glasses of pinot noir. The fabulous food was the creation of the culinary genius Michel Richard. As they ate, Paul kept the conversation focused on Allison's work and the paper she was presenting the following day about her excavation in Israel. They had made some remarkable discoveries, and there was no longer any doubt that Allison was uncovering a town from King Solomon's time. *Archeology Magazine* had called it "one of the most significant discoveries in decades." Allison had earned a major place for herself in the archeology world, and she spoke about it with joy and enthusiasm.

For dessert, they split a chocolate mousse, digging in together from the same bowl. Allison asked Paul whether he was still working at the Department of Justice and what he was doing. He told her about the favorable settlement he had gotten in a big case with Jenson from Martin's law firm on the other side.

"Good for you," she told him. "If I remember right, Jenson always made your life miserable when you were at the law firm."

"You have a good memory," Paul said with a smile. "I got a measure of revenge."

"The pup grows up."

"What's that from?"

"*Le Mis.* I'm happy for you."

After lunch, they walked along Pennsylvania Avenue. It was a bright, sunny day. As she lowered her sunglasses, Paul saw she had a smile on her face. He had never seen that before.

He spotted a deserted bench. Ironically, it was right in front of the FBI building. "Can we sit here and talk for a while?" he said. "I have something to tell you."

"Sure, I'm free until this evening. Then I have to attend the convention banquet."

This won't be easy, Paul thought.

"I need your help with something," Paul began.

She looked puzzled. "What's that?"

"Please treat all this as confidential," he continued, speaking softly.

"Of course."

"Right now I'm involved in a major project at work that deals with Chinese spies in the United States."

As soon as the words were out of his mouth, he noticed the smile had left her face, replaced by a taut expression. "Did you say Chinese spies?" she asked.

"Yeah, I'm working on national security issues."

She grimaced and picked at a fingernail.

"I'm sorry to do this to you," he continued, "rehashing unpleasant memories from last November, but I have no choice."

"We always have choices."

"That's true. Will you at least hear me out?"

"I owe you that much," she observed. "After all, without you I would never have fingered Jasper as the SOB who went to Anguilla with Vanessa. In return for that, I'll listen."

"I think the people chasing you may now be involved in a new operation," said Paul. "In November, you and I never talked about the Chinese involvement. Once you established it was Jasper, you took that story to the *Post*, and we never discussed those events again. I realized there was more to the whole business, but it was obvious you didn't want to talk about it, and I never pressed you."

She looked around anxiously. "That's right."

Pedestrians passed on the sidewalk, but nobody paid any attention to them.

"I also knew you were terrified," Paul said. "And you had a right to be after the attacks in Washington at the DuPont Circle Metro and in Anguilla."

Paul stopped talking. He waited for Allison to respond. When she didn't say a word but continued picking at her fingernail, he resumed speaking. "What I firmly believe now," he paused and turned sideways, looking straight at her, "is that whatever spy operation the Chinese were running that Vanessa stumbled across, did not die with Senator Jasper. It is continuing, and the only chance we have of stopping them now is by learning what you know. You once told me that your father instilled in you a love for our country. That was why you took a year off after college to compete and play for the US field hockey team in the Barcelona Olympics."

Allison nodded.

"I'm appealing to that patriotism in seeking your help. I wish we had another way, but unfortunately, we do not. You're our only chance. And I promise fully to protect you if you're still at risk."

Allison still didn't say anything, and he couldn't tell what she was thinking.

"If you decide not to talk to me," Paul added, "I'll understand."

"In high school," Allison began in a soft voice trembling with emotion, "my dad was a star halfback in Oxford, Ohio, and was awarded a football scholarship to Ohio State. It was during the Vietnam War. He could have stayed in Ohio and pursued his dream of playing college and maybe even pro football. Instead, he enlisted in the Marines. While in service, he took a bullet in the knee saving two of his wounded comrades. He received medals for what he did, but his dream died that day. He couldn't play football anymore. Still, he was never bitter. In fact, he was proud he served his country. He died two months ago."

"I'm sorry. I had no idea."

"When I came back from Israel for his funeral, I thought of calling you. Then I remembered how broken up you were at Vanessa's. I decided to spare you being back in that cemetery again. He was buried next to her."

"How's your mother?"

"Same bitch. A part of her died when they buried Vanessa. Hard as nails, but she keeps on trucking. She'll probably outlive me with her brain swimming in vodka." She sighed deeply. "You're a good lawyer, Paul. You pushed the right button. Patriotism. You must be skillful at manipulating witnesses to get them to open up."

He reddened. "That wasn't my intention."

She shook her head. "It doesn't matter. I believe you when you say that you have no other way. So I should help you. I have to help you. Let's go to your office, it'll be easier to talk there. Besides, I'm getting a stiff neck from looking at you sideways on this bench."

"I'd like to have someone join us. Her name's Kelly Cameron. You can trust her."

"If you tell me that, I believe you. I'll do what I can to help."

*   *   *

In view of the all-time crummy day Kelly was having, she was happily surprised to get the call from Paul asking her to come to his office and join him in talking to Allison.

Crossing Pennsylvania Avenue to go to Paul's office in the Justice Department building, she cautioned herself against being too hopeful. After Harriett, and then the CIA report, would this be more bad news?

When Kelly arrived, Paul introduced her to Allison as a senior FBI agent and task force director.

"Okay," Allison said, sounding upset.

I guess we won't be best friends, Kelly thought.

After they sat down at a table, Paul said, "I told Allison we really appreciate her talking to us. If she needs protection or any other help, we'll provide it to her."

"Absolutely," Kelly replied.

"Where do you want to begin?" Paul asked Allison.

She sighed deeply. "Before my twin sister, Vanessa, went off to Anguilla for her fatal weekend with Senator Jasper, she forwarded to my office at Brown a CD she had secretly recorded in Tokyo. In the CD, Liu Guan, the minister of state security of China, is recruiting Senator Jasper to hand over top secret US documents relating to our military operations in Asia."

Kelly, who had been leaning forward to hear each word Allison, speaking softly, delivered, almost fell off the edge of her chair.

"I was chased and pursued by Chinese men who wanted to get the CD even before I knew about it. When I finally located it, I turned it over to Andrew Martin, the Washington lawyer. He promised to deliver it to the FBI director, Jim Forester, which I gather he never did. Another of his lies."

"Why did you give it to Martin?" Kelly asked.

Before Allison had a chance to respond, Paul jumped in, "That was my doing. I was working for Martin at his firm at the time. I thought, wrongly in retrospect, Martin was honorable, knew Forester, and would deliver it to him." Paul sounded chagrin.

Allison picked it up. "My guess is Martin told the Chinese about the CD. I imagine he destroyed it."

Kelly now understood what had happened. "So the Chinese, realizing that Jasper was no longer a valuable source but a liability, arranged for Jasper's murder."

"That's the most likely conclusion," Allison said.

"Martin has represented the Chinese government for many years," Paul interjected.

"You didn't disclose these facts about the CD to the *Washington Post* or to the FBI in November, did you?" Kelly asked Allison.

Allison looked down at her hands on the table. "That's correct, I did not. But you can't blame me for that. I was scared. Paul couldn't assure my safety, he was an associate in a law firm then, working for Martin. To protect myself, I told Martin that if anything happened to me, the CD would be delivered to the *Washington Post*."

"But I thought you gave Martin the CD," Paul said.

"Allison made a copy," Kelly said, "and secretly gave it to someone. Am I right?"

Allison nodded.

"That's what I would have done in your position," Kelly observed. "Listen, Allison, I won't ask you for the CD. We're grateful for your help. We don't want you to feel at risk."

Allison looked visibly relieved. "I appreciate that."

For Kelly, that was an easy decision. They were trying to identify the mole who succeeded Jasper in working with the Chinese, and the CD wouldn't help them do that. Kelly also realized she was now at a critical crossroads. One alternative was to focus on Andrew Martin, who might be involved in the Chinese spy operation with Jasper's successor, and to attempt to force him to divulge what he knew. The problem with that approach was Martin would no doubt stonewall them, and he would be a tough nut to crack. The other alternative was to zero in on the Chinese individuals involved. That had another advantage—Kelly and Paul now had Allison, and she was willing to talk. Later on, Allison might be back in Israel or unwilling to cooperate, so Kelly decided to focus on the Chinese side.

She told Allison, "You said a few minutes ago you were chased and pursued by some Chinese men. Is that right?"

"Yes. Two of them, or maybe more, on four separate occasions in Washington. Three occasions besides the DuPont Circle Metro. One was in a churchyard near DuPont Circle, the second in a Capitol Hill restaurant, and the third in an alley downtown."

Kelly pulled an iPad out of her bag and turned it on. "I have access to the State Department's file containing the roster of individuals on the Chinese embassy staff, including photos. If I were to run through those photos with you, do you think you could recognize the men who pursued you?"

"One for sure."

"Why's that?"

"He had a scar on his left cheek. He was the worst one."

Allison's words hit Kelly like a powerful hammer. Allison was identifying Xiang. Kelly was stunned. Xiang, the only man she had ever loved. Xiang, the man she had wanted to marry. Xiang, the man she had eaten lunch with three months ago. How could Xiang have done these heinous things? Kelly was so startled that she was paralyzed. Her fingers froze on the keyboard.

"What's wrong?" Paul asked. "Are you okay?"

Kelly realized how terrible she must have looked. She had to suck it up and do her job. Her fingers began moving. "I'm fine."

In a minute, she pulled up Xiang's photo, the scar visible on his left cheek. She turned the iPad toward Allison. "Is this the man?"

"Yes," Kelly replied without hesitation. "What's his name?"

"Xiang Shen, assistant economic attaché."

"That's probably a cover for an intelligence agent," Paul said.

Kelly was too shocked to tell them she knew the man. She was reeling.

"I'll tell you something else this Xiang did," Allison said with contempt. "I mean besides attacking and threatening to kill me, he also searched my sister's apartment looking for the CD. He didn't find it, but he took a pair of yellow silk panties."

For Kelly, the pounding continued.

"Why would he do that?" Paul asked.

"Use your imagination, Paul," Allison said. "Turn off your legal mind and think creatively. He saw pictures of Vanessa in the apartment, saw how gorgeous and sexy she was. You of all people know that. Xiang is a pervert."

Kelly thought she would be sick. For sure, she couldn't tell them about her prior relationship with Xiang.

"Can you think of anything else?" Kelly asked.

"That's all at this point," Allison replied. "If I do, I'll let you know."

"Would you like us to provide protection for you?"

"Thanks, but that's not necessary. I'm going back to Israel in two days. I'll take my chances here until then. Once I get to Israel, I'm not worried. As of last week, we have guards at the excavation site because of the value of the artifacts we're finding. In town, the hotels and restaurants all have security."

"Well, thanks for your help," Kelly said. "I'll leave the two of you to talk." Then she staggered out of the office.

Kelly spent the next couple of hours in her office wondering how she could have been so wrong about Xiang. What she had learned from Allison confirmed that Xiang had been following her that Saturday in January when she and Julie went to the Spy Museum, following her because he knew she was heading a Chinese espionage section at the FBI. He had been very interested in Julie, too. Had he been signaling to her that he would move against her daughter if Kelly posed a threat to their operation? How in the world could she deal with what she had learned from Allison?

She called her father. "Where are you, Dad?"

"Home, pulling together some notes from my work in Germany. A screenwriter wants me to collaborate with him on a Cold War movie."

"Can I come by and talk to you?"

"Sure. What's going on? You sound like hell."

"I'll tell you at the house."

Driving to Chevy Chase, she decided she had to defer confronting him about Fritz Helfund and his lies. She would do it, but not now. She had to get through this thing with Xiang first.

Chevy Chase, Maryland

Her dad was at the desk in the study when Kelly walked in. "Wine or beer won't do," she said. "I need a real drink."

"Scotch?" he suggested.

"Yes."

He poured her a glass over ice and one for himself. Then they sat down in the den.

"What happened?" he asked, sounding concerned.

"Remember Xiang, the guy I was in love with when I was at Carnegie Mellon?"

"How could I ever forget the pain he caused you?"

"Well, let me tell you what just happened."

For the next fifteen minutes she spoke, relaying to him the encounter with Xiang in January and what Allison had just told her. At the end, she said, "I'm compromised. I love my work on the task force, but now I'll have to resign, maybe even from the bureau. I'm sick about this."

He raised his hand. "Not so fast, Kelly. You're not resigning from anything."

"But . . ."

"Listen to me," he said firmly. "My turn to talk."

"Okay," she acquiesced. "Go ahead."

"What Allison told you may explain what happened to you in college and your romance with Xiang."

"I don't understand. What do you mean?"

"My experience and instinct tell me that Xiang was a Chinese intelligence plant at Carnegie Mellon. They wanted him to become familiar with the States. After graduation, he would come home and advise them on US issues. Maybe later, they would send him back to the US to serve in their embassy. It's straight from the KGB playbook. During my time, the Russians regularly did that. He made an error and interfered with their game plan when he fell in love with you. Once his supervisor found out about his relationship with you, they decided it would nullify their investment. They would lose it all if he married you and stayed in the States, so they ordered him to break it off with you."

"If he really loved me, why didn't he tell them to stuff it and stick with me?"

Her father sighed. "My guess is his spymasters in China had control over his parents or another family member. They no doubt made it clear to Xiang when he went back to China to visit that if he told them to stuff it—to use your words—they would take action against those family members."

Kelly thought about Xiang's close relationship and concern for his parents. Her dad might be right.

When Kelly didn't respond, he added, "Believe me, I'm not trying to defend Xiang. I wanted to kill the bastard for what he did to you, and I still feel like that, but I'm trying to work with you to understand what happened."

Kelly nodded. "Now what do you think about him following me to the restaurant in January and having pizza with me and Julie?"

"Probably instigated by your appointment to head up the Chinese espionage section. Or conceivably, but less likely, he was still carrying a torch for you. Perhaps both."

She paused to sip her drink while considering the situation. "Everything you've said makes sense, but I still have to resign from the task force."

"Don't be ridiculous. I learned long ago it's sometimes possible to turn coal into gold."

"Meaning what?"

"Trust your instincts. You know the real Xiang."

"I didn't know someone capable of doing all those horrible things to Allison," said Kelly, shaking her head.

"He was no doubt following orders and being closely monitored."

"And the yellow panties?"

"When thirtysomething men are serving in foreign countries, lonely, and deprived of sex, they do ridiculous things. That's why the honeypot works with so many unlikely candidates."

"I don't understand where you're going with this."

"You may be able to turn Xiang," her father said.

"You're reliving your Cold War days."

"Have people changed in forty or fifty years? Are Chinese people different than Russians? Or Americans, for that matter?"

Kelly was beginning to understand what her father had in mind. "Xiang did offer to have dinner with me. He even gave me a personal cell number. I suppose we could meet for dinner. Then, while he's with me, I could have FBI agents search his apartment. Hopefully, they would find material I could use to threaten him."

"Exactly."

"How do I do this without telling the members of my task force about my personal relationship with Xiang in college?"

"Set a task force meeting for tomorrow morning. Tell them what Allison said. Also, that by a fortunate coincidence, you knew Xiang in college. Just knew. You had a class together. That's all."

"Why didn't I tell this to Paul today?"

"Allison was there. No reason for her to know."

"Okay, and then?"

"Tell your colleagues on the task force you want to use that relationship to schedule a dinner with Xiang and at the same time try to obtain information you could use to turn him."

"That makes sense. I'll have Paul get a search warrant. I can drag out dinner to enable agents to search Xiang's apartment."

"For the yellow panties?"

"That and a pair of New Balance running shoes. I have treads from the Jasper murder scene. A match will give me evidence to establish he killed Jasper. With that evidence, I'll own Xiang."

"You definitely are turning coal into gold."

A little while later, driving home, she thought about her father's last mission in East Germany. The real story. Charles Cameron did what he thought was best. He concealed information and even lied to his superiors if *he* thought it was the best thing to do, and that's what he had persuaded her to do here. She hoped this ended better for her than it had for him.

That night Kelly slept poorly. She was still torn about following her father's advice. She felt trapped between a rock and a hard place.

Washington

After Kelly had left Paul's office, Allison said to him, "Listen, Paul, you don't have to worry about me tonight. My archeology convention is having a banquet at the Grand Hyatt. That's where I'm staying, and where the convention is."

"Sounds okay."

"I had a thought," she added. "I have a plus one, and I'd love for you to come."

"It would be my pleasure," he said with a smile. "Also, I can be on the lookout for anything suspicious."

At six, he met Allison in the lobby of her hotel. He'd never seen her dressed up before, and he was blown away by how beautiful she was. Other than her hair color, brunette instead of blonde, she reminded him so much of Vanessa.

During the cocktail hour, Paul was also struck by the high regard with which she was held by her colleagues, most of whom were male, and many at least twenty years her senior. She introduced Paul as a "Washington lawyer friend of mine." Paul, who had grown up in New Haven and attended both Yale College and Yale Law, ended up in a protracted discussion with a Yale professor about whether the university should have done more to improve the city. At dinner, Paul and Allison were seated next to each other at one of the twenty round tables.

The keynote speaker focused on how new technologies were affecting archeology. "The reality is," the speaker said, "that to be a successful archeologist, a student has first to become an IT expert." He was followed by the organization's president, a man in his late sixties, Paul guessed, with a neatly trimmed gray beard sprinkled with black. He was wearing a three-piece suit with a gold chain across the vest.

"I have the honor," he said, "of announcing the organization's Archeologist of the Year Award. And the winner is," he declared while opening an envelope, "Allison Boyd, for her discovery of a town from King Solomon's time."

Paul saw Allison gasp with surprise. Everyone was on their feet applauding as Allison came up to the podium to accept the medallion, which the president draped around her neck.

She made a short acceptance speech, thanking colleagues who had helped her obtain funding and who "despite the doubters, never weakened in their support for this project." She also thanked the Israeli government for being welcoming and helpful.

Watching her speak with such self-confidence, Paul was feeling an attraction to Allison he hadn't felt before.

When the banquet ended, people milled around offering Allison congratulations. After most had left, Paul said to her, "How about a drink to celebrate?"

"Sure. I'd like that."

He thought she definitely seemed interested. As soon as they sat down at a table in the bar, a waiter came over and asked what they wanted to drink.

Paul looked at Allison, who was beaming. "You want champagne?" he asked.

"Thanks, but I've already had two glasses of wine. That's my limit. Just a Perrier."

Paul ordered an armagnac.

As the waiter left, Paul looked at Allison curiously. "Funny you said that two glasses of wine was your limit," he remarked.

"Why funny?"

"Vanessa never had any limit. Your sister was something else. We'd have a bottle of wine at dinner, sometimes two, and she'd drink most of it. Then a couple of cognacs. And after all that, which would have put anyone else to sleep, she was a terror in bed. Sometimes, she even . . ."

Allison raised her hand. "Okay, Paul. That's enough."

"I'm sorry. I guess I got a little carried away."

"For sure."

Allison quickly drank her Perrier, then said, "Listen, Paul, I am really exhausted. I have a tough day tomorrow, presenting my paper, so I better call it a night."

She stood up. "It's been great being with you."

"When can I see you again?"

"I fly out tomorrow afternoon. Call me if you or Kelly need any more help." She said it in a businesslike tone, then turned and walked away.

Well, I blew that one, Paul thought sadly. Allison is beautiful, she just won a top award, she liked me, and all I did was ramble on about her dead sister. It's no wonder she dismissed me. God, was I stupid.

*   *   *

Andrew Martin glanced quickly at his watch. It was only 7:50 on Tuesday morning. He had ten more minutes to go and his knee was killing him. He didn't know how he would make it.

He looked across the net at Senator Bill Lawson preparing to serve. With his tall, rangy figure and long arms, Bill was a formidable tennis player with a rocket serve. Martin was thrilled to be hanging in with Lawson at 5-5 in the first set. He was helped by the soft courts at Kenwood Country Club, which were kept well-watered and slowed down the ball.

Lawson placed his first serve to Martin's backhand, the weakest part of his game. When Martin's response was a short ball, Lawson attacked, moving up and putting it away. Martin's knee was throbbing and slowing him down. He shouldn't be playing tennis, but he had to do it. He needed the time alone to talk with Lawson after the match.

Lawson won three of the next four points, then they switched sides. Lawson was up 6-5. Martin figured this would be the last game. Wanting to tie the match, Martin got a shot of adrenalin from his competitive juices and aced his first two serves. After those two, he could barely move around the court. Lawson returned Martin's next three serves for winners. Following a sustained rally on the next point, Lawson moved up to the net and ended the match with a powerful smash.

As they shook hands courtside, Lawson said, "You're a gutsy guy, Andrew, to keep going with that gimpy leg."

"I didn't notice much sympathy."

Lawson laughed. "Well you're ahead of me, lifetime, twenty-eight to twenty-five."

Martin laughed as well. Lawson had pulled those numbers out of the air.

They went to the snack bar inside the tennis facility where they each picked up some fruit, a roll, and coffee. Then they headed to a table outside on the deck overlooking the courts. The deck was deserted so they could easily talk. Martin stretched out his leg on an adjoining chair and plunked an ice pack on it, which he had brought in his tennis bag.

"I'm glad to see you're back as a player," Lawson said, "and I don't mean a tennis player. That Jasper business would have knocked others out of the game."

"Yeah. Word of my demise was definitely premature."

"Personally, I think you got a bum rap. From what I know, you were just trying to help out an old friend."

"You certainly have that right. I got screwed trying to help Wes, then bam, he was dead in a robbery in Rock Creek Park."

"I liked Wes, so don't get me wrong," Lawson mused. "But it was a stupid thing to do. I mean with that girl in Anguilla. Hell, lots of guys on the Hill have a little piece on the side, but they have to know the risk. My old man ran a small country store in Nashville and his buddy used to say, 'play, you gotta pay.' But *you* didn't do a damn thing wrong. Ah well, we all live in glass houses now."

"Thanks a lot. I appreciate that, it means a lot to me," said Martin. And it did. Lawson was the ranking Republican in the Senate.

"Anyhow, Andrew," said Lawson, tearing his roll in half, "you had something you wanted to talk to me about."

"General Cartwright," Martin began, "asked me to become his advisor and strategist in his presidential bid."

"And you want my support," Lawson remarked.

"You know how to cut to the chase pretty damn quick."

"After thirty-two years in Washington, I hate the bullshit of beating around the bush. Let me give you a couple of reactions. One, though I'm no fan of our waffling president, I was stunned by how Cartwright pissed on Braddock in his press conference. Two, I expected the public to circle the wagons around Braddock and reject Cartwright, but the early polls show people seem to love Cartwright. Ordinarily, April would be too late to seek a nomination with a convention in August. However, my party is so fucked-up and deadlocked that it's still wide open. The primaries thus far have been inconclusive. A brokered convention may be inevitable. So there you are. Now my real question, and maybe you can help me, is whether the general is up to the job."

Martin took a sip of his coffee before responding. Be careful, Martin told himself. Don't oversell. "I think he is. He grew up in modest circumstances. Oconto Falls, Wisconsin. Dad was a mechanic with a pulp mill. All he wanted to do was fly planes for the US Air Force. Got himself into the Air Force Academy where he graduated first in his class."

"What about the Princeton degree I read about in the paper?"

"The Air Force sent him to Princeton for a degree at the Woodrow Wilson School of Public and International Affairs. His paper on the advantages and disadvantages of an air war in the Middle East was published in *Foreign Affairs* magazine. He's been invited to lecture at Harvard, where he wasn't booed or heckled, despite being in uniform. In other words, Cartwright is damn smart.

"Also, like Eisenhower, he's aware of the limitations of US military action. Personally, I think it would be an advantage for the country to have a military man in the White House in this era of constant foreign policy clashes—someone who understands what our military can and can't do. If you had water leaking throughout your house, you'd call a plumber, not a lawyer."

Lawson laughed. "Careful now. Remember, like you, I was a damn fine lawyer before I got into politics. I figure we can do anything."

"Which is why the country is in such a mess."

"What do you want from me, Andrew?"

"Your endorsement for Cartwright. No one has more respect in the party than you do. It won't assure him of the nomination. On the other hand, it will go a helluva long way."

Lawson wrinkled his forehead. "Let me think about it, Andrew. I want to take some soundings before I decide. And I'd like to do a little due diligence of my own on Cartwright. I might be willing to go with you on this. I want us to beat Braddock. Although we have good people fighting hard for the nomination, quite frankly, I don't see any of them winning in November. Cartwright could be our white knight."

Martin was pleased. This was as much as he had hoped for.

*   *   *

Kelly knew Forester usually arrived at the office at 7 a.m. So at 6:45 she was perched outside his office in the still deserted secretarial suite. His secretaries, Linda and Carolyn, had yet to arrive.

When Forester walked in fifteen minutes later, he looked at her and smiled. "Are you in trouble with Harriett again?" he asked.

"No, sir," she said. "I need your approval on our next step before I present it to the task force."

"And I suppose this step could blow the case wide open."

"That's right, sir."

"I definitely need coffee before listening to you."

He walked over to a shiny espresso machine on a credenza alongside Carolyn's desk and said, "Linda and Carolyn just got this gadget. They tried to show me how to use it, but I'm hopeless. We could wait until they get here or we could try it ourselves. What do you think?"

"I have one like it at home," said Kelly. "My dad gave it to me for Christmas."

"I didn't think I'd be happy to see you first thing in the morning, but now I am. You can come any day as long as you use two packets of espresso."

"Yes, sir," said Kelly, hiding a smile.

Kelly made the coffee and brought the cups into Forester's office. She handed him one and sat down in front of his desk.

"Okay. Now what do you want to do next?" he asked.

She explained about the meeting she and Paul had with Allison. Then she followed her father's script, telling Forester that she wanted to use her relationship with Xiang from college to schedule a dinner with him while FBI agents searched his apartment for evidence.

Everything was going smoothly with Forester nodding from time to time until the director said, "How well did you know Xiang in college?"

Kelly hesitated. Charles Cameron would have replied, "We had a class together." The moment of truth had come for Kelly, and she wasn't Charles Cameron. She would never have violated orders, crossed into East Germany, and gotten herself wounded and Fritz Helfund killed. Besides, Forester had always been straight with her. She had to do the same with him.

She blushed and said, "When we were both juniors at Carnegie Mellon, we had a serious romance. We were not engaged, but we talked about getting married. He broke it off during the summer after our junior year, following a trip to China. I assumed it was because his parents were opposed to him marrying an American. That may have been it, or he may already have been under the control of Chinese intelligence, and they directed him to end our relationship."

"I see," Forester said. He picked up his hand and held it against his chin.

"I'm prepared to resign from the task force," she said, gritting her teeth.

Leaving her words hanging in the air, Forester took a large gulp of coffee. She was afraid he might ask for her resignation. Even if he did, she wouldn't have second thoughts about leveling with him. She had to do it for herself.

Finally, Forester said, "When you knew Xiang in college, did you then or do you now have any basis for believing he was a spy at that time?"

"No, sir."

"Were you romantically involved with Xiang after college?"

"Not at all. We only saw each other twice, briefly at Washington restaurants."

"Do you think your prior relationship with Xiang would preclude you from doing this operation objectively?"

"No, sir. Not in any way," Kelly said staunchly.

"Then don't worry about it," said Forester. "Your romantic involvement with Xiang in college could be an advantage. It may make it easier for you to turn him."

Kelly breathed a sigh of relief. "I think so, too."

"I appreciate your giving me a full explanation. I realize this has been difficult for you."

"Thank you for understanding."

"Okay, so we're all set. Pitch to the task force your idea and keep me informed."

As Kelly started toward the door, Forester said, "One other thing."

She turned around. "Yes, sir?"

"Don't go into detail with the task force about your relationship with Xiang. Keep it simple. You knew each other when you were students."

"Thank you, I appreciate that."

"It's not for you. We don't want to give Dr. No—I mean Wilkins—a reason to try and kill our best hope of discovering the mole."

*   *   *

"We finally caught a break," Kelly said.

The task force was assembled in a conference room at FBI headquarters. Around the table, Wilkins and Farrell looked at her with anticipation. She explained what Allison had told her and Paul. At the end, she added, "I knew Xiang when we were both students at Carnegie Mellon."

If Paul was wondering why she hadn't told him that yesterday, he didn't say anything. Happily, no one asked how well she had known

Xiang, so she pushed on. "Xiang and I have had a couple of chance meetings over the last year at restaurants. He clearly remembers me, and I want to build on that."

"How?" Wilkins asked.

"I want to arrange dinner with him. While we're at the restaurant, FBI agents will search his apartment, looking for the yellow panties that could link him to the attacks on Allison, and the New Balance sneakers that could tie him to Jasper's murder. They'll also look for anything else that could establish his espionage. If I get a positive response, I'll threaten to disclose publicly what Xiang's done unless he agrees to cooperate. My hope is that he'll be so frightened of his superiors that he'll prefer working with us in order to conceal the information and to save his life. What do you think?"

"I like it a lot," Farrell immediately said. "Liu, the head of MSS, is brutal toward agents whose failures are disclosed."

"Ditto for me," Paul replied.

Wilkins looked troubled. "You can't search his apartment without a warrant, and Xiang has diplomatic immunity. This chase down the rabbit hole has the potential for being a serious incident with the Chinese government."

"We're not charging Xiang with a crime," Paul said, supporting Kelly. "We're looking for evidence relating to the murder of Senator Jasper. I'm confident I can find a judge who will give me a warrant."

"Will Xiang's diplomatic immunity be an issue?" Kelly asked.

"It shouldn't be," Paul replied. "Xiang's apartment isn't Chinese government property."

"You better be right on this," Wilkins said.

"I'll get the warrant. Trust me," said Paul.

Despite his words, Kelly thought Paul sounded nervous.

"What do you hope to get out of Xiang?" Wilkins asked Kelly.

"I want to find out if he was involved in the information leak relating to the East China Sea incident. Also, I want him to supply the names of all the Americans spying for China in this operation. Finally, I want to nail down Jasper's murderer."

"Sounds like a child's Christmas wish list," Wilkins pointed out. "Is there any conceivable chance he'll give you all of this?"

"He's our best chance. What do we lose?"

"You'll be showing our cards."

"C'mon George, we're at a dead end. Xiang's the only card we have left."

"What's happening with the Peterson surveillance?" Wilkins persisted.

"Not a damn thing." What is Wilkins' problem, Kelly wondered. She decided to ask. "What are you so worried about?"

"You'll be poisoning relations with China."

"If they arranged a spying operation in the US, then they bear responsibility for what happened," Kelly countered.

"Has Forester approved this?" Wilkins asked.

"Absolutely. I spoke to him earlier this morning."

Farrell jumped in on Kelly's side. "She's right. We have to at least try."

Wilkins sighed in resignation.

The task force meeting broke up and Wilkins returned to the White House. Kelly gave Paul Xiang's address, an apartment on Connecticut Avenue in Cleveland Park, and he left for the courthouse to get the warrant.

Farrell gathered up his papers.

"Do you have a few more minutes?" Kelly asked.

"Sure, as long as you want. You seem upset, what's wrong?"

Kelly was annoyed at herself for not doing a better job of concealing her emotions. She ignored his question and said, "I gather you're a China expert at the Company."

"That's right," Farrell confirmed, "which is why the director assigned me to this task force."

"With your knowledge of Minister Liu of MSS, do you have any thoughts as to how Xiang could have changed so much since I knew him in college?"

Farrell nodded. "Okay, I get it. Xiang was a decent guy when you knew him. Maybe you were even friends. Now the man's a monster. What happened to him in the intervening years?"

"Uh-huh."

"Obviously, I don't know his personal situation," Farrell began, "but I can tell you this. Whatever you've heard about training in the US for Navy Seals, Special Forces, and Marines—it's infinitely worse for MSS recruits. Their objective is to squeeze every ounce of humanity out of their people. They are trained to be hard, cruel, killing machines, if that's what the job requires. And they are good at accomplishing this. Add to this one other element—they seek to hold one or more family members as virtual hostages. If the MSS member doesn't obey orders, the family member dies. It's as simple as that."

Kelly recalled how much Xiang had loved his parents. Undoubtedly, Liu had control of Xiang's parents.

"Anyhow," Farrell continued, "I hope that answers your question."

"I'm afraid it does."

"Even with all of that, it's still tough to see the change in someone you liked."

"Thanks," said Kelly with a sad smile. "It took a little while, but I'm getting used to it."

"Let me know if you need anything else."

"I will, and by the way, thanks for forwarding the file on my dad."

"Most of the older people who knew him still revere him. I'd like to meet him some day," said Farrell.

Back at her own office, Kelly took a deep breath and removed one of the many burner phones from her desk. Then she dialed the private number Xiang had given her.

"Yes," Xiang answered.

"It's Kelly. You suggested we have dinner together, and I was wondering if this evening would work."

"That would be great." The surprise was evident in Xiang's voice. "Tell me where and when."

"Well, we both like Italian. How about Sette Osteria at Connecticut and R at seven?"

"Sounds good," said Xiang.

"I'll make a reservation."

After hanging up, her next step was to meet with Agent Rolfe. She summoned him to her office.

"I have a tough assignment for you this evening," she said. "Paul Maltoni is down at the courthouse trying to get a warrant to search the apartment of a Chinese diplomat, Xiang Shen, on Connecticut Avenue this evening. Assuming he obtains it, I want you to get a couple other agents and go into Xiang's apartment at seven when I'm having dinner with him."

"Okay, I can do that," Rolfe agreed.

"The tough part will be that you'll have to find and seize the items I'm looking for within an hour, an hour and a half max. Then call and let me know. Hopefully, I'll still be at the restaurant with Xiang."

"What am I looking for?"

"A pair of New Balance running shoes with a tread that matches one I'll give you, and," she paused for an instant.

Rolfe waited patiently for her to continue. Finally, she gulped and said, "A pair of women's yellow panties."

"Does this Xiang live with a woman?"

"I don't think so."

"What is this, a sex crime?" Rolfe asked.

"It's espionage."

"Sometime you'll have to let me know what yellow panties have to do with espionage."

"Sometime I will."

"What else am I looking for?"

She was glad Rolfe didn't pursue the panties. "Anything that would show Xiang was involved in espionage."

"Okay. I understand. But let me ask you this, suppose Maltoni doesn't get the warrant. Do we still go in?"

Charles Cameron would have said yes. Not Kelly. "It will be Director Forester's decision. I'll let you know."

She didn't know what Forester would do. She hoped Paul came through.

*   *   *

Paul selected Kathleen McCardle to consider his request for the warrant. He had last appeared before Judge McCardle in an insider trading case in January when he was the DOJ lawyer representing the United States. Jenson had been the opposing lawyer. Paul believed the judge liked him; she had forced Jenson's client to accept a settlement very favorable to the government in the amount of $500 million.

The judge's secretary ushered him into McCardle's chambers.

"Paul Maltoni," she said with a smile as she looked up from some papers on her desk.

"Thanks for agreeing to see me, Judge."

"What's on your mind?"

"The government is requesting a warrant to search an apartment on Connecticut Avenue. We're looking for items related to the murder last November of Senator Jasper of Colorado."

"That occurred in Rock Creek Park."

"Yes, Your Honor."

"What are you looking for?"

"Running shoes with treads that match imprints taken at the scene." Paul decided not to mention the yellow panties. The link between those and the Jasper murder was too tenuous.

"Whose apartment is it?" she asked.

"The man's name is Xiang Shen." Paul had no intention of misleading the judge or acting as if he was hiding relevant information, so he added, "Xiang is an assistant economic attaché at the Chinese embassy."

"I presume Xiang has diplomatic immunity."

Paul coughed and said, "Yes, Your Honor."

He handed her a page he had hastily put together with a brief discussion of two relevant cases.

"These don't convince me, Mr. Maltoni."

"We're not charging Xiang with a crime."

"And I suspect you never will because of his diplomatic immunity. Am I right?"

"Yes, Your Honor."

"So far you've given me no reason to issue your warrant."

Paul's heart skipped a beat. If he didn't turn the judge around, Kelly's plan would go up in flames. But he wasn't sure what to say.

The judge decided to help him out. "What is this really about, Mr. Maltoni?"

Paul took a deep breath and said, "Espionage."

"Involving Senator Jasper?" she asked.

"Yes, and others in the US government."

"Do you have a basis for believing Xiang owns the running shoes that were at the scene of Senator Jasper's murder?"

"We do. We have a witness, Allison Boyd, who linked Xiang to the Jasper murder."

"Boyd," mused the judge. "Is she Vanessa Boyd's sister? The Allison Boyd who killed a Chinese man at the DuPont metro station?"

"Yes, Your Honor. That was self-defense."

"Hand me your warrant."

As Paul did, he had no idea what the judge would do.

She read it, then reached for her pen. She signed it with a flourish and handed it back.

"Since we're off the record, I'll tell you, Mr. Maltoni, I don't like government officials who commit espionage. I hope you catch all of them."

* * *

As Xiang showered and dressed for dinner with Kelly, he could hardly believe his good fortune.

She had sounded enthusiastic about having dinner with him. Perhaps she had remembered how much fun they once had together, and how sincere he had been at the restaurant where they had pizza in January. Maybe now she was ready to resume their relationship. He was thrilled.

That still didn't solve his problem with Liu. If they began sleeping together, he had no intention of trying to obtain top secret information from her and passing it along to Liu. But at least his reports would sound more authentic.

He realized he was playing a dangerous game. But if he could see Kelly again, that would justify the risks.

* * *

Kelly approached the restaurant on foot, walking north on Connecticut Avenue. It was an unusually warm, humid evening for April. She spotted Xiang coming from the opposite direction. They met at the corner of Connecticut and R in front of the restaurant.

"Glad you called," he said.

"It'll be good to catch up," she replied. "Should we eat inside or on the patio?" Kelly asked.

"Could rain," said Xiang. "I vote for inside."

"You're still risk averse, I see," she said, tongue in cheek. That wasn't a smart comment; but she couldn't resist.

Inside was also less crowded, which suited her. The maître d' led them to a dimly lit corner table, then a waitress hustled over with menus and a wine list.

Kelly had to drag out dinner to give the agents enough time to search Xiang's apartment, so she said, "Let's start with a bottle of wine. You used to like reds."

"I still do."

Kelly handed him the wine list, and he selected a Barbera d'Alba.

"Your daughter is a very cute kid," Xiang said.

Kelly tried to conceal her concern. Why was he so damn interested in Julie? Because that was her weak spot? "She's a terrific," Kelly replied. "Loves baseball and any other sport."

"You were pretty athletic as I remember. Track team at CMU."

She forced a smile. "I enjoyed it but didn't win too many races."

"It was a question of training," Xiang remarked. "You were busy studying while your opponents spent every afternoon on the track. I realized that from attending a couple of your races."

When the wine came, the waitress asked if they were ready to order.

"Give us a few minutes," Kelly replied.

She didn't want to alarm Xiang, so she decided to ask him about what he had done since college. She calmly asked, "Did you join your country's diplomatic corps after CMU?"

"Right after," he replied. "I liked living in the United States, and I hoped it would be a way to get back here."

For the next fifteen minutes they talked about his diplomatic career. She wondered how much of it was true. She didn't want to seem as if she were interrogating him, so after a while she shifted the discussion to China's economy.

Xiang sounded pleasant and personable. The problem for Kelly was that as she listened to him and thought about how he had broken up with her, leaving her in New York that awful summer, she became enraged. She cautioned herself to keep it under control. She had assured Forester she could be objective. Even though it was tough, she damn well would do it.

The third time the waitress returned, they ordered: pasta, then fish for both of them. Over dinner, Xiang asked Kelly what she had done after graduation. She told him about her husband and failed marriage. She talked about her FBI career in broad, sweeping terms, being careful not to disclose anything of consequence.

Her phone was in the bag resting at her feet. It was open to make sure she heard the ring. So far, Rolfe hadn't called. Growing anxious, she stole a look at her watch. They had already been in the restaurant close to an hour and a half. What was taking so long?

While they were eating dessert, chocolate gelato, her phone rang. She pulled it out, looked at the caller ID, and told Xiang, "I'm sorry. This is about Julie, I have to take it."

With the phone in hand, she walked away from the table and toward a deserted corner of the restaurant. She turned her back to Xiang in case he read lips.

"Bingo," Rolfe said. "Can you talk?"

"Yes, go ahead."

"We found a pair of yellow panties under the mattress of Xiang's bed. He has a pair of New Balance running shoes. They match the tread from Rock Creek Park."

"Where are you?"

"Out of the apartment. We took both objects."

"What else did you find?"

"Several different cell phones, some encrypted. We fixed them so we'll be able to pick up any calls made on them, and left them in place. That's all of interest."

"Good. Thanks."

She now had everything she needed to destroy Xiang's life. And he deserved what would be coming to him, not just to even her personal score, but because her former lover was a killer and a spy. She turned her phone to the record mode. Glancing out of the restaurant window, she saw that it wasn't raining.

When she returned to the table, Xiang asked, "Is Julie okay?"

"She's fine. We're always negotiating about her bedtime," Kelly explained. "It looks like the weather has cleared. Let's wander down to DuPont Circle."

"Good idea."

Xiang wanted to pay, but she insisted on splitting the check. As they got up from the table, she slipped her phone into the open pocket of her light windbreaker where it would be able to pick up their conversation.

The sidewalk on Connecticut Avenue was crowded, mostly with young people.

"Being with you is like old times," Xiang said.

"Dinner was nice," she replied.

A few minutes later they entered DuPont Circle. Scores of people were milling around. Some were tossing Frisbees or balls. She led Xiang to a deserted bench.

When they were seated, he reached for her hand, but she yanked it away. The act was over.

She decided to hit him straight on. "We have to talk, Xiang. You're in trouble, a lot of trouble. But I can help you."

He looked stunned. "Tr-trouble? What kind of trouble?"

"While we were having dinner, FBI agents searched your apartment. They found the yellow panties you took from Vanessa Boyd's apartment. That ties you to attacks on Vanessa's sister Allison. We also found a pair of New Balance running shoes with treads that match those at the scene of Senator Jasper's murder. That implicates you in his murder."

She waited for him to deny it. He didn't. Instead, he looked angry, very angry. Glaring at her, he said, "You're good. You devious bitch. You're really good. You should go into the theater. And this says a lot about your American democracy, to have people sneaking into someone's apartment."

"That's pretty funny coming from a representative of the country which is one of the worst violators of human rights on the planet. For the record, you'll be interested to know we had a warrant. You'll pay dearly for what you've done."

On a roll, she kept going and tried a shot in the dark. "We know the spy operation you're involved with didn't die with Jasper. Recently, you passed information about what response the US would make to an incident in the East China Sea between China and Japan."

He didn't deny that either. Instead, defiantly, he said, "You can't do anything to me. I have diplomatic immunity."

Kelly had anticipated his words. She immediately responded, "That's correct, so what we'll do is present these facts to your government, we'll disclose them in the press, and we'll expel you from the US. When you get home to China, I'm sure you'll be severely punished for getting caught."

Xiang now looked horrified.

Recalling what Farrell had told her, she continued, "And they'll punish your parents as well." Kelly had no idea whether this was true. Her objective was to frighten Xiang as much as possible.

He put his hands over his face, lowered his head, and started shaking. "I never wanted to do those things," he said. "I never wanted to kill Senator Jasper. I'm not that kind of a person."

She had no sympathy for Xiang. "Since I've been in law enforcement, I can't tell you how many times I've heard those words from criminals. It's disgusting. You know what I tell them?"

"What?"

"So why did you do it?"

He raised his head. "Minister Liu. You don't understand. He's a cruel man. He didn't give me any choice."

"If Minister Liu is a cruel man, then I'm sure you don't want to be expelled and sent home to China."

"You said you would help me. How?"

"You tell me what you know about your government's spying operation in the United States, and I'll ask my superiors to arrange for you to have a new identity. We'll resettle you somewhere in the United States far from Washington where your government can't find you."

"You could do that?"

"We do it all the time for people in what's called the witness protection program. You'll have a new life here. In order to qualify, you have to tell me everything you know about the spying operation, and that means everything."

Xiang didn't respond. Two minutes passed, but still he didn't say a word. Kelly didn't want to disturb him while he was weighing her offer.

Finally, he said, "I'll tell you everything I know on one condition."

"What's that?"

"First, you have to get my parents out of China. Bring them here to the US and resettle them with me under your witness protection program."

Xiang was asking for a lot from Kelly. She had no idea whether she could even deliver immunity and resettlement for Xiang now that she knew he had killed Jasper, a US Senator. On top of that, he was asking the US government to attempt a complex rescue operation in China for Xiang's parents. The decision would be Forester's and Larkin's. Before teeing up the issue for them, she needed to know what information Xiang could provide.

"I'm willing to try to arrange an operation to bring your parents here," she finally said. "To do that, I'll have to let my superiors know what information you'd be giving us."

"If I tell you everything now, you won't bring my parents. I don't trust you."

"Fine," she said through clenched teeth. "Then you can go back to China. I'll take great pleasure in putting you on the plane myself. When you arrive, you can explain to Minister Liu how you got caught and exposed his spying operation because you stole a woman's panties. To do what with, I can only imagine. If you don't explain it to him, I will."

"No," Xiang said plaintively. "Please."

"Then tell me what your role is in this."

He took a deep breath and began speaking. "When Jasper was alive, he passed me documents in Rock Creek Park or left them in a concealed drop site."

"How creative."

"I didn't make the rules."

"What kind of documents?"

"Military intelligence. Jasper was the chairman of the Senate Armed Services Committee. I had no idea what was in the documents. He delivered them to me in a sealed envelope. That's how I forwarded them to Minister Liu in the diplomatic pouch."

"So why did Liu order you to kill Jasper?"

"Everything was fine until Jasper's mistress, Vanessa Boyd, told him she secretly made a CD of Liu's meeting with Jasper in Tokyo."

"And then?"

"Liu decided Jasper was a liability."

"What happened to your spy operation after Jasper's death?"

"Nothing for two months. Until January."

"And then?"

"I was instructed to meet with an American from time-to-time in Washington. He would deliver sealed envelopes to me. Unlike Jasper, he wasn't the source of the information. He was merely the conduit."

Kelly was leaning close to Xiang. Hearing so much valuable information and knowing it was being recorded, she was excited. Still, she tried to appear calm. All she needed now was the identity of the source and the conduit.

"Who's the source?" she asked.

"I don't know. I asked Liu on a trip to Beijing, but he didn't want to tell me. The conduit knows."

"Who's the conduit?"

Xiang shook his head. "That's all I'll tell you this evening. When my parents are safely in the US, I'll tell you who the conduit is."

"I can try, but it will be difficult."

"I don't see why. Thousands of Chinese tourists visit the States every year. Also, my parents can say they're coming to see me."

"They'll need passports and visas."

"They have passports. I insisted they get them. You'll have to provide the visas and airplane tickets. I'll give you their names and address."

He took a piece of paper from his pocket, wrote the information down in English and Chinese, and handed it to her.

"It will take time," she said.

"I'm in no hurry. You are."

"Let's say, if I get the approvals I need, your parents will arrive in Washington in two weeks on a Tuesday."

"How will I know if you get the approvals?"

"I will call you on your private cell phone and say, 'Your package of books is being shipped.'"

"Do you think it's likely, or is this a dream of yours?" Xiang asked skeptically.

She hesitated for a second, then said, "Very likely." She believed she could bring the AG around to approving it, and Farrell could pull off the rescue.

"I want to meet their plane."

She thought about his request. Her first reaction was that it might be too dangerous. On the other hand, if his parents were visiting him, it would be natural. Anything else would raise red flags. Besides, once his parents were off the plane, they were on US soil. She would be in control of the situation.

"You can meet their plane," she said.

Xiang nodded. "Okay."

"One other thing," Kelly added. "Don't even dream about leaving the US or flying to China. We'll be watching the embassy and your apartment. If you try to flee, we'll arrest you and hold you as long as possible, until your embassy can free you."

He looked at her with hostility. "Even after all you've learned from me, you still don't trust me."

Kelly reached into her jacket pocket and turned off the recorder. "There was a time when I not only trusted you, I loved you. You destroyed that trust and love. It took me a long time to get over your sudden and unexplained breakup. I have plenty riding on this as well, and I won't be burned by you a second time. Now reach over and give me a hug so we can look romantic in case someone is watching. But don't you dare kiss me."

Beijing

Liu had a special encrypted phone that connected him with Wu at the Chinese embassy in Washington. When it rang today, Liu was in a meeting with two of his advisers discussing an operation being planned to support a Chinese energy business in Brazil. He asked the others to leave the room.

"Yes," Liu said tersely as he picked up the phone.

"We have a serious problem involving Xiang," Wu said.

"What did he do?"

"He had dinner and then a lengthy conversation in a park with a blond American woman. One of my people observed them in the park. He took pictures of Xiang, who seemed agitated. You had instructed me to watch Xiang carefully and to call you if we detected any breach of security."

"Send me all the pictures," Liu said.

Seconds later, he had them. Liu immediately recognized Kelly Cameron as the blond woman with Xiang. So Xiang was meeting with her, he mused. Perhaps Liu had been wrong. The reports Xiang had been sending may not have been bogus.

"Unfortunately," Wu said, "there was no way for our people to get close enough to overhear their conversation."

"I understand. Keep watching Xiang closely and let me know if you see anything else or pick up anything from his phones or email."

"Yes, sir."

Once Liu hung up the phone, he scrolled through the twenty-five pictures Wu had sent. He didn't need audio, Xiang's facial expression told the story. And there was a picture of him with his head in his hands. He appeared to be crying. Liu wasn't fooled by the hug in the last photo—this was no romantic encounter. That blond American was trying to persuade Xiang to betray his country. Liu didn't know whether she had succeeded. That would be determined by what he learned next.

In the meantime, Liu focused on the leverage he had over Xiang. Liu knew that Xiang, an only child, had a great love for his parents. When Liu had first sent Xiang to Washington, he had moved Xiang's parents to a comfortable apartment in Beijing. MSS paid all the expenses. It was Liu's way of controlling Xiang. He already had a bug on the phone line into the parents' apartment, and neither the mother nor the father had a cell phone or email. Xiang communicated with them by calling the landline in their apartment.

He instructed one of his people to increase surveillance on Xiang's parents.

"Have someone watch their apartment around the clock. If either one leaves, follow them and let me know."

Two hours later, the surveillance bore fruit. Liu received a transcription of a phone call Xiang had made to his parents, persuading them to come visit him in Washington. From only one reading of the transcript,

Liu deduced what had happened. Xiang had made a deal with Kelly. He would tell her everything if she brought his parents to the US. Xiang was a fool who had grossly underestimated Liu.

Liu decided not to move immediately. Right now, the Americans would be highly vigilant. He would wait the full two weeks, hoping to lull the Americans into a false sense of complacency, figuring their plan was working. Then he would make his move.

Washington

Immediately after leaving Xiang in the DuPont Circle park, Kelly called Farrell. She had to know whether a plan to rescue Xiang's parents was viable. She asked Farrell to come to her office at six the following morning.

The next morning when he arrived, Kelly poured him a cup of coffee and led him into her office where she reported on her conversation with Xiang.

The minute she finished, Farrell told her, "Now I know why you wanted to see me. You're hoping the CIA can get Xiang's parents out of China."

"That pretty well expresses it. What do you think?"

"In some respects, the world's most populous country is like a giant prison. In this regard, it's diametrically opposed to the US. In the US, it's easy to get out and hard to get in. In China, it's relatively easy to get in, but hard to get out."

"You're stalling," said Kelly. "Can you do it?"

"We have had some successes. The good news is that Xiang's parents aren't dissidents who have been targeted for that reason by the regime. The bad news is that they're family members of a security agent posing as a diplomat. Those people are sometimes under surveillance."

"Would you be willing to try?"

"Absolutely. I'll need the director's approval, but I'm confident I can get that. You have to recognize the risks are large, and the stakes as well. I'm talking, of course, about the lives of Xiang and his parents."

"Wouldn't it be natural for them to visit their son here? After all, large numbers of Chinese come each year."

"Listen, Kelly, in view of how important this is to the task force, you can be sure I'll pull out all the stops. We have good people in Beijing. I'll use our best."

"That's all I can ask."

"You want me to get started now?"

"I'll call you after my meeting with the AG."

*   *   *

Kelly was waiting for Forester when he arrived at his office an hour later. He hung on every word of her report on her meeting with Xiang.

"That is terrific," he said at the end.

"I met with Farrell a little while ago," she added.

"Don't you ever sleep?"

"Not much, sir. Farrell is ready to go. I called Maltoni, and he's in favor."

"Which means we have to cross the street and get Arthur on board."

Kelly was thrilled to hear Forester use the word "we." That meant he would be coming with her.

Forester called the AG's secretary and found out he had time at 10 a.m. That was when Kelly, Forester, and Paul walked into Arthur's office.

"I thought good things are supposed to come in threes," the AG quipped.

"Oh, you'll be thrilled when you hear what we have to say," Forester replied. "Why don't you kick it off, Kelly?"

She was always amused how so many of the men she worked with used sports metaphors. Tee it up; kick it off; play hardball; get it over the goal line.

Kelly did more than kick it off. She described her entire conversation with Xiang. At the end, a scowling Arthur said, "Let me get this right. You now know who killed Senator Jasper and you not only want to give him a walk, but you want the US government to enhance his life and that of his parents by letting them benefit from the witness protection program?" He shook his head. "Are you out of your fuckin' mind?"

"Don't hold back, Arthur," Forester said, "tell us what you really think."

As Arthur's words reverberated, her heart sank. She had gone out on a very long limb to forge this deal with Xiang. He may have already told his parents in reliance on what she had said. Now Arthur was threatening to cut it off. She glanced to her right at the large stone fireplace as if help could magically float down the chimney.

"Kelly's proposal makes perfectly good sense," Paul said in a combative tone, ready to do battle with his boss.

"You're smoking the same thing she is."

"Let's discuss this rationally," Paul said, pushing back. "We know Xiang killed Jasper. We can't prosecute Xiang because he has diplomatic immunity. We desperately want to know the identity of the mole in the US government. Xiang can lead us to that mole. QED."

"Invoking Latin never helps a weak argument."

"Why is it weak?"

"Because you and Kelly have no basis for believing Xiang can deliver the mole. In fact, Kelly said Xiang told her he doesn't know the identity of the mole, only the conduit. Am I right?"

"You are," Paul replied, hanging tough, "but the conduit could lead us to the mole."

"I notice that you said could, not will," Arthur remarked.

"It's the only chance we have, sir."

Larkin looked at Forester. "What do you think, Jim?"

"I'd like to try it, although I have some real doubts about the operational details."

"Meaning what?"

"Getting Xiang's parents out of China will be one tough assignment. Xiang's parents aren't sophisticated people. They could wither under questioning by passport control agents."

"If they get that far," Arthur said.

"Farrell is prepared to run the Beijing part of the operation," Kelly said. "They have had good results getting out some scientists and dissidents."

"And a lot more failures," Arthur responded.

The AG sprang out of his chair and paced around the cavernous office, running his hand through his hair. They all sat in silence, waiting for the verdict.

"I should have listened to my mother," Arthur said. "She wanted me to be a doctor."

"You don't think doctors have hard decisions?" Forester said.

"Okay. Do it," Arthur finally said with resignation. "And listen, Kelly, you can get moving on this right away. You don't have to wait for me to clear it with the president. You know why?"

"Why?"

"Because I have no intention of telling Braddock," Arthur said gruffly. "If the press gets hold of this and a Senate committee starts investigating why we treated with the killer of a member of their club, I want Braddock to be able truthfully to say he had no knowledge of this totally misguided operation. Do you understand that, Kelly?"

"Yes, sir."

"Good, then you also understand that my ass is now on the line."

"I'll do my best, sir, I promise you that."

"Hopefully that will be good enough. At this point, I could never pass the MCATs to get into medical school," Larkin said.

The meeting broke up. On the way out, Kelly took Paul aside and said, "Thank you. I really appreciate you going to bat for me."

"C'mon, we're on the same team here. We back each other. Don't be upset by Arthur's rough way of talking. That approach served him well as a New York trial lawyer. Deep down, he's actually a nice person."

"You could have fooled me."

As soon as Kelly got back to her office, she called Farrell. "We got a green light from the AG," she said. "You can proceed."

"That's great. I already made some calls to Beijing. They haven't moved yet, but they're in prep mode prep mode."

"Excellent. What can I do to help?"

"Cross your fingers and toes. If you're religious, I'd recommend that you pray."

Washington, One Week Later

At nine in the evening on Tuesday, Andrew Martin opened the front door of his house on Foxhall Road for General Cartwright.

This was a critical day for Cartwright's campaign. Thanks to the strong endorsement and intervention of Senator Lawson, Cartwright was able, albeit very late, to get on the ballots for the Republican presidential primaries in Pennsylvania, Ohio, Georgia, and California—four pivotal states, all of which had primaries that day. It was a high-risk strategy Martin had urged Cartwright to pursue, recognizing he might lose big today because he hadn't much time to campaign. If he did, his presidential bid would be finished. The general had spent the last week campaigning hard in those four states, never sleeping except for on airplanes.

He looks totally washed out, Martin thought when Cartwright walked into the house and slumped down in a chair in the living room. Martin immediately brought him a scotch on the rocks, then fixed one for himself.

Over the time Huan had been living with Martin, he had learned what an amazing cook she was, using exotic spices and ingredients that she purchased at a market in Chinatown. Francis had been a good cook, Martin thought, but Huan was even better. Guessing Cartwright would be hungry, Martin had asked Huan to prepare a feast for the general.

Cartwright raised his glass and said, "Here's to victory tonight, Andrew, my friend."

"I'll drink to that."

"What in the world smells so good?"

"Huan is in the kitchen working up something special for us," Martin explained.

"That's great, I'm famished."

Fifteen minutes later, Martin opened a bottle of Vietti Barolo and the three of them sat down at the dining room table.

Half a dozen platters were in the center. Martin recognized duck, shrimp, and beef. He had no idea what the other ingredients were; the vegetables were all unfamiliar to him.

The general asked Huan where she had grown up.

"Shanghai," she said. "My father taught history at a university. During Mao's Cultural Revolution, he was sent to the countryside for indoctrination. He suffered dreadfully. When he came back, his mind had stopped working. He couldn't do anything."

"Mao was a horror," Cartwright said.

"We agree on that," Huan acknowledged.

"Andrew told me you're writing a novel."

"That's right."

"Tell me about it."

And she did. Martin drank wine and relaxed, happy that Huan was taking Cartwright's mind off the tension of the campaign.

At two minutes to ten o'clock, Martin said, "This is all very interesting, but the election coverage will be starting in a couple of minutes."

Wine glasses in hand, the three headed toward the living room.

It had been twelve years since Martin had been actively involved with a candidate running for president. He had forgotten how you hung on the results from each state.

Pennsylvania, Ohio, and Georgia were coming in first. In all these states, six names were on the ballot. Martin held his breath as results began flashing on the screen.

Everywhere, Cartwright was running first, and by a good margin. Early returns showed Cartwright not only first, but with twice as many votes as the next candidate. Cartwright and Martin congratulated each other excitedly.

Sensing that the drama had ended, Huan retreated to the dining room to clean up dinner. A little while later, she reappeared to say goodnight before heading upstairs.

For the next two hours, the general padded his lead in Pennsylvania, Ohio, and Georgia. Finally, early returns and exit polls started coming in from the big enchilada—California. And they showed Cartwright solidly ahead.

Martin heard movement coming from upstairs. Concluding that Huan wasn't asleep, he went up to tell her the good news about California. He had taken off his shoes in the den and was walking up the carpeted stairs quietly. At the top, he heard the sound of Huan's voice speaking in Chinese coming from the room she used as a study. Martin walked down the hall. From the doorway, with her back to him, he saw her seated at the desk, the phone up against her ear, engrossed in a conversation.

"Hey Huan," Martin called out, intending to interrupt her just long enough to give her the good news.

Surprisingly, she immediately ended the call, stood up, and turned around. Martin, who as a trial lawyer had observed the demeanor of plenty of witnesses, thought she had a guilty expression on her face.

"Sorry I disturbed you," Martin said.

"Oh, no problem," said Huan. "I was just talking to my mother. She's not feeling well."

"I'm sorry to hear that."

"Nothing serious."

"Well, I just wanted to tell you General Cartwright's leading in California."

"That's wonderful. I'd be surprised if he doesn't end up taking the presidency."

"I hope you're right."

Martin went back downstairs, convinced that Huan was lying about the call.

Half an hour later, California was even more solidly for Cartwright.

The general yawned. "I'm going home to bed. I can't thank you enough, Andrew, for getting Lawson's support and pushing me into these primaries. I owe you big time for all your strategic help."

Martin was thrilled with the evening's results. Cartwright had a good chance of winning. Ever since Dale Scott had written in the *Wall Street Journal* that Martin was Cartwright's top advisor, a score of new clients had flocked to him at the firm. He now saw himself as President Cartwright's confidante and top informal advisor, which would mean more legal business for Martin. At the intersection of the Washington world of high-stakes law and politics, nothing mattered as much as *access*. To be sure, legal knowledge and analytical problem-solving were important, but the ability to prepare and frame an argument meant little if the advocate couldn't get in the door to the decision maker.

All of that was good, Martin thought. However, something had occurred that evening that was troubling him. What in the world was Huan up to? If she'd been talking to her mother, why would she end the call so abruptly and look so guilty?

There was only one explanation, and it confirmed Martin's suspicions. Huan was a plant of Liu's. She must have been reporting to her control on the phone. Martin was furious at himself for not detecting this earlier. How could he have been so foolish? It was right under his nose, and he hadn't seen it.

Well, he did now, and that gave him an advantage. As long as he didn't tell Huan, she wouldn't be aware that he knew. That way he could keep his eye on her and use her to mislead Liu if the situation arose.

Washington, One Week Later

During the two weeks since Kelly had told Farrell he could proceed, he had provided her with a constant stream of information he was receiving from CIA agents in Beijing. Everything seemed to be on schedule for the operation to rescue Xiang's parents.

Kelly had thought that was good news. Not Farrell. "It's going too smoothly," he said. "That makes me nervous."

That evening, Xiang's mother and father were scheduled to land at Dulles Airport at 10:15 p.m. It was now eight in the morning. Xiang had arrived at the embassy at seven, going to work as if it were a normal day.

For the last two weeks, Kelly had arranged surveillance on the street outside of the Chinese embassy and Xiang's apartment building. FBI agents loosely trailed Xiang everywhere he went. Nothing suspicious or out of the ordinary had occurred, nor had any calls been made on the encrypted phones which Rolfe had found and tinkered with in Xiang's apartment.

Ordinarily Kelly would have viewed that as more good news, however, Farrell's attitude was contagious. If it seemed to be going too well, she thought, something must be wrong.

Today, the plan was for Farrell, who was in touch with the CIA operatives in Beijing through a secure line, to tell Kelly when Xiang's parents were on the plane. She would then call Xiang on his personal phone and give him the flight number and arrival time.

In the meantime, Kelly decided to beef up surveillance. Worried there might be a hitch, she tried to prepare for any eventuality. She now had what looked like a computer repair van with tinted windows parked a block from the embassy. Rolfe was in the van along with three other agents. One of them was operating a camera which could send real-time video feed to the FBI conference room, where Paul and Farrell were with Kelly. Wilkins was "much too busy at the White House," he said, to join them.

Kelly glanced across the table at Paul and Farrell. Both were standing in front of the screen built into the wall at the far end of the table. Displayed from the video feed in the van was the Chinese embassy. The six-floor, gray stone structure was by far the largest in Washington's new embassy row off Van Ness Street in upper northwest Washington. It had been constructed by Chinese contractors to minimize the risk of bugs being planted in the structure.

Anxiously, Kelly stared at the clock on the wall. At 8:15 a.m., she said to Farrell, "Shouldn't you have heard from your people in Beijing that Xiang's parents are on the plane?"

"Maybe they're waiting for it to clear Chinese airspace. We'll give them another hour. Have some more coffee," Farrell suggested.

"Good idea. I've already had six cups. I'm strung tighter than a piano wire."

Paul laughed and said, "You can be funny, Kelly. Has anyone told you that?"

"Only you. Two other times."

At five minutes to nine, Farrell's phone rang. Kelly glanced at the grim-faced CIA agent as he replied somberly, "Yes . . . Yes . . . I understand." He put down the phone on the table with a thud.

"Bad news?" Kelly asked.

"These are the words my colleague in Beijing just told me, 'Your package will not be arriving. The government will not let it leave the country.' It's obvious that Xiang's blown."

"Shit," Kelly said.

"My sentiments exactly," Farrell replied.

"We have to warn Xiang," Kelly said, "and get him out of that building."

She called Xiang's personal phone with one of her burner phones, but to her horror, she heard, "This line is not in service," on the other end.

Kelly asked one of the FBI's Chinese translators, a Chinese man who had been born in Beijing and did not have an American accent, to call the embassy and ask for Xiang, explaining he was with IBM corporate and wanted to discuss an investment in China.

When he called, he was told, "Xiang is in a meeting and cannot be disturbed."

Then one of the FBI's IT technicians rushed into the room carrying a sheet of paper. He handed it to Kelly saying, "Ten minutes ago Xiang received a call on one of the encrypted phones Rolfe had fixed. Here is a transcript of the conversation."

Kelly read:

"Xiang, this is Minister Liu."

"Yes, sir."

"I want you to fly home immediately for consultations."

"Can I come tomorrow?"

"No, it must be today. A seat has been reserved for you on the 2 p.m. Air China flight to Beijing. Go to the airport now. That's an order."

"But—"

"I have an urgent matter to discuss with you, do you understand?"

"Yes, sir."

Kelly felt sick, realizing she had destroyed Xiang's parents. Still, she didn't want to let Xiang leave the country. She hoped she could get him to talk, even though his parents wouldn't be coming.

She called Rolfe in the van. "We're expecting Xiang to leave the embassy and go to Dulles Airport. Follow whatever vehicle he's in. Once he's a good distance from the embassy, stop the vehicle and get him into your van. Then call me."

"Will do."

They waited for Xiang to move. Two hours later, he still hadn't left the embassy.

"What the hell's going on?" Kelly said aloud.

"Xiang is refusing to go," Farrell said. "Knowing Liu, he's decided Liu has control of his parents. Also, Liu must have learned about your DuPont Circle encounter with Xiang. Even if he goes, what's the point? Liu will torture and kill him as soon as he gets to Beijing."

"He may be too paralyzed with fear to move," Paul chimed in.

"So what will happen to him if he stays in the embassy?" Kelly asked.

"They'll kill him there," Paul said. "Fifty years from now when the building comes down, somebody will find his remains in the basement."

His words made Kelly cringe. "That's certainly a comforting thought," she said.

Farrell interjected, "Sorry to disagree, Counselor, but you're in my area. I've studied Liu and the MSS, which I guess is why I landed on this task force. Liu will want to get his hands on Xiang to find out personally what Xiang knows and what you told him in your DuPont Circle meeting. He won't trust people at the embassy to do that."

"So what will he do?" Kelly asked.

"He'll try to smuggle Xiang out of the country. The same as the Israelis did with Eichmann, even though it would have been a lot easier to kill him in Argentina."

"They wanted a show trial."

Farrell nodded. "And Liu wants to vacuum Xiang's brain about what he knows."

"So how will he do it?" Kelly asked.

"Look for a van of some type to pull up in front of the embassy. They'll try to slip him on that 2 p.m. Air China plane probably in a heated and ventilated baggage container."

Kelly was convinced Farrell was right. "So we have to seize him from the vehicle taking him to Dulles."

"Exactly," said Farrell. "He'll be drugged. He's probably already been drugged."

Kelly got moving. She called Rolfe on the secure phone and gave him the game plan. "Remember, we need Xiang alive," she cautioned.

"Understood."

She put William, another agent, on the street near the embassy, then she sent half a dozen agents to Dulles. She also enlisted the help of the Virginia state police, who were responsible for the road to Dulles. Thirty minutes later, she had everything in place. Kelly, Paul, and Farrell sat silently, staring at the TV screen.

At ten minutes to twelve, Kelly began to have doubts. Maybe Farrell was wrong.

As if reading her mind, Farrell said with confidence, "Patience, Kelly. These logistics take time. They're not operating in their own country."

"Okay."

"I'm getting a stiff neck," Paul said.

"Then take a walk in the corridor," Kelly told him. "We'll cover the screen."

"How about lunch?" Paul asked.

"You always think about food," Kelly chided.

"We need energy."

"Personally, I can operate on adrenalin, but I'll order pizza in," she said, picking up the phone to call her secretary with the pizza order.

After Kelly made the call, a movement on the screen caught her eye. "Hold on," she said.

A white van with "ACE CARPET CLEANING AND REPAIR" painted on the side pulled up to the front of the embassy. Two Chinese men dressed in jeans and checked shirts got out of the van and approached the locked metal gate leading to the courtyard in front of the embassy. One man flashed an ID and the gate immediately swung open. Then they crossed the courtyard and walked into the building.

Kelly grabbed her iPad immediately.

"Check on Ace Carpet Cleaning and Repair," Paul told Kelly.

"That's what I'm doing."

Kelly found a company with that name in Silver Spring. She called and told the receptionist, "I'm Kelly Cameron with the FBI. I want to know if you're scheduled to do work in the Chinese embassy today."

The woman replied in a worried tone, "We are not, but one of our trucks has gone missing. I can't get the driver on the phone."

Kelly gave the woman her phone number and said, "Please let me know if you locate the truck." Then she put down the phone and said, "Farrell's right on point."

She picked up her phone again and called William. "Move now. The carpet van."

"Roger that."

On the screen, she focused on William, an African American agent who was dressed as a student from the nearby University of the District of Columbia, complete with a bulky backpack. Kelly held her breath as she watched William approaching the carpet van. Without breaking pace, he stuck a small, black homing device onto the bottom of the rear bumper, then passed out of view of the camera.

She exhaled with relief and called Rolfe at his position in the back of the van. "Tracking in place. You ready to move?"

"Absolutely."

"It won't be long now. I'll keep this line open."

She was feeling more confident. At least this was proceeding as planned.

Ten minutes later, the front door of the embassy opened. The two Chinese men from the carpet van walked out. They were carrying a rolled up carpet, straining as if it were heavy. By the time they approached the van, Kelly saw perspiration dotting one man's forehead and sweat dripping down the other man's face.

"Must be a heavy carpet," Farrell remarked.

"Yeah, real heavy," Paul agreed.

As Kelly watched them load the carpet into the back of the van, she thought about having FBI agents move in now and seize Xiang in front of the embassy. But ultimately she decided against it. Chinese security personnel would undoubtedly be watching from embassy windows and might use force to try and bring Xiang back into the embassy compound. It would be better to grab him on the way to Dulles, she concluded.

She watched the van drive away.

"They're moving," Rolfe said. "Tracking device is working. I have them on the screen. Proceeding east on Van Ness . . . turning south on Connecticut. You want me to follow?"

"Hold your position for two more minutes, then follow. But maintain your distance."

"Roger that."

Rolfe kept Kelly apprised of the carpet van's location. Fifteen minutes later, he said, "Crossing Memorial Bridge."

"Good, they're heading to Dulles Airport."

Another twelve minutes and they were on the Dulles Access Road.

"We're hanging back about ten car lengths," Rolfe said. "They are definitely in excess of the speed limit."

"Excellent. Traffic stop is about ten miles down the road. Focus your camera on the carpet van. I want to see what's happening."

"Roger that."

As Kelly watched the screen along with Paul and Farrell, the carpet van passed an unmarked dark blue Virginia state police car parked along the side of the road. Kelly had instructed the state police to pull over the van. As the dark blue car moved onto the highway, the driver affixed a flashing light to the roof and turned on his siren. He motioned for the carpet van to pull over.

It complied, stopping on the right apron. Rolfe pulled over as well, but held his position, still about ten car lengths' back.

Two uniformed Virginia state troopers got out of the car—one on each side of the front. The driver was holding a bullhorn. He called to the men in the carpet van.

"Out of the van, both of you. Hands in the air."

The troopers then approached the van. Both had guns holstered at their waists.

One of the Chinese men jumped out on the passenger side, a gun in his hand. Without saying a word, he raised his gun and shot both troopers. Then he quickly climbed back into the van. It roared away before the FBI agents had a chance to stop them.

Kelly hadn't figured on this. She immediately called her Virginia police contact to get medical help for the two troopers. What to do now? They could set up a roadblock, bring in a chopper, and try to stop the carpet van on the road. But there was too much risk of harming Xiang and other motorists that way, Kelly decided. Better to pretend the police didn't know the men who shot the troopers were in the carpet van, then wait until they reached Dulles Airport and stopped driving. They couldn't put a carpet like that on a plane. They would have to take the carpet to a freight forwarder to be packaged for shipment to China.

Kelly told the others in the room and Rolfe what she planned to do. Fortunately, she had stationed six agents at Dulles. She told three of them to take up positions along the road which housed two freight forwarders. The other three she directed to East Asia Shipping, one of the freight forwarders. She gave them all a warning. "The two men in the van are armed and extremely dangerous. They have shot two Virginia troopers."

Fifteen minutes later, the carpet van pulled up in front of East Asia Shipping. Kelly, Paul, and Farrell were following what was happening on the television screen. Rolfe's van, which had been trailing closely behind, stopped ten yards away. Leaving the carpet in the back of the van, the two Chinese men got out and walked toward the front door.

They never made it inside the building. Guns in hand, the three FBI agents converged on them. The two Chinese men pulled out their own guns and opened fire, but it was too late. Both went down in a hail of bullets fired by the FBI agents.

Rolfe and another agent jumped out of their van and raced over to the carpet van, opening the rear door. Slowly and carefully, they pulled out the rolled up carpet and placed it on the asphalt surface of the parking lot. Kelly watched them unroll it. Xiang was inside, and he wasn't moving.

Rolfe and the other agent, who had medical training, examined Xiang.

"He's alive but unconscious," Rolfe told Kelly.

"I have a chopper in the area," said Kelly. "I'll have him land close to your location. I want you to load Xiang inside, then accompany him to the safe house near Charlottesville. I'll meet you there."

While she waited for the chopper to land, her phone beeped. She had a text message—the two Virginia troopers would live.

As soon as Xiang was en route to the safe house, Kelly ordered a second chopper to take her there.

Charlottesville

In the chopper, Kelly had arranged for a doctor from Charlottesville to meet them at the safe house. He examined Xiang immediately after arrival and told Kelly that they had given him a powerful sedative.

"How soon do you think he'll be able to talk to me?"

"Give him another hour, two at most."

The doctor's prognosis proved to be accurate. An hour and a half later, Xiang came around and sat up in the bed. Kelly was sitting in a chair next to him.

"My mother and father," were Xiang's first words. "Liu will kill them if he hasn't already."

"Maybe not," Kelly said. "That won't help Liu." She tried to sound hopeful.

"You don't understand Liu. He won't care, he's a vindictive bastard. He'll do it to get even with me.'" Xiang was crying now. "That's why I didn't follow orders to fly home. It's hopeless, they're probably already dead."

Xiang's crying intensified to sharp, racking sobs.

Kelly sat in silence, waiting for the distraught Xiang to recover. He closed his eyes, not saying a word.

After twenty minutes, she asked, "Would you like something to eat or to drink?"

"No, I don't want anything from you. *You're* the one who caused my parents' death."

"We don't know they are dead," Kelly reasoned.

"I know. I understand Liu. You do not. Believe me, they are dead, and you are responsible."

His comment infuriated Kelly, but she kept calm and didn't say a word, holding on to the hope that he would eventually talk.

Beijing

An MSS official at the embassy in Washington forwarded to Liu clips from American news programs and links to articles in the online *Washington Post, New York Times,* and *Wall Street Journal.* All carried the same story: Two Virginia state policemen had been shot and seriously wounded on the Dulles Access Road. Two Chinese men, found without any identification, had been shot and killed in front of the East Asia Shipping freight forwarder building at Dulles Airport. The FBI had released a statement that both incidents were under investigation. Reporters were speculating that the two incidents were related, but the FBI spokesman refused to confirm.

Once Liu had been informed that Xiang was refusing to fly to Beijing, he had given the order to drug Xiang and put him on the plane in the baggage compartment. Liu didn't know precisely what had happened, but the result was clear: the fools on his staff in Washington had bungled the assignment, and the Americans now had Xiang in their possession.

In a white rage, Liu picked up the gun on the table behind his desk. He holstered it at his waist, then ordered his driver to bring the car around to the front of the building. He would go to Xiang's parents' apartment to deal with the situation himself. He didn't trust his underlings to do the job. He just hoped he was in time, and that Xiang hadn't already spilled his guts to Kelly Cameron.

Half an hour later, gun in hand, Liu burst into the apartment.

"Your son is a traitor," he cried out.

The two of them cowered in a corner, the man shielding his wife. Liu grabbed Xiang's father by the neck and said, "You're the father of a traitor, but I will give you a chance to save your life, and your son's life."

Xiang's father looked at Liu, his eyes wide, and nodded.

"Call your son," Liu instructed. "Tell him you didn't come to Washington because his mother was sick, and you didn't think she could make the trip. But perhaps you will come in a couple of months. Do you understand?"

"Yes . . . I understand," Xiang's father choked out.

Looking at the woman, Liu added, "Then you will tell him that you hope to be feeling better soon."

Xiang's mother nodded.

Liu pushed the father toward the phone. Then he slammed Xiang's mother down onto a chair, standing next to her and holding the gun against her head.

"You say one wrong word, father of traitor, and I blow her brains out."

Charlottesville

Kelly, sitting next to the bed of the silent Xiang, was trying to decide how much longer to stay when she heard a phone ring in his pocket. Xiang pulled it out, looked at the caller ID and said, "It's my parents' number."

She decided to let him take the call.

The call, conducted in Chinese, was brief, Xiang saying little while mostly listening. When the call was over, Kelly asked him to tell her about the conversation.

"My father called to say he was sorry they couldn't come to Washington. My mother has been sick, and he didn't think she could make the trip, but they will try to come in a couple of months. He put my mother on the phone, and she said she thought she'd be feeling better soon."

Kelly was relieved they were still alive. "That's great that they're okay," she said, trying to put on an optimistic front.

"You are so smart about some things, Kelly, and so stupid about others."

"Listen, Xiang, believe what you want, but I am tired of wasting time with you. Here is your situation. I will explain it clearly. I have arranged with my government to give you a new life under the witness protection program. We will resettle you with a new identification, even plastic surgery if you would like, anywhere in the United Sates—your choice. In order to have this, all you have to do is to tell me what you've been involved in and who the conduit is. And by disclosing those facts, you will be getting revenge on Liu."

"I won't tell you anything," Xiang said defiantly.

Kelly had held out the carrot for Xiang, but it hadn't worked. It was time for the stick.

"Fine, that's your choice," she replied. "Then let me tell you the alternative."

When Xiang didn't respond, Kelly continued. "I'll be going back to Washington, but other agents will remain here with you. For one month, you can remain in this house. They will have food for you—eat or not, that's your decision. At the end of thirty days, if you're not willing to talk to me, we will give you a powerful sedative and place you on a plane to Beijing. We will inform your embassy that we have repatriated you, and give them your flight number. I'm sure they will have a welcome party waiting for you at the airport."

When he still didn't respond, she stood up, adding, "Enjoy the comfort of this house, because you won't experience anything like it when you return to China."

Then she left the room.

Washington

After returning to Washington, Kelly was feeling despair. She had failed to persuade Xiang to tell her about the current spy operation and to identify the conduit. She immediately convened a meeting of the task force.

In the conference room, Wilkins looked tense. "Listen," he said, "we have a crisis going on involving new Russian threats to Poland. I have to get back to the White House ASAP. I hope this is important."

"It is," Kelly said. In a somber voice, cracking with emotion, she reported to Wilkins, Paul, and Farrell, what had happened in Charlottesville. "I'm so sorry," she said at the end. "I've failed you."

"Failed us how?" Farrell said.

"I couldn't get Xiang to talk."

"Don't be ridiculous," Farrell replied. "You played it brilliantly. I've been in the same situation with prisoners before. Giving them time to make up their mind to cooperate is precisely the right thing to do. It lets them feel as if they're making the decision. And you held out the threat of repatriation to China. In my situation, I threatened shipment to Guantanamo. It's the same principle."

"Xiang refused to eat," Kelly added.

"He's no ideologue," Farrell replied with a shrug. "He'll eat. And he'll come around. My guess is that it will take about three weeks. I assume you'll have Rolfe watching him closely and keeping you informed?"

"Correct," Kelly confirmed. She couldn't think of another way to find out who the conduit was, and after what Farrell said she was hopeful Xiang would come around. "Okay," she continued. "Let's suspend our operation while we wait for Xiang to break. We can all do other work in the meantime."

"That makes sense," Paul said.

"I'm in agreement," Wilkins added. "Meantime, anything new on the Peterson surveillance or the other documents?"

"Not a thing," Kelly replied.

"If Xiang doesn't talk," Wilkins said, looking at Kelly, "we won't have a damn thing to show for all this effort."

"Thank you, George, for expressing it so succinctly."

When the meeting broke up, Kelly needed a change of pace and a release from the tension. She went for a run along the mall, but she couldn't stop thinking about Xiang. She wanted to believe Farrell was right, and that Xiang would come around. But deep down, she was worried. His attachment to his parents was so great that it had led to their breakup in college. He would do everything possible to keep them alive, and that meant staying silent.

She was prepared to wait a month, hoping Farrell's prediction panned out. In the meantime, she had to address her father and his lies about his dismissal from the CIA. Julie would be at school tomorrow, so it seemed like as good a time as any to talk to him alone.

She called him and said, "We have to talk. How about your house tomorrow at one?"

"Sounds ominous," he replied.

She didn't respond.

Chevy Chase, Maryland

Before getting out of the car on Leland Street the next day, Kelly glanced in the rearview mirror. She looked sad and unhappy. That matched her mood.

"I made some sandwiches," her dad said when she walked in. "Turkey and Swiss cheese. Let's go in the kitchen and talk."

When they were seated at the table, he said, "What's wrong?"

She took a gulp of water, cautioning herself to present this calmly and unemotionally. Sure, she was upset, but that wasn't the issue; it was his lies.

"One of the members of my task force is from the CIA. When we were at dinner one night in Saint Michaels he asked me if I was related to Charles Cameron, and he told me what really happened on your last mission with Fritz Helfund."

She watched her father carefully, but he showed no emotion, looking at her and waiting to hear what came next.

"What did he say?" he finally asked.

"That you were fired from the agency as a result of that operation. His account was so different from what you had told me that I was sure he was wrong, so I asked him to send me the file. He forwarded the judge's decision from the administrative hearing related to your termination. I couldn't believe what I read."

"Continuing with that operation and going across the border was a difficult decision for me."

"I understand that," said Kelly. "I also understand that you were on the ground and believed you were justified in disobeying orders coming from Langley. Of course I know that operations go wrong. I don't care about those things. It's the lies you've told me all these years. How could you have done that?"

He looked at the floor, his expression sad. When a minute had gone by and he had yet to respond, she continued. "I thought we had a relationship based on honesty and trust, and now I realize it's all based on lies. How could you have done that to me?"

He took a deep breath and said, "I had to fabricate that story because of your mother."

"What do you mean?" Kelly asked.

"She was never happy about me being in the CIA. I was always downplaying the risks for her, telling her I had a desk job in the safety of US headquarters in West Germany. If she had ever found out I was lying to her, it would have been the end of our marriage. That's why I never fought the agency's decision to terminate me—it would have blown up the whole affair and she would have found out how dangerous my work really was. I couldn't let that happen. So even though I believed, and my CIA counsel concurred, that I had a good chance of reversing their decision to terminate me, I didn't fight it. I walked away from the agency in silence."

Recalling her parents' battles about her dad's work, Kelly realized what he said made sense. Her mother was constantly urging him to quit and take "a safe job" in his father's candy business. But that didn't excuse him with her.

"How about after Mother's death? You should have told me then— especially when I went into national security affairs. You had to know that sooner or later someone would tell me and I'd look like a fool."

"You're right," he agreed. "I'm sorry I didn't tell you after your mother died. Really, I am."

From the sound of his voice, she didn't believe he was sorry. "There's a 'but,' isn't there?" she asked.

"Yeah," he said reluctantly. "Now I'm being perfectly honest. I didn't want you to know that I left the agency in disgrace. I didn't want you to be disappointed in me. Most parents don't want their children to be disappointed in them."

"If you had explained the circumstance to me, don't you think I would have understood?"

He shrugged. "I didn't think so. You're much more of a straight arrow than I am. You follow the orders of your superiors. Also, you would have been upset that I was responsible for the death of Fritz Helfund, a valuable scientist."

"That's ridiculous," she said, raising her voice. "Those explanations don't justify the lies you told me for so many years. I thought there was more to our relationship. Obviously, I was wrong."

"I believed I was doing the right thing," he maintained.

"You were treating me like a fool," countered Kelly, shaking her head. "You could have explained that you were trying to give Fritz Helfund a new life and freedom, and that you were willing to risk your life for him."

For a full minute, he didn't respond. Then he said, "You're absolutely right. I realize now that I was wrong, and I'm sincerely sorry. I hope you'll forgive me."

She thought about his words and Julie's relationship with him. "I have to," she replied. "You're the only family I have."

He seemed relieved. "Not meaning to change the subject, but let me point out the parallel to your situation now."

"What do you mean?" Kelly inquired.

"You just said that I was trying to give Fritz Helfund a new life and freedom. Isn't that what you're trying to do for Xiang?"

PART III

May, the Following Month

Beijing

Sitting in his office smoking cigarette after cigarette, Liu had thought long and hard about the consequences of Xiang's seizure by the Americans for Operation New World Order. He was persuaded that having Xiang's father call Xiang to let him know they were still alive would convince Xiang not to talk. However, regardless of what Xiang did, Liu was convinced everything could still proceed as planned. Xiang only knew the identity of the conduit, not the source, and Liu had a way to protect the source. Besides, they were already in the next phase, and he didn't want to turn back.

Liu did have one problem, and that was President Yao. Though Yao only paid attention to the Chinese media, he would no doubt learn of the Dulles Airport incident and Xiang's seizure. If he didn't learn it from the media, the Chinese ambassador to Washington was scheduled to be in Beijing next week for a Party gathering. He might mention it to the president, who would be furious at Liu for not telling him. Still worse, in the kind of impulsive, irrational decision he sometimes made, Yao might shut down the operation. It would be far better for Liu to break the news to Yao himself. Then he would be able to add the appropriate spin. So with trepidation, he arranged a meeting with Yao at his office.

When Liu arrived, Yao was with his top science advisors reviewing plans for a space launch in two months to put Chinese men on the moon. Liu sat through the end of the meeting, noting how Yao was bursting with pride at what they hoped to achieve. Perhaps Yao would be less critical, Liu thought, since he was in such high spirits.

When the others had gone, Yao said, "You wanted to see me?"

"We've had a development in Operation New World Order."

Yao frowned. "More bad news obviously."

"The Americans have seized Xiang, who had been in charge of collecting the information missives from Andrew Martin."

"Will Xiang tell the Americans about Martin?" Yao asked.

"I have taken steps to preclude that. Nevertheless, I can't be positive."

Yao closed his eyes and rubbed his forehead. When he opened them, he said, "Won't this put our entire operation at risk? Perhaps it's better to call it off."

"I don't think so. We have made so much progress in the second phase."

"Will our American agent be willing to continue and stick with what he has promised?"

"I'm sure of it," Liu replied, presenting a confident veneer for which he had no basis.

Yao shook his head. He wasn't buying. "You will meet with him to make sure he's willing to continue," Yao ordered.

Liu didn't like that idea. Word of their meeting could leak out. He was trying to decide how to frame his response when Yao resumed speaking.

"Do you have any leverage over our source, so that he won't walk away and he'll do what he promised?" Yao asked.

Liu shook his head. "I am convinced of it from talking to him."

"That's not enough," Yao snapped. "You need leverage. Figure out how to get it. You and the American have the most to lose if Operation New World Order fails. He will be sentenced to life in prison, and you will face a firing squad." Yao spoke in a cold voice that cut through Liu like a knife.

"I've always found," Yao continued, "that people perform better when they have an understanding of what is at stake for them."

Charlottesville and Washington

From the time she had left Charlottesville, Kelly stayed in close contact with Rolfe, who briefed her several times a day. On the second day in the safe house, Xiang resumed eating.

Xiang wanted to walk on the trails in the woods that surrounded the safe house, which Kelly approved. Xiang would be followed by two armed agents, one of whom had a Doberman on a leash.

Meantime, Kelly caught up on other work, receiving reports on possible operations being run by China. She had lengthy conversations with people in the San Francisco office. However, she also worked a shorter day, from nine to five thirty, which meant she could walk Julie to school in the morning. With Julie's help, Kelly also cooked dinner each evening.

On the weekends, she took Julie to the indoor pool at Kenwood Country Club, where her father was a member, and taught her how to dive. Her dad joined them on Sundays. After swimming, he rewarded Julie for her good diving with pizza, followed by a banana split at a local Bethesda Häagan-Dazs.

Kelly was trying to enjoy herself, but it was difficult. Each time Rolfe called, it increased her anxiety level. What if Xiang escaped? What if he decided not to talk as Farrell had predicted?

Calm down, she told herself. You've given him a month, and it's only been two weeks. Unfortunately, Kelly wasn't a patient person. She continually agonized over whether Xiang would talk. Each night she tossed in bed, imagining how awful she would feel putting Xiang on a plane back to China if he didn't talk.

Kelly continued like this for another week, watching Farrell's three week target pass. She was becoming increasingly depressed as she started to truly believe that Xiang would never break.

Then, on day twenty-five, Rolfe called her at her office at three in the afternoon. "Xiang wants to talk to you," the agent said tersely.

"Good, I'm on my way."

On the road in an unmarked FBI car, Kelly dared to hope Xiang would be willing to tell her what he knew and, most importantly, to identify the conduit. That was what Farrell had predicted would happen. She tried to tamp her excitement.

When she arrived, Xiang was sitting in a rocker on the verandah in the back of the house. Rolfe was there as well.

Kelly had a gun in her bag. She told Rolfe, "I can take over now."

He went back into the house and she sat in a wooden chair facing Xiang. "You wanted to talk to me?" she said.

"Yes, first let me explain why."

"Okay, I'm listening."

"My father is a peasant," Xiang began. "A simple man, without any education, but still wise. I never told him what I was doing in the United States, but somehow, he understood I was working for the State in security matters. He knows what the Party and its leaders are like. Mao is gone, but some things remain the same. He knows that anyone who works in the security area is always at great risk."

Kelly had no idea where Xiang was going with this, but she didn't interrupt.

"The last time I was home in January," Xiang continued, "my father took me outside his apartment building where we could talk freely. He told me he understood the State had given him and my mother a comfortable apartment at no cost and a payment each month because they represented the State's control over me. My father, who had never asked me for anything, made me promise that if I was ever faced with a choice between saving their lives or my own, I must choose my own. 'For many years we have lived comfortably, thanks to you, my son,' he told me, 'in a style we could never have afforded. You have most of your life ahead of you, but ours is behind us. If you do not choose life for yourself, I will never forgive you.'"

Xiang paused, then said, "You no doubt wonder why I'm telling you this."

"That's right," Kelly acknowledged.

"Because on the phone, when my father called me the last time you were here, he didn't just tell me my mother was sick and they couldn't come. He said, 'Remember when you were here in January? I took you outside and told you about your mother's health.' In fact, we had never discussed my mother's health. He was recalling the conversation we had in January to remind me of my promise. He was signaling that he and my mother were under Liu's control, and I should honor my promise to him and save myself. It took me this past month to decide I should honor my promise. It is horrible for a child to accept that he will be sentencing his parents to death."

Xiang wiped tears from his eyes. "In addition to my promise to my father," he continued, "I am also aware that if you were to put me on a plane to Beijing, all three of our lives would be over. So now I'm ready."

Kelly understood.

Xiang continued, "Tell me how your witness protection program works."

Though she was pulsing with excitement, Kelly kept calm. "We give you a new identity—birth certificate, driver's license, Social Security card. Credit cards, for which you have to pay the bills of course. Plastic surgery to touch up your face if you want it. And you pick the place. Anywhere in the US that you want to live, we'll buy you a house there. It will be in your name, fully paid off, no mortgage. And we'll give you some cash to get you started until you get a job. That's pretty much it."

"And what do I have to do in order to get all this?" Xiang asked.

"Tell me everything about the spy operations you've been involved with in the United States and identify the conduit in the newest operation."

In silence, Xiang rocked his chair back and forth for a few minutes. Then he said, "I want this agreement in writing. I want it to include immunity from prosecution for any crime I may have committed up to this point, and I want it to be signed by a lawyer with the Department of Justice." Xiang apparently knew how the American legal system worked.

"I can arrange that," Kelly said with confidence. This was the deal Arthur Larkin had already approved in his office.

"Good. Do it. When I have the document in hand, I'll talk to you."

She called Paul and explained what she wanted. Fifteen minutes later, the document was faxed over with Paul's signature. She handed it to Xiang, who read the document and nodded.

"Let's go inside to talk," Kelly said.

They sat down across from each other at the dining room table. Kelly took a recorder out of her bag and placed it on the table. She also took out her iPad to take notes.

For the next hour and a half, Xiang spoke, interrupted occasionally by Kelly. He began with his birth in a small town in Western China, then covered his recruitment by Liu.

"Liu directed me to apply to three American universities," Xiang explained. "I was admitted to all three, and chose Carnegie Mellon. At CMU, Liu must have had someone watching me, maybe another student. That was probably how he found out about us. When I went back to China to visit my parents before joining you in New York, I was taken to Liu's office. He said if I went back to the US, married you, and defected, he would kill my parents. I had no doubt he meant it. They were his hostages. Liu had made an investment in me, and he wasn't about to lose it."

He stopped talking and looked at her. "Believe me, Kelly, when I say I was very much in love with you. Breaking off our relationship was incredibly painful. It was the hardest thing I have ever done."

She believed him. He had chosen his parents' lives over his relationship with her. Could she blame him for that?

"Tell me about your operation with Senator Jasper," Kelly said.

Xiang explained how Jasper had passed secret information to him that he had obtained as chairman of the Armed Services Committee. "The operation went awry when Vanessa threatened Jasper with the CD," he said.

Xiang also told Kelly about his involvement with Allison leading up to Jasper's murder. Kelly knew most of this, but it was still useful to let Xiang set forth the entirety of the operation.

"I killed Jasper in Rock Creek Park. I put the gun and Jasper's wallet in a storage locker in the basement of our embassy."

"What happened after that?" Kelly asked.

"I killed Jasper in November. I didn't hear anything further from Minister Liu until January, two months later, when he asked me to fly to Beijing. He wanted me to play a critical role in a new operation in Washington, which was similar to the Jasper operation though somewhat different."

"Different how?"

"This time I would not know the source of the intelligence, I would be getting it from a conduit. No dawn meetings in the park, instead I would be going to the office of an important Washington lawyer who did legal work for the embassy. It would be natural for me to be there, since my official title was assistant economic attaché. The lawyer would call me each time I was to come to his office, then when I arrived, he would hand me an unmarked envelope. I have no idea what was inside any of the envelopes. I took them to the embassy and placed them in the diplomatic pouch to be opened only by Minister Liu."

"How many of these meetings did you have with this lawyer?"

"Eight all together."

"Over what period of time?"

"The first was in January," Xiang recalled. "The last was a week before the April incident over the East China Sea.

"And since then have you had any contact with this lawyer?"

"No."

"What is the lawyer's name?" Kelly asked, leaning forward in her chair.

Xiang looked over the document he had gotten from Paul. They had reached the moment of truth. Xiang no doubt recognized, Kelly thought, he was about to surrender the only chip he had left. She hoped he wasn't having buyer's remorse.

"Andrew Martin," Xiang blurted out.

Kelly sat up with a start. Martin was not only one of the most prominent lawyers in Washington, but he had been heavily involved in the Jasper affair. With the Chinese government as his client, it made sense he would be the conduit.

But the disclosure was only valuable, Kelly realized, if she could use it to ascertain the mole. That was the information they really needed.

*   *   *

At ten o'clock the following morning, Kelly convened a meeting of the task force. Everyone came, even Wilkins, although he grumbled about the short notice.

While Kelly gave a detailed report of her discussion with Xiang, Wilkins frowned and Paul looked angry. She didn't know whether it was at her for accusing Martin, or at Martin himself. Farrell, at least, was nodding with approval. The minute she finished, she had her answer.

"That dirty bastard, Martin," Paul burst out. "He's worse than I ever thought."

Kelly was relieved to hear his words. "I want to arrest Martin," she said. "Haul him down to jail. After he spends a night behind bars, he'll identify the source of the info he was passing to Xiang."

"Arrest him for what?" Wilkins asked.

"Espionage."

Wilkins shook his head emphatically. "You have to be kidding. I'm no lawyer and even I know you don't have a damn bit of evidence to justify that. All you have is the word of a spy and a murderer. Besides, Xiang has no idea what was in the envelopes he was receiving from Martin. Martin would blast our case out of the water in about three seconds. He'd never spend an hour in jail. He'd find a friendly judge to give him a hearing and then we'd end up with egg on our faces."

Kelly felt like a kid whose balloon had just been punctured. "So what do you propose we do?" she asked.

Before Wilkins had a chance to respond, Paul said, "Well, I learned a lot practicing law with Martin. Now I want to use some of those lessons."

"Like what?" Farrell asked.

"Anatole France, who Martin was always fond of, once wrote, 'The best evidence is perjured evidence.' Martin used to tell me if we don't have either the facts or the law on our side, then we have to skew the facts—just enough to get the job done."

"Could you please speak English instead of that legal gobbledygook?" Kelly requested.

"Okay," Paul said. "Here's what we should do. You and I go see Martin at his home this evening. You'll be carrying a pair of handcuffs, telling Martin we're here to arrest him for espionage."

"Then what?"

"When Martin demands to know what evidence we have," Paul continued, "I tell him that Xiang is prepared to testify that Martin handed him envelopes containing classified information, knowing full well that Xiang would pass them on to Minister Liu. Xiang opened the envelopes before putting them in the pouch to make sure they contained the information Liu wanted. Xiang told us that the last installment contained the memo from Camp David stating the US would not intervene on the side of Japan in a dispute over the islands."

"You'd be willing to tell him that?" Kelly asked. "Knowing it's not true?"

"Of course," said Paul with a shrug. "I won't be in a courtroom, I'll be in his house. I can say anything I want as long as he believes me. And he will, because we know that top secret military material was in those envelopes he was passing to Xiang. It's not like he was passing on a list of DC's best restaurants."

Farrell laughed.

"After the way Martin treated Allison and me in dealing with Vanessa's murder," Paul continued, "I don't owe that prick a damn thing."

"But where are you going with this?" Wilkins asked, sounding skeptical.

"I know Martin," Paul replied, "he'll never take the fall to save the Chinese government or Liu. Once he hears what I have to say, and he sees Kelly standing next to him with handcuffs, he'll want to cut a deal. He's the quintessential deal maker, and he'll do what he has to in order to save his own ass."

"What do you want to offer him," Kelly asked, "in return for giving us the name of the mole?"

Paul thought about it for a minute, then said, "I had better talk to Arthur Larkin to see what we can offer him."

Paul pulled out his phone and dialed Arthur's number. Kelly heard him say, "This is Paul Maltoni. Can I speak to Attorney General Larkin? . . . Oh, okay . . . Yes, I understand."

Paul put down the phone and said, "Bad news. Arthur is on his way home from Moscow. His plane arrives at 11:10 this evening, so we'll have to wait until tomorrow morning."

"I don't want to wait," Kelly said.

"Okay," Paul told her. "You and I will confront Martin this evening. We'll see what he's seeking, then I'll tell him that I'll check with Arthur and get back to him in the morning."

Wilkins stood and looked at Farrell, "Are you on board with this deceitful plan of Paul's?"

"Absolutely," Farrell affirmed.

"Well, for the record," Wilkins said, "I'm opposed. I can't believe the three of you want to do all this to Martin based on Xiang's word. Talk about presuming somebody is guilty. Now I have to get back to the White House."

When he was gone, Farrell said, "Has that guy ever supported anything we wanted to do?"

"I can't think of one," Kelly replied.

"Do you think Wilkins is the mole?" Paul asked.

"From observing his demeanor with us," Farrell responded, "I would say it's unlikely. But let's keep peeling the onion. He may be at the rotten core."

"I agree with that," Kelly said.

"But meantime, I have a problem with the plan for Martin," Farrell added.

"What's that?" Paul asked.

"If Xiang's right about Martin being the conduit for a Beijing spy operation, after you confront him, he might take off during the night, hop a plane to Beijing, and we'll never see him again. That's what Philby did."

"To prevent that, we should take him into custody overnight," Kelly said.

"I have a better idea," Paul responded. "We put guards at his house overnight and we tell him that if he tries to leave the house, they'll arrest him."

"I don't like it," Kelly said.

"Why not?"

"Too risky. What's wrong with putting him in jail overnight? It'll be late. He'll never get a judge to spring him."

"I know Martin," Paul said stubbornly. "We'll have a much better chance of him cooperating if we leave him at home."

Kelly still didn't like it, but she reluctantly deferred to Paul. "Okay, we'll do it your way. I just hope to hell we don't lose him."

"Don't worry, we won't," Paul insisted.

Hong Kong

Liu had to create leverage over the American mole. That was what President Yao had demanded. After wracking his brain and coming up empty, Liu decided he needed help. He had only one place to turn: Andrei. That meant a trip to Hong Kong.

On the plane, Liu thought about Andrei Mikhailovich. The Russian was a former power in the KGB and then in the FSB until he had a falling out with President Fyodor Kuznov. Once he learned that Kuznov had directed a group of thugs to kill him, Andrei shifted all of the money he'd stolen from Russia to banks in Singapore, Switzerland, and Andorra. Then he bribed a pilot to fly him to Singapore. From there, he got to Macau, which was where he had arranged to meet Liu for the first time. Both men loved to gamble, and Andrei just happened to be at the craps table of the "invitation only" high rollers room in the back of the casino at the Mandarin Oriental Hotel when Liu was playing.

The deal they struck was simple: Liu agreed to give the Russian a secure hideaway to avoid the killers Kuznov had sent for him. Andrei, in turn, agreed to help Liu reshape China's MSS along the lines of the KGB. He had also informed Liu about his past work and what he knew from friends in the FSB regarding what was inside Kuznov's kimono. The hideaway Liu had prepared for Andrei was a walled compound in Hong Kong, formerly the residence of a powerful British industrialist during the days when Britain called the tune there. Though Andrei had escaped with billions from Russia's treasury, Liu paid the expenses for the Hong Kong villa and supplied it with two gorgeous Chinese women, as Andrei had requested.

"Why two?" Liu had asked.

"One for three nights every week."

"There are seven nights. You're planning to rest on Sunday?"

The Russian had laughed. "No, I'll have them both together on the Lord's Day."

"Whatever you want," Liu had said. "I take care of my friends."

Andrei had also promised always to be available if Liu wanted to talk. So when Liu had called earlier that day, Andrei had said, "What time does your plane get to Hong Kong?"

"Around 6:30 p.m."

"Come right to Happy Valley. The first race is at 7:15. They have some outstanding horses running tonight. My box is 22. We can talk there in privacy and eat well. If we're lucky, we'll take home a little cash. What could be better?"

Liu liked that plan. He loved everything about Happy Valley Racecourse—the crowds, the skillful jockeys, the physical beauty of the location, and the magnificent horses. The only thing he didn't like was that the track had been opened by the British in 1846. He hated the British and the humiliation they had inflicted on China. Well, that was over now. China was close to being the dominant world power and the British were on life support.

When Liu entered the box, which was closed off by glass walls and a wooden door, he saw Andrei holding a racing paper and studying the track below.

"The first race is about to begin," Andrei said.

"Is there still time to bet?"

"Yeah, but you don't want to. My rule is that I only bet on races where I know something the unwashed masses don't."

"Sounds like a strategy," Liu remarked.

"Wait for the third race," Andrei advised, "then bet the farm on Noble House. Meantime, let's eat."

"Good, I'm hungry."

Andrei ordered lavishly. They had scallops, Peking duck, and a smoked pork dish with garlic shoots, all full of the bright, nuanced flavors and textures of Hong Kong cuisine. Then they washed everything down with cold Tsingtaos. After dinner, Liu lit up a cigarette.

Andrei told him, "You did a good job of putting down the protests in January. It's been quiet since."

"That's what I hear," said Liu.

"The only way to stop those people is with live ammunition. Nothing else works. I'm glad you realized that."

They talked for a while about the long-term future of Hong Kong. "Now that Shanghai is a financial center, Hong Kong has become redundant," Liu said.

Andrei agreed.

"Time to bet the third race," the Russian said.

They each put up 100,000 RMB on Noble House to win. The horse went off at 8 to 1. Noble House started slow. Though Andrei had never let him down, Liu was feeling a bit anxious.

"Jockey's holding him back," Andrei said.

By the time they rounded the final turn, Noble House was coming up on the outside. Then he took the lead and never lost it, thundering down the track at the finish three lengths ahead of the second horse.

After the race, a young woman delivered their winnings.

"Thank you, Andrei," Liu said.

Andrei nodded. "Okay, now let's talk business. Why'd you want to see me?"

While Andrei sipped his beer, Liu spoke for half an hour, describing what had happened in Operation New World Order. Andrei was familiar with the operation, having approved it before Liu presented it to Yao. Liu also told Andrei about his latest meeting with Yao.

"The Americans snatching Xiang is an unfortunate complication," Liu said.

"True, but you played it right with his parents," said Andrei.

"I wanted to shoot them myself," Liu seethed.

"Of course you did. Nevertheless, you were smart to keep them alive."

"At this point, it seems to be working," Liu acknowledged. "I haven't heard anything to suggest Xiang has talked to the Americans."

"Even if he does, I assume you have the firewall around Martin we discussed."

"Correct, she's in place. Still, I have the question of whether I meet with the mole again, as Yao suggested, or not. I want to know your opinion."

Andrei thought about it for a few seconds, then said, "Yao is setting you up to take the fall if Operation New World goes bad. Meet with the American at some neutral site in Western Europe. It's essential to protect yourself."

Liu was puzzled. "How? I don't understand."

"If the mole is reluctant to continue after what happened to Xiang, you have to abort the operation."

"Even if he is willing to continue now, he could still change his mind later on."

"That's where Yao's suggestion is right on the mark," said Andrei. "You need leverage over the mole to prevent him from walking away."

"Tell me how to create that leverage."

"Establish an account in a Caribbean bank in the mole's name. Deposit ten million dollars, with the funds coming from a Chinese bank, preferably one controlled by the PLA. Don't tell the American about it. Forge his signature electronically on the documents opening the account. Later, if you think he intends to turn on you or go back on your deal, threaten to disclose the existence of the account to the American media. If they discover it, they will conclude that he was accepting money from the Chinese government. No one will believe he didn't know about the account. He'll have to do what you want to avoid the disclosure."

Liu thought the idea was brilliant, and he told Andrei that. A waitress brought them two more beers.

When she was gone, Andrei said, "You have another problem besides the American."

"What's that?"

"The blond woman directing the FBI investigation, the one who met with Xiang in the park and managed to snatch him away from your people—she's a real threat. You have to go after her and block her investigation."

Liu wasn't surprised to hear Andrei's advice. Intimidating and coercing prosecutors and investigators with brute force was a typical Russian move.

"I would prefer not to do that except as a last resort," said Liu. "It raises political complications for Yao."

"As you wish. But I've always found that if you want to stop a snake, it's best to cut off its head."

Liu nodded. Andrei, as usual, was right. He would go after Kelly.

As Liu was preparing to leave, Andrei said, "I have a little gift for you, something else to give you additional leverage over the American. This will make your trip to Hong Kong even more worthwhile."

"What's that?" Liu asked eagerly.

"I still keep in touch, very discretely of course, with one of my former KGB buddies who's with the FSB now. He hates Kuznov as much as I do."

"And?"

Andrei reached into his pocket and pulled out a picture of a gorgeous, buxom blond woman, completely naked, facing and posing for the camera. He handed it to Liu.

"Who is she?" Liu asked.

Andrei smiled as he began to explain.

Washington

At nine in the evening, Kelly drove to Martin's house with Paul in the front seat. The skies had opened up an hour before they left, and the windshield wipers were working furiously in the blinding rainstorm. The prediction was for two days of hard rain in the Washington area.

Kelly had decided to let Paul take the lead in confronting Martin. He knew the man, and he was a lawyer. Late in the afternoon, Paul had suggested to Kelly that he call Martin's secretary, Alice, to find out if Martin was in town and would be home that evening. Kelly vetoed the idea for fear of tipping off Martin and having him flee. "If he's not home, we'll park and wait near his house," she said. "Sooner or later he'll come home."

She had been busy making sure everything was ready before they left the FBI for Martin's house. Besides reporting to Forester, she had set up a tap on Martin's house phone and a monitor for any call or email to or from the house. Out of an abundance of caution, she asked Rolfe and another agent to follow her to Martin's house. They would monitor surveillance while she and Paul were in the house.

Driving north on Foxhall Road, its large stately homes set back from the road, they passed the Field School, then a museum housing the late David Lloyd Kreeger's art collection. Kelly saw lights on both upstairs and on the ground floor as they approached Martin's house. That told her someone was probably in the house. Hopefully, it was Martin. But she had to know before they went in.

She dialed Martin's home phone. A man answered. She heard him say, "Yes?" in a terse voice.

"I'd like to speak with Andrew Martin."

"I'm Andrew Martin."

"I'm with a charity that—"

Click. The phone went down.

"Showtime, Paul. Let's go."

Paul led the way with Kelly following two steps behind, a gun holstered at her waist and handcuffs in the pocket of her raincoat. Following their script, Paul rang the bell.

"Who's there?" Martin called from inside the house.

"Paul Maltoni."

The door opened and Paul quickly entered, Kelly close behind. Looking around, she saw a table in the living room with a chessboard. On one side sat an Asian woman. Judging from the board, they were in the middle of a game.

"What are you doing here, Paul?" Martin asked. "And who's she?"

Kelly pulled her FBI ID from her raincoat pocket and showed it to him. "Kelly Cameron, FBI, Mr. Martin." She put it back into her pocket and pulled out the handcuffs. Following their script, she said, "We're here to arrest you for espionage."

"You're what?" a startled Martin asked.

She repeated, "We're here to arrest you for espionage."

Martin looked at the terrified woman sitting next to the chessboard and said, "Huan, why don't you go upstairs? These people have made a mistake. It's nothing. I'll sort it out with them."

The woman got up and left, climbing the staircase rapidly.

Martin turned back to Kelly and Paul. "Why don't the two of you take off your coats and sit down. We can talk about this. And for God's sake, put away those handcuffs. You certainly won't need them."

Standing in the living room, Kelly and Paul took off their coats, but Kelly kept the handcuffs in her grasp. She unbuttoned the jacket of her pantsuit to reveal the gun holstered at her hip.

"You two want a drink?" Martin asked. "Maybe a glass of wine, Paul? Some of that Saint-Joseph you like?"

He's smooth, Kelly thought, just as Paul had warned her. That was, no doubt, how he had gained Allison's confidence.

"Listen, Andrew," Paul said forcefully, "this isn't a social visit."

"Then why are you here?" Martin asked.

"As Kelly said, to arrest you for espionage."

Martin looked bewildered. "You're kidding, right?"

"Look, Andrew," Paul said. "Don't play games with us. We have a witness, Xiang Shen, who's prepared to testify that on eight separate occasions you called and asked him to come to your office. There, you gave him an envelope to forward to Liu Guan, the Chinese minister of state security. Before sending the envelopes, Xiang examined the contents. Inside were copies of classified US defense documents. The last one contained a memo from a Camp David gathering at which a decision was made not to respond militarily if China should attack Japan over the islands in the East China Sea. This is enough evidence to arrest you for espionage. We will now be taking you into custody. Kelly, you won't need the handcuffs. Andrew, get your coat, you're coming with us."

Through the corner of her eye, Kelly noticed the Asian woman, mostly concealed, crouched near the top of the stairs, no doubt listening. Kelly made eye contact with her, and she quickly disappeared from Kelly's sight.

"Don't be in such a hurry," Martin said. "Let's sit down and talk about this."

Kelly thought about Paul's words this afternoon. Martin was "the quintessential deal maker." So far, it was playing out exactly as Paul had predicted. He knew Martin well.

"I'm getting a scotch," Martin said. "You two sure you don't want a drink?"

They both shook their heads.

Martin fixed a scotch from the cart, pointed to chairs in the living room, and the three sat down.

"Now, Paul, let's talk about this like a couple of lawyers," Martin said. "You don't really have a case based on what this fellow Xiang told you."

"Why not?"

"For starters, he's a member of the Chinese diplomatic corps in the US and has diplomatic immunity. He could easily leave the country and you couldn't stop him. If he wanted to stay and testify, the Chinese could persuade the State Department to release him into their custody and they would send him back to China. I know Jane Prosser, the secretary of state, very well. That's what she'll do. Then, poof, your case is gone."

"I disagree," Paul said firmly. "These charges are so serious that Prosser would never sweep them under the rug. Jane Prosser may have once been a friend of yours, but I'll bet she's not too wild about you after you lied to her to get her to call off the DC police when Allison was attacked in the DuPont Circle Metro Station in November. And neither President Braddock nor Arthur Larkin is a big supporter of yours."

Kelly saw Martin cringe. It was definitely a break in the veneer. Paul charged ahead. "This isn't some small matter like a scuffle at the DuPont Circle Metro. That time you could persuade Prosser to do what you wanted, but not anymore."

"I never—" Martin started.

"C'mon, Andrew," Paul cut in. "Don't try to bullshit me. Besides espionage, we will be charging you with conspiracy in the murder of Senator Jasper."

"Are you crazy?" Martin sputtered. "Wes was one of my best friends."

"He may have been, but Allison Boyd is prepared to testify that before Jasper was murdered, she gave you the CD her sister had made of Liu's conversation with Jasper. You destroyed it, and we have enough circumstantial evidence to prove you tipped off the Chinese about the CD, which led to Jasper's murder. You're going down for that as well, Andrew. Two trials, two convictions."

Watching Martin's face as Paul had been pouring it on, Kelly thought that Martin was shaken. His bravado was gone. She understood why Paul was a good lawyer. He spoke clearly, forcefully, and persuasively.

"Perhaps, we can work something out," Martin said.

"I'm listening," Paul replied.

"I don't want this to be recorded."

"It isn't being recorded," Kelly said.

"If you give me your word on that, Paul, I'll accept it," said Martin.

"You have my word."

"All right." Martin took a deep breath. "What you really want is the name of the US official who provided me with the envelopes I turned over to Xiang, correct?"

"That's right," Paul acknowledged.

"I'll give you his name. In return, I get immunity from prosecution for espionage as well as the events surrounding Jasper's murder."

His words were music to Kelly's ears. She didn't care squat about Martin. All she cared about was the identity of the mole. She would have grabbed the deal in a second, but Paul had one big constraint: he needed Arthur Larkin's approval.

"That's a ridiculous opening position," Paul said.

"It's not an opening position, it's the only deal I'll make," Martin replied.

"You're asking for a lot."

"And giving even more in return."

"It's not my decision."

"I'm aware of that," said Martin. "I'm happy to meet with Arthur and present it to him myself."

Paul shook his head. "That's my job."

"I understand Arthur has issues with me," Martin remarked.

"You can't blame him," said Paul with a shrug.

"Will you recommend it to Arthur?"

Paul looked at Kelly. She nodded.

"Yes, I will," he said. "I should have an answer for you in the morning."

"You'll spend tonight in jail," Kelly said. "You'll have your own private cell."

She realized she was going back on the arrangement she and Paul had made, but she didn't trust Martin. This lawyer was too slick. He could still have something else up his sleeve. Even as she said the words, she realized Paul had the final word. It was a legal issue.

Martin shot to his feet. "Screw that! The deal is off. You can prove your case in court, Paul."

Paul glanced at her, then turned back to Martin. "We'll strike a compromise," he said. "You turn over your passport, and we'll have agents watching your house until we get back in the morning. If you try to leave before we return, they'll arrest you. That's what we'll do."

Kelly bit her tongue and didn't say a word.

Martin said to Kelly, "I'm going into the study to get my passport. You want to follow me?"

"Yes." And she did.

When they left Martin's house, the heavy rain was still falling. She got into the back of Rolfe's car and told the two agents what they had agreed on. "If Martin leaves the house before I return, arrest him," Kelly instructed. "Sorry to do this to you in the rain, but one of you will have to watch the back entrance to the house. The other one can watch the front of the house from the car."

"Don't worry, we'll take turns," Rolfe said.

"You want me to get a second team?" Kelly asked.

"We can handle it."

She got into her own car. Paul was already there.

"I thought we agreed we wouldn't arrest Martin tonight," he said. "You went back on that."

"I don't trust him."

"You made your point. It's my ass on the line." He sounded angry. She chalked it up to the tension and what they had at stake.

"Where do you want me to drop you?" she asked.

"My house in Georgetown, so I can pick up my car. When you were talking to Rolfe, I called Arthur's house. His wife is expecting him home around midnight. As soon as I told her that I needed to speak with him about an urgent matter, she told me to come over and wait for him at the house."

"Okay. I'll take you to your place. Call me when you're finished with Arthur, no matter how late."

"Will do."

Kelly suddenly felt weary. The adrenalin rush she had experienced in Martin's house had dissipated. She was uncomfortable leaving Martin at home overnight. In her gut, she believed they had made a mistake, and that they should have taken him to jail. But she didn't argue with Paul anymore. It would be futile. Besides, it was done. She just hoped that it wouldn't come back to bite them.

Washington

As Martin closed the door behind Kelly and Paul, he realized he was in deep trouble. However, he was confident he could cut a deal. If Paul couldn't get Arthur to agree, Martin would do it himself. But it wouldn't be easy. On the other hand, he had something they desperately wanted: the identity of the mole.

That was only one of Martin's problems. The other was Huan. After he had told her to go upstairs, he had seen her peeking out to listen. That, in addition to the suspicious phone call she had made when General Cartwright had been there to watch the primary, had him worried.

But he didn't want to be paranoid. Perhaps she had been listening because serious charges had been made against a man she cared for deeply. Still, it was far more likely in Martin's mind that she was Liu's plant. He had to know for sure.

Martin called upstairs to Huan, "They're gone now, you can come down."

When she returned to the living room, she looked worried. "Are you okay, Andrew? Those people accused you of a serious crime."

"It was all a mistake," he said smoothly. "They apologized. No cause for concern. They mixed me up with another Washington lawyer."

"Well, I'm glad to hear that."

"Enough about all this nonsense. You know what I'd like?"

"No. Tell me."

"You make the most incredible soufflés, and that's really an art. Last week your Grand Marnier was fabulous. Would you do that again?"

"Now?" Huan asked.

"Sure, it's still early. And I'll open up a half bottle of Château d'Yquem Sauterne, the nectar of the gods. That will go perfectly with the soufflé. What do you think?"

"Sure."

"Great. You get the soufflé ready and I'll go up and shower."

Once Martin heard her busy in the kitchen, he went up the stairs.

Though they slept together in the master bedroom, she kept her clothes and other things in another bedroom and bath down the hall. Moving quickly, he looked through the drawers she used, then the closet. He didn't find anything suspicious.

He then went into her bathroom. She had showered before Paul and Kelly had come, and the floor was wet. He didn't see anything unusual on the sink. In the closet, he saw a black Tumi bag.

Martin took it out, placed it on the sink, and opened it. It had cosmetics, lotions, soaps, creams, and perfumes. That made sense, he thought.

Then he reached around inside the bag. At the bottom, he felt a zipper. Martin pushed aside the cosmetics and opened the bottom compartment. To his horror, he saw a syringe and a clear liquid in a small, unmarked bottle. Martin unscrewed the top, reached his finger inside, moistened it slightly, and touched it to his tongue. It tasted salty. Potassium chloride, he guessed, used to cause a heart attack when injected with a syringe.

He reached into the bottom compartment again and found a small bottle with three pills. Martin opened it and held it up to his nose. He detected the unmistakable odor of cyanide. Everything now fell into place. There was no doubt about it. *Huan was Liu's plant.*

Beijing

When his encrypted phone rang and Liu saw that Huan was calling, he quickly left a meeting with top military officers and went outside the conference room to the corridor.

"Yes?" he said.

"Xiang gave them Martin," she told him tersely.

"Will Martin cooperate with the American government?"

"He's willing to negotiate for immunity. It's unclear whether he will succeed."

Liu cursed under his breath. "I see."

"What do you want me to do?"

"Get rid of him. Call and tell me when it's done. Then get on the first plane to China."

"It will be done," she said. "I will call you in exactly one hour to report."

Huan was intelligent and tough. Liu had selected her carefully, and he fully expected her to succeed.

Washington

Staring at Huan's bag, Martin realized he had behaved stupidly with her. It should have been obvious to him that she was Liu's plant. From the moment she called to say she was coming to Washington, he should have had nothing to do with her. Unfortunately, he had been ruled by his libido.

"What are you doing, Andrew?"

Andrew whipped his head around and saw Huan standing in the doorway. He had been so absorbed by his discovery that he hadn't heard her coming up the stairs.

"Discovering why you're really here," Martin said, his voice quavering.

Huan had a terrifying, menacing look on her face. Martin clutched the Tumi bag as she moved toward him. She's going to kill me, he thought. She lifts weights, and she's strong.

Before she could act, he swung the bag at her face with all the force he could muster. It smashed against her nose and knocked her off balance. She fell to her knees on the wet floor.

Martin dropped the bag and tried to get out of the small bathroom, but she was blocking his way. She staggered to her feet and reached for his neck, as if to strangle him.

Before she could get a hold, he shoved both of his hands against her chest with all of his might, pushing her away. She slipped backwards and fell, her head smacking hard on the side of the bathtub.

Her body shook once, then it went still.

For a full two minutes, Martin was paralyzed. He stood staring at her, unable to move.

Then he walked over and checked her pulse.

She was dead!

Martin was shaking so badly that he could barely stand. What should he do now? He felt completely unglued, as though his mind were unraveling.

He thought about going outside to the FBI agents and telling them what had happened. Or calling 911. But he couldn't bring himself to do either of those things. It was as if his mind were frozen. He just wanted it all to go away.

He left the bathroom and closed the door, as if in a trance. Then he staggered down the stairs and went into the den. Grabbing a bottle of scotch, he collapsed on the floor against the couch, nursing the bottle as though it were his last chance for salvation.

Beijing

Still meeting with the generals, Liu checked his watch. Huan should have called five minutes ago. He had to assume she was either dead or that she had been taken into custody. He couldn't risk calling her for fear that her encrypted phone had fallen into the hands of the Americans. He wasn't worried that they would learn about earlier calls, since all info was deleted after the calls were concluded and could not be recovered. He also had to assume Martin would cut a deal with the Americans.

He remembered what Andrei had said. It was time to cut off the head of the snake, but not until after his Paris meeting. Only then would he know whether Operation New World Order was still viable. Still, he could take one action now. As soon as this meeting ended, he would call one of his aides and give him the order: Kill Xiang's parents.

Washington

Paul was dozing on a couch in the living room of Arthur Larkin's house on Tracy Place in the luxurious Kalorama area. Arthur's wife had gone to bed shortly after Paul arrived at 11 p.m.

Paul woke with a start as he heard the front door open. He sprang to his feet as Arthur walked in, disheveled after his long flight from Moscow. His hair was messy, his shirt open at the neck, and his shirttail hanging out in the back. He looked exhausted.

When he saw Paul, he did a double take. "Just what I was hoping to see when I got home," he said sarcastically.

"Well, sir, I wouldn't have come if it weren't urgent."

"I don't imagine you would have. Did your FBI friend Kelly pick the lock to let you in?"

"No, sir. Mrs. Larkin very graciously did."

"And this couldn't have waited until morning?" he said gruffly.

"I don't think so."

Arthur sighed. Then he took off his suit jacket and tossed it onto a chair. "I should be hospitable and offer you a drink."

"No thanks. Mrs. Larkin already did. I'll tell you what I came for and then go home and let you get some sleep."

"That would be considerate."

Arthur led Paul into his study. Once they were both seated and Arthur had a cognac, he asked Paul, "Okay. What's this about?"

"I suggest you take a good belt of that drink and grab the arms of your chair tightly," said Paul.

Arthur complied. "Go ahead."

"Remember how we hoped Xiang would identify the conduit for us?"

"Of course I remember, I don't have dementia. Not yet, at least. Although if I work with you a little longer, I might lose my mind. Who the hell is the conduit?"

"You ready for this? It's your old tennis buddy Andrew Martin."

Arthur stood up and flung the glass into the fireplace where it shattered into a myriad of pieces. "It wasn't bad enough that he made me look like a fool with Braddock last year when he was being considered for chief justice. Now you're telling me he's a spy for the Chinese?"

"Correct."

"We'll throw the book at Andrew Martin," Arthur seethed. "He'll go to jail for life. *No possibility of parole.* I'll argue at the sentencing hearing myself."

"With all due respect, sir, I don't think we should do that," reasoned Paul.

"Why the hell not?"

Paul repeated the same explanation he had given Kelly and Farrell that afternoon as to why they didn't have a case against Martin.

Arthur was shaking his head. "I'm not buying what you're saying."

"With all due respect, sir—"

"Stop staying that," Arthur cut in.

"Okay. The fact is we'll never be able to make a case against Martin."

"If you don't think you can prove the case, I'll give it to another lawyer."

Paul hesitated for a second, then took a deep breath as if he were preparing to plunge off a high diving board, or more accurately, get himself fired. Still, he had an obligation to tell the attorney general of the United States what he thought. "Sorry, sir but . . . I think your anger at Martin for what he did to you last November is clouding your judgment."

Arthur pointed a thick finger at Paul. "I don't give a shit what you think. Here's what you're going to do. Tomorrow morning at nine, you and Kelly will drive to Martin's house. You will arrest Andrew Martin and the two of you will take him to the courthouse. Time your arrival for ten o'clock. Once you call and tell me you've arrested him, I'll notify the press that I have an announcement. When you arrive at the courthouse, I will be standing in front with reporters and television cameras. They won't know why they've been summoned. As you lead Martin into the courthouse, they will film him and I will make a statement. That's what's going to happen."

"But it's more important we learn the name of the source leaking information to Martin," Paul protested. "And Martin's willing to give us that. I know Martin. If we arrest him, he'll never tell us."

"Oh don't worry, Paul," Arthur assured him. "He'll divulge the name of the mole after he's sat in jail without bail for a couple of days. Lest you think I'm being motivated solely by vindictiveness, let me tell you that I intend to cut a better deal with him than what he no doubt offered that you snapped up. I'll get the name out of Martin in return for a plea bargain with him doing a minimum of five years' jail time to avoid a life sentence for espionage."

When Paul didn't respond, Arthur added, "I am old, tired, angry, and vindictive. Nevertheless, this is still a better result for the United States and more satisfying for Arthur Larkin. Now go home and get some sleep. We don't want you to have bags under your eyes in front of the TV cameras."

"I have another idea," Paul said.

"I hope this is better than the last one."

"Well, here it is. You give Martin only conditional immunity."

"Conditional?"

"Yeah. He only gets it if he not only gives us the name of the mole, but helps us build a tight case against that individual, too. Meantime, we keep him under house arrest."

Paul could tell Arthur was considering his new proposal. He decided to push. "Believe me Arthur, I'm not trying to help Martin. I loathe the guy after the way he treated me and Allison. I just honestly don't think we have a strong case against him. To bring it and lose before a jury would be a disaster. And you know juries."

"Okay, okay. Enough," said Arthur, waving his hand. "Tell you what, I'm reserving judgment. I'll meet you and Kelly at Martin's house tomorrow morning at eight. I want to confront the bastard myself. Then I'll decide what to do."

Miami

Despite meeting with supporters until midnight, plus another hour in a hotel bar with a couple of reporters, General Cartwright was up at 5:30 in the morning. After a glass of orange juice and a cup of black coffee, he put on running clothes and met Chris Mallory for a run along the trail that paralleled the ocean.

Cartwright loved his early morning runs with Mallory and tried not to miss a day. Mallory, a former Air Force captain and pilot, had been Cartwright's aide when the general had been chairman of the Joint Chiefs. When Cartwright had resigned from the military to run for president, Mallory had resigned as well to serve Cartwright in his new role. Mallory was also Cartwright's private pilot, flying the plane Cartwright used for the campaign.

Cartwright particularly enjoyed running with Mallory because his thirty-three-year-old aide didn't talk unless Cartwright addressed him. That meant Cartwright could use the hour they ran as time for reflection on the campaign and what he was doing.

That morning, Cartwright was euphoric. Last night's speech at the Fontainebleau Hotel to two hundred Latino businessmen had been a huge success. Cartwright had addressed them in Spanish, recounting how he had always treated every Latino officer with whom he had served with respect and dignity.

"I won't make sweeping promises," Cartwright had said. "I will tell you, however, that I want to forge a new inclusion coalition for the Republican Party, and I want the Latino community to be a critical part of that new coalition."

His speech had received a standing ovation. Florida's governor had attended and, following the speech, had announced his support for Cartwright.

On the path by the ocean, Cartwright and Mallory passed a couple of runners heading in the other direction. "We're with you, General Cartwright," one called.

"God bless you," the other one said.

When they returned to the hotel, Cartwright and Mallory split up. Mallory had to shower and head to the airport to prepare the plane for a morning flight to Charlotte.

Back in his hotel suite, Cartwright showered and drank some coffee, then took out his phone. He wanted to report to Andrew Martin on developments in Florida, particularly how well last night's speech had gone and the governor's endorsement.

Despite Martin's congratulations, Cartwright thought the Washington lawyer sounded strained, as though he were not really concentrating. Cartwright asked about the status of the white paper on immigration, but Martin didn't seem to know what he was talking about. He was obviously preoccupied, but Cartwright could forgive him after all he had done for the campaign. They talked a little about the day's schedule, and then Cartwright clicked off.

In a few minutes waiters would be wheeling in a table for breakfast and Juan Lopez, the Republican Senator from Florida, would be arriving for what Cartwright expected to be a contentious breakfast meeting. Juan wanted Cartwright to pledge that if elected, he would reimpose the US trade embargo against Cuba until the government changed its policy on human rights.

Cartwright's expectation about the meeting with Lopez proved to be correct. Before Cartwright had a chance to eat any of the gorgeous melon he had selected from the breakfast table, Lopez said, "Let me be perfectly blunt, General. Our opening to Cuba has been a disaster, and it hasn't done squat for the political rights or economic well-being of the Cuban people. Unless you clearly and unequivocally announce your support for reinstituting the embargo, you will not receive my endorsement, nor will you receive the backing of the Latino community or Florida's votes for president."

Cartwright took a deep breath and replied, "Let me be equally blunt, Senator. The Cuba embargo was bad policy. It achieved nothing for the Cuban American community or the Cuban people. Our only hope for political change in Cuba, which we all want, is by engaging the government and helping them on the path toward prosperity, which will in turn lead to political change. I agree not much has happened along those lines yet, but we have to give it time."

Growing red in the face, Lopez took the linen napkin from his lap and tossed it onto the table. "If you announce this position, General, I—and the Cuban American community—will bury you."

Rather than responding angrily, Cartwright calmly said, "Unfortunately, Senator, your views are passé. You follow the antiquated ideas of the older members of your community. I have seen surveys and conducted polls among young voters, and they overwhelmingly support my position." Cartwright was confident in what he said. Also, with the endorsement he had received last evening from Florida's governor, he expected to carry the state.

"Show me the surveys," Lopez said defiantly.

Cartwright walked over to the desk, removed a file, and handed it to Lopez. "I commissioned these surveys to be taken by the University of Miami Public Affairs Group. Their credibility cannot be questioned."

Lopez looked through the materials and grimaced.

"My train is leaving the station," Cartwright said. "Either you get on, or you get left behind."

"I have to think about it," Lopez replied reluctantly.

"Don't take too long. You face a tough reelection battle in November. I'm sure you'll want my support and you'll want me to come down here and speak when I'm the Republican candidate for president."

"I'll let you know."

"Good. Now let's eat some breakfast."

While they ate, they discussed other topics, including economic and environmental issues, on which they were in agreement, and Lopez's mood improved. By the time the senator left, Cartwright was confident he would receive his endorsement.

After breakfast, Cartwright dressed, then a car took him to the airport. Waiting for him on the tarmac was Dale Scott, the *Wall Street*

Journal reporter whose interview with Cartwright had launched his campaign. On the flight to North Carolina, Cartwright planned to give Scott his views on the Middle East for publication in the *Journal*.

Once the plane took off, Scott moved up to the table across from Cartwright with his pen and reporter's pad in hand. Cartwright had told Scott this interview would be on the record.

"How do you view the conflicts in the Middle East and what the United States should be doing?" Scott inquired.

"First of all, Dale," Cartwright began, "let me say that Israel is our strong ally and a democratic nation, the only one in the region. They deserve our unqualified support. Unfortunately, Israel's conflict with the Palestinians is only a minor sideshow in the Middle East."

"What is the main event, to use your metaphor?"

"The conflict between Shiites and Sunnis, which has been raging since the death of Mohammad fourteen hundred years ago. We can no more stop this conflict than we can halt the tides in the ocean. As a military man, I am familiar with the horrors of war. If I become president, I will not send our men and women off to the Middle East to die and be wounded in a centuries-old conflict we cannot end."

"What about using air power?"

"To some extent that may be possible, but again, from my experience and reading of history, I am aware of its limitations."

Scott looked squarely at Cartwright. "It sounds to me as if you are calling for a new isolationism. Is that correct?"

The general smiled. "I am calling for a new pragmatic foreign policy. Let's be realistic about the Middle East. We are blessed with an abundance of oil and natural gas here at home. We no longer need the Arabs' oil to preserve our way of life. That's what has changed. We cannot be the world's policeman, and we no longer have to be the arbiter between Sunnis and Shiites. We must reshape our foreign policy around what is important and what we can achieve. Our position in the world is not what it was sixty years ago, though we might wish it were. It's time to modify our thinking and policy to accommodate that."

Scott put down his pencil. "When this appears in the paper, you may get a strong reaction from hawks in your own party."

"That's okay," said Cartwright. "I'm running for president to do what's in the best interests of the United States, even if others don't agree. I love this country. Never forget that."

Washington

Kelly arrived outside of Martin's house before Paul or Arthur got there. Fortunately, the rain had decided to take a hiatus.

She saw Rolfe sitting in the car and walked over and climbed inside. "Where's Clarence?" she asked.

"In the back of the house."

"Anything happen last night?"

"Not a thing," said Rolfe. "All quiet. Are you going to arrest Martin?"

"I don't know, it's the AG's call. When we go into the house, I want you to stand at the front door, just in case."

"Will do."

Ten minutes later, Paul and Arthur arrived. She expected the AG to step in front of her and lead the way to the door, and she was right. Paul fell in behind his boss, with Kelly pulling up the rear. The lawyers had taken charge.

As Arthur had asked, her jacket was unbuttoned, her holstered gun visible, and she carried a pair of handcuffs conspicuously. Her prediction, which she wasn't sharing with anyone, was that sleazy Martin would find a way to wiggle out of this unscathed.

Arthur rang the bell, but nothing happened. Impatiently, he rang it again. Finally, Martin opened the door.

Martin looked like hell!

The usually well-dressed, dapper, and groomed Washington lawyer was disheveled, his hair uncombed, shirt buttoned improperly, and his eyes puffy and red. He was clutching a mostly empty bottle of scotch. It appeared as though he'd had quite a night.

As soon as he stepped into the house, Arthur said, "What happened to you?"

"She tried to kill me," Martin blurted out.

"Who tried to kill you?"

"Huan, the Chinese woman living with me. She was a plant by Liu. Once she heard what Paul and Kelly said last evening, she knew I was blown. She must have had orders to kill me if that happened."

Kelly was convinced Martin was telling the truth.

Arthur said, "What kind of bullshit story is this?"

Kelly couldn't tell whether Arthur was serious or just posturing. With the AG, you never knew.

Martin collapsed into a chair, "I killed her first. I had to save myself."

Kelly stepped forward, "Where's Huan's body?"

"It was an accident, I swear." His breath was coming in short spurts and he sounded panicked. "We struggled, and I pushed her. She slipped and hit her head. It happened upstairs in one of the bathrooms. I closed the door and stayed down here all night." He was looking at Kelly. "I'm no killer, I had to save my life."

Kelly sat down in a chair, close to Martin, pulled out a recorder and said, "Why don't you tell us in detail what happened."

Martin described how he had gotten suspicious of Huan, what he had found in her black bag, and how they had struggled in the bathroom. At the end, Martin said, "It was a clear case of self-defense."

Kelly couldn't help but crack a small smile. Martin was always the lawyer.

"That's for a court to decide," Arthur interjected.

"Let's go upstairs," Kelly told Martin. "Show me the body."

"No way," said Martin, shaking his head emphatically. "Top of the stairs and turn left. You can't miss it."

"I'll go up myself." She turned to Paul. "Keep your eye on Martin."

"I'm going with you," Arthur said.

In the bathroom, Kelly looked at Huan's still, lifeless body. The black bag was close to her on the floor. Kelly didn't touch a thing. It all seemed consistent with Martin's story.

Arthur looked pale. She led him out of the bathroom and into a bedroom down the hall. "I'll get a forensic team out here," she said, "and an ambulance to take the body away."

"Arrange for them to pull the ambulance into the garage and use unmarked cars. If we're going to make a deal with Martin, we can't let this turn into a media circus. Happily, there's a lot of space between the houses and the rain has started again. I doubt if anybody will be out walking the dog and become nosey."

"Will do."

"Good. We'll wait to talk to Martin about the mole until they've taken the woman's body away."

An hour later, the forensic team was wrapping up. Kelly went to tell Arthur. He was in the study with Martin. She hoped that the AG wasn't cutting a deal himself. Eavesdropping, she heard Arthur say, "I won't discuss what we do with you until I have Paul and Kelly with me."

"I understand."

"I'm glad you understand something, Andrew, because I can't comprehend a damn thing about you."

"What do you mean?" she heard Martin inquire.

"How someone with all you had going for you at the pinnacle of the legal profession could have fallen so far, so fast. Seven months ago you were admired by everyone. Now you're a spy, your wife's gone, and you killed your mistress."

"She wanted to kill me."

"That's irrelevant to my point. If somebody wanted to be kind to you, they would say it's sad. I just think what you've done is stupid. You used poor judgment making that call to Anguilla for Jasper, and then you kept compounding your error. I have no sympathy for you."

"Shit happens."

"Don't you dare say that. You did it all to yourself. Nobody did it to you."

Still listening, Kelly was anxious to hear how Martin responded.

After a few moments of silence, Martin said, "You're right, Arthur. I've been a fool. Now I've hit rock bottom." Kelly thought he sounded contrite. "If you give me a chance, I'll do what I can to help you. I want to work my way back up."

"We'll see about that," the AG said. "Now wait here. I'll let you know when we're ready to talk to you."

Kelly moved quickly away. She didn't want Arthur to know she had been listening.

Fifteen minutes later, they sat down at the dining room table, Martin and Arthur at the ends, Kelly and Paul across from each other.

Arthur pointed to Kelly. "Tell Andrew where you are in your investigation and what you need from him."

She coughed and cleared her throat. "We've established that you received, on eight separate occasions, secret military and political information from a high-level government official. Each time, it came to you in a brown envelope. We also know you passed those on to this man."

She showed him Xiang's picture. "His name is Xiang Shen, and he's an assistant economic attaché at the Chinese embassy. We have him in custody and he's cooperating. One of the pieces of information you passed is the memo from Camp David regarding the islands in the East China Sea."

"In other words," Arthur said, "we have an ironclad case against you for espionage."

Martin shook his head. "That's what I like about you, Arthur. You always puff up your case. What can you really prove? That I passed sealed envelopes. You won't be able to prove I knew what was in them. And in fact, I did not. Besides, your whole case depends on Xiang. At the end of the day, the Chinese will find a way to snatch him away from you. Wilkins will no doubt convince Braddock to trade Xiang for something more important we want from the Chinese."

Kelly feared Martin was right about Wilkins. She decided to step in and help Arthur out. "You were also involved in Jasper's murder."

"That whole business is so complicated even the great lawyer Paul Maltoni could never convince a jury of that."

Looking angry, Paul shot to his feet. Arthur waved him down.

"And we also have a charge against you for killing the Chinese woman."

"That's ridiculous."

"We'll see what a jury decides."

Martin didn't reply.

"If you tell us," Arthur said, "who gave you those eight envelopes, I'm prepared to recommend a minimum sentence for you. Five to ten years."

Martin laughed, but Kelly thought it seemed forced. "You're not even close," he replied. "What I have is huge—the identity of a spy at the top of the American government. Only I can give it to you. Here's what I want."

"Go ahead," Arthur said.

"Complete immunity for espionage and the Jasper murder. In return, I'll not only name the spy, but do everything I can to help you build your case against him."

Kelly looked at Arthur. She had no idea how the AG would react. Her best guess was that he would come down hard on Martin and say, "No way."

But she was wrong.

"Listen, Andrew," Arthur said, "let's not waste a lot of time posturing. I'll cut right to my bottom line."

"Which is?"

"You give us the name of the spy and you get conditional immunity for both espionage and Jasper's murder."

"What do you mean conditional?"

"You not only give us a name, but you agree to cooperate with us to build a bulletproof case against that individual as you proposed a minute ago. Once we have that case, your immunity becomes effective."

"Why do you want that?" Martin asked.

"To make sure you identify the correct individual."

"You don't trust me?"

"You have that correct, and there's more." The AG sounded firm and self-confident. "Until we have that bulletproof case, you're under house arrest. Here in this house. We'll have an FBI agent in the house at all times. You can't leave. You'll have to tell people that you have a bad stomach virus. Phones and email will be controlled and monitored."

Martin looked angry. "Why the hell do you need that?"

"I'll give you three reasons. One, I don't want you tipping off the Chinese. Two, I don't want you skipping out on us. And three, I don't want you to end up like Huan. Those are my terms, and they are nonnegotiable."

Kelly listened intently for the next half hour while Martin tried to persuade Arthur to back off the house arrest, but the AG didn't budge. Not one inch. While this was happening, Kelly noticed Paul was working on his iPad.

Finally, Martin folded. "I want the deal in writing."

Paul spoke up. "I've already drafted it," he said pointing to his iPad.

"Let me see it," Arthur said.

Paul carried it around the table and handed it to the AG to read.

When he was finished, Arthur said, "You do good work, Paul."

"Who do you think trained him?" Martin said.

Ignoring Martin's comment, Paul said, "I can send it to the printer here in the house."

"Do it."

Minutes later, Arthur and Martin had signed the document.

"Now give us the name," Arthur said.

"Can I pee first?"

"Sure, but Paul goes with you."

"Do you really think I would pop one of those cyanide pills Huan had?"

"I no longer have any idea what you would do."

After Martin and Paul left for the bathroom, Arthur headed toward the kitchen, asking Kelly to accompany him.

"Espresso?" he asked.

"Sure, thanks."

He fixed them each one. While the machine was brewing, he said, "What do you think?"

"You did a good job of negotiating. I'm glad you hung tough."

"I'm still worried."

"About what?"

"I don't trust Martin, he could give us a phony name. His moral compass is so fucked up, anything is possible. So you and Paul will have to build the bulletproof case against whoever Martin fingers. If you find out he's lying, we'll go back to Martin and try again."

"How will you get him to break then?"

"Ever hear of waterboarding?"

Kelly didn't know whether the AG was serious.

He smiled. "I had you there, didn't I?"

Kelly gulped down her espresso and followed Arthur back to the dining room where Paul and Martin were seated.

"Nice of you to help yourself to my coffee," Martin said. "You could have at least offered me some."

"Okay, stop screwing around," said Arthur. "Who's the Chinese spy?"

For thirty seconds, Martin didn't respond, letting the suspense build. Finally, as if he were pulling the pin out of a grenade and placing it on the table, he said softly, "General Cartwright."

"Oh my god," Arthur blurted out.

Kelly had the same reaction. She couldn't believe that this famous American military man, and the likely Republican presidential nominee, was a Chinese mole.

Arthur recovered quickly. The trial lawyer was on his feet, ready to interrogate the witness. "Tell us what you know about Cartwright's involvement."

"In January I was summoned to Hong Kong. I met there with Justice Minister Jiang, followed by a meeting with Liu Guan, the minister of MSS. Liu wanted me to pass sealed envelopes from Cartwright to Xiang from time to time."

"And you agreed?"

"Yes."

"Why?"

"They sharply increased my law firm's retainer."

"C'mon, Andrew, don't bullshit me. You didn't do it for the money. You've banked much more from law practice than you could ever spend."

Martin hesitated.

Arthur moved up close to him. "What really made you do it?" he insisted.

"If I didn't agree, Liu threatened to disclose my involvement in Jasper's murder to the American authorities. I had no choice."

"How did this work? The exchange of information?"

"General Cartwright called and arranged a meeting at my office. He delivered a sealed envelope to me. I called Xiang, asked him to come to my office, and gave him the sealed envelope. I had no idea what was in any of the envelopes."

"How often did you do this?"

"Eight times altogether. General Cartwright delivered seven of the envelopes. Once, he had a last minute summons to the White House so he sent his aide, Captain Mallory, with the envelope."

"I need proof of all of this. Do you have records of these handoffs?"

Martin shook his head. "No, of course not."

Paul spoke up. "Do you have any other evidence to establish that Cartwright was the spy?"

"Just my word. That's plenty."

Paul turned to Arthur. "You, Kelly, and I have to talk."

"There's a patio in the back, under cover. Let's go out there," Kelly suggested. "I'll get Rolfe in the house to watch Martin."

When they reached the patio, Arthur said to Paul. "What's bothering you?"

"I think that sleazebag Martin is conning us with Cartwright. He hasn't given us any real evidence it's Cartwright. He must have had scores of meetings with Cartwright about the general's candidacy even before he announced it. Martin's trying to link those to his eight Xiang meetings."

"Suppose each Xiang meeting occurred immediately after a Cartwright meeting?" Kelly said. "The next day, for example. That would be powerful circumstantial evidence to prove Cartwright was the spy."

"I agree," Paul said, raising his voice and sounding emotional. "But we don't have the evidence."

Arthur lifted his hands in a time-out signal. "Listen, Paul. When I was in private practice, my secretary kept careful logs of every call or meeting I had, and I was damn glad she did. They saved my ass more than once in billing disputes. You worked for Martin at his firm. Do you know whether his secretary did something similar?"

Paul shook his head. "I have no idea."

"How well do you know Martin's secretary?" Kelly asked.

"Alice Taylor is her name. I liked her. We ended up chatting from time to time while I waited for Martin to finish up a call or a meeting so I could talk to him. We always got along well."

"Could you visit Alice at home this evening and ask her if she has logs like this and to forward them to you electronically if so?" inquired Arthur.

"Sure, but why not ask Martin to have her get them for us?" Paul asked.

Kelly saw a smile on Arthur's face. She realized he viewed Paul's question as a lob to the net. He was about to put it away. "Because I don't trust Martin either," he said. "If there's a name other than Cartwright's linked with the Xiang visits, and Martin knows we're focused on the logs, he might delete that name before we obtain them."

Listening to Arthur, Kelly decided on her own next moves. She had to brief Forester. Unfortunately, he was in Phoenix that day. She could see him first thing the following morning.

She also planned to wait until then to brief Wilkins and Farrell at a task force meeting. Expecting Wilkins to be a problem, she wanted to find out whether Martin's secretary kept logs and to have Paul's analysis of them before that meeting.

*   *   *

Paul decided not to call Alice, merely to show up at her house and hope she would talk to him. Having delivered documents to her house for Martin about a year ago, he remembered that Alice lived alone, or at least she had at the time.

Driving to Alice's house at seven in the evening, Paul thought about how much the neighborhood called Logan Circle had changed. Ten years ago, the sturdy red brick row houses, built to endure for decades, had been predominantly inhabited by African Americans like Alice. Now, the neighborhood was mostly white. "Gentrification," it was called, with white professionals moving in to displace the African Americans and driving up real estate values. It was all part of the shifting racial composition of the District of Columbia, which had decades ago been overwhelmingly African American. Soon, whites would be the majority.

When Alice opened the door for Paul, she had a startled expression, but he had expected that.

"Paul Maltoni, what in the world are you doing here?" she asked.

"I hate to bother you," he said, "but I have a confidential government matter to talk to you about."

"That sounds serious."

"I'm afraid it is."

"Well c'mon in. Would you like something to drink?"

"No thanks, I'm fine."

She invited Paul into the living room and they both sat down.

"I was very sorry you left the firm," said Alice. "Everybody liked you."

"Thanks a lot," Paul acknowledged.

"I've been following your career since you left," she added. "I hear you're involved with national security issues at the Justice Department now."

"That's right."

"I'm actually glad you came this evening," she remarked.

It was an odd comment, Paul thought. It sounded as if she had something she wanted to tell Paul. He decided to let her begin. He could ask about the logs when she was finished. "Please tell me why."

"Well, you know I have always been very loyal to Mr. Martin, and I've always kept his secrets to myself."

"Of course, I understand that."

"However, my country means even more to me than Mr. Martin," she continued. "My husband was career army until his death two years ago, and we both shared a love for this great country."

Paul wondered where Alice was going with this.

"I've been troubled about some things and didn't know who to tell," she said. "Since you now work in national security matters, I'm afraid you won the lottery."

He smiled. "I'm glad you selected me. Why don't you tell me what's bothering you?"

"Well, as you know, Mr. Martin always kept the door to his office open when he had meetings with other firm lawyers or even clients, including company CEOs. Since he was at the end of the hall in a corner office, no one except me could hear what was said."

Paul nodded, recalling that in the years he had worked with Martin, the senior partner had closed the door only when he was at a critical point in dealing with the Jasper affair.

"But in the last three months," Alice continued, "Mr. Martin has had eight meetings with a man by the name of Xiang, an economic attaché at the Chinese embassy. As you know, Mr. Martin represents the Chinese government. Each time Xiang came, Mr. Martin shut his door."

"Did he close it for anyone else?"

"Once, when this Chinese woman called Huan came. She's the woman he's now living with. It's too bad about his personal life. I liked Francis, and this strumpet was younger than his daughters. I'm sorry to digress. Anyhow, once when she came, she shut the door. Now, I'm no prude, but they were both straightening their clothes when they opened the door and left to go to dinner. I couldn't believe it. Well, anyhow, that's one thing that bothered me. Here's another."

"Please tell me."

"In January, after Francis left him, Mr. Martin suddenly, with no advance notice, flew to Hong Kong for business. After that, he started having secret meetings with this man Xiang. Then that woman moved into his house. Today he called and told me he'd be out for a few days with a bad stomach virus. He didn't sound convincing. I figured he might be slipping off for another meeting with these Chinese people and that he didn't want me to know about it." She paused. "If you think I'm reading too many spy stories, let me know."

"Unfortunately, you're not," said Paul. "Martin is mixed up in some serious matters, and we're watching him very closely. I can't tell you more than that, I'm afraid."

"That's too bad," Alice replied. "I'm sorry to hear it. Until this business with Senator Jasper, he was on top of the world. When the mighty fall, they sure fall hard."

For an instant, Paul thought she might cry. But she pulled herself together and said, "What can I do to help you?"

"Do you keep logs of Martin's meetings on a daily basis?"

"Absolutely. Every meeting and phone call. It's been useful for billing purposes. Until a few years ago, it was paper entries. Now it's all electronic."

"Do you have a computer here?" Paul asked.

She pointed toward the next room. "In my study."

"Can you access those logs from here?"

She smiled. "I'm the only secretary in the firm who can access firm records remotely. It's a perk of working for the boss."

Paul gave her the relevant time period and she pulled up the logs of all of Martin's meetings, printed them, and put them in a folder for Paul.

Then he thanked her and left.

Washington and Bethesda, Maryland

Three hours later, Paul, working in his office at the DOJ, had analyzed the logs. They corroborated Martin's story. Paul listed each of the eight dates Martin met with Xiang. For seven of them, General Cartwright had met with Martin the day before. For the eighth, Captain Mallory had met with Martin the previous day. Paul carefully scrutinized the logs to determine whether Martin had meetings with any other individuals on the days immediately before his eight Xiang meetings. There was no one.

As he made a chart of the meetings, he was convinced this couldn't be a coincidence. It was confirmation that General Cartwright was the mole.

Paul noted that Martin had plenty of other Cartwright meetings unrelated to Xiang meetings, but that didn't trouble him. Martin was a key advisor to General Cartwright's campaign.

Paul placed his analysis and the supporting logs in his briefcase and called Kelly. "Where are you?" he asked.

"At home."

"I want to show you something."

She gave him the address and twenty-five minutes later Paul walked into Kelly's house, clutching his briefcase.

"Wait 'til you see this," he exclaimed.

She raised a finger to her lips. "Julie just got to sleep. She was having nightmares."

She led him into the den where he spread out the papers and went through his analysis.

At the end, he said, "Complete confirmation. Cartwright is our mole."

"Listen, Paul, let's take this slowly."

"You were convinced this morning. Now you're sounding hesitant. What happened?"

"I still think that's the conclusion, but General Cartwright is the closest thing this country has to a war hero. That's bad enough. Blowing up a presidential election is even worse. We have more work to do."

"The evidence is clear," Paul insisted.

"And very circumstantial," countered Kelly. "I accept your conclusion, but we have to be realistic. It's not the bulletproof case the AG wanted."

"What do you think we should we do next?" Paul asked.

"I'm calling a task force meeting for eleven tomorrow morning. I have to brief Forester before then, and I urge you to report to Arthur about the logs. You and I are about to climb out on a very long limb, and we need whatever protection was can get."

Washington

After Paul had left Kelly's house the previous evening, she had called her dad. "You running tomorrow morning?" she asked.

"Five thirty sharp. Starting at Candy Cane City."

To preserve his knees and hips, her dad had stopped running on pavement and confined himself to a dirt track which circled a grassy area in Rock Creek Park near ball fields, tennis courts, and a children's play area known as Candy Cane City.

"Good. I'll be there," she said.

When she arrived, her dad was stretching next to his parked car. She pulled in beside him.

"Glad you called," he said. "We haven't run together in a long time."

"Yeah, that's true. I have to warn you, though, this isn't for father-daughter bonding."

"You have a problem?"

"A big one."

They jogged over to the track, which was deserted. Once they began running side by side, he said, "Tell me about it."

And she did.

When she was finished explaining about Martin, Xiang, and Cartwright, the first words out of his mouth were, "Holy shit."

"Meaning what?" she asked.

"I'm surprised as hell. I really like Cartwright. I would have never guessed it."

"Do you think there could be another explanation? That we're missing something?"

For a full minute her father didn't answer. Then he said, "It's conceivable that Martin got the information he gave to Xiang outside of the office and that his Cartwright meetings were only about the campaign."

"Look at the timing on eight meetings. That would be a helluva coincidence."

"You're right," he conceded. "Cartwright has to be the mole."

Kelly was breathing hard. She hated to admit it, but the old man was in better shape than she was. "Can we reduce the pace a little?"

"Sure." He glanced at her. "With Cartwright as the likely Republican presidential nominee, this is huge."

"That's an understatement."

"Make sure you keep Forester in the loop."

"Damn right. That's where I'm going from here."

She recalled her testimony before Senator Dorsey's subcommittee. Either that pompous ass or someone else in Congress would skewer her if she were wrong about this.

Her father suddenly stopped running and clutched her arm. "Listen, Kelly, you like to grab a ball and run with it, which is usually good. I'm all for being aggressive. I also always believed in doing what I thought in my gut was right, even if my bosses in Langley didn't agree. Despite all of that, this time I'm telling you to go slow. You've already had one dustup in this operation over Peterson and that Saint Michaels business. You were going after a little fish then. Now you're about to challenge the biggest shark in the sea. I don't want you to get hurt."

*   *   *

FBI Director Forester was a good listener. Kelly guessed that had made him an excellent US district judge. While sitting in front of his desk, she told him about what had happened with Martin. Then she told him about the logs Paul had acquired from Alice.

Forester jotted notes while she spoke without saying a word. When she was finished, he said, "Your conclusion that Cartwright is the spy seems right, but you're a long way from having a case for espionage against him. We need more evidence."

"I agree. Any suggestions about where we go next?"

"Mallory. Get his background ASAP and arrange an interview. You and Paul should do it together, and in a way that Cartwright won't find out."

"What do we hope to learn from Mallory?" Kelly asked.

"For starters, find out what he knows about the reason for his one meeting with Martin. Then see where it goes. Let Paul take the lead, he'll know how to do the interrogation. And do not, I repeat, do not under any circumstances confront Cartwright until we have pulled together all of the evidence against him."

"I understand."

"And I want you to keep me informed."

"For sure." She stood up to leave.

"Let me tell you one other thing, Kelly," said Forester.

"Yes, sir?"

"I don't play the 'cover your ass' game like so many people in Washington. I'm right with you on this."

"I appreciate that."

"If we hang, we hang together," he said.

Forester's words were jarring for Kelly. She wished the director hadn't used that metaphor.

*   *   *

When Kelly entered the task force conference room, Paul was already there. Farrell and Wilkins had yet to arrive.

She told Paul what Forester had said, then added, "I've asked our research people to prepare a profile on Mallory ASAP."

"That's good."

"What happened with Larkin?"

"I told him about my analysis of the logs Alice turned over. He said, 'Full steam ahead and keep me in the loop.' I asked him if he planned to brief the president."

"What'd he say?"

"It was pure Arthur Larkin. In that gruff tone, he said, 'You do your job. I'll do mine.' I interpreted that to mean he wants Braddock to be able to say he didn't know we were moving up on Cartwright, even if

Arthur does tell him, because then no one would be able to contradict him except Arthur himself. He's prepared to take the bullet to protect his president."

"Sounds like Watergate with John Mitchell as the AG."

"Don't you love these Washington games?"

"I think they stink," said Kelly, "but that's the way it goes. It's the same in every administration—Democrats or Republicans. Only the names are different."

Farrell entered the room and sat down next to Paul across from Kelly. Wilkins was right behind him. He took a chair at the head of the table.

"My time's tight," Wilkins said. "The president wants me back for a noon meeting with a congressional delegation about Middle East policy."

"We'll talk fast," Kelly said. "I don't think you'll want to miss this."

"What's so important?"

She turned to Paul. "You tell them what we learned from Andrew Martin and from Alice. Then I'll describe our next step."

She put her iPad on the table, wanting to see the profile on Mallory as soon as the research department sent it. She was planning to jump in if Paul missed anything, but it wasn't necessary.

The instant Paul was finished, Wilkins pounced. "The charge that General Cartwright, one of the most courageous and heroic American warriors, is a Chinese spy is the most absurd and ludicrous thing I've ever heard in my life."

Paul was ready to defend their conclusion. "Eight meetings cannot be a coincidence."

"That's ridiculous," said Wilkins, raising his voice now. "I'm sure Cartwright was meeting with Martin a lot more than those eight times. Martin is the top advisor for Cartwright's presidential campaign."

"We know that," said Paul, "but the eight all occurred before Cartwright announced for presidency."

"So what? They were no doubt planning for the announcement and campaign. Candidates always do lots of prep work before they announce."

"What seals it for me," said Paul, "is that no other individual met with Martin with regularity around the time of the Xiang meetings."

Wilkins turned to Kelly. "Are you buying this bullshit Maltoni is selling?" he asked in a surly tone.

"Absolutely," Kelly replied. "He's right."

"What about you?" Wilkins asked Farrell.

"It may not be definitive. On the other hand, it sure sounds plausible."

Wilkins pounded the palm of his hand on the table. "I'm going over your heads to Forester and to Larkin."

"We've briefed both of them," Kelly replied. "They told us to pursue it."

"Well at least you should give General Cartwright a chance to explain about these meetings before you do anything else."

"Director Forester does not want to do that."

Wilkins said, "Humph. What will you do next?"

"Talk to Captain Mallory. See what he has to say about his meeting with Martin." She glanced at her iPad. "I just received a bio on Mallory."

"What's it say?" Wilkins asked. He checked his watch. "And talk fast, I have to get to the White House."

"Christopher Mallory is fourth generation military. Very distinguished record at the Air Force Academy and as an Air Force pilot. Cartwright served with Mallory's father. Mallory was Cartwright's assistant when he was chairman of the Joint Chiefs. When Cartwright left the military to run for president, Mallory resigned to be Cartwright's aide and private pilot."

Wilkins was shaking his head. "Everything's going to hit the fan when Cartwright finds out why you're talking to Mallory. This is Washington, everything sees the light of day." Wilkins pointed a bony finger at Kelly. "To quote John Mitchell, you're gonna get your tit caught in a wringer."

Kelly was planning a sharp retort, but before she had a chance to deliver it, Wilkins was on his feet, heading out of the door.

"What's his problem?" Paul said, shaking his head.

"He's probably friends with Cartwright," Farrell said. "He doesn't want to believe his good buddy can be a Chinese spy."

"Forget about Wilkins," Kelly said. "Time to move up on Mallory. Anybody have a connection at DOD?"

"Let me check out the lawyers at the Pentagon," Paul said, picking up his iPad. After a few moments, he said, "The Air Force GC is Carol

Bailey. She went to Yale Law about ten years before me. We can start there."

Paul took out his cell and called her. After introducing himself, he said, "Kelly Cameron from the FBI and I would like to talk to you about a confidential matter."

"Sure, I'm free now."

"We're on our way. We'll be there in about twenty minutes."

*   *   *

Carol Bailey was a tough looking woman with short gray hair and wire-framed glasses. She was dressed in a navy pantsuit. Paul remembered meeting her once, but he couldn't recall where or when until she said, "Hey Paul, about five years ago, didn't I meet you at a reception for the Yale Law School dean at Andrew Martin's house up on Foxhall? You were working with Martin at the time."

"Yeah, that's right."

"A shame about Martin and the Supreme Court appointment."

"He seems to be carrying on." Paul was unwilling to tell her that what they were doing there related to Martin.

After introducing herself to Kelly, Carol asked them to take a seat.

"From your title, Paul, I assume this is a national security matter," Carol said, cutting to the chase.

"Correct."

"And you probably can't tell me what it's about."

"Correct again."

"I understand," she said. "I've been in this job for five years now, and that's been par for the course. How can I help you?"

"We'd like to interview Christopher Mallory, recently resigned from the Air Force."

"You mean General Cartwright's assistant?"

"You know him?" Paul asked.

"I know of him. Cartwright was a presence here, and Mallory was close to the general. The Air Force hated losing them both."

"We'd like to interview Mallory without him tipping off Cartwright."

She nodded. "I get the picture. Let me see what info we have for Mallory in the system."

She checked her computer. "I have a cell number and email. I could contact Mallory and ask him to come down here to sign some papers related to his benefits. How's that sound?"

"Perfect."

"I'll try his cell. When do you want to meet with him?"

"As soon as possible."

She picked up the phone and dialed.

Paul listened to her telling Mallory what they had agreed on. A few seconds later, she said, "Okay, call me when you get back to Washington."

She put down the phone. "This afternoon Mallory is flying Cartwright to Paris in his private plane. He's not sure when they'll be back, but he thinks it'll only be a couple of days. He'll call me when they return."

Paul thanked Carol, and they drove back to Washington.

In the car, Kelly said, "Don't you think that's odd?"

"What's odd?" asked Paul.

"Cartwright taking off for Paris in the middle of his campaign."

Paul thought about it for a minute. "Yeah, it is. Let's see what Mallory has to say about it."

Paris

At seven in the evening, Cartwright got out of a limousine and walked into the Bristol Hotel. Mallory was two steps behind. Both were dressed in civilian clothes.

Before leaving Washington, Cartwright had arranged their accommodations: a suite for himself on the sixth floor, and a room for Mallory on the second.

Once they had checked in, they headed toward the glass door elevator.

Cartwright told Mallory, "You have the evening off. Enjoy Paris. We'll leave here tomorrow morning at eight to go back to the airport. Then we're flying home. Let the people at Orly know."

"Yes, sir," Mallory replied.

On the second floor, Mallory exited the elevator. As he left, Cartwright said, "Don't get into trouble with those French women."

The sixth floor suite was one with a view of the center courtyard. Cartwright checked his Rolex. The call was scheduled to come at eight. With time to kill, he took a long shower, then fixed a scotch from the mini bar.

Sipping it, Cartwright thought about his one previous meeting with Minister Liu, which had occurred in Singapore at the Raffles Hotel six months previously. That had been a secret meeting, too. Only Mallory, his pilot, had known that Cartwright was going to Singapore.

Cartwright had initiated the Singapore meeting following an incident in the South China Sea. A Chinese fighter jet had brought one of its wingtips within twenty feet of a US patrol aircraft. Cartwright was fearful incidents like this would lead to war. He had asked President Braddock to call the Chinese president and seek an immediate meeting, but the president had refused to do anything more than file a formal complaint. From their discussions following the incident, Cartwright had concluded that Braddock, who had been the governor of New York, might be adept at dealing with domestic issues, but he was naïve and totally in over his head in matters of foreign policy. Cartwright, who had studied world and military history in depth for decades, was convinced that many of the wars resulting in the deaths of millions were avoidable. They occurred because civilian leaders, like Braddock, kept kicking the can down the road, and never faced the difficult choices they had to make until a confrontation broke out. At that point, it was too late.

Cartwright loved the United States, and he was determined to do what he could to avoid having it dragged into a horrendously destructive war with China. Enraged by Braddock's passivity in response to the near miss between the US and Chinese planes, Cartwright had decided to arrange a secret meeting with General Piao, the head of the People's Liberation Army. Piao had selected Raffles Hotel in Singapore for the meeting.

Cartwright had decided to conceal the meeting from Braddock; only Mallory, who would fly Cartwright to Singapore in an Air Force plane, would know that Cartwright was going to Singapore. Then Cartwright had dismissed Mallory so he could meet Piao alone. He and Piao had spoken for about an hour, comparing their backgrounds, what they had each done to serve their countries, and finding many similarities in their careers. At the end of their discussion, Cartwright and Piao had agreed that their two great nations had to find a way to get along. Piao had then left the room, returning a few minutes later with Liu Guan, the minister of state security. After introducing Liu, Piao had withdrawn.

Liu had begun by explaining to Cartwright how China had only in the last twenty years emerged from two nightmares: first, a century of humiliation by the Western powers; second, the outrageous and stifling rule of Mao. At the end, Liu had said, "Our nation has come too far economically and as a world power in these last two decades to risk losing it all in a mutually destructive war with the United States."

"We share that goal," Cartwright had said. "That's why I'm here. I'm a student of history, and it sounds as if you are as well."

"Absolutely," Liu had agreed.

"Then I'm sure you will agree that wars are never inevitable."

"Correct, they can always be avoided. And I have a plan for avoiding a war between the US and China."

"I would like to hear it."

"At the end of the Second World War, the US and Britain met with Russia at Yalta and reached an agreement to carve up Europe into spheres of influence in a way that would avoid a war between them. Under that agreement, Russia emerged with control over Central and Eastern Europe, and the Soviets agreed not to threaten the Western European nations. That agreement was successful. It produced forty years of peace in Europe. In 1989, it had outlived its usefulness and the Berlin wall came down. Since then, there has been no agreement with Russia. Kuznov threatens his neighbors, and a conflict between Russia and Western Europe is again a real possibility."

Cartwright agreed with everything Liu had said, but he wondered where Liu was going with this.

"What I am suggesting," Liu continued, "is that it's time for the creation of a new world order in which China and the US divide up the world into spheres of influence to avoid a war with each other. The US would stay out of Asia, and in return China would avoid becoming involved politically or militarily in Europe or the Western Hemisphere."

"What about Africa and the Middle East?"

"Those are miserable and chaotic places. I would hope that with our broader agreement we could cooperate there."

Cartwright had stood up and begun pacing with his hands in his pockets as he thought about what Liu had said. In concept, it made sense; however, if Liu thought that Cartwright could influence Braddock to agree with this approach, he was sadly mistaken. The two men intensely disliked each other. Cartwright realized it was impossible for Braddock to accept any proposal of Cartwright's, and the same was true in reverse.

Cartwright stopped pacing and turned around. Still on his feet, he stared at Liu. "I assume you are speaking for the Chinese president."

"Correct."

"Well, your proposal has merit, and I'm flattered you presented it to me. Unfortunately, I am not the US president, and I don't have the clout to persuade Braddock to accept it. In fact, to be perfectly honest, my support would doom your proposal."

"I'm aware of that." Liu paused for a moment then continued, "On the other hand, you could become the US president."

Cartwright had laughed. "I'm no politician, and I've never even considered it."

"That doesn't matter," Liu had replied. "Other US military leaders have made the transition to president—Washington, Jackson, and Eisenhower, for example. The point is that the American people will embrace a military hero in troubled times, and that's what these are."

"Even if I wanted to run, the timing is unfortunate. As I'm sure you're aware, the election is in November. I'm a Republican and my party's campaign is already in full swing."

"However, it's still wide open," Liu had countered. "You and I both know your elections are decided by money. Suppose I were to guarantee you an unlimited amount of money for your campaign—and it would all be perfectly legal. What would you say?"

Cartwright sat back down. "I'm listening," he said.

"You've no doubt heard of the wealthy American businessman Carl Dickerson, who is based in Los Angeles."

"Of course."

"Dickerson is very interested in geopolitical issues. He also has many investments and businesses in China and throughout Asia. He would be willing to provide you with all the funding you would want for your campaign, and it would be legal under US campaign finance laws."

Cartwright could guess at Dickerson's motive. A war between the States and China would damage his business interests. Beyond that, Liu might have offered Dickerson incentives relating to his future operations in China in order to secure his support.

"You seem to have considered everything," Cartwright noted.

"Well, what do you think?"

Cartwright had closed his eyes and pondered the offer. It was enticing. Through the years, he had often thought he could do a better job as president than the incumbent. Now he was being given a chance. He thought of the movie *The Manchurian Candidate*. He would be the Beijing candidate. Nobody would ever know.

Before Cartwright responded, Liu added, "In return for my arranging with Dickerson to provide you with unlimited funds for your election campaign, I would like an expression of good faith on your part."

"What's that?"

"Until you launch your campaign, I would like you to supply me with confidential military information concerning US involvement in Asia."

"You mean become a spy for China?"

"I wouldn't express it that way."

"Then how would you?"

"It will be the beginning of our cooperation, the means to avoid a war between our two great nations. You wouldn't have to worry about being caught. You will be passing the information to a well-respected Washington lawyer, Andrew Martin, who represents my government in Washington. Then later, when you announce your candidacy for president, you can employ Martin as an adviser."

Cartwright had asked Liu for an hour to think about the proposal. He had then gone back to his room where he listed pros and cons on a sheet of paper. At the top of the positive reasons was: "good chance to be president of the US" followed by "avoiding a war with China."

For the cons, he listed: "could get caught and charged with treason; might not be elected president."

He weighed them carefully, then tore up the paper and flushed it down the toilet. Then he had returned to Liu's room.

"I'm in," he had told the head of MSS. In doing so, Cartwright did not view himself as a traitor to the United States. Rather, he saw himself as helping to create a new world order in which China and the US could find a way to coexist peacefully.

"I will talk to Dickerson," Liu said, "and have him reach out to you without indicating that the funding has been arranged. This will help establish an alibi in case anyone ever questions the legality of his funding you. My involvement, of course, cannot be known, so when you meet with him it would be best to act accordingly and assume your every move is being watched."

The next day, Mallory flew Cartwright from Singapore back to Washington. Cartwright was confident that no one other than Mallory knew he had gone to Singapore.

Now, six months later, Cartwright sat in his Bristol Hotel room finishing up his first scotch as he thought about pouring another. He decided against it. He had to be sharp for his upcoming meeting.

When it approached eight o'clock, Cartwright nervously eyed the phone in the room. Precisely at eight, it rang. Cartwright grabbed it. He heard, "Room 724," in a voice unmistakably Liu's. Then the phone went dead.

Cartwright put on his tie and jacket and left his room. He rode the elevator up to the seventh floor, then stepped out, looking around anxiously. The corridor was deserted except for a Chinese man sitting outside one of the doors. Cartwright figured that had to be Liu's room; the man was probably part of Liu's security detail. Approaching the man, Cartwright saw a bulge under his jacket confirming Cartwright's assessment. He remembered seeing a similar guard outside of the hotel room in Singapore.

As Cartwright came closer, the guard stood and tapped on the door of room 724. It opened from inside and the guard gestured for Cartwright to enter. As he did, the door quickly closed behind him.

Liu was waiting for him in the center of the suite's living room. "Cognac?" he asked in a curt voice, a snifter in his hand filled with amber liquid. There were no greetings or pleasantries from the Chinese spymaster, but Cartwright was expecting that. He had behaved the same way in Singapore. Cartwright responded in kind, not saying a word. He walked over to the bottle of Remy Martin on a table and poured himself a glass.

Once they were seated, Liu said, "We've had a complication."

"What happened?" Cartwright asked.

Liu explained about Xiang, and how Kelly Cameron had turned him. "She now knows that Andrew Martin was the conduit to pass envelopes to Xiang," Liu continued. "However, I have no idea whether Martin has identified you as the official who provided him with the envelopes."

"I strongly doubt that Andrew would turn on me."

"I hope you're right."

Cartwright could tell that Liu wasn't convinced.

"I'm confident of it," Cartwright said. "I know Andrew Martin. And even if I'm wrong, they couldn't build a case on his testimony. He never would have opened those envelopes, so he would have no idea what was in them."

"I agree with that," Liu replied, nodding. "Still I had to tell you what happened. You have a choice."

"What's that?" Cartwright inquired.

"Either continue with our joint operation, or terminate it. Of course, I hope you will continue."

As Cartwright processed the information, he realized this wasn't much of a choice. Even if he were to drop out of the presidential race, the FBI would no doubt continue their search for the mole in the US government. Indeed, he would be even more exposed. As a candidate, he at least had a chance that the gutless Braddock would call off the dogs to avoid charges that this was all politically motivated. More than that, he genuinely believed in what he was doing. He decided to reiterate that for Liu.

"Let's go back to basics," said Cartwright. "I joined with you in our project because I am terrified for my country, and the world, that the US and China could end up in a cataclysmic war that no one wants and no one would win. I see our working together as a way—the only way—of avoiding that. So I'm still in to the end."

Liu nodded with approval. "Good. How do you assess your chances of being elected?"

"Excellent. My campaign is going well. I know you like to gamble, so I will tell you Las Vegas has me as the favorite—ahead of Braddock."

Liu cracked a tiny smile that surprised Cartwright. He'd never seen the grim-looking Liu smile before.

"That's good," Liu said. "I want you to know I have eliminated one possible obstacle to your campaign."

"What's that?"

Liu reached into his pocket and removed a photo of a naked blond woman. He handed it to Cartwright, who immediately recognized Helena from that unfortunate night in Prague when she had ended up in bed with him after he had too much to drink. Cartwright turned pale.

"This was given to me by a close friend in Russian intelligence," Liu explained. "Once he saw we were clashing with the US over the East China Sea, he told me what had happened between you and Helena in Prague, how Helena had broken into your computer and forwarded sensitive emails to Moscow. He thought I might want some leverage over you. I told him positively not, and that I didn't want anything to happen which would embarrass you. He owes me a favor so he promised that Helena would be relocated to Siberia. You do not have to worry about any of your political opponents coming forward with this."

"That's good to know," Cartwright said weakly.

Liu handed him the photo. "I have no need for this. Now let's talk about Kelly Cameron. We can't underestimate her. We have to take certain precautions."

"What kind of precautions?"

"First of all, if you sense that Kelly Cameron is getting close, or you have to get a message to me for any other reason, I want you to call Mario's Pizza in Washington." Liu handed Cartwright a slip of paper with a phone number written on it. "Ask for Mario and tell him you would like a pizza with Chinese spices from the Szechuan province. A delivery man will come an hour later. He will be a member of my staff. Tell him what you'd like passed on to me verbally. Understood?"

"Yes," agreed Cartwright as he committed the phone number to memory.

Liu walked across the room to a brown leather Berluti bag. He pulled out an envelope and handed it to Cartwright.

"Open it," Liu commanded.

Inside, Cartwright found a Hong Kong passport, credit cards, and a driver's license for someone named Virgil MacMillan. Opening the passport and staring at the driver's license, Cartwright noted that MacMillan did not look like him. He pointed this out to Liu. In response, Liu reached into his pocket and took out a piece of paper. He handed it to Cartwright. It contained an email address and a phone number.

"This is for a Chinese woman in New York City. She calls herself Melody. She's a theatrical makeup artist. If you contact her and tell her where you are, she'll drop everything and get to you as soon as possible. She will make you look like Virgil MacMillan. Then get yourself on a plane to Hong Kong. Victoria Bank will have twenty million dollars in an account for Virgil MacMillan."

"I'm not doing this for the money."

"I understand. Nevertheless, if you have to escape, I want you to live comfortably. I take care of my friends."

Cartwright was convinced Liu's motive wasn't altruism. Liu would prefer that Cartwright not remain in the United States where he could tell the authorities about Liu and his program.

"You'll turn me into a modern day Philby," Cartwright remarked.

Liu sat up straight, grimaced, and said, "Would you prefer being dead or in a prison for life?"

Liu's words hung in the room, a blunt reminder of what Cartwright had at stake.

Cartwright took the elevator to the lobby of the Bristol, exited the hotel through the front door, then turned right. As he walked along Rue St. Honore, he stopped from time to time to look into shop windows, making certain he wasn't being followed. He took out his phone and dialed a number from memory. "Agnes," he said. "I'm in Paris. I'll be there in another two hours or so."

"I'll be waiting for you."

Fifteen minutes later, on Rue Artois, he entered the majestic gray stone chateau that housed Restaurant Apicius, one of the premier dining establishments in Paris.

"I'm meeting Mr. Dickerson," he explained to the tuxedo clad maître d' who greeted him.

"This way, please."

Carl Dickerson was seated at a table facing the garden in the center room. He stood as Cartwright approached. Cartwright had known that Dickerson and Liu had a close relationship, so he wasn't surprised when Dickerson had invited him out for dinner once his meeting in Paris with Liu had been set. Still, Cartwright wondered why Dickerson wanted to meet with him.

Now that Cartwright's presidential campaign had taken off, thanks to Dickerson's funding, Cartwright expected Dickerson to seek the promise of an appointment from him should he win. Perhaps he wanted to be secretary of the Treasury. Cartwright would never agree to that. He'd need someone from Wall Street who was in banking for that post. Secretary of commerce would be okay. Dickerson couldn't get into trouble at the Department of Commerce. He hoped he wouldn't end up in a conflict with Dickerson on the issue.

During dinner—an outstanding crab dish followed by rack of lamb and accompanied by a 2000 Latour—Dickerson asked Cartwright about his military career. He listened in admiration as Cartwright spoke before confessing that he had dodged the draft during the Vietnam War so he could play baseball in the Yankees farm system. As far as he ever got was AAA. Eventually, he hung up his cleats and joined his father's business importing consumer products from Asia. Dickerson seemed to be mesmerized by Cartwright's discussion of what happened in the first and second Iraqi wars, as well as in Afghanistan.

At the end, Cartwright said, "One of the primary lessons I learned is to recognize the limits of outside military intervention in places where conflicts have spanned centuries."

"Is that why you were willing to work with our mutual friend?" Dickerson asked in a soft voice.

Cartwright paused to sip some wine, then he replied, "That's a large part of it."

"I'm very pleased at how well your campaign is going."

"Thanks to your support, which I appreciate." Cartwright decided to take the bull by the horns. "If I win," he continued, "I'd like you to be secretary of commerce in my administration."

Dickerson smiled. "I would never try for any position requiring Senate confirmation. That would mean exposing every business deal I ever made to congressional scrutiny. Not in a million years."

Cartwright was relieved to hear that.

Dickerson added, "I'll tell you what I would like."

Cartwright's stomach tightened. "What's that?" he asked.

"A bedroom at the White House."

Cartwright's head snapped back. "What's that mean?"

"Access. A chance to talk with you when I'm in Washington."

"You've got it. I'll always be available for you."

"I won't come or call often," Dickerson continued. "What I'll really gain from your presidency is a chance to grow my business in Asia. War is a destabilizer and very bad for a business like mine."

"It also kills people," said Cartwright. "Often for no good reason."

By the time coffee came, Cartwright was getting antsy. All he could think about was Agnes in her apartment, naked between the silk sheets, waiting for him. Finally, Dickerson called for the check.

After they parted ways, Cartwright took a cab to Agnes's apartment. On the street in front, he saw a trash bin. Reaching into his pocket, he took out the photo of Helena that Liu had given him and tore it into a myriad of little pieces, then tossed them into the can.

The whole Helena business Liu had raised was troublesome. Liu had pretended to be helping Cartwright, but the general realized Liu was doing something else entirely. He was letting Cartwright know he held a card that could damage Cartwright immeasurably. If Cartwright didn't follow the plan and do Liu's bidding, he would play that card. And it would be easy to do. Liu undoubtedly had another copy of that photo. Even worse, Helena was probably still alive. If she had been sent to Siberia—which was questionable—the Russians could bring her back at any time and display her in front of television cameras to tell the story of her Prague adventure.

Also troublesome, Cartwright thought, was that if the Chinese had been able to find out about Helena, would someone in the US media or a political opponent learn about her as well, notwithstanding the promise of the CIA director?

Cartwright felt vulnerable. Nevertheless, he had to continue in his quest for the presidency. He was getting close enough to touch the ultimate gold ring. There was no turning back now.

Arlington, Virginia

Kelly was behind the wheel of an unmarked black SUV on the way from the FBI building to the Pentagon to interview Captain Mallory. Seated beside her was Paul, glancing at a notepad and reading through the questions he planned to ask Mallory. They had decided that Paul would take the lead for what was, in essence, a witness interview.

Kelly crossed the 14th Street Bridge, then took the exit ramp. It was ten in the morning. Rush hour was over; traffic was light. She slowed to merge into traffic on the parkway.

Off to the right, just ahead on the side of the road, she spotted a battered dump truck loaded with debris. The driver had his turn signal on, indicating he was planning to enter the parkway. Kelly reduced her speed to let the truck pull in ahead of her SUV, but the truck didn't do that. Instead, the driver turned sharply to the left, coming right at Kelly's vehicle.

"Hey, you—what the hell!" she cried out as, at the last possible second, she cut the wheel sharply to the right, hoping to avoid a collision. She almost succeeded, but as the truck barreled towards her, it hit the front driver's side of the SUV. The sudden impact turned the car on its side, the momentum rolling it over into a grassy area along the side of the road. Kelly gripped the wheel hard as the car spun, until it finally lurching to a stop on its right side. The airbags had failed to open, and Paul was pinned against the door. Kelly could tell that he wasn't moving.

Dazed, she struggled to unfasten her seatbelt. Groping along the floor, she got a hand on her bag, reached in, and pulled out her phone. She called the FBI agent emergency line and said, "This is Agent Kelly Cameron. My car was hit on the GW Parkway, coming off the 14th Street Bridge. My partner is pinned in the car."

"We'll get someone right there," said the voice on the other end.

After hanging up, Kelly continued struggling. Finally, she managed to get the door open and climb out. Her whole body ached and her hands were scratched. She looked at the road in both directions. There was no sign of the dump truck.

She turned back to the SUV. Paul still wasn't moving. She briefly thought about trying to get him out of the vehicle, but ultimately decided against it. She might make his condition worse—if he was even still alive. No, she had to wait for help.

Five minutes later, two Virginia State troopers arrived, followed soon after by a tow truck and an emergency medical unit in an ambulance. Red lights flashed and sirens blared as she directed the two EMTs to Paul. He was now stirring and calling out for help. Thank God, he was alive, Kelly thought.

While the mechanics and medical people worked on freeing Paul, Kelly showed one of the troopers her FBI ID. "My colleague pinned in the SUV is Paul Maltoni. He's a lawyer with DOJ."

"What happened?" the trooper asked.

"A dump truck swerved into our vehicle, and then took off."

"Intentional?"

She wasn't willing to involve the state police—the task force work was too confidential—so she lied. "I have no reason to believe that," she replied.

"Where were you going?"

"The Pentagon."

"Did you get a license number on the truck?" the trooped asked.

Kelly shook her head. "It all happened too fast."

"Description?"

"Gray, dirty, filled with debris."

"That's not much to go on," said the trooper. "You think the truck was banged up from the collision?"

"Hard to say, but if so I doubt very much."

"I'm not optimistic," the trooper told her, pulling out a phone, "but I'll put out an alert."

Kelly nodded. "Let's see how my partner is doing," she said, moving closer to the SUV. They were extracting Paul with great care as he rubbed his head, blinking his eyes slowly. His face and arms were scratched and bleeding.

"I'm okay," he said, catching sight of Kelly.

One of the EMTs said to Paul, "We'll take you to the hospital in the ambulance."

"No way, I'm fine," he protested. "Just give me a couple of Band-Aids."

"Listen, mister, you undoubtedly suffered a concussion. You have to get checked out."

"I told you I'm okay."

The medical official turned to Kelly. "Can you talk to him?"

"Listen, Paul, I think he's right," she said.

"It's my decision, and I'm not doing it."

"You could have a serious head injury."

"I'm all right. We have a meeting to get to."

"Don't be a fool," said Kelly.

"I've made up my mind," Paul replied, raising his voice now. "Stop telling me what to do. I hate it when people tell me what to do."

She realized arguing with Paul was hopeless. While the EMS personnel cleaned him up, she approached one of the police officers. "Can you give us a ride to the Pentagon?" she asked.

"If that's what you want to do," the officer responded.

Over the continued protests of the EMS personnel, they climbed into the back of a police car for the ride to the Pentagon, Paul sporting a bandage on his forehead. Kelly called Carol Bailey. "We had a problem," she told her. "We'll be a little late."

When they got out of the car in front of the Pentagon, Kelly asked Paul, "You sure you're okay?"

"Absolutely."

"You could have fooled me," Kelly retorted. "You look like hell."

"I wouldn't miss this for the world. Let's go."

"Wait a minute. You and I have to talk first."

She led Paul into a snack bar where they sat in a deserted corner.

"Are you okay to do this interview?" Kelly asked.

"Absolutely. Test me."

She held up three fingers. "How many fingers up?" she asked.

"Sixteen," said Paul, rolling his eyes.

"Okay, smartass," said Kelly, clearly annoyed. "You realize that was no accident. Either Liu or Cartwright just tried to kill us. You were probably looking at your notes and didn't see what was happening, but that truck was coming right at us. It was intentional."

"You're right, I didn't," Paul acknowledged.

"Trust me, this was attempted murder. They didn't want us to talk to Mallory."

"How'd they know where we were going?"

"Did you make the arrangements with Carol Baily by cell phone?"

"Yeah."

"My guess is they've hacked into your cell. Mine is encrypted, and tough to break into."

"I just have an ordinary iPhone. What should I do?"

"Put it in your desk drawer and leave it there," said Kelly. "I'll give you one of ours. Meantime, I have something else to do."

After the attempt on their life, Kelly's reasoning kicked into high gear. If they were unable to take Kelly and Paul out immediately, it was possible they would also implement a backup plan. Kelly's first guess was that they would try to get collateral in the form of an important bargaining chip—and the most effective candidate for that was incredibly vulnerable. She took out her phone and called her father.

"Where are you?" she asked.

"Fourth green at Kenwood."

"Listen, Dad, someone in a dump truck just tried to kill me and Paul near the Pentagon."

"Are you okay?" he asked, alarmed.

"Yeah, I'm fine. Paul is banged up. I want you to get Julie and keep her in your house until this is all over. Don't let her out."

"Of course. Where is she?"

Kelly's mind was still foggy. She thought about it for a moment, then said, "In school. I'll call and let them know you're coming for her."

"I'll be there in fifteen minutes."

"Will she be okay at your house?" Kelly asked, the worry in her voice tangible.

"I have enough weapons for a small army," he replied. "Julie will be safe. You worry about yourself until this is over."

"Don't say anything that will alarm her."

"Why do children always think their parents are morons?"

"Thank you, Dad."

*   *   *

When Paul and Kelly entered Carol Bailey's office, Carol asked Paul, "What happened to you?"

"He ran into a door," Kelly said before he could answer.

Carol smiled. "You should be more careful."

"Yeah," said Paul. "I've always been awkward."

"You want to have one of our doctors out here look at you?"

"Thanks," he replied, "but I've already been checked out."

Carol led them to a small conference room with a view of the parking lot, then departed. Mallory was waiting at a table, dressed in a suit and tie. He could have come from central casting, Paul thought. He had a sandy brown crew cut and was sitting ramrod straight, looking directly ahead. As soon as they entered the room, Mallory stood up.

Paul thought Mallory looked tense. He wondered how the former Air Force officer would respond when he realized he'd been hauled to a meeting under false pretenses and was being questioned about his former commanding officer, a man he admired enough to leave the military for. From Paul's own relationship and disillusionment with Andrew Martin, Paul could sympathize with Mallory.

"I'm Paul Maltoni," he said, reaching out a hand to shake Mallory's, "a Justice Department lawyer. This is Kelly Cameron, from the FBI."

"This isn't about my benefits, is it?" Mallory said, looking worried.

"No, it's not," Paul agreed. "We want to ask you some questions about General Cartwright. We can't compel you to talk to us, however, we hope you will."

"Yes, sir," Mallory replied. He didn't seem surprised.

How odd, Paul thought. In the next few minutes, Paul expected to find out why.

"Please sit down," said Paul

Mallory took a chair on one side of the table, and Kelly and Paul sat across from him. Paul picked up his legal pad, bent and battered from the crash, and a pen. Before he asked his first question, Mallory said, "Let me be clear about one thing. I have a great deal of respect and admiration for General Cartwright. However, I have an even greater love for my country."

Paul concealed his surprise. "Do you have reason to believe the two are inconsistent?" he asked.

Mallory hesitated for a moment, then said, "I do have some concerns, and didn't know who to talk to. So this meeting is in some ways a relief."

"We appreciate your candor," said Paul. "Do you mind if Kelly takes notes on her iPad?"

"No, not at all."

"Why don't you begin by telling us about your concerns."

Without any hesitation, Mallory responded, "Are you familiar with the *Wall Street Journal* article the day after the incident in the East China Sea?"

"Yes, we both read it," said Paul with a nod.

"In my opinion, what General Cartwright said was inappropriate. President Braddock is our commander in chief."

"Even after his interview, you still decided to leave the military and to work for General Cartwright in his campaign?" Paul inquired.

"Yes, sir," Mallory replied. Then, after a pause, he added, "I had given General Cartwright my commitment to join with him about twelve or so hours before the article appeared. I thought about reversing that decision, but I didn't think it would be right to go back on my word. Since then, I've seen some very troubling things."

"Please tell us about them."

"Two days ago, I flew General Cartwright to Paris on a secret trip. He told me it related to the campaign. He also told me I wouldn't be attending meetings with him. That was unusual. He had only done it once before in November, six months ago, when we took a trip to Singapore. Usually, I attend meetings and take notes. General Cartwright had also been acting strangely in the few days before we went to Paris."

"Strange how?" Kelly interjected.

"Nervous. Anxious. That wasn't like him."

Paul resumed the questioning. "What happened in Paris?"

"We arrived at the Bristol Hotel at about seven o'clock in the evening and checked in. I was given a room on the second floor. Cartwright was on the sixth. Before we went to our rooms, he dismissed me, telling me to enjoy an evening in Paris."

"And?"

For an instant, Mallory looked away from Paul. Then he turned back, "I did something I shouldn't have," he said, sounding defensive.

"What was that?"

"I was concerned about General Cartwright, so I climbed up to the sixth floor using an inside staircase. I hid in the staircase with the door open a crack, watching General Cartwright's room. I've never done anything like that before."

"What happened then?"

"About an hour later, General Cartwright left his room. He looked around suspiciously, then walked to the elevator. When he got inside, I ran down the corridor to see where the elevator was going. It went to the seventh floor. I raced up the inside stairs and looked out. At that moment, I saw General Cartwright go into a room with an armed Chinese guard in front. From the layout of the floors, I believe it was room 724, sir."

"What did you do then?"

"This will sound ridiculous."

"Go ahead."

"I was so upset that I went to a local bistro. I could barely eat, however I drank almost two bottles of wine. After leaving the bistro, I threw up in the gutter along the street. Back at the hotel, I collapsed into my bed. I was sick from what I saw. I haven't told anyone about it until now."

"Any idea who Cartwright was meeting or why?" Paul asked.

Mallory shook his head. "But obviously you think he's doing something wrong or you wouldn't be here."

Before Paul could respond, Kelly said, "Tell us about the Singapore trip."

"This was also top secret," Mallory replied. "Last year on November 20th, General Cartwright had a confidential meeting at the hotel we were staying at, the Raffles Hotels. Again, I was excluded. I don't know who he met with."

Paul turned the focus to Mallory's meeting with Martin. "On one occasion, you met with a Washington lawyer named Andrew Martin in his office on Pennsylvania Avenue."

"Yes, sir."

"What was that about?"

"General Cartwright had to attend a meeting with the president at the White House. He asked me to deliver an envelope to Andrew Martin."

"What did it look like?"

"Standard brown, eight and a half by eleven. It was sealed and had Andrew Martin's name on the front. No other markings."

"Do you have any idea of the contents?"

"No, sir. General Cartwright asked me to deliver it personally to Andrew Martin, not to a secretary."

"And did you do that?"

"Yes, sir."

"Did you speak to Martin?"

"Only to introduce myself as General Cartwright's aide. Mr. Martin seemed busy. He thanked me and I left."

Paul looked at Kelly.

"Are you aware," she said, "of any other meetings General Cartwright had with Chinese officials?"

"No, ma'am, I'm not."

"What about newspaper interviews or speeches he gave that dealt specifically with China?"

Mallory thought about it for a moment, then said, "Last year, November 5th, General Cartwright gave a speech at West Point to the senior class and the faculty. I was in the audience, but the press was not invited. In his speech, he said it was imperative that the United States find a way of dealing with China's rising military power."

"Do you have a copy of the speech?" Kelly asked.

"It's in my computer. He wrote it himself, but he asked me to review his draft and make suggestions."

"Did you?" she inquired.

"Only minor ones."

"Could you forward it to me?"

"Yes, ma'am."

Kelly turned to Paul. "Do you have anything else to ask Captain Mallory?"

"Nothing, I just want to thank you," Paul said. "This has been very helpful. Please don't discuss this interview or what we said with anyone else."

"Of course not."

Kelly gave Mallory a card with her encrypted cell number and the email address where he could forward the West Point speech. He promised she would have it within the hour.

"If you recall anything else you think we might like to know," said Kelly, "please call me any hour of the day."

"Yes, ma'am."

When Mallory left the room, Kelly turned to Paul. "I want to check hotel records for confirmation of Mallory's statements, however I think it's clear that General Cartwright is our mole."

"No doubt about it," Paul agreed.

"This is a horrible situation. Cartwright is very popular and the likely Republican presidential candidate. We'll take a lot of heat over this. People always like to shoot the messenger."

"You can start with Wilkins. He's a big buddy of Cartwright's."

"He may be," said Kelly, "but he'll have to accept the fact that Cartwright is guilty. We'll give Wilkins the news at a task force meeting tomorrow morning at ten."

"Better wear your Kevlar vest."

"Good idea. I'm staying at my dad's house tonight. I'm sure he'll have one. Also, I would like to set up security at your house."

"Do you think that's necessary?" Before she had a chance to respond, he added, "Okay, do it."

At Kelly's request, Carol Bailey arranged for a car and driver to take them to their offices in Washington. The whole way, she kept her hand on her gun, but nothing happened.

Washington

Back at FBI headquarters, Kelly briefed Forester on the crash and the interview.

Alarmed, he told her, "You need more protection. What do you want?"

"I'm okay for now."

"Don't be foolish. I'll authorize whatever you need."

"I understand. Thank you."

As soon as Kelly got to her office, she checked her computer. Mallory had forwarded Cartwright's speech. It was titled, "The United States and China: Is War Inevitable?" Kelly began reading.

"The single greatest challenge our nation faces is the rising economic and military power of the People's Republic of China. Nothing else—not the Middle East or Russia—poses an existential threat to the United States. Somehow, we must find a way of reaching an accommodation with Beijing. There is much about the regime in Beijing that is reprehensible. For example, their record on human rights and free speech and their intimidation of neighboring countries. However, we cannot permit the world's two superpowers to drift into a destructive war with horrific casualties on both sides. Nor can we let this occur by a miscalculation in Beijing or in Washington.

"Ever since the end of the Second World War, the United States has called the shots in establishing international order. But that is changing with rising Chinese power. In many respects, the situation is similar to the rise of Germany after 1870 that challenged the British-led world order. Those nations did not reach an accommodation, and their failure to do so was one of the leading causes of the First World War.

"We must meet with the leaders in Beijing and structure an agreement that will eliminate the threat of war. We have a useful precedent—we were able to reach such an agreement with Russia at the end of the Second World War. As a result of the courage of our leaders then, and their willingness to compromise, we were able to avoid a costly nuclear war with Russia, which at the time seemed inevitable. That compromise, which ceded control over Central Europe and Eastern Europe to Russia, was met with enormous criticism from many Americans. But in retrospect, it was clearly the correct decision.

"Unfortunately, I am not optimistic that our current leaders have the same courage, wisdom, and foresight to make the necessary compromises with China. Let me be clear: I am not urging surrender to China. Instead, I want us to reach accommodations, and those will mean making concessions."

The remainder of Cartwright's speech followed the same approach. When Kelly finished reading it, she felt sick. She was now entirely convinced that General Cartwright had been spying for China. In his hubris, he believed he was wiser than President Braddock, the man the American people had elected. And in his view, that superior wisdom entitled him to usurp the role of the president, as he had done in the East China Sea incident. And that same rationale permitted him to accept campaign money arranged by Beijing in order to capture the American presidency and to impose his accommodations with China on the country.

The reality, Kelly realized, was that Cartwright might get away with it. It was also possible, she thought, that their task force was the only thing that could stop him.

Beijing and Countryside

To implement Andrei's idea of establishing a Caribbean bank account for $10 million in General Cartwright's name, Liu enlisted the assistance of Yue Choi, the director of China's Latin American investments.

Yue, who had thick glasses and a scholarly look, seemed frightened when he entered Liu's office. "You can relax," Liu told him. "No one is questioning your actions." That made Yue smile.

The spymaster disclosed as little as possible about what he was doing. "For reasons I will not explain," he began, "I want to open a bank account on a Caribbean island in which we have significant investments, one where we will be able to find a cooperative bank."

Without hesitating, Yue replied, "That's an easy decision. Trinidad is the place."

"Tell me why," Liu commanded.

"Trinidad is industrial, not a beach resort for rich Americans," Yue explained. "It has significant oil deposits, and we've entered into long-term contracts to acquire much of that oil. Trinidad is also close to Venezuela, where we now have a strong presence."

"Do you have a bank you've worked with particularly in Trinidad?"

"The National Bank of Trinidad and Tobago. Its CEO is Alistair Singh."

"Can you trust him?"

"About as well as you can trust anybody in that part of the world."

Liu snarled. "Fine," he said. "Here's what I want you to do. Establish an account at that bank in the name of an American, Darrell Cartwright. Then transfer in ten million dollars from NRW bank in Shanghai."

"Singh will need a card on file electronically with an address and signature for Cartwright."

"List his address as Washington, DC. I assume Singh will accept that?"

"If I tell him to. What about the signature?"

Liu thought about it for a moment, then recalled that Cartwright had signed a document forwarded by Xiang in one of the eight envelopes. He could have one of his handwriting experts forge the signature from that. "I'll send it to you electronically."

"That should be sufficient. I'll forward it to Singh."

"Give Singh one other instruction," said Liu.

"What's that?"

"He shouldn't disclose when the account was opened or the source of the funds to anyone unless you expressly authorize it. Is that clear?"

"Absolutely."

Later that day, Liu went to see President Yao, who had left the heat and smog of Beijing behind for his house in the mountains.

They walked along a lake near the president's house, security guards trailing behind—close enough to provide protection, but far enough so they couldn't overhear what was said.

"We now have leverage over General Cartwright," Liu told President Yao.

"How? Tell me."

Liu explained about the Trinidad bank account.

Yao immediately understood. "So if Cartwright would like to drop out of the presidential race, or if he is elected and intends to renege on his commitments to you, then you can threaten to disclose the Trinidad account to the American media. Knowing that would destroy him, Cartwright would have to do your bidding."

"Precisely."

"Excellent," Yao said.

That was the most complimentary thing Yao had ever said to Liu. "Wait, there's more," said Liu as he reached into his pocket. He pulled out a picture of Helena and showed it to Yao. "She was a Russian girl Cartwright slept with in Prague. That night, she gained access to his computer and forwarded emails to Moscow. Disclosure of that, too, would destroy him."

"Without any doubt," agreed Yao. "You have done well. Now we have total control over him—this man who is likely to be the future president of the United States."

Chevy Chase and Washington

The night after the attack was uneventful for Kelly. As a result of her father's CIA work, he had installed an extensive security system in and around his house, including an invisible electronic fence at the perimeter. Forester also stationed two agents in a car in front of the house. Kelly felt secure sleeping in her old room with Julie next door.

Kelly was up at 5:30 the following morning. After making a pot of coffee, she was on the computer. Working with the IT people at FBI headquarters, she was hacking into hotel computers. By seven o'clock, she had established that Minister Liu had been registered in room 724 at the Bristol the night that Cartwright and Mallory had stayed there.

Mallory had told her that he and Cartwright had stayed at Raffles Hotel in Singapore on November 20th. Hacking into the Raffles computer system was difficult, but Kelly kept going until she got what she wanted. Minister Liu had also stayed there that night.

The case against Cartwright was getting stronger.

"Good luck," her father told her when she left the house at seven. Julie was still sleeping.

"Thanks," she said. "I'll need it."

At ten, she started the task force meeting. Kelly began by presenting the evidence she and Paul had assembled.

Farrell quickly agreed with them. "Cartwright is our mole, no doubt about it," he said.

But not Wilkins. As she had anticipated, the national security adviser was furious. "You're slandering an innocent man, a military hero of the United States."

"Look at the evidence," Kelly insisted.

Red-faced and raising his voice, Wilkins pointed to Paul. "You're the damn lawyer. Explain to her that if you presented this evidence to a judge, he'd toss out your case."

Before Paul had a chance to respond, Farrell's phone rang. He glanced at it and said, "It's the CIA director's secretary. I better take it."

He moved into a corner with the phone. Kelly heard him say, "Yes, sir, I'll be there in thirty minutes." He put away the phone and turned to Kelly. "Director Harrison wants a briefing about the task force and what we've done. I'll have to tell him about Cartwright."

"Absolutely," said Kelly. "Go do it."

Once Farrell was gone, Wilkins bore in on Paul. "You know I'm right. All you have is circumstantial evidence, at best."

"It's strong," Paul said. "The eight meetings with Martin, and then Xiang comes the next day to pick up the envelopes."

"Cartwright must have had scores of meetings with Martin."

"The Bristol Hotel meeting with Liu," Paul continued.

"You have no idea what was said," Wilkins retorted.

"I doubt they were discussing the Olympics."

"Oh, bullshit. You don't have nearly enough to prove a case beyond a reasonable doubt, and you know damn well I'm right."

When Paul didn't respond, Wilkins pressed on. "Arthur Larkin couldn't possibly be ready to go for an indictment."

"I was waiting until after this meeting to present it to him."

"I'm sure you were. You'd like to gain some support for this absurd conclusion so the AG doesn't toss you out of his office."

Kelly watched Paul beginning to wither. They had to get more evidence.

"Fine," she said. "We'll apply the old Washington adage. Follow the money."

"What do you mean?" Wilkins asked.

"We know from press accounts that Carl Dickerson, an LA businessman, has been giving Cartwright tens of millions of dollars for his campaign through super PACs. Paul and I will fly out to LA and meet with Dickerson."

"For what reason?" Wilkins asked.

"To prove that some of this is Chinese money, or that the Chinese are leaning on Dickerson to give money to Cartwright. It's all part of a conspiracy to commit espionage."

"Yeah, right," Wilkins said. "To me, it sounds like a waste of time and taxpayer money."

He looked at this watch. "Sorry. I have to get back to the White House."

"It's been swell," Kelly mumbled under her breath.

When Wilkins was gone, Kelly said to Paul, "I intend to do one other thing. I'll ask Joanne Moore at the Treasury to canvass offshore banks and determine whether Cartwright has an account funded by the Chinese. That would really help nail down our case."

*   *   *

For his campaign headquarters, Cartwright had taken over a suite of offices on the top floor of a new building in the Penn Quarter, Washington's hottest downtown real estate, having ousted Gucci Gulch on K Street for that designation. It was only a couple blocks from Andrew Martin's office at Eighth and Pennsylvania, which had been a factor in Cartwright's choice.

That morning, Cartwright was in a meeting with his chief pollster, Kenny Thornton. All of the news was good. Cartwright was surging in the polls.

"Bottom line," Kenny said, "is that if you got the nomination and the election were held today, you'd beat Braddock by 55 percent to 41 percent, with 4 percent undecided. That's a huge lead."

"There's still a long way to go," Cartwright noted.

"True. But wouldn't you rather be ahead than behind?"

"For sure. However, we can't let up, we have to keep pushing."

Cartwright's phone rang. He saw that the call came from a blocked number. "Hang on a minute," he said to Kenny. "I have to take this."

As soon as Cartwright heard Wilkins voice, he asked Kenny to leave the room.

"Yes, George," Cartwright said.

"We have to talk."

"Sure. I can come to your office, unless you prefer mine."

"A remote location would be better."

Cartwright quickly understood that Wilkins had something highly confidential to tell him. When he had begun his campaign, he realized that meetings like this would occur, so he had arranged with Senator Haywood, a second-term Republican from South Carolina, to use the senator's Georgetown house whenever he needed a venue for secret meetings. No one would raise an eyebrow if Cartwright or Wilkins went to the senator's house. The powerful always mingled in Washington. Also, Haywood's frequent entertaining, including his lavish dinner parties, were a mainstay of the capital social scene. Guests regularly came from across the political spectrum.

"Meet me at Senator Haywood's house in Georgetown, this evening at seven," Cartwright said.

"I'll be there."

*   *   *

Senator Haywood greeted Cartwright when he arrived at the house at 6:30 that evening.

"The polls look great," Haywood said. "You are definitely on a roll, my friend."

"I can't lose momentum."

"Don't worry, you won't. Now let's talk about this evening. Lance, my congressional aide, said you wanted to schedule a meeting here, which is of course fine with me. How many people?"

"Just one and myself." Cartwright hoped Haywood wouldn't ask who was coming.

"I'm going out in a few minutes," said Haywood. "Make yourself comfortable in the study. Joseph will bring you a drink and lead in your visitor when he arrives."

"Perfect. Thanks, Senator."

"My pleasure. I said I'd do anything to help your campaign, and I meant it."

Wilkins arrived promptly at seven. Cartwright thought he looked frazzled and distraught. He asked Joseph for a bourbon and water, which the butler prepared from the bar located along one side of the room. He also topped off Cartwright's drink with some additional liquor. Then he quickly departed, closing the door behind him.

Wilkins took a gulp. "I have the damnedest thing to tell you."

"Okay, I'm listening."

"Immediately after the incident in the East China Sea," Wilkins began in a halting voice, "the Japanese prime minister convinced Braddock that the Chinese have a mole planted at the top of the American government."

Cartwright cautioned himself that it was critical to pretend he had no idea of any effort the government had made to uncover the mole. His only source of information had been Liu, who had told him about Kelly Cameron.

"What evidence do the Japanese or Braddock have for that supposition?" Cartwright asked, sounding surprised.

"A voice intercept of a conversation between two Chinese pilots that didn't justify the conclusion. However, Braddock appointed a secret task force with Kelly Cameron, a hard-driving FBI agent, a real ballbreaker, in charge of this witch hunt."

"Who else is on it?"

"Paul Maltoni from DOJ, Lance Farrell from the CIA, and me."

Cartwright leaned forward in his chair. "Has your task force identified the mole?"

Wilkins coughed, cleared his throat, and took another gulp of scotch. "You're never going to believe this."

"Try me."

"Kelly, Paul, and Farrell are convinced it's you."

As soon as Wilkins words were out, Cartwright shot to his feet. "What?" He raised his voice, sounding indignant. "You've got to be kidding."

"I wish I were. I argued against them, telling them they were slandering a patriotic and loyal American. But I've gotten nowhere. That's why I had to tell you."

"What do they base this absurd conclusion on?"

"They have circumstantial evidence."

"What evidence?"

Wilkins hesitated for a moment, then spit it out. "They arrested Xiang, a Chinese embassy official who was on the receiving end of the material being passed. He said he received his information from Andrew Martin. They've established from Martin's secretary's records that you had meetings with Martin right before Martin passed the info to Xiang."

Cartwright snarled. "That proves nothing. I've had lots of meetings with Andrew Martin for months. He's my top campaign advisor."

"Precisely what I said."

"What else do they have?"

"Kelly and Paul talked to Mallory, your pilot. He told them about a secret trip you took to Paris a few days ago. There, according to Mallory, you met with someone in the Bristol Hotel who had a Chinese guard in front of his suite."

Cartwright kept his anger against Mallory in check. "That's total and utter bullshit."

"You mean you didn't go to Paris?"

"I went and I did meet with a top Chinese official. There was absolutely nothing improper in that meeting. Now that I have a good chance of being president, I've begun an outreach to the Chinese. They're the second most powerful nation in the world, and I'm a military man. I didn't want them to be alarmed. I want to assure them that our great nations can work together cooperatively. I know you'll agree that engagement makes sense."

"Absolutely. Who did you meet with?"

"Jiang, their justice minister. He was there as a representative of President Yao." Cartwright was certain Wilkins would never check with Jiang. He added, "I'm telling you this because you're my friend. I'd appreciate it if you didn't share it with anyone else, even on the task force. In this witch hunt atmosphere, they could take it out of context."

"Of course, I won't. My advice as a friend is that you defer further meetings with Chinese leaders until after the election."

"For sure. I had no idea any of this was occurring."

"I knew there had to be a good explanation."

"What other so-called evidence does this Kelly Cameron have?"

"That's all at this point. However, Kelly and Paul Maltoni are going out to Los Angeles tomorrow to meet with Dickerson, your big contributor."

"What the hell for?"

"They want to establish a link between Dickerson and the Chinese. They hope to prove Dickerson's money is Chinese money."

"They won't find a damn thing, because there is nothing."

"I didn't think so." Wilkins took a deep breath and exhaled. "Now you know the whole story. I have so much respect and admiration for you, General Cartwright. That's why I had to warn you that these people are gunning for you."

"Thanks, I really appreciate it. And please arrange another meeting with me if you have anything else to share."

"Oh, I will. In my job as head of the NSC, I'm not political. I'd be as comfortable working in your administration as Braddock's. Even more so, because our views are so closely aligned."

Wilkins' blatant pitch for a job in the Cartwright administration confirmed that he was the front-runner.

"I'm glad you told me that," said Cartwright. "I'll bear it in mind."

Ten minutes after Wilkins left, Cartwright thanked Joseph and left the senator's house. Cartwright's car and driver were waiting outside.

"Take me home," Cartwright said.

In the back of the car on the way to Arlington, Cartwright replayed in his mind what Wilkins had told him. He was particularly outraged by Mallory's perfidy. His instinctive reaction was to fire him, but he quickly rejected that. It might tip his hand to others that he knew Mallory had spoken to Kelly and Paul. Besides, now that he knew Mallory was a traitor, he might be able to use him to his own advantage.

Cartwright's bottom line assessment was that Kelly and Paul didn't have enough evidence to charge him. Without a solid case, they didn't dare file charges. If they did, the Republicans and many in the media would scream this was all politically motivated by Braddock, who was behind in the polls.

That's where matters stood now. However, the meeting Kelly and Paul were having tomorrow with Dickerson worried Cartwright. If Dickerson had violated campaign funding laws, which were complex as hell, they might be able to induce Dickerson to cut a deal in return for immunity. Cartwright couldn't let that happen without giving Liu a chance to shore up Dickerson.

As soon as Cartwright walked into his house, he picked up the phone and dialed Mario's pizza.

"Please deliver one pizza to me with Chinese spices from Szechuan," he asked.

"Address?"

Cartwright gave it.

"Pizza will be there in an hour."

For most of the hour, Cartwright paced in the living room. Finally, the doorbell rang.

"Pizza delivery," Cartwright heard through the closed door.

When Cartwright opened it, a Chinese man entered and handed him a box with pizza.

"You have a message for me," the delivery man said.

"Yes, the message is that Kelly Cameron and Paul Maltoni are flying to Los Angeles to meet with Dickerson tomorrow."

Beijing

Liu was disturbed but not upset when Wu called from Washington to relay the message from Cartwright. He had been furious at Wu for failing to take out Kelly and Paul when they were en route to their interview with Mallory. By now, he knew Kelly well enough to realize that a failed attempt on her life would never get her to back off. He had to go after her with all possible weapons.

He told Wu, "Kelly Cameron has a daughter, Julie. She's eight years old. I want you to kidnap her."

"I already thought of that. It won't work."

"Why not?"

"Kelly stashed the girl with her father, a former big shot in the CIA. He has his house fortified like a military base. We'd never succeed, and we'd get some awful press if we tried and were caught."

"Have your people keep watching that house. Sooner or later you'll get a chance." Meantime, Liu had to shift his focus to Dickerson and Los Angeles. He told Wu, "Stand by the phone. I'll get back to you."

Liu reached Dickerson in his Los Angeles office on an encrypted phone. "I heard you're having some visitors from Washington."

"That's right. Tomorrow at two. Paul Maltoni from DOJ and Kelly Cameron from the FBI are coming out. We're meeting in my office. My guess is they'll press me about my contributions to Cartwright's campaign. I intend to have my LA lawyer, Ken Norton, there. This shouldn't be a big deal. I'm clean. One of Andrew Martin's partners who specializes in political contributions set it up. Norton understands the structure, and he confirmed it's perfectly legal. I'm only giving my own money to Cartwright, not company money. They're barking up the wrong tree."

"To continue your metaphor," said Liu, "these are attack dogs. They'll try to intimidate you—force you on the defensive about your relationship with Chinese governmental officials."

"They won't get anywhere. I'll enjoy slapping them down."

Liu hoped Dickerson wasn't getting too self-confident. "Don't underestimate these two, particularly Kelly Cameron."

"I won't, believe me. You don't have to worry."

But Liu was worried as he put down the phone. Dickerson was a weak link in his plan. He had to know how weak. He called Jiang, the justice minister.

"We have to talk," Liu said.

Indicative of the relative power between security and justice in the Chinese government, Jiang didn't suggest that Liu come to his office. "I'm on my way to you," Jiang said.

*   *   *

Liu explained the situation to Jiang. "You went to law school in the US and you understand their system. How much of a problem can Dickerson be for us?"

"Under US laws, foreigners cannot contribute to US elections."

"I haven't given any money. It all came from Dickerson. He's an American citizen."

"Did you have meetings with Dickerson in which you discussed him contributing to Cartwright's campaign?" When Liu didn't respond, Jiang said, "I won't repeat what you tell me."

"The answer is yes."

"And you promised Dickerson benefits for his business in China if he contributed to Cartwright's campaign?"

"Not in those precise terms."

"Nevertheless, he understood that, didn't he?"

"I suppose so."

Jiang rubbed his forehead as if that could help frame his judgment. After a few moments, he said, "The American prosecutors could argue that Dickerson was your agent and his contributions to Cartwright's campaign were, in effect, Chinese contributions."

That would blow up my entire operation, Liu thought. He couldn't let that happen. But how to stop it? Going after Dickerson wasn't an option. He had only one possible action.

As soon as Jiang left, he called Wu back in Washington. "Listen carefully," he said. "Kelly Cameron and Paul Maltoni have a meeting in Beverly Hills tomorrow at the office of Carl Dickerson. I want you to fly to Los Angeles as soon as possible. Here's what I want you to do . . . ."

Los Angeles

The headquarters of CDI, Carl Dickerson Industries, occupied an entire eight-story building on the corner of Wilshire and Beverly in Beverly Hills. Wanting to keep the work of the task force secret, Kelly decided that rather than having a team of agents shepherd her and Paul around, which would have meant lots of explanations and filling out paperwork, she and Paul would fly commercial and rent a car at the Los Angeles airport when they arrived Friday at noon. They would enter the city under the radar, quietly get in, have their meeting with Dickerson, and get out.

Once they had arrived, they parked their rental across the street from CDI and walked into the building. A guard in the lobby directed them to the eighth floor. When they stepped out of the elevator, Anna, a smartly dressed young Chinese woman, met them and escorted them to Dickerson's corner office.

Dickerson was waiting with Ken Norton, his lawyer. Both men were dressed in white shirts, ties, and suits, which Kelly guessed cost more than all the clothes in her closet.

"We've met before," Norton said to Paul.

Paul stared at Norton, then said, "That's right. About two years ago when I was with Martin and Glass, I was assisting Andrew Martin, who was retained by Universal in an antitrust litigation. You were Universal's regular outside counsel. We had one meeting with you at the beginning of the case."

"Good memory. You and Martin did an outstanding job for Universal."

Kelly hated it when her lawyer became chummy with the lawyer on the other side. She didn't want Paul to drop his guard.

"That was in my former life," he said tersely.

"Let's get started," Norton said, taking charge. He pointed them to an octagonal table in one corner of the office.

As they sat down, Anna reappeared, offering coffee, tea, or water. Paul seemed like he'd accept, but Kelly responded first. "We're not here to socialize. This is all business."

Following their script, Paul began, "We want to talk to you, Mr. Dickerson, about your massive spending on Cartwright's presidential campaign."

"For what reason?" Norton responded.

"We want to determine whether there have been violations of campaign finance laws."

"Mr. Dickerson is under no obligation to talk to you."

"We can do it here or down at the courthouse."

"That's ridiculous. My client—"

Dickerson waved his hand and cut off Norton. "I'm happy to talk to these people, Ken. I have nothing to hide. I'm merely exercising the First Amendment rights I have under Supreme Court decisions relating to presidential campaign financing."

Norton came back in. "In case you're not familiar with those decisions, Mr. Maltoni," he said in a condescending voice, "they permit an

American a citizen to give unlimited amounts to a super PAC to fund advertising for a presidential election. That is precisely what my client has been doing."

"Thank you for explaining the law to me," Paul said in a voice dripping with sarcasm.

Kelly was happy to hear that Paul wouldn't be steamrolled by Dickerson's high-priced lawyer.

"Are we finished then?" Norton asked.

"Of course not," said Paul. "The Supreme Court cases don't permit an American citizen to pass through funds from a foreign government."

"That's not relevant to this situation," said Norton.

"We think it is," Paul returned.

"Which government do you have in mind?"

"The People's Republic of China."

Dickerson was smiling. He looked amused. "Sorry, Mr. Maltoni," he said, "you're way off the mark. Every dollar I've given to General Cartwright's campaign came from a personal account of mine at Wells Fargo. My accountant and an officer at Wells Fargo will confirm that and provide you with documentation."

Paul let Dickerson's words hang in the air for a few moments. Then he said, "Well, let me ask you this, Mr. Dickerson. You do a great deal of business in China, don't you?"

"Of course I do, Mr. Maltoni. I also do business in Japan, Singapore, Korea, and many other countries throughout the world. All of that's a matter of public record."

"Did any Chinese official urge you to make these contributions to the Cartwright campaign?"

Norton reached out and put his hand on Dickerson's arm. Dickerson pushed it away.

"Absolutely not," Dickerson said.

Kelly was watching Dickerson's face as he delivered those words. The self-confident swagger was gone. His expression had tightened. From his face, she was confident he was lying.

Paul pressed on. "Did they promise you additional business if you made the contributions?"

"Absolutely not."

Another lie, Kelly decided.

Kelly broke in. "Would you submit to a polygraph, Mr. Dickerson, for these last two questions?"

"You've got to be kidding," Norton said.

This time, Dickerson didn't overrule his lawyer.

Paul pulled a pad from his briefcase and glanced at it. "Please identify for me all of the Chinese government officials you met with in the last year."

Norton responded, "You're asking my client to provide you with sensitive business information that's not relevant to your inquiry."

"I disagree. It was at those meetings that Chinese officials urged Mr. Dickerson to contribute to General Cartwright's campaign."

"He already told you no one asked him to do that."

"Then tell us who he met with."

"Irrelevant."

"I could get a court order to compel him to answer," said Paul.

"I doubt that."

"We could convene a grand jury and force him to answer."

"Attorney General Larkin would never authorize it," Norton countered. "Even if he did, the press would see this for what it is: a lynch mob going after the likely Republican nominee who's leading Braddock in the polls. You people are desperate. Have you ever heard of Watergate? This is another campaign dirty trick."

Paul looked at Kelly to see if she had any more questions. She shook her head.

"Okay, we're finished," Paul said.

"I'll buzz for Anna," Dickerson said. "She'll show you out."

When they were alone in the elevator, Paul told Kelly, "He was lying through his teeth."

"Wait until we're outside."

Once they were on the sidewalk on Wilshire Boulevard, Paul repeated himself. "He was lying through his teeth."

As they crossed Beverly to get to their car, Kelly said, "I agree, but we'll never be able to prove it. And I don't know how you'll break him."

Once they were almost at their car, Kelly took the keys out of her bag and pressed the unlock button. After doing so, she suddenly looked up. Across the street, on the roof of Dickerson's building, she spotted a Chinese man holding a cell phone and preparing to push a button.

Paul said, "There has to be a way for us to—"

On instinct, Kelly reacted. She shouted, "Paul, move quick," pointing to the open door of a nearby building.

When the lawyer didn't move, she grabbed him by the arm and pulled him away from the car toward the doorway. Just as they passed the threshold, their car exploded. A fireball shot into the air. As glass debris flew in their direction, Kelly ducked, shielding her face with her arms. People on the sidewalk were screaming—it was pandemonium.

Kelly desperately wanted to chase the man who had detonated the bomb, but she was afraid to leave Paul. He was in shock and bleeding from his face, arms, and abdomen. She only had minor scratches. She called for an ambulance and remained with Paul.

Minutes later, it arrived. Kelly flashed her FBI ID and climbed into the back with Paul. Fortunately, they were close to Cedar Sinai Hospital. When they reached the hospital, Paul was rushed into the emergency room. Kelly was furious at herself for not arranging maximum security for her and Paul. *Stupid, stupid, stupid,* she chided herself.

Well, better late than never. With a few phone calls, she arranged for her and Paul to have protection 24–7, for as long as they were in LA, on the plane back, and then in Washington. She also beefed up protection at her father's house where Julie was staying. After that, she called Forester to tell him what had occurred.

"I'll mobilize law enforcement in LA," he said. "We'll get right on trying to find out who's responsible. Also, I'll tell Arthur Larkin. Call and let me know Paul's situation."

"Yes, sir. Will do."

An hour later, she got the prognosis on Paul. He was now fully cognizant. He had multiple cuts and bruises, which had been stitched up, and a concussion. The doctor said that he should remain in the hospital overnight. As she walked into Paul's hospital room, she was startled by his appearance. He had bandages on his face, arm, and chest.

"I'm so sorry," Kelly said. "Really, I am, Paul. I blame myself for not arranging protection for us in LA."

"Don't," he said. "I could have suggested it. My fault as well."

When Kelly told him she'd be taking the red-eye to Washington, and he'd be flying back tomorrow, Paul shouted, "No way, I'm fine. I'm going back with you."

"C'mon Paul, don't be ridiculous. You were already banged up once when that truck hit our SUV. Now this makes two. You have to rest and let them check you."

"No fucking way. I have to get even with the bastards who did this to us."

Paul was a grown man. Neither she nor the hospital could keep him against his will, so they compromised. He would rest in the hospital until nine that evening when the two of them would leave for the airport. But the doctor made it clear that Paul was flying against her advice.

While Paul rested, Kelly sat alone in the office she had commandeered at the hospital, drinking coffee and trying to evaluate what had occurred. The more she thought about it, the more convinced she became that there was a leak in the task force. The Chinese who were running the Cartwright operation must have known she and Paul were coming to LA. Farrell didn't even know about this trip, because he had left the meeting before they had discussed it. That meant it had to be Wilkins.

The conclusion was clear: Wilkins had told someone about their trip to Los Angeles. Cartwright, Dickerson, or Liu? But why? What was Wilkins' motive? Did he genuinely believe Cartwright was innocent, and he wanted to help Cartwright? Or was Wilkins in bed with the Chinese as well as Cartwright? She didn't know, but she had to find out.

Kelly recalled at one of the first task force meetings that Wilkins had supported Cartwright's version of what occurred in the White House Situation Room involving the incident in the East China Sea. He reaffirmed the story that Cartwright had told the *Wall Street Journal* reporter, which made Braddock look weak and frightened. She wondered whether it had really occurred this way, or whether it was another instance of Wilkins backing Cartwright.

She recalled that in addition to the president, Cartwright, and Wilkins, one other person had been in the Situation Room that day: the president's chief of staff, Chad Vernon. She called Vernon and arranged a meeting with him for the following morning at the FBI.

Washington

The plane carrying Kelly and Paul, accompanied by two FBI agents from the LA field office, landed at Dulles at 6:20 on Saturday morning. Passing a newsstand, she saw that the Los Angeles explosion had made the front page of the *Post*, *Times*, and *Wall Street Journal*. She grabbed copies of all three. Then she insisted that Paul, accompanied by one of the security men, go home to sleep for a few hours while she went to her office to meet with Vernon.

In the car on the way to FBI headquarters, she read the papers. Her and Paul's names had been withheld, and the explosion was described as possibly gang related.

When the president's chief of staff heard she wanted to talk about the meeting in the Situation Room, his face lit up. "I'm damn glad somebody finally wants to hear about that."

Vernon's reaction took her by surprise. "Why, what happened?" Kelly asked.

"The story Cartwright told the *Wall Street Journal* was not only horribly insulting to the president, it was also a pack of lies."

"In what respect?"

"Cartwright said the president was indecisive, shaking, and perspiring, that he was panicked by having to make a decision. Nothing could be further from the truth. In fact, the president was very calm and cool."

Kelly wasn't sure she believed Vernon. She was concerned he might be trying to defend his boss. She told Vernon that Wilkins had corroborated Cartwright's account in a task force meeting.

"Then Wilkins was lying as well."

"Why should I believe you against both of them?" she asked.

He pulled a phone from his pocket. "Because I have proof I'm right."

"What proof?"

"I recorded the discussion in the Situation Room on my phone. I'll play it for you now."

"Go ahead."

Listening to the recording, Kelly realized Vernon was correct. Braddock did sound calm and cool. Initially, the president had wanted to repudiate the Camp David decision and engage the Chinese. In response to the president's proposed action, Cartwright was shouting in an emotional tone, "These fucking pieces of rock aren't even islands. Going to war with China over them would be the height of stupidity." At the last minute, Braddock yielded to Cartwright. He reverted to the Camp David decision and ordered the US pilots to break off from engaging the Chinese pilots.

When the tape was finished, Vernon said, "I certainly don't want to impugn General Cartwright's patriotism. However, you have to admit, Kelly, that the general did a good job of representing Chinese interests on this issue."

Kelly couldn't argue with Vernon. She was happy to have the recording, because it was further corroboration that Cartwright was in bed with the Chinese.

"Is President Braddock aware of this recording?" Kelly asked.

"I played it for him as soon as the *Wall Street Journal* article appeared. I pleaded with him to let me release it to at least one reporter, but Braddock refused. He claimed it would be viewed as a political act against Cartwright, and people might not understand the nuances. Also, he felt that if we released the tape, it would keep the whole incident alive. This way he hoped it would die down quickly."

"Can I have the recording?"

"For sure. I'll send it to you electronically right now."

"Don't you have to check with Braddock?"

"He already told me to cooperate fully with your task force investigation. If you need anything else, call me any hour of the day or night. In my job, I never sleep—as my wife often reminds me. She's working on a book, *The Nonexistent Sex Life of a Presidential Chief of Staff*."

When Kelly didn't respond, he said, "You were supposed to laugh."

"Sorry," she said, cracking a smile. "I had a tough day in LA yesterday followed by a red-eye. I'm afraid I've lost my sense of humor."

Once Vernon had gone, Kelly pondered what to do about Wilkins. Some government people were fond of saying, "That's above my GS level." These words summarized Kelly's situation. She couldn't deal with Wilkins on her own. It was a matter for Forester.

She took out her phone and called upstairs. The director's secretary said, "Director Forester had a meeting outside of the office this morning. He'll be able to see you at two in his office."

"I'll be there," Kelly replied.

*   *   *

Kelly, accompanied by a heavily bandaged Paul at her side, walked into Forester's office at two o'clock on the dot.

"We had no success finding the man who detonated the bomb," the FBI director said.

"I'm sorry to hear that," Kelly told him. "We have another problem."

"What's that?"

She explained the basis for her conclusion that Wilkins had leaked word of their LA trip.

An initially perplexed and then irate Forester rolled his hand into a fist and pounded on the top of his desk. "I'm going to call Wilkins over here and confront him."

Forester picked up the phone. Kelly heard him say, "I don't care how busy you are, either you get your ass over here right now, or I'll send two agents to the White House to arrest you for treason." Forester slammed down the phone. "Wilkins is on his way."

Ten minutes later he arrived. Kelly and Paul were sitting in front of Forester's desk, facing the director. A third chair for Wilkins was off to one side.

"There must be some mistake," Wilkins said, entering the room. He was pale and looked flustered, his usual arrogance gone.

"There is no mistake," Forester said in a booming voice. "Thanks to you, Kelly and Paul were almost killed yesterday in Los Angeles."

"What are you talking about?"

"You saw the news stories about the bomb that went off in Beverly Hills."

"Yeah, it was gang related."

"Wrong. That was the story I gave the press. A Chinese man standing on the roof of Dickerson's office building detonated a powerful bomb in the car Kelly and Paul had been using. It's a miracle the two of them weren't killed."

Wilkins collapsed into the empty chair. "Did you catch the person who set off the bomb?" he asked.

"Not yet. So far, we've established that *you*," he paused to point a finger at Wilkins, "leaked the information of their Los Angeles meeting with Dickerson to the Chinese."

"I did no such thing." Wilkins sounded indignant.

"Don't you lie to me. You and I were the only ones who knew Kelly and Paul were going to LA to meet with Dickerson. I sure as hell didn't leak that information to anyone."

Wilkins raised his right hand. "I swear that I didn't tell the Chinese about the meeting."

Before Forester had a chance to respond, Kelly figured it out. "You told Cartwright we were going to meet with Dickerson, didn't you?" she said.

As Wilkins sat mute, Forester went back on the attack. "That's treason, Wilkins, I could arrest you for that."

"I never thought there would be any danger to Kelly or Paul," he replied weakly.

"That's absurd. You've been on this task force from the beginning. You know they've built a solid case against Cartwright for being a Chinese spy."

"I never believed that. General Cartwright is a military hero. He's spent his life defending the United States. I rejected their conclusion because I thought it was wrong."

"Are you a Chinese spy, too?" Forester asked.

Wilkins shot to his feet. "Absolutely not." He threw up his hands for emphasis. "That's ridiculous. I'm no spy."

"Sit down and cut the histrionics," Forester said.

Wilkins returned to his chair.

"This is the second time we were attacked," Kelly said. "The first was when we were going to the Pentagon to interview Mallory. Did you tip Cartwright off about that, too?"

"Positively not."

"But you did tell Cartwright about the Dickerson meeting," Forester said.

"I thought an innocent and courageous American was being railroaded."

"And that gave you the right to tip off Cartwright about their trip," said Forester.

Kelly interjected, "You've been a pain for us in the task force from the beginning. You fought against everything we wanted to do."

"That's not right," Wilkins protested.

"You always thought you knew better."

"If you're not a Chinese spy," Forester said, "then why did you tell Cartwright? Is it because you thought you were smarter than Kelly and Paul, even with all the evidence they had assembled against Cartwright?"

Wilkins screwed up his face, but didn't respond.

Forester shook his head. "No, that's not it. I know why you did it."

Everyone was looking at Forester, waiting for him to continue.

"You think Cartwright will defeat Braddock and become the next president. You want a big job in Cartwright's administration, maybe secretary of state. That's it, isn't it?"

Wilkins still remained silent.

"You're pathetic," Forester hissed.

Kelly thought Wilkins would break into tears.

"Get out of my sight," said Forester.

Wilkins sprang to his feet and raced to the door. He had to be relieved he wasn't being sent to jail, Kelly thought.

After Wilkins left, Forester asked Kelly, "What do you think we should do to him?"

Before she had a chance to respond, Paul said, "We should string him up by the ankles and pull out his fingernails. Then we'll find out if he's been spying for the Chinese."

Paul sounded serious. Kelly could hardly believe he meant it, but obviously he had gone through a lot because of Wilkins' indiscretion.

"What about you, Kelly?" Forester asked.

"I believe him when he says he's not a Chinese spy."

"Agreed," Forester said.

"We should toss him off the task force," Kelly continued. "Also, I recommend that you tell Arthur Larkin and President Braddock about what Wilkins did. Let them devise the punishment."

The director was shaking his head. "I don't want to do that."

"Why not?" Paul asked. He sounded incredulous.

"Because we're nearing the end game with Cartwright. For now, we're better off leaving Wilkins in place with surveillance. If I tell Braddock and Larkin, they're likely to take some immediate action against Wilkins. Cartwright will undoubtedly find out. He might hop on a plane and fly to China ala Kim Philby. I don't want that to happen."

"What do we do about Wilkins in the meantime?" Kelly asked.

"Freeze him out. Let Wilkins think he convinced us. Don't give him any more information. When this ends, which will be soon, there will be plenty of time to punish him."

Paul opened his mouth to protest, but Kelly cut him off. "That makes good sense to me."

Her phone rang. She looked at her caller ID and saw that it was Joanne Moore at the Treasury. Kelly had given Joanne an assignment to try and find an offshore account in Cartwright's name, funded by the Chinese government.

"We found something," Joanne said.

"Go ahead, tell me." Kelly held her breath.

"Cartwright has an account in a Trinidad bank, the National Bank of Trinidad and Tobago, with ten million dollars."

"When was it opened?" she asked.

"I couldn't find out."

"Source of the funds?"

"Ditto for that. The bank president refused to tell me. When we hacked in, we hit a firewall for that account."

"Do you have any agents in Trinidad?"

"A Treasury investigator by the name of Chas Cohen. We've been worried about drug money finding its way into the Trinidad banks, so we sent him down. Chas spent twenty years in Special Forces before he joined Treasury. We need somebody like that because the drug lords play rough."

Kelly was getting an idea. "How would Chas like a visitor from Washington?" she asked.

"I'm sure he'd love it," said Joanne. "It gets lonely with the hot sun beating down on your head all year long. Let me know who's going down and when."

"Will do," said Kelly, putting down the phone and reporting the discussion to Forester and Paul.

"You okay with me going?" she asked Forester.

"It could be risky."

"We have to find out when the account was opened and the source of the funds. That info could establish beyond any doubt Cartwright's involvement with the Chinese. Tomorrow's Sunday, but I could fly down Monday morning when the bank is open."

Forester thought about it for a minute. Finally, he said, "Okay. Do it."

"I'm going with her," Paul said.

"No way," she replied. "You had a concussion in LA, and probably one before that from the crash on the parkway. You're staying in Washington to rest. If you fight me on this, I'll lock you up in one of those jail cells we have downstairs."

Forester looked at Paul. "The lady plays rough, and I think she means it. Those cells downstairs aren't too comfortable. If I were you, I'd go along with what she's asking."

"All right," Paul grumbled.

Forester turned to Kelly. "You can use my plane," he said. "You want to take security with you?"

"Coming in a private plane, I can bring a gun with me. Chas Cohen will no doubt be armed. With his Special Forces background, we should be okay."

"You're taking a helluva chance."

"On the other hand," said Kelly, "if I come in with a whole entourage, the locals may circle the wagons around the bank."

"Okay, do it your way. But make sure you keep the plane fueled in Trinidad and ready for a quick escape."

The cell phone in Kelly's bag rang. Taking it out, she saw that the call was coming from her father's cell.

"Yes, Dad."

"It's Julie, they grabbed her," came her father's horrified voice.

Panicked, Kelly shot to her feet. "What happened? Who grabbed her?"

"We went to the movie theater, and—"

"Goddammit, I told you to keep her in the house!"

"She really wanted to go, and I thought I could protect her."

Kelly had to get a hold of herself and find out quickly what had happened. "Then what?" she probed.

"We were in line to get popcorn when she said that she had to go to the bathroom. Since I had a clear view of the path to the ladies room, I let her go. I was watching her walk away when I felt a pinprick on the back of my neck. It must have been a powerful sedative. When I came to, emergency medics were helping me, and Julie was gone."

"Did you see anyone suspicious behind you in line?"

"Nothing, everything was normal."

"What about the guards who had been at your house?"

"Two came with me to the theater. They were waiting outside on the street, right in front. I don't know how they missed her."

"How could you have let this happen?" Kelly screamed.

"I'm so sorry, Kelly. But at least I know where Julie is."

"What do you mean?"

"Before we left the house, I attached a tiny tracking device to one of her sneakers. The receiver shows she's at a location in Rockville."

"Unless, of course, they found the device and tossed away the sneaker."

"Unlikely. It was concealed."

Kelly detected the uncertainty in his voice. He had to realize the sneaker might have been abandoned. Whoever had done this with the pinprick sedative would be sophisticated enough to detect a tracking device. If they had, Julie could be anywhere. And Kelly had no idea where to begin looking. This was her worst nightmare.

But even smart perps make mistakes, she had learned. She had to hope that the kidnapper had, and that Julie was still wearing the sneaker.

"What's the location?"

"216 Elm Street."

"Okay, I'll tell Forester. They have people trained to deal with situations like this."

"What can I do to help?"

"Nothing, you've already done enough damage. Just stay away from the area."

Kelly put the phone down. Struggling to keep her emotions under control, she explained the situation to Forester. The instant she finished, he picked up his office phone.

"Listen, Bill," he said, "I want you to set up a hostage rescue right now. It's the eight-year-old daughter of Kelly Cameron."

After Forester provided all the details, he put down the phone. Narrowing his eyes, he looked straight at Kelly. "That was Bill Pierson who heads up hostage situations," he said. "I know how difficult this is for you, so against my better judgment, I'll let you watch from a distance. But I don't want you to play any part in this operation."

"I understand."

"And you'll comply?"

"And I'll comply," she said reluctantly.

"I'm serious, Kelly."

"Yes, sir, I know you are."

Rockville, Maryland

An hour later, the FBI hostage rescue team, headed by Bill Pierson was in place. Four heavily armed men, along with Kelly, were in an unmarked van with one-way glass parked half a block away from 216 Elm Street. It was a shabby, rundown house with a for sale sign in the front. The small front yard was overgrown with weeds. Mixed in with them were a couple of beer cans. Pierson had called the broker on the sign and learned that the house was deserted, the owner having moved to California a month ago.

Another van was parked half a block away in the alley behind the house. One man in each van was watching the house through binoculars, but the curtains were drawn. Neither agent could see inside the house. The plan was to wait another thirty minutes, hoping the kidnappers would bring Julie out. If not, they would break into the house from the front and back. Per Forester's orders, Kelly would remain in the van.

What kept running through her mind was the possibility that the kidnappers had taken Julie to this house, then found the sneaker, left it behind, and taken off with her.

She raised that with Pierson, a grizzled veteran of thirty years with the FBI. "Let's take it one step at a time," he said.

That was certainly reassuring.

She couldn't believe this was happening. It was horrible—truly her worst nightmare. She kept looking at the cell phone in her bag, expecting it to ring with the kidnappers' demands. She tried to guess what they would want. The likeliest scenario was that they would offer to trade Julie for Xiang. She had no idea how Forester would react.

When her phone remained silent, she thought of another, worse scenario: the kidnappers didn't want to deal; their plan was to kill Julie, expecting that to sideline Kelly from the investigation. Surely, they had to realize others in the FBI would pick it up, but there would be a delay and time might be critical for them.

Ten more minutes until Pierson and his men would move. Suddenly, a brown Washington Gas truck drove down the street and parked in front of 216 Elm. A man in a Washington Gas uniform and cap sprang out of the van and quickly climbed the three crumbling stone steps to the front door.

"What the hell," Pierson blurted out. "This idiot could wreck everything."

Kelly grabbed a pair of binoculars and focused on the man approaching the front door. She felt a chill run down her spine. From her vantage point, it was difficult to see his face. Oh no! It couldn't be. *It was. It was her father.*

She wanted to yell at him to get away from the house. But he'd never hear. Even if he did, he wouldn't obey. The kidnappers would surely kill Julie if they were in the house with her. How could he be so stupid?

Horrified, she watched him smash his shoulder against the door, blasting it open. Then, he pulled a pistol from a chest holster. Gun in hand, he went into the house.

"Move now," Pierson told his men in the two vans. As she watched, holding her breath, Pierson and the other three climbed out of the van and ran toward the house.

Only Kelly was left in the van. She grabbed her own gun and jumped out of the van, then stood next to it and watched the house. She wanted to be ready in case the kidnappers slipped out with Julie.

Please God let her be safe.

Ten minutes later, the longest ten minutes of Kelly's life, her father emerged from the house holding Julie in his arms. The girl looked terrified.

Kelly ran toward them.

"She's perfectly okay," her father said. "They didn't harm her."

"Thank God for that."

He handed Julie to Kelly. Julie was crying. "I was so scared, Mommy."

"I know you were. It's all over. You're safe now," Kelly said, hugging her tightly.

"What happened to the people in the house with her?" Kelly asked her dad.

"Nobody was in there besides Julie. Your FBI friends are collecting evidence. The kidnappers blindfolded her and locked her in a closet downstairs, then they left the house."

Kelly had to control her shaking. The kidnappers had figured no one would find Julie. "Bastards," Kelly blurted out. They had planned to kill her, letting her suffocate or die of starvation. Days from now, they would have called to tell Kelly where to find Julie's body, or maybe not even that.

Pierson approached them. "You may be the girl's grandfather and a former CIA agent," he said, "but I should arrest you for what you did."

"I don't think so," Charles Cameron said.

Calmly, he walked back to the Washington Gas truck and drove away.

Anger directed at Liu, who she knew must have masterminded Julie's kidnapping, surged through Kelly's body. She rolled her hands into fists. She was even more determined than ever to wreck Liu's operation.

Trinidad

Monday morning, with Kelly as the sole passenger, Forester's sleek jet approached Piarco Airport. She had spent Sunday with Julie at her father's house. Two armed men were in front, and another two in the back, around the clock. All was quiet, and Julie didn't seem to be suffering any ill effects from her ordeal. Kelly had made her father swear on two Bibles that he wouldn't take or let Julie out of the house until this was all over.

The airport was on the northwest corner of Trinidad, which along with Tobago, formed the twin island nation off the coast of Venezuela. The capital, Port of Spain, was twelve miles from the airport. The previous evening she had done a little research about the Caribbean island republic and learned that it had been a British territory until it had been granted independence in 1962. Trinidad was the largest island in this republic, with a Creole culture and a diverse African, Indian, and European population totaling 1.3 million.

From the air, Kelly saw oil and gas drilling rigs. Those commodities had made Trinidad one of the wealthiest places in the Caribbean. According to a CIA report Joanne had forwarded, oil and gas reserves had made Trinidad a target for Chinese government investments. Beijing, with extensive oil investments in neighboring Venezuela, had been pushing hard to lock up the oil and gas in Trinidad and gain a foothold in the Caribbean, close to the United States. That report also said that with the plunge in oil prices, hard times had set in and crime had escalated.

Kelly walked off the plane into bright sunlight and intense heat. A slight breeze was blowing off the ocean.

Once she had cleared customs, she saw a man with a shaved head and wire-framed glasses dressed in a suit and tie. She immediately recognized Chas Cohen from the picture on the bio Joanne had forwarded the day before.

After a no-nonsense cursory greeting, Chas led her to his black Range Rover. Kelly climbed into the front seat next to Chas.

As they exited the parking lot with Chas driving, he said, "Joanne wouldn't give me much information about the purpose of your trip down here. She said you'd explain."

Kelly laid it out for Chas, then added, "The good news is Joanne arranged a meeting for me with Alistair Singh, the President of the National Bank of Trinidad and Tobago at his office in Port of Spain. The bad news, Joanne told me, is that I'll have an uphill battle to get Alistair to talk to me."

"She's right about that."

"How well do you know Alistair?"

"His family came here from India four generations ago. He was educated at the London School of Economics. He's extremely intelligent. At the same time, he's venal and corrupt. That makes him a good partner for Mexican drug lords and—" Chas abruptly stopped talking and made a sharp left turn. "Hmm," he said.

"What's wrong?"

"I think we have company. A gray Toyota has been following us since we left the airport. I have binoculars in the glove compartment. Grab them and get a line on our friends."

As Kelly did, she noticed they were climbing a steep hill. Once she had located the binoculars, she looked through the window in the back. "Two Chinese men in the gray Toyota."

"That's what I was afraid of. My guess is they'll try to prevent you from getting to your meeting with Alistair."

"What do you want to do?"

"Are you armed?"

"I've got a gun in my bag."

"Good. Grab it."

"Maybe they're just following us," Kelly suggested.

"I know the territory. Trinidad is a great island with lots of wonderful people, but it also has some real thugs. I promised Joanne I'd take care of you, so stop talking and get ready."

Pulling out her gun, she said, "What will you do?"

"I'll take a detour away from town along a narrow road that runs up into the hills. You climb over the seat into the back and roll down both back windows. Let's wait for them to commit. We'll have an advantage with the more substantial vehicle. Make sure you get off the first shot."

"Will do."

Ten minutes later, they were almost at the top of a steep hill. Chas cut his speed to a crawl, hugging the road on the left. That was when the Toyota made its move, acting as if it intended to pass the Range Rover on the right.

When the Toyota was alongside the Range Rover, Kelly saw the man on the passenger side raise a gun and point it directly at Chas.

"Now!" Chas screamed.

Before the man in the Toyota had a chance to shoot, Kelly opened fire, hitting him square in the chest. Next, she shot the driver, who lost control of the Toyota. It veered off the road, flew over the cliff, and down the hill.

Chas put on the brakes and they sprang out of the car. They watched as the Toyota became airborne, hit a rock, and exploded, sending flames high into the air.

"You don't have to worry about them any longer," Chas said.

"What do we do we do now?" Kelly asked.

"We'll go see Police Chief Kasim and tell him what happened."

"Won't I be in trouble?"

"Not at all. Kasim is a friend of mine. He'll believe my story. Besides, Kasim has a Creole background. He figures this is his island, and he hates the Chinese. He thinks they're trying to take over Trinidad's oil and gas through a combination of money and intimidation. I'm hoping Kasim will help you convince Alistair to talk."

Despite what Chas had said, Kelly was more than a little nervous when he turned around, drove into Port of Spain, and pulled up in front of police headquarters. It might not go as smoothly as Chas thought. After all, she had just killed two people. She didn't want to torpedo this Trinidad mission before it got off the ground.

Kelly followed Chas inside the gray cinderblock building where he introduced her to Kasim as "an FBI agent from Washington." Kasim stuck out a large hand. Shaking it, Kelly felt as if her hand was in a powerful vice.

Chas said, "Kelly has a meeting with Alistair Singh, but a couple of our local Chinese friends didn't think she should keep it. They tried to force us off the road and ended up losing control of their car and crashing down the hill. It's a real shame they weren't better drivers."

Kasim smiled. "I heard about an exploding car. Thanks for the explanation." Turning to Kelly he said, "I'm sorry about that. This is a friendly island. What happened to you isn't the usual way we treat visitors."

"Thank you. I didn't think so."

"I assume Alistair knew you were coming."

"Right. We have an appointment."

"So we have to assume he tipped off the Chinese," Kasim said.

"That's what I was thinking," Kelly agreed.

"I don't want you to have any more problems, Ms. Cameron. As a result, I'd like personally to accompany you to your meeting with Alistair. That okay with you?"

"Absolutely."

"Good. I might even be able to assist you if Alistair isn't cooperative, which sometimes happens. Then I'll be forced to invoke Trinidad rules. I'll bet you don't know what those are."

"I have no idea," said Kelly.

"Well, you're in for an education," said Kasim. "Let's go. We can all ride in my car."

Kelly was relieved there were no repercussions from the incident on the road, and delighted to receive Kasim's help.

As Kasim navigated through heavy traffic in the frenetic, noisy capital city, he waved and shouted greetings to people.

After fifteen minutes, the three of them climbed the steps to the National Bank of Trinidad and Tobago. Once they were inside the building, Kasim pushed his way past the receptionist to the elevator, Kelly and Chas following behind.

Kelly understood that Kasim was one of those people who never stopped for red lights, which was okay if you're the police chief. With Kasim in the lead, the three of them barreled past Alistair's secretary without saying a word. Kasim opened a closed door, and they entered the banker's office.

Startled, Alistair Singh, who was on a phone call, quickly hung up and shot to his feet. Short and squat, Alistair reminded Kelly of a tank. He was wearing a shirt and tie, but no jacket.

"Have you ever heard of knocking?" the banker asked.

"You're just lucky Kelly Cameron wasn't murdered on her way to meet with you," Kasim said.

"I have no idea what you're talking about." Alistair came over and held out his hand to Kelly. "Happy to meet you, Ms. Cameron."

She refused to shake his hand and left it hanging in the air.

Once they were seated—Alistair behind his desk and the other three in front—Kelly began. "What I want is real simple. You have an account in the name of Darrell Cartwright, which has ten million dollars in it. I want to know when it was opened and the source of the funds."

Alistair shook his head. "I'm very sorry, Ms. Cameron. Information about our customers is maintained in the strictest confidence. I think you can understand that."

Chas was scowling. "Don't play games with us. We're very close to blacklisting your bank because of drug money laundering. Failure to cooperate with us will push you over the edge. Blacklisting means no US bank will be able to do any business with you. You might as well shut down your bank at that point. Is that what you want?"

Despite the comfortably air-conditioned room, Kelly noticed moisture forming under Alistair's arms. When he didn't answer, Kelly imagined he was weighing in his mind who could hurt him more, the US Treasury Department or the Chinese government.

After a minute of silence, Kasim turned to Kelly and said, "Remember when I told you I might have to invoke Trinidad rules?"

"I sure do."

Without saying another word, Kasim flew out of his chair and over the desk. He forced the startled Alistair in his chair back against the credenza behind the desk. Then he grabbed the terrified banker's throat with both hands.

"Tell her what she wants to know," Kasim commanded.

"All right," Alistair choked out, gagging for air. "All right, I'll tell her. Just get your hands off me!"

Kasim released Alistair and returned to his chair.

The banker turned to his computer and began punching keys. After a minute, he said, "The account was opened three days ago." He turned around the computer. "Here's the card opening the account signed by Cartwright."

"Does that mean he was here?"

"It was done by remote, electronically."

"I want a copy of that card."

Alistair hesitated for a moment, then hit print. He wheeled around to the printer on the credenza to hand it to her.

"Source of the funds?" Kelly asked.

"NRW Bank in Shanghai."

Chas winced. "Are you sure of that?"

"Yes, I'm sure."

Kelly glanced at the computer screen again. It confirmed what Alistair had told them.

"Do you want to know anything else?" Kasim asked Kelly.

"No, I have it all."

When they reached the street, Kasim asked Kelly, "Where can I take you?"

"The airport, if it's not too much trouble."

"No, of course not."

The three of them climbed back into the police chief's car. The ride to the airport went by without incident. She thanked Kasim, and Chas walked her to Forester's waiting plane.

"You were surprised to hear it was NRW Bank in Shanghai," Kelly remarked to Chas. "Why?"

"Because that bank is controlled by PLA, the Chinese People's Liberation Army."

"Meaning that?"

Chas completed the sentence for Kelly: "Cartwright is clearly on the take from the Chinese government."

Chas's conclusion made sense, but as the plane took off, knifing through the clouds, Kelly was troubled. If the Chinese had wanted to transfer funds secretly to Cartwright, they would have done so by employing a bank that couldn't be linked to them. Using a bank owned by the PLA made no sense at all. It was as if they wanted anyone who checked to reach the conclusion Chas had. But why?

No matter how hard Kelly thought about the issue, she couldn't come up with another explanation.

Washington

As Kelly reported on her trip to Trinidad to Forester and Paul in the director's office, she expressed her misgivings regarding Chas's conclusion that Cartwright was on the take from the Chinese. "There has to be another explanation," she said. "We're dealing with sophisticated people—both Cartwright and Liu. This is too clumsy."

The director was shaking his head. "It always amazes me how smart people sometimes do really stupid things that lead to their getting caught. I've seen it over and over again," he said, dismissing Kelly's concerns.

"Get your handcuffs, Kelly," said Paul. "It's time to arrest Cartwright."

"Not so fast," Forester replied. "We're not arresting Cartwright without explicit approval from the attorney general."

As the director picked up the phone, Kelly wondered how it would go. She heard him say, "It's Forester. I have to speak to Arthur." After a pause, the director said, "Listen, Arthur, the task force is ready to make an arrest. They need your approval . . . Sure, we'll be right over."

*   *   *

Arthur looked grim, Kelly thought, as they walked into his office. He must have had a premonition of what they were about to tell him.

Staring at the bandaged Paul, he said, "I'm sorry this happened to you, Paul. Why don't you take some time off?"

"No, sir. I have to see this through."

After they were seated around the conference table, Forester said, "Kelly, why don't you summarize what you and Paul have learned in the last couple of days?"

Kelly was pleased to hear him say this. She had been afraid he might ask Paul to brief his boss, and she didn't think Paul was firing on all cylinders.

She took the AG through it in detail. At the end, Kelly said, "We're here for your approval to arrest General Cartwright."

Arthur stood up and paced around the office, one hand in his pocket, the other ruffling his hair. When he didn't reply, the director added, "We clearly have enough evidence against Cartwright to make the arrest."

"Of course you do," said Arthur, "but this is Washington. Politics comes above everything else." Arthur continued in a somber voice, "A presidential campaign is going full blast. You're asking the attorney general, close friend, and confidante of one of the two leading candidates, to order the arrest of the other one. Cartwright's supporters will claim I'm worse than John Mitchell."

"Surely," the director said, "you're not suggesting we excuse Cartwright's espionage."

"Of course not. What I'm saying is the decision on arresting Cartwright has to be made by President Braddock."

"I disagree," the director replied forcefully, "you are this country's top legal officer. The decision is yours."

Kelly was happy to hear Forester's words. Arthur was trying to play the old Washington game of CYA, cover your ass, and she was glad the director wouldn't let him get away with it.

Arthur turned to Forester. "You have been both a successful lawyer and a federal judge. Normally I would never disagree with you, Jim. However, as I said, this is not a legal matter."

The director was ready to fire back. It was as if they were the only two in the room. "Have you considered that you might not be doing your friend Braddock a favor by dropping this hot potato into his lap?"

"That thought has been running through my mind. I'm sure pundits and historians will debate it. For me, the decisive factor is if I were Braddock, I would want to know about it before the arrest were made. Also, let's face it, after hearing about the issue, Braddock may want to make a decision on arresting Cartwright, but pretend he didn't know about it. He'll tell the press I did it on my own. That's his prerogative as president, and I'll be happy to take the heat. I'm giving him a chance to do that."

Forester made a couple more efforts to move Arthur, but the AG wouldn't budge. Finally, Arthur called Braddock.

After the call, he reported back to them. "The president agreed to cancel a meeting with the Treasury secretary over fiscal policy. He'll see us in an hour. I told him the four of us would be coming, and to have Vernon there, but not Wilkins."

*   *   *

Walking into the Oval Office, Kelly couldn't believe how much had happened in the three months since she had last been in this room for the ceremony honoring her and the members of her team who had thwarted the terrorist attack at Walter Reed.

In the car on the way to the White House, Arthur had told her, "Braddock selected you to be chairman of the task force, so I want you to summarize everything the task force has done and all the evidence against Cartwright. Then end with your recommendation that *you* arrest Cartwright. We'll hear Braddock's reaction."

Kelly felt like a calf being led off to slaughter. Stay calm, she told herself. As she looked around, she was struck by the simplicity and dignity of the office. The deep blue oval shaped carpet had the presidential seal in the center. Most imposing was the dark wooden desk with thick legs that curled at the bottom, which had been used by several other presidents, including Franklin Roosevelt. Two black leather chairs were in front of it. Behind, there was a credenza flanked by an American flag with pictures of the president's family—two married sons and one granddaughter—just in front of the three floor-to-ceiling bulletproof windows facing the south lawn. Off to one side was an informal meeting area with an upholstered sofa, four chairs, a coffee table, and a couple of end tables with lamps.

When they were all seated, Kelly followed Arthur's script, telling the president in chronological order how their investigation had unfolded. She laid out all the evidence establishing that Cartwright was a spy for China, beginning with the eight meetings Martin had with Cartwright and Mallory followed by meetings with Xiang. She talked about Xiang's story. Then she summarized what Mallory had told them, reporting on Cartwright's meeting with Liu in Paris and in Singapore. She told him about their meeting with Dickerson, and how she and Paul had been attacked in Los Angeles because of Wilkins.

Braddock had been listening in stony silence, his face showing no emotion, until she got to Wilkins. Then he turned beet red. "Do you think George is also a spy for the Chinese?" Braddock asked Kelly.

"I don't know whether he's a spy or just taken in by Cartwright, Mr. President," Kelly replied.

Forester spoke up. "Regardless of whether Wilkins is a spy or not, what he did is reprehensible."

"Well, when this is over," Braddock said, "I intend to fire Wilkins. And I hope Arthur can come up with some charge that will let me arrest him."

"I'll look into that, Mr. President."

Kelly resumed talking, and finished her report with the ten million dollar bank account in Trinidad, explaining that she had a copy of the signature card opening the account. At the end, she said, "I'm prepared to arrest Cartwright for espionage if you give me that order, Mr. President."

Braddock turned to Arthur. "How strong do you think the legal case is against Cartwright?"

"Persuasive, but like most, it's not bulletproof."

Thanks, Arthur, Kelly thought.

"What's been worrying me," Braddock said, "about Kelly's excellent report, is that all the evidence seems to be sound, yet there's no smoking gun. There's nothing to grab the public."

"How about the ten million dollars in a Trinidad account which came from the Chinese?" Forester said.

"That's true. However, I'd like a little more."

Here was another gutless politician. Kelly was ready to scream.

Arthur turned to Vernon. "Where is Cartwright today?"

"I know from press people covering his campaign that he's in New York City today and this evening. This morning he flew into Teterboro in his private plane with his pilot Mallory. He's speaking at the Waldorf this evening at eight, and he'll be staying at the St. Regis tonight. Tomorrow, he's flying out of Teterboro at noon for Chicago and several Midwest campaign appearances."

"All right, I have an idea," Arthur said.

All eyes were on the attorney general.

"What would nail down the case against Cartwright," Arthur said, talking slowly, selecting each word carefully, "is if we had a recording of Cartwright giving an order to his pilot to fly him to China to avoid being arrested. People would then unequivocally understand he was a traitor. Everybody knows about Kim Philby. That's what he did, secretly flew off to Russia."

"That's an excellent idea, Arthur," Braddock said with enthusiasm. "How do you propose to make that happen?"

Arthur smiled. "I have no idea. That would take a younger and more supple, agile mind. I'll bet Kelly will be able to devise a plan."

Forester said, "Kelly, would you like to strangle Arthur, or would you prefer I do it?"

Everybody in the room laughed except for Kelly. Her mind was racing. She was grateful to the director for his humorous comment. It gave her a few additional seconds to come up with a plan.

Now all eyes shifted to Kelly.

"Here is my proposal," she said.

The room was deathly still.

"Andrew Martin is obligated to help us build the case against Cartwright to gain his immunity, and Cartwright has great confidence in Martin. I will meet with Martin and tell him to inform his buddy Cartwright that Arthur Larkin just called him and laid out the case against Cartwright. Martin can summarize that case. He can also tell Cartwright the president has given the order to arrest him. However, the president doesn't want it done until 4:00 p.m. tomorrow, because Braddock wants to ensure he has time to set it up for maximum publicity. Sound good so far?"

Forester was nodding.

"You think you can trust Martin to deliver that message?" Braddock asked.

"I believe he'll do whatever it takes to redeem himself. In any event, I will be standing next to him, gun in hand, when he makes that call."

"Okay. What's next?" the president asked impatiently.

"I will work with Mallory, Cartwright's pilot, to install a recording device on Mallory's phone and also on Cartwright's plane," Kelly continued. "Any discussions between Cartwright and Mallory will be broadcast to a van at Teterboro. What I'm hoping is that after Cartwright hears from Martin, he will give Mallory an order to fly to China or somewhere else in Asia. Once Cartwright gives that order, we'll block his plane from taking off. Then we'll move in and arrest Cartwright."

"Suppose Cartwright doesn't give that order and he tells Mallory to fly to Chicago, as planned," Braddock said. "What will you do at 4:00 p.m. tomorrow?"

"Mr. President, I would recommend arresting Cartwright with the evidence we now have."

"I'm not ready to make that decision," Braddock said, shaking his head. "We'll discuss it tomorrow at 3:30."

Here was another famous Washington tactic, Kelly thought. Next to CYA, it was one of the most popular in Washington, referred to as "kicking the can down the road."

"What do the rest of you think?" Braddock asked.

"I like it," Forester said.

"Arthur?" Braddock asked.

"I see only one possible downside."

"What's that?" Kelly asked.

"I'm worried that Cartwright will escape after he hears from Martin. You may not be able to arrest him."

"We'll have agents watching Cartwright and his hotel around the clock."

"Nothing's foolproof," Arthur pointed out.

Kelly was getting a sick feeling in her stomach. Would Arthur, and perhaps even Braddock, prefer that Cartwright escape to avoid the PR and legal nightmare they would have if Cartwright were arrested? Would they even help him escape? She hoped she was wrong. They couldn't be that cynical. However, she didn't know either of them well enough to decide if that was what they were thinking.

After the meeting, she raised it with Forester. He didn't dismiss her suspicions. "It's a troubling possibility," he told her. "As an alternative to escape, no doubt Braddock and Arthur would prefer that Cartwright took his own life. If he were dead, they wouldn't have to deal with the consequences."

Kelly didn't articulate what was running through her mind. Would Braddock and Arthur arrange to murder Cartwright and make it look like suicide?

*   *   *

Kelly took Paul with her to Martin's house.

"What happened to you?" Martin asked the bandaged Paul as they walked in.

"Let's just say that the woman who wanted to kill you had some friends."

Kelly doubted that Martin felt sorry for Paul.

"To what do I owe the honor of this visit?" Martin asked.

"We're moving into the endgame," Kelly said. "Here's your chance to seal your immunity deal."

"What do I have to do?" he asked.

"Lie," said Kelly. "That shouldn't be too hard for you."

"That wasn't justified," Martin replied, raising his voice. "I've changed. I've come over to your side. I'm one of the good guys now."

"Save the posturing and listen carefully. You're going to make a call to your friend Cartwright. I'll give you the script, and I'll be standing next to you, gun in hand, to make sure you follow it. You make one tiny departure, and you're on the way to jail. It's real simple. Do you understand?"

"Yes."

"Okay, here's what you're going to say." Kelly handed Martin the written script. She had decided not to elaborate on what they hoped to achieve with this call to Cartwright, although Martin might be able to figure it out by himself. Still, she wanted to minimize the chance of him tipping off the general.

Fifteen minutes later, they were all set. With Kelly standing next to him, Martin placed the call on a landline in his house. Paul was listening in on an extension in the next room. If Martin tried to tip off Cartwright, Kelly would immediately grab the phone from his hand.

New York

Cartwright was alone in the back of a limo traveling from the St. Regis to the Waldorf for a campaign speech when his phone rang. He saw from caller the ID that it was Andrew Martin.

Cartwright asked the driver to slide up the glass partition separating him from the driver. Once it was raised, he answered the phone.

"Can you talk?" Martin sounded upset.

"Sure, go ahead."

"I just came from a meeting with Arthur Larkin, the attorney general. Arthur and I have been good friends for a long time. Arthur told me the most incredible thing."

"What's that?" Cartwright asked.

"Braddock is out to get you and to destroy your campaign. He's had the FBI come up with phony evidence that you're a Chinese spy, and that the Chinese are paying you off."

"You have to be kidding."

"I wish I were."

"What's their supposed evidence?"

"Xiang from the Chinese embassy told them the envelopes you passed through me contained military secrets. And your pilot, Mallory, claims you met with Chinese spymaster Liu on your recent trip to Paris."

Mallory's perfidy infuriated Cartwright. He swallowed hard and said, "Mallory is lying."

"And finally," Martin continued, "they claim you have a ten million dollar account in a Trinidad bank with funds that came from a Chinese bank run by the People's Liberation Army."

"That's total and utter bullshit." Cartwright was shouting now. "Braddock must have directed his people to open the account and make it look like Chinese money."

"They have your signature card."

"They could have forged it."

"The president has given the FBI an order to arrest you at four o'clock tomorrow afternoon."

"Why is he waiting until tomorrow?" Cartwright asked.

"They want to make their case airtight and maximize publicity."

"You don't have to worry, Andrew. I'll fight those bastards and their phony evidence every step of the way."

"I'll be right there with you, leading your defense."

"Thanks. I know I can count on you."

When he put down the phone, Cartwright replayed the conversation in his mind. He had to admit, it all made sense except for one thing: the bank account in Trinidad. Liu had never said anything about setting up a bank account for Cartwright, and the general would never have agreed to it. Not only was there great risk of it being discovered, but Cartwright wasn't in this for the money. And he never had been, as he had repeatedly told Liu. Dickerson's money went directly to Cartwright's presidential campaign. Not a cent flowed to the general personally.

The Trinidad account, Cartwright decided, must have been set up by Braddock's people to frame him. Here was another presidential campaign dirty trick like Watergate. Without it, they only had a circumstantial case.

Regardless of all that, Cartwright realized Braddock was still the president. He could commence espionage proceedings against Cartwright, which would be difficult to defend. He had no choice. Cartwright had to activate his escape plan.

He picked up his phone and called Dickerson. "I need your help."

New Jersey

Kelly had to admit that Martin was convincing in the call with Cartwright. He had fulfilled his end of the bargain. Following the call between Martin and Cartwright, Paul reported to the AG, who agreed that Martin's immunity deal was final. Martin seemed enormously relieved when Paul told him.

"However," Paul said, "we want you to remain under house arrest until Cartwright is taken into custody."

Martin didn't argue.

Kelly, with Paul in tow, left Martin's house. On the street, she phoned Mallory. "Where are you?" she asked the pilot.

"A motel near Teterboro Airport in New Jersey."

"What's your departure time?"

"Noon tomorrow for Chicago."

"Can you meet me in the private plane terminal at Teterboro in an hour, maybe less? I'm heading out to Reagan to take a private plane there."

"I'll be here waiting for you."

When she told Paul, he said, "You better go up alone. I don't want to slow you down. I'll stay here and rest, then join you at Teterboro in the morning."

*   *   *

Moments after her arrival, Kelly found Mallory sitting in the lounge area sipping a can of Coke.

"Let's go out to your plane to talk," she said.

She signaled to the two techies who had flown up with her to accompany them.

Once the four were in the plane, Kelly said, "Here's what I want to do."

Mallory raised his hand. "Time out. I have some new news about our plans."

"Go ahead."

"A little while after you called me, Cartwright phoned. He told me that tomorrow morning I should make sure the plane is fully fueled. 'We're not going to Chicago,' he said. 'We're going to an international destination. I'll tell you where after I board the plane at noon tomorrow.'"

Kelly was ready to scream with joy. Cartwright had taken the bait. Her plan was working. Once Cartwright got on the plane tomorrow at noon, he would give Mallory the order to fly him to China. His words would be recorded. They would move in and block the plane from taking off, then arrest Cartwright.

She explained to Mallory that they would be hooking up a concealed recording system on the plane, as well as a recording device on his phone. Mallory didn't ask why she was doing it. He was smart. He had probably pieced it together—or, being a good military man, he didn't question orders.

While the techies were wiring the plane, Kelly arranged for New York field agents, armed with Cartwright's picture, to watch all three New York airports in case he slipped away from her. She had people at headquarters checking manifests for all flights out of New York, but there was no reservation for Cartwright.

Once the plane was wired, Kelly told Mallory he could go back to his motel. Then she took over an empty office in the terminal building and installed a cot. That's where she planned to spend the night, gun in one hand, phone in the other.

In the meantime, she checked with Felix, her lead agent in Manhattan from the FBI's New York field office.

Felix told her, "Target is speaking now in the Waldorf ballroom. I have men on the floor watching him. Others will follow him when he leaves the Waldorf."

An hour and ten minutes later, Felix called back. "Target is leaving the Waldorf in a limo. We're following."

"Good. Stay on the line with me."

Fifteen minutes later, Felix said, "Target's car pulled up in front of St. Regis . . . Target is shaking hands with well-wishers in front of the hotel . . . Entering hotel, and . . . Hold on for a minute. My man in the lobby reports that he took the elevator to the fifteenth floor. His suite is 1501. Looks like he's calling it a night."

"Good. What are your assets in the hotel?"

"I have one man inside the lobby. He'll be replaced in five hours by a woman. Nobody abandons their post, not even for an instant."

"What about outside the hotel?"

"We have a car parked on 55th Street in front of the main entrance and another midway down the block at the employee entrance. If the target leaves, they'll let me know and follow him. I'll report to you."

"I want those men replaced in five hours as well."

"They're two of my best. They would never abandon their position."

"Don't argue," she said sharply. The tension was getting to her. "Just replace them. My ass is on the line, and now yours is as well. We can't let the target escape."

New York

In his suite, Cartwright waited until 11:30 in the evening to take out his phone and call the theatrical makeup specialist whose contact info Liu had given him.

"Is this Melody?" he asked.

A woman replied in English with a Chinese accent. "Yes. Where are you?"

"St. Regis hotel."

"I know where it is. Room number?" she asked.

"1501."

When Cartwright had returned to the St. Regis from the Waldorf, he observed a man sitting in the lobby who was no doubt FBI. Even though Cartwright had seen many Chinese guests in the hotel, that agent would be sure to look at which floor the elevator stopped if a

Chinese woman got on. So Cartwright added, "Take the elevator to the twelfth floor and walk up the last three flights."

"I'll be there in thirty minutes," she said before hanging up.

Exactly thirty minutes later, Cartwright heard a knock on the door.

He opened it and admitted a young, bespectacled Chinese woman carrying a briefcase. He hung the "Do Not Disturb" sign on the knob before shutting the door.

"Did anyone in the lobby notice you?" he asked.

"No. Fortunately two Chinese women and one man came into the hotel right after me. I tried to blend in with them."

"Good."

"It's time to go to work," she said. "Strip down to your briefs, I don't want to leave any residue on your clothes."

Cartwright did what she said, then went into the bathroom where she was setting up. She directed him to a chair in front of a small table with a mirror above it. Then she took out a picture of a gray-haired man with glasses, which was identical to the Virgil MacMillan on the passport Liu had given Cartwright in Paris. She taped it up on the mirror.

Working slowly and carefully, she changed Cartwright's facial appearance, his hair, and his eyes. She was a perfectionist, working for nearly an hour. When she was finished, she carefully cleaned up everything with her own towels, then put them back into her bag. He thanked her and told her to walk down three flights before taking the elevator back to the lobby.

Alone again in the suite, Cartwright sat down at the desk in the living room. He turned on his iPad and checked the Amtrak schedule. Seeing a 9:00 a.m. express train to Montreal from Penn Station, he made a reservation for a first-class seat for Virgil MacMillan, which he paid for with a Virgil MacMillan credit card. When the transaction was complete, Amtrak gave him a confirmation code to use in picking up his ticket. He jotted the confirmation code on a small St. Regis notepad on the desk, tore it off, and put it into his pocket.

Cartwright decided to wait until 4:00 a.m. to leave the St. Regis. Until then, he sat in the still room, staring at the ceiling. As he did, the enormity of what he was doing came driving home and hit him hard.

He had no close family in the United States—his wife had died a year ago, and they had no children. Still, he loved the United States. He had spent his life serving his country. And now he would be remembered as a traitor, not a hero.

All of that was true. However, Cartwright believed he had pursued a path that was best for his country, and he had almost succeeded. In his view, the world was divided into those who had the courage to do what they believed in, and those who talked about it. Cartwright was a doer. He had courage. In war, he had taken risks. Most of the time, he had succeeded. Sometimes, he had failed. In his new life, he hoped Liu and his Chinese colleagues would listen to Cartwright's pleas not to risk war with the United States, but he wasn't confident of that.

At ten minutes to four, he used the bathroom and washed his hands. His eye itched from the makeup, so he wiped it gently with the corner of a towel. He put his cash, along with the Virgil MacMillan passport, credit cards, and a small pistol in his pocket. Leaving the "Do Not Disturb" sign on the door and carrying only his iPad in his hand, Cartwright exited the room.

He walked confidently along the deserted corridor to the staircase, climbed down four flights, then took the elevator to the lobby. Calmly, he exited through the revolving door and down three stairs to 55th Street, not paying attention to the car parked in front with two men inside.

Melody had done a good job. No one stopped him.

On the sidewalk, he turned right. Coolly, with even, measured steps, he walked to the corner of Madison, never looking over this shoulder. Then he turned right and walked south on Madison for twenty-two blocks before turning west on 33rd Street and walking until he reached Penn Station.

Inside the station, he found an isolated area and sat on a wooden bench, waiting until the ticket windows opened at five o'clock. Then he provided his confirmation code to the agent, who gave him his train ticket. Once shops opened, he purchased two cell phones and a small wheelie suitcase so he would look like a traveler. He then used one of the phones to call Air China and purchase a first-class seat on their flight from Montreal to Hong Kong later that evening in the name of Virgil MacMillan. He also purchased several newspapers.

Back on the bench, Cartwright held up a newspaper close to his face, pretending to read. As soon as the train was available for boarding, he went down to the track.

He was safe. Kelly Cameron would never catch him.

New Jersey and Connecticut

Kelly slept sporadically, a total of an hour, she guessed, on the cot. Paul arrived at Teterboro at 9:30 in the morning. "I had to be here when you arrested Cartwright," he told Kelly.

"The general hasn't left the St. Regis yet," she said to Paul. "He told Mallory they'd be flying out at noon, so I don't think he'll be here until a little before that."

Kelly was calculating time. With traffic from Manhattan to Teterboro, he'd have to leave the St. Regis no later than 11:00 a.m.

She called Felix. "Let me know the instant the target leaves the St. Regis," she instructed.

"Will do."

At 10:30, Felix called and told Kelly, "Cartwright's limo just arrived. It's waiting in front of the hotel."

So far so good, she thought.

At 11:15 she became worried. Mallory hadn't heard from Cartwright. She called Felix, who checked with his agent in the lobby. "No sign of Cartwright at checkout."

At 11:30 she called Forester to report. "I want your authorization to have Felix go in with a couple of agents and arrest Cartwright."

"He may have taken his own life," the director said.

"I hope not. I want to arrest the bastard."

"Wait fifteen more minutes," Forester said. "Then do it."

The hotel management was cooperative, so at 11:45, Kelly told Felix to have a bellman open the door. "And keep me on the line for real-time reports."

As soon as Felix and two of his agents were inside Cartwright's suite, Kelly heard Felix shout, "Son of a bitch!"

"What the hell does that mean?" she asked.

"Cartwright's not in the suite. He left all his clothes behind."

She kicked a nearby wall so hard her foot throbbed. Paul was holding his head in his hands. Kelly was furious. She couldn't let Cartwright get away.

"Get all your people into that suite," Kelly said to Felix. "Check it with a fine-tooth comb for any hints about where he might have gone. Meantime, I'll increase our vigilance at New York airports."

Kelly also checked with Terry, the head of travel at FBI headquarters. Cartwright's name wasn't on any airplane reservations or manifests anywhere in the United States.

He couldn't have vanished into thin air.

Kelly thought about taking a chopper to the St. Regis, but ultimately rejected the idea. She was better off at this command center. Fifteen minutes later, Felix called back.

"I have a couple of things for you," he reported. He sounded excited.

"Go ahead."

"One of my guys noticed indentations on a St. Regis notepad. It seemed as if something had been written on the page above and torn off. They worked hard on the pad."

"And?" she asked, holding her breath.

"Somebody wrote K32PZ7R."

Kelly scribbled it on a piece of paper.

Felix cautioned, "We don't know it was Cartwright. It may have been a prior guest."

"What else do you have?"

"This is a little more speculative."

"Tell me."

"Jennifer Coughlin, one of my agents, is confident that there was a smudge of makeup on a hand towel. She also claims she detected the odor of hair spray. However, none of my guys can smell a thing."

Kelly was sure this meant that Cartwright had changed his appearance, explaining how he had departed the hotel undetected. "Give Jennifer a big thank-you for me," she said before putting down the phone. She stared at the piece of paper on the table. *K32PZ7R.* She showed it to Paul. "Perhaps it's a code to access Chinese help," he mused.

That didn't seem right to her. It could be an online confirmation code. She called Terry in travel at the FBI and read her the number.

"Amtrak confirmation," Terry immediately said.

"You sure?"

"Positive."

"Can you get passenger details from Amtrak?"

"Stay on the line, I'll have it for you in two minutes or less."

Waiting for Terry to come back on, Kelly tried to think of where Cartwright could be going on Amtrak. One answer leapt into her mind: Montreal. It was the closest and easiest foreign destination to reach by train from New York. In Canada, he would be outside of the FBI's jurisdiction. And from Montreal, he could fly to China or any other country.

Then Terry was back. "It's a reservation for a first-class seat for Virgil MacMillan on Amtrak train 271—a train to Montreal that left Penn Station at 9:00 a.m. He's a resident of Hong Kong traveling on a Chinese passport."

Now that Kelly had the alias Cartwright was using, she asked Terry to check all flights to Hong Kong, Shanghai, and Beijing from Montreal to see if they had a reservation for Virgil MacMillan. If not, she would ask Terry to check other destinations. Meantime, Kelly frantically pulled up the Amtrak schedule on her iPad. The train should be crossing the border into Canada in about ten minutes. She couldn't let that happen. The Canadians could be sticky in complying with US extradition requests, especially when China, now their biggest oil customer, was involved.

She used another phone to call Forester and give him a report. Before she had a chance to tell him what she wanted, he said, "I'll get a hold of Amtrak and stop that train. Stand by."

Terry was on the other phone. "Virgil MacMillan is on Air China this evening from Montreal to Hong Kong."

Seconds later, Forester was back. "Amtrak will stop the train on the US side of the border. They'll tell the passengers there's a mechanical problem."

"Perfect."

"Are you still at Teterboro?"

"Yes, sir. And I have a chopper on hold."

"I know you want to be there to arrest Cartwright," Forester said. "Take that chopper up to the train along with Paul and as many agents as you can get inside. I'll send up another chopper or two from the New York field office with more agents. We won't let Cartwright get away."

Walking to the chopper to explain the plan to the pilot, Kelly's euphoria about catching Cartwright gave way to a sickly feeling. It was all too easy. The indentation on the notepad, the reservations on Amtrak and Air China. She was afraid Cartwright had left her a false trail. If this really was his escape plan, he was too smart to make it so obvious. He didn't have to write down the Amtrak confirmation on the notepad. He didn't even need an advance reservation a few hours ahead. He could have gotten his ticket in person at Penn Station. Even if he made it to Canada, he couldn't be sure the Canadians wouldn't extradite him to the US.

She tried to put herself into Cartwright's mind. How best for him to escape the US and get to China? She pondered the question for a moment and recalled that Cartwright was a top Air Force pilot. He could fly a plane himself out of the US to China.

Once inside the chopper, she told the pilot to hold. "We're not going anywhere yet." Then she called Forester. "Cartwright won't be on that train," she said with confidence.

"What do you mean?"

She explained her analysis.

"Let's confirm," the FBI director said. "I'll get the Amtrak conductor from the first-class car on the phone. You hold."

While she waited for Forester to come back on, she tried to think of where Cartwright might get a plane. One of his Air Force buddies? Unlikely. A rental? Tough on short notice for long range. But Cartwright's big supporter, Dickerson, no doubt had a fleet of long-range aircraft. Cartwright wouldn't be flying commercial to Asia.

Forester was back. "You were right. Cartwright left the train at Poughkeepsie. I have somebody checking car rental companies near that station. Also, the conductor gave me a description of Virgil MacMillan."

"Good. Can you have someone from our civil aviation branch check the status and location of Dickerson's planes?"

"Good thinking. I'll get back to you."

Kelly pulled up a map of the Eastern United States on her iPad, focusing on cities close to Poughkeepsie. Her theory was that Cartwright would be driving to the airport he intended to use, and it would have to be large enough for a big plane to take off. He wouldn't choose JFK, LaGuardia, or Newark, because he'd want to get out of the New York area and FBI surveillance. But it couldn't be too far from the point at which he left the train, or the driving time would be too long.

Forester called to say Cartwright had rented from Hertz, but they had no way of tracking the car. She glanced at her watch. Time was her enemy in view of Cartwright's head start. She quickly narrowed the possibilities to Hartford and Philadelphia. Hartford was closer and an easier drive. It was also a smaller airport, and less likely to have delays on flight takeoff.

Without waiting to hear back from Forester, she told the chopper pilot, "We're going to Bradley Airport outside of Hartford. Right now."

"Roger that."

Fortunately, the day was crystal clear with a robin egg blue sky. When they were twenty miles from the airport, Forester called Kelly again.

"One of Dickerson's planes, a Boeing 767, arrived at Bradley Airport at six this morning," he said. "The plane was fueled a few minutes ago and is heading toward the runway right now. The pilot is General Cartwright. He must be confident we'll never catch him."

"He's certainly sticking it to us by using his own name."

"Cartwright filed a phony flight plan for Miami. I asked the tower to order him back to the gate."

"He'll never comply."

"Agreed. I'll have the Air Force scramble a couple of jets to bring him down once he's airborne."

"Good idea. But you may not need them. I'm only ten minutes out."

"Way to go, Kelly. If Cartwright doesn't return to the gate, you have my approval to stop him from getting airborne. Do whatever it takes."

As she approached the airfield, Kelly immediately sized up the situation. Only one plane was near the runway. It was a sleek Boeing 767 with Dickerson Industries painted in large blue letters against a white background. All the other planes had moved to the side of the airfield.

Fire trucks and emergency medical ambulances were on standby adjacent to the terminal.

Cartwright's plane was taxiing toward the runway. He hadn't complied with orders from the tower. She asked the tower to patch her through to the cockpit.

"General Cartwright," she said, "this is Kelly Cameron with the FBI. I'm in a chopper closing in on the airfield. I've been ordered by FBI Director Forester to block your takeoff. Even if you manage to get airborne, two Air Force jets have been directed to bring you down. Your game is over. Stop now and turn yourself in."

When he didn't respond, she looked at the runway. Cartwright's answer was there. His plane was positioned for takeoff. She directed the helicopter pilot to move in close to the runway and hold. One shot is all I'll get, she told herself. It better be good. She heard the roar of the engines on Cartwright's plane. As it thundered along the runway, she took aim at one of its engines. Yes. Now. Fire. She pulled the trigger and held her breath. It was a direct hit. The plane skidded off the runway and burst into flames.

Fire trucks and mechanics with movable stairs raced across the airfield to the plane. The door opened from the inside. Stairs were pulled up alongside the burning plane, and Kelly watched Cartwright stagger down them, disguised as Virgil MacMillan. She held a pair of handcuffs in her left hand and a Glock in her right. As soon as he reached the ground, Cartwright pulled a pistol from his pocket.

"You're under arrest, General Cartwright," Kelly called out. "Drop the gun."

He looked at Kelly and raised the pistol in his right hand, aiming at her. Kelly's finger was on the trigger. There was no way she would let him get off the first shot. And this time, she'd hit him in the right shoulder. She wouldn't make the mistake she had at Walter Reed.

Suddenly, Cartwright rotated his arm and held the pistol against the side of his head. Kelly couldn't let him shoot himself.

"Drop it," she cried out. She aimed for his right hand, but before she had a chance to pull the trigger, he tossed the gun away.

"I have nothing to be ashamed of," he said. "I'm no traitor. Everything I did was in the best interests of the United States."

"A court will decide that."

EPILOGUE

Having been granted immunity, Andrew Martin represented Cartwright in negotiating a plea agreement with Arthur Larkin. Under its terms, Cartwright dropped out of the presidential race and agreed to a five-year jail term with the possibility of parole after two. Paul presented the agreement to Judge McCardle, who immediately signed it.

Wilkins was fired from his post as national security advisor, and the ten million dollars disappeared from the Trinidad bank. Alistair Singh claimed he had no idea where it went.

Once Cartwright's plea agreement was accepted by the judge, Kelly knew she would not need Xiang as a witness. The next day, she drove to Charlottesville in an unmarked car with two US marshals. Their plan was to pick up Xiang at the FBI safe house and drive him to Dulles Airport, where he would be taking a plane to his place of resettlement under the witness protection program. The marshals had all of the papers, identification, and cash that Xiang would need to start a new life.

In the car, one of the marshals explained to Kelly, "Director Forester told us not to provide you with this man's new name or his place of resettlement. He said that was for your protection. We will take Xiang to the airport, and Agent Rolfe will drive you back to Washington."

Kelly understood. If Liu ever decided to find and kill Xiang, he might use Kelly to do so. It would be better if she didn't know his name or location.

Xiang was standing on the porch in the bright sunlight with Rolfe when Kelly and the marshals arrived. She asked the marshals to remain in the house while she went out to talk with Xiang one final time. Rolfe nodded at Kelly as she approached and withdrew into the house.

"It's all over," she told Xiang. "They're taking you to Dulles Airport to fly you to your resettlement location."

"I was hoping we could be together from this point on," Xiang said.

"That's not possible."

He nodded. "I understand. You should know that I'm extremely grateful to you. You've given me a new life and freedom."

His words echoed what her father had tried and failed to do for Fritz Helfund.

"Return to being the person you were our junior year at CMU," she said.

"I will, and I'll never forget about the Kelly Cameron I fell in love with that year."

One of the marshals stepped out onto the porch. "Ms. Cameron, we have to leave to make his plane."

She looked at Xiang and said, "Go now."

Xiang reached for her hand and squeezed it. Then he walked through the door and into his new life.

Watching him go, Kelly tried to imagine what her life might have been if Xiang had defected fifteen years ago.

About the Author

Allan Topol is the author of thirteen novels of international intrigue. Two of them, *Spy Dance* and *Enemy of My Enemy*, were national best sellers. His novels have been translated into Chinese, Japanese, Portuguese, and Hebrew. One was optioned, and three are in development for movies.

In addition to his fiction writing, Allan Topol coauthored a two-volume legal treatise entitled *Superfund Law and Procedure*. He wrote a weekly column for Military.com, and has published articles in numerous newspapers and periodicals, including the *New York Times*, *Washington Post*, and *Yale Law Journal*.

He is a graduate of the Carnegie Institute of Technology who majored in chemistry, abandoned science, and obtained a law degree from Yale University. He became a partner in a major Washington law firm. An avid wine collector and connoisseur, he has traveled extensively researching dramatic locations for his novels.

Since his graduation from Yale Law School, Allan Topol has been a Washington lawyer observing the Washington power play.

For more information, visit www.allantopol.com.